Copyright © 2025 by Ben Farthing

All rights reserved.

No part of this book may be reproduced in any form or by any electronic or mechanical means, including information storage and retrieval systems, without written permission from the author, except for the use of brief quotations in a book review.

Cover art by Luciano Fleitas. Typography by Ruth Anna Evans.

ALSO BY BEN FARTHING

Series: *I Found Horror*

I Found a Circus Tent In the Woods Behind My House

I Found Puppets Living In My Apartment Walls

I Found Christmas Lights Slithering Up My Street

I Found a Lost Hallway in a Dying Mall

I Found the Boogeyman Under My Brother's Crib

Trilogy: *Horror Lurks Beneath*

It Waits On the Top Floor

They Cling To the Hull

We Hide Our Faces

Standalone Books

The Twitching House

The Piper's Graveyard

Those Who Dwell Below the Sidewalk

Crowded Chasms: Tales In Terrifying Places

THE 31ST TRICK-OR-TREATER

BEN FARTHING

PROLOGUE

Up until 7:31 p.m., it's a normal Halloween in the neighborhood of Maple Creek.

Trick-or-treaters and their bobbing flashlights parade up and down the HOA-maintained sidewalks.

Young moms and dads film iPhone videos of their toddlers dressed up like Bluey and Bingo, Spin and Ghost Spider, Elsa and Anna.

Older kids are costumed to scare, masquerading as wasteland ghouls, Cordyceps zombies, and Art the Clown.

The air is chilly enough that the moseying parents are wearing jackets, but for the kids, it's that wonderfully perfect temperature where the exertion of Halloween joy keeps them warm.

Outside Maple Creek, trick-or-treaters have largely abandoned the Richmond area's residential streets. A nationwide celebration of the spooky has diminished into sporadic participation.

But here in this used-to-be-affordable neighborhood, parents share with their children the same Halloween fun they had as kids.

There's only one adult Halloween party scheduled in Maple Creek this year—Betty and Tim Witt have invited a few neighbors and work friends.

For most of the three hundred and twenty-three homes in Maple Creek, Halloween is 100% about the kids.

Of course, after the kids are in bed, plenty of the grown-ups plan to relax in front of a scary movie.

Or the more daring will join the teenagers to get shepherded through the old elementary school, which can be reached from Maple Creek via a short walk through the woods. For the first time, the Chester brothers have transformed Old Pine Elementary into the fun and terrifying Crimson Corridors haunted attraction. Butterflies dance in parents' stomachs—those who aren't so sure about what they've signed up for. But for now, they're following their little princesses and ninjas and superheroes from house to house. Candy is filling up pillowcases and pumpkin buckets. Shrieks of joy are echoing between the namesake trees of the neighborhood.

Yes, it's safe to say that up until 7:31 P.M., Maple Creek is still a neighborhood that knows the happiness of Halloween.

∼

At 7:25 P.M., Bob finally gives in to his two-year-old's begging to be carried.

Her McDonald's ghost bucket is full of candy, her purple Asha dress is dragging on the sidewalk, and her feet are tired.

"Come on up, Emily," Bob says, wishing he'd brought the stroller.

Emily's older brother and sister still have enough energy to walk, but after more than an hour of trick-or-treating, Optimus Prime and Elphaba are dragging their feet.

At the corner of the block, Bob's middle daughter looks down the street and squeals in excitement. One house is decorated in a *Nightmare Before Christmas* theme, including a 12-foot-tall Jack.

That movie is Mary's current obsession.

"There's Sally!" She hops up and down, pointing to a yard decoration behind the Pumpkin King, a plastic version of the wide-eyed reconstructed corpse who helps save Christmas and Halloweentown. "Come on!" Mary shouts. "Let's trick-or-treat that house!"

Mary grabs her brother's hand, but Sam is worn out. He jerks his arm back.

"It's too far away. I want to go home and count my candy."

"Come with me," Mary whines. She's always been timid, and Sam usually takes pride in holding her hand through moments of nervousness. Not tonight, apparently.

Bob considers reprimanding Sam, but he wants Mary to practice going after what she wants, even when it scares her. In this case, it's only to go see a Halloween yard display of a movie she likes, but still—if it's only nervousness holding her back, then Bob wants her to go.

A gaggle of middle school kids runs from porch to porch, skipping the sidewalk to maximize candy-getting time. They approach the *Nightmare Before Christmas* house, ring the doorbell, and receive candy from a man dressed as Santa Claus.

Mary's face lights up as she hears their laughter. "I'm gonna go trick-or-treat there," she tells her dad.

"Stay off the grass." Bob watches his daughter run down the sidewalk, candy bucket in one hand, the other outstretched for balance. Pride wells inside him that she's pushing past her nerves.

He walks behind Mary, carrying Emily and dragging Sam.

Mary cuts up the house's driveway, slows to gawk at Jack and Sally, and then marches up the steps to ring the doorbell.

There she is, Bob's brave little witch, standing on a stranger's porch, waiting for Santa to bring her candy.

Halloween is a strange holiday, but nothing makes Bob so happy as witnessing his kids grow.

Sam tugs on Bob's arm, distracting him from the image of Mary waiting patiently in her black dress and pointy hat.

"I want to go hooooome," Sam whines.

Bob looks down to tell his oldest to be patient.

When he looks back up, Mary is gone.

Bob's heart skips.

Can anything jerk you from calm to panic like suddenly not knowing where your child is?

Bob quickly reassures himself that Mary must be just out of sight. She couldn't have gone far.

Emily bouncing in his arms, Bob hurries toward the closed front door. It's black with a glass storm door in front of it. A novelty lightbulb colors the porch orange.

Mary's pointy black hat sits on the cement.

Sam stops his complaining long enough to notice, "Where's Mary?"

His son's words allow panic to flood into Bob. He rushes between the towering Jack and Sally, stomping over the grass. Emily fusses in his arms. Sam hops and jumps to keep up.

Boxwood bushes with their tiny, evergreen leaves line the front of the house, with old, dry mulch beneath them.

There aren't any missing four-year-old witches behind the bushes.

"Mary?" Bob calls, wanting desperately to race to her. Other families and flocks of children notice his panic from the sidewalk.

One couple dressed as the Joker and Harley Quinn walk their little Batman toward Bob, parents ready to help out another parent.

"Mary!" Bob yells.

"Daddy?" Emily whines into his ear.

Behind Mary's pointy hat, the black front door opens.

The neighbor dressed as a Santa holds his bowl of candy. The orange porch light reflects in the glass storm door, obscuring Santa's face.

Bob asks, "Where's my daughter?"

It's an accusation. Of course it is. Mary is nowhere to be seen so she must have gone inside.

She can't possibly have slipped in during the half-second Bob looked down to tell Sam to be patient, but where else could she have gone?

Santa Claus opens the storm door. It pushes Mary's hat aside.

Santa sees Emily and Sam. "Look at the princess and the Transformer. I love Transformers!"

"Where's my daughter?" Bob demands. Never mind that the positioning of Mary's hat means that she couldn't have been snatched inside.

Santa furls his bushy white brow, looks at Emily and then back at Bob. "I don't—"

Joker and Harley reach the porch.

"Trick or treat!" shouts their little Batman.

Harley says, "He's looking for his daughter."

Joker says, "We saw what happened. I mean, we both looked away for a sec and then your daughter had disappeared."

"There wasn't time for this guy to open the door, yank her inside, then position her hat outside and somehow shut the door," says Harley. "She's got to be outside somewhere."

Joker adds, "We'll find her. Maybe around the back?"

"She didn't get that far unless she's an Olympic sprinter," Harley says.

"Trick or *treat!*" Batman insists.

Bob doesn't care about this other family's opinions on where his daughter's gone. He wants her back, *now*.

His fingers clench. Emily shifts uncomfortably. Mary has to be right here. She couldn't have gone anywhere. He wants to pick her up. It's an intense, blinding need that has no release, no end. Bob is left on this edge and he will remain there for a long, long time.

From a few houses up the road, he hears a man shout.

In the other direction, a woman screams.

Next door, the flock of middle-schoolers burst into commotion.

Santa Claus cranes his neck to look past his yard full of *Nightmare Before Christmas* decorations. "What's going on?"

Mary isn't the only disappeared trick-or-treater. Not by a long shot.

As parents' panic drips down to despair, someone else walks the roads of Maple Creek.

He's slender, probably not yet in his twenties, although impossible to tell since he keeps the hood of his burnt orange sweatshirt pulled low over his face.

One hand keeps warm in the hoodie's front pocket.

In his other hand dangles a lantern made from a giant turnip.

A length of curved wire is stuck into either side, and he holds the middle of it.

The turnip itself has been hollowed out. A crude face is carved into the front of it—one triangle eye bigger than the other, and the mouth an exaggerated, toothless grin.

A candle glows inside the turnip, but it's not a flickering yellow. Instead, it's the warbling pink of neon in glass. It casts its dim light onto the asphalt before the slim man.

He walks down the center of the road, right down the middle of Maple Creek's denial and grief.

Only one pair of eyes spot him:

An eight-year-old boy named Sam, who doesn't understand how his sister Mary could have vanished so quickly and completely.

But the skinny man in the hoodie doesn't know he's been spotted, and so he keeps on with his evening, reveling in the first steps of justice being done against the people of Maple Creek.

OCTOBER 1ST

Bob can't sleep.

October starts tomorrow.

He checks his phone. 12:01 A.M.

Correction: October starts today.

"Thirty-one days of Halloween," scream the movie channels.

Meanwhile in the Wilson household, they've spent all summer dreading the changing of the leaves. Not that they need any more reminders. It's been eleven months without their Mary.

Bob sits up, puts his feet on the cold wood floor.

Next to him, Joann touches his back. He's disturbed her.

They sleep lightly now. They have two children who still might need them at any moment.

Three children, Bob reminds himself. He hasn't given up on Mary. He tries not to resent that his wife did long ago.

Bob gets out of bed.

"Bob," Joann says. She's fully awake. Maybe she never fell asleep last night. "Where are you going?"

"Checking on the kids." He knows his lie is obvious.

She knows where he's going.

Well, the gist of it. Not the details. Better she never knows the details.

Of course, before he leaves, he does check on the kids. He steps quietly into Sam's room.

His son is asleep on his back, covers tossed aside after he got hot in his flannel Minecraft pajamas.

Bob goes to the girls' room. Lately, Emily has been sleeping on her side, cheek resting on her hands which she holds flat together as if in prayer. She did this even before Joann started taking her to church this year.

Mary slept that same way when she was three.

After Bob verifies that both Sam and Emily are present and breathing, he stands by Mary's empty bed.

Her pink comforter is tucked under the mattress all around. Emily has claimed most of Mary's plushies, but nobody has touched the stuffed ghost dog Zero. Last fall, Mary was obsessed with Zero.

"Stay brave," Bob says above Mary's empty bed. "I'll find you."

He puts on his coat, grabs his backpack and flashlight from his office, and heads out into the night.

∼

FROGS SHRIEK in the chilly air.

Clouds obscure the three-quarter moon, but Bob knows his way across the yard, to the sidewalk.

If he takes the truck, the cops would be more likely to notice him. Walking is better.

The Wilsons still live one street over from the house where Mary disappeared: 4490 Ash Lane. That's where Bob heads now.

His phone buzzes in his pocket.

He assumes it's Joann, but when he checks, he sees a message from someone else.

"*It says you're online. Are you going out again?*"

It's from Bob's YouTube channel's private WhatsApp group. When he got out of bed and started using his phone, the app must have turned his yellow "idle" icon to the "active" green.

He taps on the notification to see who sent the message.
Username: 99LaughBaboons.
Not just one of his viewers, but a Maple Creek resident, police officer, and co-investigator, Karl.
Another message.
"Dude, let the heat die down before you go out again."
Last week someone had spotted him creeping through their neighbor's yard and called it in.
Karl sent a message to Bob before any unfriendly cops showed up and he booked it back home. In his recent career of breaking-and-entering, that's the closest Bob has come to getting caught.
The last thing his family needs is for him to get arrested.
Joann has asked him to stop his evening walks. She knows he's looking for Mary. She must know that he's breaking the law to do so, but they never say those words aloud. It's easier not to talk about it. And lately, they don't talk much at all. So much of Joann's mind is occupied by imagining a future, heavenly reunification with Mary.
Bob knows their marriage is hanging on by a thread, but what is he supposed to do? Stop looking for their daughter?
Fuck. That.
He walks to the end of his street, then turns down Maple Creek Road, the main drag from which all the other streets of the neighborhood branch off.
He doesn't bother responding to Karl. Karl worries too much. Considering that Karl doesn't have any skin in this game, so to speak, it's impressive that the man is willing to risk his job on the police force to help Bob conduct his own investigation. Bob's grateful for Karl and the rest of his YouTube community who have watched Bob's videos about Mary and are trying to help.
But tonight, Bob is alone.
The streets don't look so different from the night Mary disappeared. Cloudy, but the three-quarter moon now peeks down on Bob, bathing the yards and houses in the faintest silver.
Thinning trees are spindly silhouettes against the charcoal sky.

They stick out alongside the pine trees, whose own branches are dense with needles.

Bob has grown comfortable sneaking around at night.

He has a system.

When he can slip out, he heads to one of thirty houses.

He checks to see if any lights are on. If there are, then he watches through the windows. He takes note of anything suspicious.

This goes into his files about each missing child, where they disappeared, who was near, and anything else that might be relevant.

If Bob arrives at one of the thirty houses where a trick-or-treater went missing and that house is dark, then he checks the driveway and garage for cars. If people are home, he moves on. After all, there are twenty-nine other houses he can check, with several neighbors each.

But, if the house is dark and no one is home, then Bob finds a way inside.

In the last eleven months, he's had lots of practice jimmying locks, confusing security systems, and finding hidden spare keys. But the easiest way to get inside a house is usually an unlocked door.

People forget. Or they don't worry about locking their door in the first place. It's not like Maple Creek is a dangerous neighborhood, if you ignore the thirty disappearances last year.

Tonight, eleven months after Mary disappeared, Bob sees a new opportunity.

He messages Karl. *"Wade is home, but his neighbor's driveway is empty."*

Wade Greenwood was Santa Claus last Halloween. He decorated his yard with those *Nightmare Before Christmas* props that lured in Mary.

Bob has already explored every inch of Wade's house—including the attic and basement. If he has anything to do with Mary's disappearance, he's hidden it well.

The neighbor to Wade's left is an elderly couple, Richard and Mallory Stoutly. Bob can't ever find them out of town, but he did notice hearing aid batteries in their trash. Google told him that those batteries last about a month, so twenty-eight days later, Bob broke in, gambling that they wouldn't hear him. They didn't. He didn't find anything.

Wade's neighbor to the right is a lady in her thirties who lives alone. Bob's never met her, but Officer Karl says her name is Sariah Fisher. Bob has never once seen her car gone from her driveway at night, until now.

His phone buzzes with Karl's response. *"Looks like the Nikolaus house is also empty tonight. That's where the Longstrum girl was trick-or-treating."*

Bob checks his notes app. He's searched that house before. He's all for searching places multiple times—especially the houses where a kid disappeared right off the porch—but Sariah Fisher lives right next to where he lost Mary, and he hasn't seen inside yet. That takes priority.

Bob tells Karl what he's doing.

Karl responds with a thumbs-up emoji, then also messages, *"There's an extra deputy patrolling nights with me now. The FBI is worried tourists and amateurs will show up now that it's October again. They asked our office to increase patrols."*

Bob reads his underlying point: If you see a squad car, don't assume it's Karl's.

And don't get caught.

Bob slips off the sidewalk into the shadows, to find a way into Sariah Fisher's empty house.

SARIAH FISHER DOESN'T LEAVE her door unlocked.

Smart for Sariah, unlucky for Bob.

He slips back off the front porch, away from the revealing glow of the porch light.

He listens for the rumble of any car motors, but hears only crickets and chirper frogs. That's not good, since he knows at least two police cruisers are driving around. How close do they have to get before he hears them?

He checks under clay planters and cement pavers for a spare key. Nothing.

He sneaks around the back.

Glass french doors lead out to a patio, but there aren't any easy ways inside.

Bob inspects the doorknob and the deadbolt.

A window at ground level catches his eye. Or rather, something inside that window.

Sariah has left a light on in the basement. It's down the hall from the room that Bob is peering into, but it's enough to reveal a massive model train table.

Bob's seen model trains before—there's a shop in town that always sets up displays at holiday festivals. But this is different. There's a simple track loop around the outer edge of the table, on which sits an unmoving train. That train is Halloween themed, along with each model house.

Again, that's not that weird.

What's weird, is that the haunted houses being circled by the train are arranged in a familiar layout. There's a main road down the middle, with smaller roads each branching off.

It's Maple Creek.

There aren't three hundred and twenty-three houses in this model village, maybe a third of that, but the representation of the neighborhood is clear enough.

Bob gets down on his hands and knees for a closer look through the window.

Not each building on the table is a house. There's a ghost tavern and a werewolf movie theater. It's a Halloween village.

Bob doesn't know what to make of this.

Nobody has decorated for Halloween this year, and he expects no one will. Even the Chester brothers—who always competed with each other for the most insane yard display before last year when they created Crimson Corridors at the old school—have enough decency not to remind the thirty grieving families of the night their children disappeared.

And Bob supposes that Sariah Fisher isn't doing anything wrong. If she likes Halloween, there's no reason she can't set up a model village in her basement.

Still. Doesn't all that make *her* uncomfortable, even if she didn't personally lose anybody?

It's possible she set this up before last year and hasn't bothered to take it down, but there's no dust on the tiny porcelain Dracula and none on his convertible. His petite coffin reflects the light from down the hall.

Sariah has been maintaining her Halloween village.

It's not evidence. It's not even worth reporting to Karl or mentioning to Bob's YouTube viewers—not that he tells them about his break-ins.

But it's got Bob's hackles raised.

It's a hunch he wants to follow.

He gets his roll of tools from his backpack. The easiest way to get through a locked door is with force, but that's also the easiest way to announce to the neighborhood that there's a cat burglar in the area. So Bob has learned to open locks with picks.

A bright white light swings across Sariah's backyard.

Bob's heart races. He ducks behind a pair of wheeled trash cans.

The light moves along behind the neighbor's house.

It's a cop's spotlight.

Karl's colleague must be cruising by out front. He must have seen something that grabbed his attention.

It couldn't have been a neighbor who spotted Bob and called it in, or else Karl would have messaged Bob.

He checks his phone. There's a notification.

While Bob was entranced by Sariah's Halloween model train village, he'd missed his phone's buzz.

Karl had messaged, "*Someone called in a stray dog. Keep your head down.*"

Bob hadn't been spotted—just bad luck.

The spotlight moves along down the street, illuminating bits of backyards.

Bob catches his breath, lets his heart rate normalize.

The spotlight darts around treetops several houses down and then starts coming back Bob's way.

The report of the dog must have been on this road.

As much as he wants to get into Sariah's basement, it's not safe to stick around.

The cop's spotlight brightens one edge of Sariah's backyard.

Bob goes still. The spotlight doesn't move on.

Karl's colleague is right in front of Sariah's house.

Bob doesn't wait for the cop to get out and walk around. He goes straight across Sariah's backyard, keeping her house between him and the source of the spotlight. He crosses over into another neighbor's yard, past their house, and onto his own street.

As Bob slinks back home, the clouds move over the three-quarter moon.

Coming home from his "outings" is always a dark affair.

Sneaking out is hopeful. He's venturing out from his castle to find his missing daughter. He's confident there will be answers in the night.

But each time, he returns home to a dreary hovel. There's an empty hole in his family, right where their nervously outgoing daughter should be. He's once again failed to rescue Mary, or even find the tiniest of clues.

It has to be somebody in the Maple Creek neighborhood. Maybe Sariah Fisher.

Thirty kids disappeared.

No one spotted anyone who didn't belong, unless you counted the guy with the jack-o-lantern who only Sam had seen, and Bob had chased that lead as far as it went, which was nowhere. No one else remembered seeing someone with a jack-o-lantern with pink light.

And no one saw any unfamiliar cars driving off. Definitely not any buses or trucks that could have carried thirty kids.

What that means is that they might still be in the neighborhood somewhere.

Bob doesn't buy it when people say they must be dead by now.

His little Mary is alive.

He didn't find her tonight, but tomorrow is another night, and Bob knows exactly where he's looking.

SAM WAKES TO OCTOBER, sees gray skies and orange leaves out the window. He's briefly thrilled about the start of Halloween season, until the reality of his life comes washing back over him.

As he changes out of his Minecraft pajamas into autumn weather clothes, he decides that his brain is perfectly capable of having opposite and contradicting thoughts, even at the same time.

Especially at the same time.

Case in point, he's picked out black pants and an orange shirt—Halloween colors—even while he's also planning not to bring up the holiday around his parents this year.

He used to *love* Halloween.

Today, he hates how the arrival of October—which to his nine-year-old mind is entirely devoted to Halloween—makes him miss Mary so bad that his throat feels clogged and his stomach gets a big rock in it.

He wants to spend Sundays flipping through the sales pages, circling costumes like Spider-Man or the creepy killers from the movies he's not allowed to watch, only to ultimately get Mom's help to make a costume himself, something that doesn't look as cool as the sale papers but makes Sam feel proud of himself as he sets out to make his pillowcase heavy with candy.

At the same time, Sam wants the world outside his head to leave him alone—Halloween included. He wants to make a fort in the woods, one with tight walls and a low ceiling, then sit inside with his eyes closed until trick-or-treating season is over.

Once summer ended and school began, the day-to-day progression of the world led like a funnel to October, and Sam used to love spiraling down that funnel like a bug in a draining bathtub.

Except this year, it's not candy and exhaustion and fun at the bottom. It's also the punch-you-in-the-face reminder that Mary is gone, and it's the physically painful guilt that Sam let her go up those porch steps by herself.

This year, October will be excitement, dread, and shame, all mashed up together, all the time.

He hears Emily in the kitchen, crying for cereal. Mom's probably still doing her morning prayers, and Dad is probably still asleep, so Sam hurries down the hall to help his little sister get started with October.

SAM WALKS HOME FROM SCHOOL, down Rolling Hill Road, past the shopping center with the Food Lion and the Chinese restaurant.

He passes the empty Old Pine Elementary School, which last year had been set up as a fun haunted house. This year, it's still empty.

Sam tries to remember if last year, Crimson Corridors already had a sign out front at the beginning of October. He's pretty sure it did. That's one more ingredient of Halloween he'll be doing without this year.

No costumes, no trick-or-treating, no trying to convince Dad to take him to Crimson Corridors.

It's just as well. Walking by the undecorated old school without even a sign makes Sam notice how empty his hand feels—he should be walking Mary home from Kindergarten, holding her hand, proud of her for making new friends even though she's shy.

Instead, he's walking home to an empty house.

Well, technically Dad is usually home, but he'll either be asleep or working on his videos that he makes about Mary and the other missing kids.

Jeff Wright from Sam's class says that all 30 of the disappeared trick-or-treaters are dead.

Sam likes that Dad is still looking for Mary. Any time Sam worries that he might be forgetting his sister's face, he can peek at Dad's computer and see her picture.

Sam often picks up Emily under her arms, straining to lift her so she can see Dad's monitor with the picture of the little girl who looks so much like her.

"That's Mary," Sam says in those moments. "That's your big sister. When Dad finds her, she'll play with you."

Emily is only three, and it's been eleven months since Mary disappeared. Sam doesn't think Emily remembers her big sister at all.

That's the sad thought occupying Sam's mind when he walks into his front door, drops his backpack with a *thud*, and sees something wrong with the TV.

Dad has mounted the 55-inch LG to the wall, an *oh-led* screen that Mom thinks was too expensive.

At first, when Sam sees the rectangular glow, he thinks it's the picture-in-picture feature which Dad has excitedly shown off. You can watch a football game on the big screen, and at the same time —in a smaller rectangle in the corner—you can watch cartoons.

But the picture on the corner of the TV now isn't a perfect rectangle. It looks like someone has taken a wide paintbrush and slobbed on an irregular patch of video.

Sam looks around the empty living room. "Dad?"

No answer.

He steps closer to the TV.

Black, reflectionless glass surrounds the patch of video.

Oh-led TVs only send light where the picture is. Sam remembers Dad saying that. This is perfectly normal. But it doesn't feel normal.

Right now, the splotch of video shows a big room with white cork ceiling, white painted cinderblock walls, and a purplish-gray, flecked tile floor.

Sam can't see any windows or doors. The room tickles memories, but he's not sure which ones yet.

He smells waxy crayons and thick construction paper.

He suddenly notices a school desk in the center of the room, the kind with a cubby underneath the desktop. Had that been there before?

Shadows warble in the desk cubby.

Sam gets close to the TV, barely registering that the blue light underneath the LG logo isn't on.

He squints, focusing on that narrow rectangle of black within the desk, within the empty classroom. And that's what it is—a classroom, only without the alphabet on the wall or a big soft rug on the floor or a bulletin board of classmates' names.

Maybe the shadows inside the desk cubby have swallowed it all.

Sam gets closer to the TV, trying to see deeper into the classroom, as if the bright section of TV screen were a window he could peer through at different angles.

He's got too close to the TV plenty of times. All pictures on the screen are made of millions of tiny dots called pixels. Sam can't make out any pixels now. The picture of the classroom is as clear as the living room he stands in.

But it's not a window. He can't see past the edges of the picture, even with his nose and cheek against the cold glass.

A dark shape fills the picture. In its center, a pink glow.

Sam falls back in shock. His heart pounds. He feels his eyes widen to assess what must be a threat.

No, he tells himself. It's Mary in her black dress.

But of course it's not.

Sam crab walks backward as a hooded head and shoulders loom over him.

It's a hood like on a sweatshirt.

Sam feels weak. He knows this figure—its dark orange hoodie, and especially the pink glow that accompanies it, lighting the figure from somewhere to the side, past the view of the screen.

Sam saw this man in the seconds after Mary disappeared, so he knows what will be in its hand as it raises it into view: a turnip carved like a jack-o-lantern, but with a fiercely bright, pink light beaming out from the triangle eyes and toothless smile.

Beams of pink light shoot out from the TV screen, into the carpet, between Sam's splayed feet.

He finds his courage and scrambles farther back, but pins himself against the couch as the pink search lights reach his feet. They creep up his legs. His skin tingles underneath where the light touches his jeans.

The lights move up his stomach, over his chest, three pink beams intersecting the open space of the living room.

They reached his chin, his cheeks, and he knows that if they touch his eyes then he'll peer through those tiny passageways across the living room, to the corner of the TV, into the turnip jack-o-lantern's eyes, which are the hooded man's eyes.

Sam won't do that.

He covers his face with his hands, refusing to believe this is real at the same time that he's desperate to escape it.

His hand tingles. The backs of his eyelids become pink. His hands are over his face but the pink light is still shining through.

It hovers there and then blinks out.

Although he can sense its absence, he keeps his eyes shut until he's crawled to the hallway. Only then does he open his eyes and turn back to the living room.

The TV is off. The entire screen.

Sam's lungs ache for air. He breathes deep.

Then he flees to his room.

MICHELLE LETS the McDonald's door swing shut behind her, all too aware that her navy blue polo smells like french fry oil.

She breathes in the October evening air. Nope, still too close to the building.

This job isn't going to work out if she can't get used to the smell.

They wanted her to stay late, but her shift ended at 7:30 and she got the hell out of there at 7:30.

As she walks toward home, she carries her jacket, on the off chance by not wearing it she won't have to wash it.

The sidewalk passes the old school and a fancy neighborhood before it leads to her apartment.

She hates walking by that empty school. The one good thing about those kids vanishing is that nobody is celebrating Halloween this year.

Michelle hates that spooky stuff.

She hears a child crying.

She looks around in the evening darkness. Someone is playing a prank. It can't be a real kid. Nobody around Maple Creek lets their kids run around after dark anymore.

But when she looks across the street at Old Pine Elementary, the moonlight is enough to reveal a tiny surgeon standing in the school doorway.

It's a child in pale teal scrubs and a surgical mask.

Michelle's heart leaps at the strange sight. She stands still, not sure if she'd come across some social media video in progress, or an early trick-or-treater.

Then she notices that the little girl is hugging her chest. Her shoulders are rising and falling gently.

She's crying. Hard.

And she was holding a white pillowcase with something heavy at the bottom. Candy.

Suddenly, Michelle knows who she's looking at.

Well, not exactly who, but she's narrowed it down to thirty.

One of the trick-or-treaters last year had been dressed as a doctor.

Michelle calls the police as she runs across the street to help this missing little girl.

OCTOBER 2ND

Mom takes Emily to a church thing and Dad is still asleep when the bus comes, so nobody notices that Sam skips school.

Today is pizza day, and also library, so normally Sam is excited for school on Thursdays. He's even been hopeful that there'd be some good Halloween books since the month just started. He was planning on sneaking them into his room where Mom and Dad wouldn't see them. They might make him sad, but he wants to try.

Still, after yesterday, he needs to be home where he can see the TV.

The man with the turnip jack-o-lantern is scary, but it's the same man he saw when Mary disappeared. He must be the kidnapper. Find the kidnapper, find Mary.

He hasn't told Mom and Dad about the TV yet. Dad wouldn't believe him—he didn't believe him about seeing the same guy last Halloween. And Mom would probably tell him to pray about it.

Sam goes downstairs. The house is quiet except for Dad's snoring coming through his bedroom door.

Back when Mom first started going to church, after Mary disappeared, Sam got weirded out by the stillness of being home alone.

He and Mary used to play pirates or Star Wars or superheroes, running and jumping and screaming while Emily squealed and staggered after them.

But once Mary was gone, the house was so quiet that Sam had to fill it up with his own noise. He sang songs from *Encanto* and from Mom's *Florence and the Machine* records, or sometimes he acted out his favorite parts from *Trollhunters* and *The Owl House*. Mom smiled at him funny at first, but then sometimes instead she went to her bedroom and cried as quiet as she could, which wasn't very quiet.

Emily would smack her little hands against the locked door, so Sam had to pull her into her room and get a board book to read together until she calmed down.

Mom always came out pretty quick. She never forgot them for long.

But Mom stopped hiding after she started going to church. Sam went with her for a couple months, but after arguing with the Sunday School teacher about whether God would hug mean people, Sam decided he liked staying home by himself. Mom still makes him go sometimes, but not when she thinks he's getting on the bus, instead of playing hooky to investigate the TV.

Sam stands on the plush carpet, staring up at the big blank TV screen. From the kitchen, the fridge hums and the dishwasher glugs.

The TV screen reflects the big white rectangle of the front window. In the black of the screen, Sam sees a dark version of his own reflection.

"Mary?" he whispers.

Only the liquid noise from the kitchen, only Dad's distant snoring.

"Mary, does that man have you?"

A car passes by out front, its reflection cruising across the TV.

Sam wonders if he should try turning it on. But that's not how it was yesterday.

Yesterday, it'd been getting dark—not yet sunset but the clouds had made dusk come early.

One time when Sam was riding in Grandpa's truck at night, Grandpa said that some radio shows reach farther in the dark.

The man in the hoodie hadn't really been in Sam's living room. It was some kind of broadcast. Maybe he can only broadcast when it's dark.

Sam closes the curtain. It squeaks on the rod.

The window's reflection is now the glowing rectangle outline of the curtain. Still not dark enough.

Sam's watch buzzes.

His stomach flips.

Mom must have realized he's not at school.

But no, the message on his watch isn't from Mom. It's from Jeremy, Sam's classmate from across the street.

Jeremy is the only person that Dad has set up Sam's watch to message—other than family.

Sam reads the message as it scrolls across his watch's screen. *"Was it Mary? Is that why you're not here?"*

Sam's confused. Does Jeremy know what Sam saw yesterday?

No, of course Jeremy doesn't know. He has to be talking about something else. Right?

"Who told you I saw something?" Sam speaks into his watch, checks that it correctly transcribed to text, and then he taps "send."

A second later comes the reply. "Everybody knows! It's all over the Maple Creek group." Jeremy means one of the Facebook groups where the neighborhood talks to each other.

Sam isn't allowed any social media yet.

He sends a reply. *"But I didn't tell anyone."*

"What?"

"I didn't tell anyone I saw that man on TV."

"What show are you talking about?"

"Not a show. The screen just came to life."

"That's super weird. I'm coming over tomorrow to see."

"Okay. But what happened that you were talking about?"

"A missing trick-or-treater came back last night. They found her walking out from Old Pine."

Sam reads Jeremy's message three times before it sinks in. When it does, he dashes down the hall. "Dad!"

An hour later, with Sam dropped off at school and a tardy slip signed, Bob drives over to Old Pine Elementary School, more recently the Crimson Corridors haunt, and even more recently, a sprawling shell of a building between Maple Creek and Sam's new school.

Bob's exhausted. He'd wanted to get back over to Sariah Fisher's house last night, but Emily had been up all night crying.

But now his hunch about that weird Halloween-themed train table in Sariah Fisher's house must come second to finding out what the hell is going on with Debbie Meyers reappearing last night.

The crumbling asphalt parking lot is full of his neighbors' cars. The crowd that's gathered around Old Pine's front doors is big enough that many of those in attendance must have walked over.

A yellow police line separates the crowd from the doors. A single cop stands behind the tape, trying unsuccessfully to calm the parents of twenty-nine missing trick-or-treaters.

Four police cruisers are parked in the old bus loop. The cops must already be doing what Bob would like to do: searching the school.

Bob has already seen on Facebook that the reappeared trick-or-treater is Debbie Meyers.

As soon as Sam had told him the news, Bob knew it couldn't be Mary—the police would have already notified them.

But the news still filled Bob with a hope he didn't know he'd been missing.

Bob thought he had refused to lose hope.

That's why he never stopped looking for Mary.

That's why he and Joann can't even talk about their middle child anymore, because Joann is simultaneously grieving and celebrating a future reunion in her newfound Heaven, while Bob is working through a list of houses he hasn't broken into yet.

It'd been a hard eleven months. Harder than Bob has let himself admit.

But now Debbie Meyers has reappeared, whole and healthy as far as Bob understands it.

That's finally real, undeniable evidence that Mary might still be alive.

Bob gets out of the car to join his neighbors in demanding answers from the police. Now that he can hear them, the crowd sounds desperate and grief-stricken more than angry.

Is Bob the only one who has hope? The only one actually doing something?

The parking lot crumbles under his steps.

His phone *dings*.

Karl's finally responded to Bob's many messages. *"All I know is a little girl was found at the front door of the old school. They haven't found anyone else."*

Bob texts back, *"Did Debbie say anything yet?"*

"No idea."

Bob switches over to his camera app. The first news in eleven months—the first breakthrough in his investigation. He needs to get a video uploaded so his network of internet sleuths can start digging.

He pushes through the crowd, past Peg Smith, whose son Donny had disappeared. He passes Maggie Thacker, whose son Andrew is missing. He bumps Rick Allan, whose missing daughter, Anna, is the same age as Mary.

All these people going through the exact same experience as Bob and Joann—why hasn't he spoke to them more?

Hell, Carlos Fuentes lives two doors down. They lost a little girl named Sofia. Couldn't be more similar, and yet they've only ever discussed their daughters' disappearance on the goddam Facebook group.

Bob reaches the police tape. The closest cop has the name "Yachuw" on his badge.

Bob catches the cop's eyes, which immediately go to Bob's upraised phone.

"What have they found inside?" Bob demands.

"Turn your camera off," Officer Yachuw growls. "Show these parents some respect."

That gets some indignant remarks from the crowd. His neighbors actually recognize him.

Bob raises his voice for the camera. "I'm one of these parents. Is my daughter in there?"

An ounce of compassion reveals itself in Officer Yachuw's relaxing expression. "I can only tell you what I've told everyone else, which is all I know: Our guys are still searching inside, but it's just as possible someone dropped off the little girl and then hightailed it out of here."

"The lady who found her—is that what she saw?" Bob hears himself sound like a real investigative reporter. It's been eight months since the last interview he did with fellow parents—no cops have ever agreed to talk to him on camera, not even Karl.

This cop scrunches his brow at Bob. The guy is torn between sympathy for a grieving parent and annoyance at a cell-phone-wielding amateur investigator.

Amped up with nerves and hope, Bob can't help but ask the question again. "Did the lady who found Debbie see someone drop her off?"

Officer Yachuw steps toward Bob, palms open in a placating gesture. "Look man, you're gonna have to wait until the department knows something. Then we'll call the parents before we make a statement to the press." He quiets his voice. "Stop recording for a second."

Bob lowers his phone but keeps it recording.

The cop says, "Nobody saw anybody drop the kid off. There's no cameras here at Old Pine anymore, but the Mickey D's across the street—their drive-through camera points this way, and nobody drove in or out of this front parking lot."

"You think someone dropped her off out back?" Bob asks.

"Well, she hasn't been here the past eleven months, has she?"

Bob pictures a basement room with the 29 other missing kids—with his little Mary—locked inside.

But that's stupid. Someone would have noticed the kidnapper coming and going. Old Pine sits on one of the busiest roads in the county, after all.

"Where are the other kids?" Bob asks, conspiratorially. "Has Debbie said anything?"

"I haven't heard," the cop says, but not in a tone that makes Bob believe him. "The department will call you once we have something to share."

Bob thanks the cop and backs into the crowd. He realizes that he doesn't trust Officer Yachuw. He doesn't trust the county police department to suddenly become competent now that one missing kid has reappeared.

This is fantastic news that Debbie is back, and maybe it's a good thing that the cops will get more serious about their investigation, but Bob's not relying on them to be even halfway useful.

He came here wanting to search the old school for himself, and that desire hasn't changed.

He'll want to talk to Debbie, too. Not sure if her parents will allow that. Definitely not today, but maybe in a few days.

But he still wants to get a closer look at that Halloween village in Sariah Fisher's basement. And now with his need to search the school, tonight is lining up to be a busy night.

OFFICER PJ FREEMAN is perfectly fine with the night shift.

As a first year officer with the Hanover County Police Department, he's got a career of unpleasant shifts ahead of him, so there's no point in stewing over his exhaustion.

Besides, babysitting a crime scene sure beats driving around to hand out speeding tickets.

He gets out of his cruiser and leans against the door. One thing he can't let himself get used to is sitting down all the time. He won't be one of those officers who lets his belly grow out so big that his kevlar vest sticks forward at a downward angle.

PJ breathes deep.

The October night air is the perfect temperature. The days are still warm, and now the nights have just the right crispness to keep him relaxed and alert.

He shines his flashlight around the Old Pine Elementary School parking lot. His lieutenant has tried to get the streetlights turned back on, but the school's been closed so long that the power company can't do it without sending someone out, which is scheduled for tomorrow. So PJ is left with his flashlight and his cruiser's searchlight.

Regular headlights drive by down the road. The McDonald's glows from across the street. Down the way, on the other side of Old Pine, the new elementary school has plenty of working streetlights. PJ can't see them, but they make the night above Old Pine a yellowish charcoal instead of a violet black.

If you ask PJ, there's no real point to this posting. The kidnapper dropped off Debbie and hightailed it out of there.

PJ had joined in the search inside, turning up nothing but dust and a few trinkets left behind from last year's Crimson Corridors haunted attraction.

A metallic squeaking pierces the air.

PJ points his flashlight over to the school's front doors. He's not above getting creeped out once in a while.

Yellow tape still blocks off the school entrance.

He hears that squeaking noise again, this time followed by a rattle and then a *thump*.

PJ's heart jumps.

He sweeps the flashlight beam over the front doors again. All closed.

Someone's fucking with him. "This is a crime scene," he yells into the dark parking lot.

Then his light falls on one of the doors. There's a face behind the dirty glass.

PJ jumps and the flashlight dances around. He brings it back steady to the doors.

Inside the old school, yanking on the locked door, is a little boy in a green, onesie dinosaur costume. He's lost his mask, which allows PJ to see the fear and desperation on the little boy's face.

PJ runs to help the missing trick-or-treater.

OCTOBER 3RD

At 3:00 a.m., Bob rolls out of bed.

Joann snores softly.

She'd gone to sleep as soon as the kids were in bed, like she normally does. Her Bible is on the nightstand.

Bob checks on Emily and then Sam. Emily is sleeping hard, mouth open, arms flung wide to either side. Sam cracks open his eyes when Bob walks in.

"Where are you going?" Sam murmurs, only half awake.

"For a walk. Go back to sleep."

Sam rolls over.

Bob goes back out into the night.

The school takes priority over Sariah Fisher's house.

He walks along the neighborhood streets until he comes to the trail that leads through the woods to Old Pine.

Moonlight is enough to light his way along the dirt path, even though many of the red, yellow, and orange leaves haven't fallen yet.

But as he nears the far end of the trail and the edge of the Old Pine parking lot, his plans run into a big hitch: the hum of a generator and the glare of work lights.

Five police cruisers are parked in the lot, along with several other unmarked cars. A circle of cops stand under the lights, sharing orders or reporting in.

Bob stands still at the edge of the woods.

Something else has happened.

He'd get out his phone to check the news and the Facebook groups, but he doesn't want the cops to notice his phone's light. If they find him heading to the school in the middle of the night, he'll become suspect number one.

But what if they've found evidence the kidnapper left behind? That could be the ticket to finding Mary.

Bob creeps back into the woods to text Karl and get the scoop.

He goes by Sariah Fisher's house, but her car is back in the driveway.

∼

SAM DOESN'T MANAGE to skip school. Dad is up too early.

Over breakfast, he tells Sam, "They found Mark Calton last night. He disappeared last year on Halloween."

Sam doesn't know how to react. That's two missing kids back. He asks the first thing that comes to his mind. "Are they going to find Mary?"

Dad gives him a long, serious look, before saying, "If they don't, I will."

Sam instantly believes him, but he knows that there's extra info Dad needs. Sam is suddenly telling Dad about what he'd seen on the TV—the empty classroom and then the man in the dark orange hoodie with the glowing pink turnip jack-o-lantern.

Sam finishes his confession. It feels like a physical weight lifted to share it with an adult.

He holds his breath while he watches Dad's eyes for a sign of whether he believes him.

But Dad frowns. "You said this was a bad dream you had?"

Sam hasn't said a thing about dreaming and Dad knows it. "No. It happened yesterday."

Dad gets up and walks to the living room. Sam follows a second later to find Dad inspecting the TV.

"You didn't imagine it?" Dad asks, which doesn't frustrate Sam because the fact that Dad is poking around the back of the TV means he's taking him seriously.

"No. The TV came on but only in a little part of the screen."

"What do you mean?"

Sam points to the corner of the TV. "That part was on. The rest was black."

Dad raises an eyebrow. He's back to not believing him. "You can't turn on a piece of the screen. It's either all or nothing."

"That's what I saw. It looked like a classroom. Do you think Mary is in the old school?"

"The cops searched it yesterday and last night. They would have found her."

"Can we go look?" Sam asks.

Dad gives him a funny smile but then says, "No, they'd arrest us for breaking in."

"But we'd be doing something good."

"They wouldn't see it that way."

Sam's noticed that Dad gets angry whenever anybody brings up the police. "Maybe Mary's in a different school. I could look around my school today."

"You said it was an empty classroom?"

"Yeah."

"Your school is overcrowded. There aren't any empty classrooms."

Dad's right.

So the video has to be from inside Old Pine. If Dad won't sneak inside with Sam, then he'll have to find someone else to go with him. His friend Jeremy is brave enough for a secret mission like this. Sam will ask him today.

∽

AFTER DROPPING Sam off at school, Bob comes home and sits on the living room couch.

He watches the blank TV.

Sam isn't a liar, nor is he delusional.

Bob didn't want to make a huge deal and upset his son, so he'd kept it mild. But if Sam really saw something, then it came from somewhere.

Someone put that video on their TV.

Someone is taunting their family.

Bob's YouTube channel invites its share of internet trolls, but this is local. Someone nearby.

Had the kidnapper been standing in Bob's own living room?

He turns on his phone and goes to his WhatsApp group to discuss these new developments.

∼

SAM DOESN'T GET a chance to talk privately to Jeremy until lunchtime.

Both he and Jeremy bring their lunch, so there's a few minutes while their other friends are still in line to get their trays of warm food.

"I wanna ask you something," Sam says.

Jeremy takes a big bite of peanut butter and banana. "You mean why I wasn't here yesterday?"

Sam blinks at his friend. He'd arrived late at school since he tried to skip until he ran to tell Dad about Debbie Meyers returning. At school he'd barely talked to anybody, spending so much time inside his own head. But Sam knows he shouldn't admit he failed to notice his friend was absent. "Where were you?"

Jeremy chews and then chugs from his water bottle full of milk. "Mom kept me home."

"Why?"

Jeremy shrugs. "Something she read on Facebook, I guess. She's worried about the kids showing up again."

That sounds dumb to Sam. "It's a good thing they're coming back. Mary might come home soon."

"But why's the kidnapper doing it? He's just letting kids go?" Jeremy tears open a bag of Cheetos. "My mom says there might be more kidnappings soon."

"That's stupid." Sam unwraps cold pizza from tin foil.

"You calling my mama stupid?" Jeremy grins, inviting Sam into a game of funny insults.

Sam's not in the mood. "Stupid and fat. But I still need your help with something."

Jeremy offers Sam a Cheeto. "As long as I'm home before dark. My mom is seriously freaked out right now. Only reason I'm in school at all is the science quiz today."

Sam groans. He's forgotten about the science quiz and hasn't studied at all. Now he's sure to fail.

But that doesn't matter. "My dad believes me about what I saw on our TV."

"Why wouldn't he?"

"Because it was super weird. In a creepy way."

"I wanna see it."

"I can't make it happen again. It was just that one time."

"Let me come over tomorrow. I can make it happen again, I promise." Jeremy does this all the time, acting like insisting he's right is some kind of evidence for his argument.

"Just like you were going to climb the pine tree in my backyard."

"Hey, those branches were thinner than you said."

"Fine. Come over tomorrow. We can stare at my TV."

∽

PJ isn't the only officer posted at Old Pine on this rainy Friday evening.

Officers Dan Yachuw and Karl Cooper are also taking regular turns, walking around the school, both inside and out.

On the off chance that last year's kidnapper sneaks another

missing trick-or-treater into the empty school, the lieutenant wants to be sure that they catch him in the act.

Old Pine is pretty much one big loop. You walk in the lobby, then you can go left or right. Both directions take a quick turn, bringing you deeper into the school, and then they turn toward each other to complete that loop. In the middle are the cafeteria and the gym.

Officer Yachuw has refused to take a turn on outside rounds. Since PJ is a greenhorn, he's not fighting Yachuw about it.

Right now, Officer Cooper is walking through the mud and rain, from exit to exit. PJ is making the same rounds, but inside.

The walls feel too close and the ceiling too short. But it's an elementary school. Doesn't need to be huge.

PJ shivers. He should have left his rain slicker in the lobby. He needs to dry off.

He walks along the back hallway, past the short hall that leads to the back doors. Those doors open, and PJ doubles back.

The sound of heavy rain enters the quiet school.

Karl Cooper, rain slicker drenched, sticks his head inside. "Officer Freeman!"

"Right here," PJ says.

Cooper squints into the lit hall. "Bring me a coffee."

They've set up a coffee machine in the lobby.

"Get it yourself," PJ says.

Cooper only has a couple years seniority. PJ doesn't need to obey him.

"Come on," Cooper switches his attempted order to a request. "It's cold tonight. I'll bring you one on your outdoor rounds."

"Come inside," PJ says. "You really think the kidnapper is going to drop a kid off with three patrol cars parked out front?"

Cooper shrugs. "He did it last night when you were here."

A bouncy thump echoes down the hallway.

"What was that?" Cooper whispers.

PJ walks in the direction of the noise. "Officer Yachuw? Is that you?"

Cooper drips on the floor behind PJ.

Another thump from behind the gym doors. It's a rubbery and echoey sound.

"That's a basketball," Cooper says.

PJ opens the gym door.

It's dark inside, but the light from the hallway spills into the gym in a wedge shape.

A boy in a pirate costume—complete with hand-drawn mustache—turns toward PJ, squinting at the light like Cooper had a second ago.

Old basketballs are rolling away from him. He's kicked them while stumbling around in the dark.

"Hot damn," whispers Cooper.

"Come here, buddy," PJ says.

The boy's eyes adjust enough that he sees the two police officers, and he runs toward them.

∾

Lauren is *pissed*.

Today, she and her sister Rachel showed their mom a Pinterest board with the coolest Halloween costumes.

Lauren pointed at a fairy costume they could make with store-bought wings and real vines from the woods! She and Rachel would look so good.

But Mom shut them down. "No trick-or-treating this year."

It's not fair.

Lauren sits in her pajamas in the den, watching a TikTok tutorial about braiding hair. Rachel sits on the floor in front of her, not even complaining when Lauren accidentally tugs too hard.

"We can go buy candy," Rachel says. "I have some money."

"That's not the point. It's not our fault those kids got taken. We should be able to dress up and have fun. I'm almost too old to trick-or-treat. Now it's like, did I already have my last year?"

"If we go the day after Halloween, the candy will be really cheap," Rachel says.

Lauren tugs her sister's hair on purpose.

"Ow!"

"You're not listening."

There's a knock at the front door.

"That's weird," Rachel says. "What time is it?"

They both know it's after nine, because they've been watching the stairs for Mom. Once she realizes they're still up, she'll send them to bed, who cares that it's Friday.

Lauren says, "Answer the door before Mom hears."

Rachel has gone real still. "You answer it. You're older."

Lauren quietly gets up.

"Faster," Rachel says. "Before they knock again."

Lauren walks softly over the carpet. She looks out the window. "No one's out there."

The knock comes again.

Both girls jump.

Mom calls from upstairs. "Did you girls drop something?"

"It's nothing!" Rachel yells back. Then she hisses at her sister. "Open it!"

Lauren opens the door.

There's a pumpkin on the front porch. No, a jack-o-lantern.

It's got triangle eyes, one bigger than the other. Its mouth is a smooth, wide smile. There's a yellow square of paper beside the mouth.

Lauren feels Rachel touch her back and peek out from behind her. "Who left that?"

"I don't know. Maybe Bradley."

"Your boyfriend?"

"He's not my boyfriend, but he knows I'm sad about Halloween."

"Tell him to bring us candy next time. Tell him I like Red Vines, not Twizzlers."

"Shut up." Lauren bends over to grab the yellow square of paper. It's a sticky note. She reads it aloud, "Surprise inside."

"He did bring us candy!" Rachel says. "Open it."

"Open a pumpkin?" Lauren asks. Normally, her sister's question wouldn't be that weird, but this jack-o-lantern doesn't have a lid. Nobody's carved open the top. They've only cut out the uneven eyes and toothless mouth.

"Weird," Rachel says. She bends over to inspect the pumpkin.

Lauren pulls her back.

"Stop it," Rachel jerks away. "What candy did you tell Bradley that you like?"

She puts her head near the porch floor so she can see inside the jack-o-lantern's mouth.

Lauren holds her breath. "What do you see?"

"It's too dark." Rachel starts to reach inside.

Before her fingers can pass between the smooth edges of the grinning mouth, Lauren grabs her. "Don't be stupid."

"What? It's not dangerous."

Now Lauren feels like a wimp. "I mean don't be stupid, it's from Bradley so it's my candy." That's what she says, but really she's worried about her sister. "I'll get it myself."

Lauren squats down. Rachel was right—it's too dark out here. The light from inside the house barely reaches inside the pumpkin. There's orange stringy mess and white seeds, but not much of it.

She reaches in. It's slimy and gross.

Lauren laughs. "Yuck."

"What?" Rachel asks.

Lauren flings some pumpkin innards at her sister. "Pumpkin guts!"

"Ugh. I hate you!" But Rachel is laughing, too.

This is the Halloween season they aren't allowed to have this year.

Lauren pats around inside. "I hope whatever candy Bradley gave me isn't open yet. It'll get all slimy."

Her fingers pat something hard and light. It's the corner of a piece of wood. "What is this?" she asks to herself.

The wood jumps and there's a terrible pain in her pointer finger.

She yanks her hand free.

Rachel screams.

Blood is pouring over her knuckles, splattering onto the cement of the porch and onto the pumpkin.

A mousetrap has snapped over her hand. Something glistens where the thick metal wire has pinned her finger.

A razor blade.

This pumpkin isn't from Bradley.

Lauren doesn't know who it's from.

Rachel yells for Mom.

As Lauren watches her hand bleed and starts to get dizzy, she really wishes Mom would get down here faster.

OCTOBER 4TH

Saturday morning, Jeremy comes over after breakfast.

Dad is still asleep and Mom has taken Emily to church.

"Alright, let's see it," Jeremy says as Sam lets him in.

Sam points to the TV. "You know where my TV is."

This is stupid and pointless, but Jeremy is so confident that Sam feels a tiny bit of hope. Maybe they'll find Mary before Dad even wakes up. That'll show Dad that Sam wasn't seeing things.

"What do I do?" Jeremy asks. "Turn on the TV?"

Sam walks up close to the dark screen. "No, it was off when I saw it. Only a little part of the screen had video going."

"Is that how your TV works?"

"No."

"That's how my uncle's projector works. You point it at the wall and it makes a TV screen. Do you have a projector in here?" Jeremy goes to the couch and starts pulling up cushions.

Sam joins him. "What's a projector look like?"

"My uncle's is a gray metal box, like this big." He holds his hands six inches apart. "It's got a glass circle where the picture shines out, and there's a bunch of buttons on top."

Stacks of Mom's books sit on the end table, all about grief and God. In between two of those stacks is some kind of dirty softball.

Curious, Sam touches it.

It's cold and scratchy under his fingertips, which can't quite reach around it. He scoops it up with both hands.

Now that he can get a good look at it, chills run up his spine.

Jeremy asks, "Is that an onion?"

"It's a turnip," Sam says.

"Oh shit," Jeremy plucks it out of Sam's hands. "Did that creepy guy leave it in your house?"

Fear floods Sam again. "He wasn't in my house. Just on the TV."

"You said it was like pink headlights in fog pointing straight at you." Jeremy flips the turnip over. "I thought he carved it like a jack-o-lantern."

"He did." Sam doesn't understand how this turnip is in his house. Has it been there since Wednesday? Does this mean the hooded man is coming back for him?

"Hey, look at this." Jeremy holds up the turnip. A glass circle has been pressed into its hard flesh. "It's like the lens on my uncle's projector."

Curiosity drowns out Sam's fear. "Are there circuit boards and whatever inside?"

While his friend holds the turnip, Sam peeks into the lens.

"Well?" Jeremy asks.

"Hold it up to the lamp."

"You're blocking the light with your big head."

"Keep it still." Sam thinks he sees circuitry. There's definitely something that's not a natural part of a turnip.

Through the lens, a soft pink glow flickers to life.

Sam jumps back. "Put it down."

Jeremy throws the turnip on the couch. "What's wrong? What did you see?"

Sam backs up toward the hallway. "A pink light inside. Like the hooded man's jack-o-lantern."

Jeremy whispers, "Is this the one he was carrying?"

Sam shakes his head. "That one had eyes and a mouth carved into it. It was a lot bigger. I don't know what this is."

The turnip lies next to a throw pillow, projecting pink light onto the gray couch cushions. That light doesn't fit with the couch's colors. It doesn't fit with the living room's cozy atmosphere. It doesn't even fit with the weakening sense of *home* that's been draining away these past eleven months.

"I have to go," Jeremy says.

"No you don't. Your mom isn't expecting you home for a couple hours. You're afraid of how weird it is, aren't you?" Sam wants to hear that from Jeremy, to know that he's not alone in facing whatever is going on.

Jeremy keeps his eyes pinned to the couch. "My mom might want me home early."

Sam feels a welling panic at being left alone, even if Dad is asleep down the hall. "You feel it, right? You know there's something wrong with it."

"It's a turnip with a pink flashlight stuck into it. I'm going home." Jeremy runs out the front door.

Sam follows. Strong wind makes his arms and face cold. "Don't be a pussy," he shouts, feeling guilty for using a bad word.

"An *unkind* word," Dad would say.

Sam is allowed to use *bad* words, or at least he was before Mom started going to church. It's *unkind* words that Dad won't let him use.

As Jeremy tromps through the yard and across the street, he turns around to shout, "You should throw that thing away. Vegetables are gross."

Suddenly, Sam remembers why he'd wanted to talk to Jeremy about this in the first place. He yells after his friend, "I think Mary's inside Old Pine. Help me go look for her."

Jeremy turns back to look at Sam like he's stupid, but Sam also sees the fear in his friend. Jeremy shakes his head and goes inside his house.

∼

BACK IN THE LIVING ROOM, Sam works up the courage to approach the turnip on the couch.

The pink light has gone out. Now it's just a vegetable with a glass lens stuck into it.

How is he possibly going to save Mary if he's too chickenshit to even move a turnip?

He takes a deep breath, picks up the turnip with both hands, and sets it back on the end table, this time in front of the stacks of Mom's books instead of hidden between them.

What's he supposed to do with this? If it's a projector and it put that video of the man in the hoodie on the TV, then how did those pink beams of light come from the TV?

He looks around the turnip without touching it. The only thing weird about it is the lens. He tries to pull it out but it's in there pretty good.

He adjusts the turnip so the lens points at the TV.

The next step is to go inside Old Pine and look for Mary. The idea of going alone terrifies him.

He sits on the couch, waiting for either the TV to light up again or to magically gain the courage to go in Old Pine alone.

Before either happens, Mom and Emily get home, and they whisk him away to an outing of Chick-fil-A and then the library.

His anxiety about what to do follows him all day.

∼

WHILE HIS FAMILY IS OUT, Bob sits in his office.

After he woke up, he cruised Facebook and Nextdoor to see people talking about a Halloween prank that went way too far. At least, Bob assumes that's what it is. The rumors people are spreading are about mousetraps and razorblades, but Bob thinks once the dust settles it'll be some kid who didn't realize a mousetrap can actually mess up a finger pretty bad.

He makes a mental note to keep an eye on it, though.

There are also rumors that when the returned kids get to the hospital, they start panicking about something. Makes sense, after being held captive for nearly a year.

After his social media rounds, Bob makes a short video, updating his viewers on the third returned trick-or-treater.

There's not much to say. For the third time, no one has spotted anyone dropping them off. The cops haven't found a cache of kids inside Old Pine. The kids are appearing alone, somewhere inside the school.

Comments come in. Theories that Bob has already checked out. Well-wishes that Mary will be home soon.

His WhatsApp group with his most devoted followers is buzzing with requests for more info. He's got hundreds of internet sleuths raring to go, but nowhere to send them.

But he appreciates the community.

It's better than what he has in Maple Creek.

Bob hasn't been invited to a cookout in years. Not that he can be harsh on his neighbors about that—he hasn't hosted a cookout in years, either.

The only neighbors he regularly talks to face-to-face are the parents of his kids' friends. Although, that happens less and less since twenty-nine of his neighbors went missing, and everyone became more protective.

But he still generally knows what's going on in Maple Creek because everyone chats on Nextdoor and Facebook.

The town square has gone digital.

He doesn't like it, would much prefer catching up with his neighbors face-to-face. But that's the way the world is and you have to take what you can get.

He goes back to skimming through those pages now.

Today, there's camaraderie in Maple Creek.

The communication is all online, but at least everyone is talking.

Three nights in a row, a missing child has reappeared.

Debbie Meyers on October first, Donny Smith on the second, Beto Esquivel on the third.

This is a pattern now.

It's repeating.

The next repeating moment is scheduled for tonight, around 7:30, at the front doors of Old Pine Elementary School.

Bob intends to be there.

Hope and fear dance in his chest. He's got the same hope that he's reading in his neighbors' posts and comments: If this pattern continues, it'll bring home his own missing child. What if Mary comes home tonight?

Forget his whole investigation, every scant clue he's found along the way. If Mary comes through those doors, then nothing else in the world will matter. He just wants his daughter back.

Bob wanders to the kitchen.

The front door opens and Joann comes inside. Emily dashes in a moment later, a hurricane bottled into a three-year-old's body.

"Shoes!" Joann calls as Emily sprints across the carpet to her dollhouse.

Joann sees Bob and offers him a genuine smile. "You slept in today. Were you out last night?"

Bob gives his normal answer, which sometimes is a lie, but today is honest. "I was up late working on videos."

Sam walks in, a stack of chapter books in his arms. He looks at Bob and quickly lowers his eyes. That sets off alarm bells in Bob's head. There's something Sam doesn't want to talk to his dad about. He'll need to ask about that.

Joann follows Emily to her dollhouse and removes her shoes. "We had a good discussion in Bible Study this morning, all about the Parable of the Lost Coin."

Bob thinks he remembers that one. A woman loses a coin, looks for it like crazy, and finds it. A little on the nose for the Maple Creek community, but he supposes most people at Joann's church don't live in Maple Creek. "Sounds nice."

Then she drops a bomb on him. "We're all going to the old school. They prayed with me that Mary will come home tonight."

It takes real effort not to let his jaw drop.

What he doesn't say is, *But you think she's dead. You GRIEVED her.*

Because that would be a terrible thing to say. He's spent eleven months wanting Joann to see that Mary must still be alive, and that's been an earnest desire. It's not that he wants to be *right* or win an argument—he wants Joann to be as hopeful as he is.

So now that Joann is so matter-of-factly stating that she'll be waiting outside Old Pine, Bob makes himself accept it completely and immediately.

"I'll go with you," he says.

Joann nods a few seconds too long, clearly deciding whether to point out that Bob doesn't care for Joann's church friends. But she doesn't, because to do so would be to point out that their relationship has become a minor priority for the both of them. For Bob, it ranks far below his search for Mary. For Joann, it ranks far below working through her grief for Mary.

But now, the missing children are coming home.

Priorities are realigning.

Emily climbs to the top of her dollhouse like an overall-wearing King Kong, Sam drops his books to run and help her balance, while their parents consider that maybe the roadtrip of their marriage isn't running out of gas after all.

∼

BOB SQUEEZES JOANN'S HAND.

They've left the kids with Joann's sister.

It's raining and dark, but they join the crowd of their neighbors around the Old Pine Elementary School front doors.

Joann's church friends hold her hand on her other side. Bob thinks they embody the word "frumpy," but of course he'll never say that out loud. No need to be a jerk.

There are cops at each entrance to Old Pine. Probably a few inside, as well.

At this front entrance, three cops stand behind yellow plastic barriers, rain jackets reflecting the super bright work lights.

There's the pissy Officer Yachuw. Next to him is a young officer who can't be older than twenty. His name patch reads "Freeman."

Beside the young cop is Karl. Bob tries to catch Karl's eye, but for obvious reasons Karl avoids him.

It's not just the camera phone that Bob keeps raised and recording under his umbrella. It's also the fact that any night, Bob might get caught breaking-and-entering. And since Maple Creek is Officer Karl's beat, nobody better see Karl ever buddying up to Bob.

Officer Yachuw raises a megaphone. "Please go home. We'll keep you updated with everything we learn. But for now, go home before you get pneumonia."

He has a point. A few of the parents are pushing sixty. But Bob isn't going anywhere. When Mary walks out of those glass doors, she'll see her mom and dad.

Someone in the crowd yells, "Let us search inside."

As if the three cops and the flimsy plastic barriers could stop fifty determined adults. But where would they go? Three kids have now appeared in the school, but not in the same place as each other. It wouldn't help anything to have all the parents wandering the premises. As much as Bob hates to admit it, they'd only get in the way of the cops catching the kidnapper.

Of course, they don't actually know that the kidnapper has snuck the kids inside the last three nights. Some of his neighbors have speculated on NextDoor and Facebook that the rest of the kids are already inside, hidden somewhere. Bob's not ready to buy into that theory quite yet. The local police force isn't so incompetent that in three nights of searching they could have missed twenty-seven kids in Old Pine.

Someone shouts from the crowd, "There's someone inside."

The cops whirl around, except for Karl, who glances Bob's way first.

A small figure is up against the interior glass doors.

When did they get there?

Their height says they're no older than ten. Even through the fogging glass, Bob sees an all-black costume.

Pants and a mask.

Not a witch's dress.

Not Mary.

He feels Joann's shoulders slump. She's noticed the same thing.

Who is this, then?

A boy in a ninja costume. Bob knows each missing child and their costume. This is Calvin Mitchel, a boy from Sam's class last year.

The cops are moving to the doors.

Calvin is leaning against the door. Bob can't make out his face, but why isn't he moving?

He hears a cry of hope. Tina Mitchel, Calvin's mom. The crowd lets her through. The cops don't try to stop her because they're all trying to get the doors open.

Calvin is leaning funny against the glass.

Bob suddenly doesn't want to record this, but he also doesn't dare turn off his camera.

Tina passes between the barriers just as the cops open the doors and the little ninja falls through. His limp body hits the sidewalk. Bob hears the boy's head thud against cement.

Tina screams.

Bob moves forward, needing to see what's wrong with Calvin, already knowing.

The cops all kneel at the boy's side as his mother arrives. They're being delicate but Tina hits the ground to lift her baby into her arms.

Calvin's head hangs limp.

As the cops pull Tina away, Bob gets a clear view of Calvin's face. His jaw hangs uneven. His eyelids cover his pupils but are open enough to show lower crescents of white.

Bob puts his phone in his pocket and rushes back to Joann, determined not to let her see their murdered neighbor.

OCTOBER 5TH

SAM WAKES up and instantly knows something is wrong.

He hears the trilly melody of the *Bluey* theme song, which means Emily is parked happily on the couch.

The tea kettle is whistling, and only Mom drinks tea.

Today is Sunday. Mom goes to church most days, but she never misses the Sunday morning service, and she always takes Emily with her.

Nerves writhe in Sam's gut. He doesn't want to know what's wrong.

But what if it's good news?

Sam gets out of bed. He walks down the hallway to the open doorway between the kitchen and living room.

The turnip is on the kitchen counter. Either Mom or Dad has moved it from the end table.

Is this why Mom is skipping church? Did the projector cut on again?

Mom stands next to the counter. She pours hot water into two cups and then sits down across from Dad. She places one cup in front of him.

Dad looks exhausted, which is pretty normal, but this morning he's left a red mark on his forehead from rubbing it so much.

The skin around Mom's eyes is puffy. She dangles a teabag over her cup.

Awkwardness hangs heavy in the air. Sam plows through it. "Why aren't you at church?"

Both Mom and Dad jump at his voice.

Mom says, "Can you go watch cartoons with Emily? Dad and I need to finish our discussion."

They haven't said a word to each other since the tea kettle woke up Sam.

Dad plops his teabag into his cup. "Sam needs to hear it from us."

"Bob," Mom says, but Dad is already talking.

"Calvin Mitchel died last night."

Sam tries to process this. "But he was missing."

"He showed up at the school, like the kids before him, but he was dead."

Back in second grade, Calvin had been in his class. They played together at recess. When he'd disappeared, it had been sad, but for Sam, his classmate's disappearance was overshadowed by Mary.

Now he's dead?

Sam thinks he should cry, but then he has a more terrible thought. "What about Mary? I thought she was coming home soon. Is she okay?"

Mom answers too quickly, "Of course she is."

Dad sips his tea and glowers at Mom. "We don't know if Mary's okay."

"Bob," Mom spits Dad's name. "A whole year of hope and now you're giving up?"

Dad sets down his cup. Sam thought Dad would be angry but he sounds more surprised than anything. "I'm not giving up. After the first three nights of kids coming home, I thought it was guaranteed that Mary would be home soon. Our year without our daughter was finally coming to an end. But after Calvin, the truth might be that our time to find Mary is running out."

Mom stands up and gently takes Sam's arm. "Don't talk like this in front of Sam."

But Sam knows Dad is right.

"What do you plan to do?" Dad asks Mom. "Pray that God brings her back?"

"As a matter of fact," Mom says, "yes! But you'll also notice that I'm not at Sunday Services today. I'm here with you to figure out what we should do. I saw Calvin just like you did. I heard Tina screaming and the police panicking."

Sam doesn't like imagining Calvin's mom screaming.

Dad's shoulders slump. "I'm sorry. I'm glad you're here."

Mom says, "Thank you," and then tries to usher Sam out of the kitchen.

Sam isn't getting excluded from searching for Mary. He didn't go up to that porch with her last year—he's not abandoning her again. "The guy in the hoodie with the turnip jack-o-lantern has Mary."

"What?" Mom asks.

Dad sighs. "Sam saw something really weird on the TV. I don't think he's making it up, but maybe he got freaked out by a YouTube video or something."

That's worse than a berating and a punishment from Dad. "I thought you believed me."

"I'm sorry, buddy. We're all so stressed out. It's hard to say what anybody's really seeing."

Sam picks up the turnip from the counter. "What about this?"

"What about that?" Mom asks. "Bob, why'd you get a turnip?"

"I thought you bought it."

"I found it on the table by the couch," Sam says. "Jeremy's uncle has a projector so he said maybe the video I saw of the school and the hoodie guy was being projected, and we found this so I think it was."

Dad cracks his knuckles. Usually when Dad does that it means he's about to say something nice but also that he's going to sound really impatient about it. "Why does a turnip mean there was a projector?"

"Because look." Sam finds the glass lens on the turnip and holds it up for his parents to see.

"What the hell?" Dad says.

"Language," Mom says but she's just as entranced as Dad. She takes the turnip and peers into the lens, then feels around the rest of the vegetable's surface. She hands it to Dad.

He inspects it in the same way. "You found this on the end table?"

Sam nods.

"It was there when you saw the video?"

"I think so. I saw the video on Wednesday but didn't find the turnip until Jeremy came over yesterday."

"Is it possible that Jeremy snuck the turnip in?" Dad asks.

Mom *tsk*s. "Why would he do that?"

"Because if he didn't, then someone else was in our house. I want to be very sure about that."

Sam thinks hard. "No. I opened the door. Me and Jeremy talked about the video while he walked inside. Then he told me about his uncle's projector, and he looked on the couch for one, and I looked on the end table. Jeremy never went to that side of the room."

Mom hugs her arms across her chest. "Should we feel better or worse about that?"

Dad shakes his head. "We've got a lot to discuss. Are you guys hungry?"

He gets out the electric griddle and the big blue bag of pancake mix.

Sam sits at the table. He's happy to not be treated like a kid, but also it would be nice to watch *Bluey* with Emily and pretend everything is okay.

⁓

BOB THINKS MORE CLEARLY while he cooks, even something simple like chocolate-chip pancakes. Keeping his hands busy lets his brain focus on what matters.

But this morning, there's so much to think about.

Once he gets some food in his stomach, maybe he should cut open that turnip.

But what's the point? Someone was inside their house, but what does that prove? It doesn't get Mary home any quicker.

If they find out who it was, it'd have to be the kidnapper, right? And if he can find the kidnapper, he'll find Mary.

He needs to get inside Old Pine.

For the thousandth time this year, Bob angrily wishes he could depend on the police.

But the cops have been useless. Even now, they've searched the old school every day, and yet each night another missing kid comes out from inside.

The obvious answer is the kidnapper is ferreting them inside, but the cops have been watching all the exits. No one's so incompetent that they could have missed a man dragging in a kicking, screaming child. Either the kidnapper has a secret way into the school, or the wackos on the internet are right, and twenty-six kids are hidden somewhere inside Old Pine.

He can't rely on the cops to find them.

Bob needs to get in before Mary's turn comes.

Joann interrupts Bob's increasingly frantic thoughts. Not with words, but with the *shunk* of a chef's knife cutting the turnip-projector in half.

"Hey," Bob says, because dissecting the turnip had been on his list of things to do, all piling onto him at once.

Inside the turnip is just turnip.

Joann cuts it again, a finger's width closer to the lens.

More turnip.

Again, only a slice at a time, as to not cut through whatever electronic guts there must be.

Finally, with both Bob and Sam watching intently, Joann slices down only three inches away from the lens.

The knife taps against something metal. Joann ever-so-carefully slices around a cylinder.

She pulls it free from the turnip.

"It looks like a miniature telescope," says Sam, and Bob agrees.

A bubble lens on one end, a two-inch cylinder behind it.

Bob picks it up to see what sort of screwdriver he'll need to get it open, but it's all one solid piece. He tries to unscrew the lens itself—maybe you access it from one end, like a flashlight.

But the lens feels glued on.

Bob has some heavy-duty solvents in the garage he can try later on, although they might damage anything inside.

"We should give this to the police," Joann says.

"No," Bob says before thinking. But he's sure of his belief. Even if the cops suddenly become competent, this would have to change hands three or four times before anybody learned anything from it. There'd be paperwork and waiting for the right specialist to take it apart. There's one kid coming home each night now, one out of four have come home dead, and there's only twenty-six kids remaining, so that means... Bob does some math in his head... something like a 3.9% chance that Mary comes back tonight. Or a 1% chance that she dies tonight.

He's not rolling the dice on his daughter's life by handing over the only piece of evidence to the cops.

"Then what do you want to do?" Joann asks.

Bob is surprised that Joann doesn't push the issue, but he's happy to have her on board. "I'll ask my YouTube viewers if they've seen anything like it. Maybe we can figure out who sells this stuff around here."

"Amazon sells stuff like this," Joann says. "This isn't nineteen-nineties *Law and Order*. We can't go question the local shopkeep."

"What's a shopkeep?" Sam asks.

"Someone who works at a store," Bob says. "Well, one of my subscribers will know how we can get any personal data off of it. At the very least, we can see the video that you saw, Sam."

"We should ask the other parents if they found anything like this," Joann says.

Bob agrees. "What about the Meyers, Smiths, or Esquivels? Do you think they'd let us talk to their kids?"

"We can ask," Joann says. "I'm sure the cops are all over them. I saw a news van by the Meyers. A reporter was using their house as a backdrop for their miracle story."

"I'm sure they're exhausted. But if those kids can tell us anything about where they've been, maybe we can find Mary in time."

"I don't personally know any of them," Joann says. "But I can reach out on Facebook. Or we can go knock on the door."

"Yes. Let's do both."

"What about your cop friend?"

Bob forgot he'd told Joann about Karl. "He's not a detective. I doubt he'll know the details of interviews, but I'll ask."

They've got a plan:

Get help from Bob's YouTube viewers about how to get information off this tiny projector.

Find out if any other parents of a missing trick-or-treater found one.

Talk to the families of the returned kids.

But even all that feels like a secondary priority to Bob.

Tonight, there's a one percent chance that Mary dies. He knows where the kids are reappearing. All his old ways of investigating must play second fiddle to actively searching for his daughter.

"I want to get inside that school," he says.

Joann shakes her head. They've never spoken aloud about his breaking into their neighbors' homes. She must know about it but doesn't want to confront it. It's wrong, it's dangerous, it's stupid.

But now she's sitting at the table, on board with the rest of his investigations—the parts that aren't illegal. Actually searching the crime scenes is essential.

"The police must be turning that place upside down," Joann says.

"Are they? Because every time I drive by, I see two or three cop cars outside, and all those anger-prone C-students are standing outside the front doors, not doing shit. They searched it at first, but they're too arrogant to think they could have missed something."

"I'm sure they've searched it again. Especially now that Calvin..." Joann trails off, glances at Sam.

Sam is a tough kid. If he wasn't eleven months ago, he's learned to be now. "I'll go tonight," Bob decides. "After the cops have given up again. After any excitement from tonight's arrival dies down."

They all three become very interested in patterns in the vinyl floor. It's better than saying aloud what they're all thinking, that tonight's arrival might be a happy reunion, but it might also be the beginning of a lifetime of grief.

Sam speaks first. "I want to help. What can I do?"

"Ask your friends if they've seen one of these." Bob holds up the metal cylinder. "Not any projector. But one that looks exactly like this."

Sam nods excitedly. "What about tonight? I can go with you, help you find the classroom that I saw on the video. There was this one desk—"

"No," Bob says. There's no way he's letting his nine-year-old break into a crime scene with him. But he's spoken too sharply. Sam has taken an impulsive step back. Bob feels like a terrible father, scaring his boy like that. "You let me worry about the old school. You be a fact-finder, okay?"

Sam says, "Okay," but Bob sees himself in the way Sam quietly, intelligently withdraws. Sam's given the answer the authority figure wants to hear. Shit. The last thing Bob needs is Sam wandering off on his own. "I mean it. There's lots of people in this neighborhood who won't open up to me, but maybe they'll talk to you. Ask your friends' questions. That's how you can best help."

"Got it," Sam says. He goes to sit by his sister in front of *Bluey*.

Joann asks, "What was that about?"

"He's gonna go off and do something stupid."

"He wants to help Mary, but he's not dumb."

"You're right. Not something dumb. Something risky."

"What's the difference?"

"Whether it's worth it."

"He's just found out his friend died," Joann says. "He's afraid the same thing will happen to his sister. Let him daydream about saving her."

Bob thinks of himself at nine-years-old, thirty years ago. "We gotta keep an eye on him."

∼

Bob spends the rest of the morning recording footage talking about Calvin's reappearance, and then footage for a separate video asking for help identifying the projector they found inside the turnip.

He edits the first and posts it, but both Sam and Emily are eager for his attention today.

Emily doesn't understand that their neighbor has died, but she can sense her family's fear.

Sam feels what he's feeling and knows it's called "grief" but knowledge is no preparation for the knotting in his gut and the enormity of life without ever seeing Calvin again and the fear that Mary will be next and one day death will come to everyone who Sam loves.

And so Bob closes his laptop and spends the afternoon building Legos with his kids.

∼

PJ Freeman is at Old Pine again, but after the dead kid appeared in the vestibule last night, the State Troopers are now involved.

They tore the place apart but didn't find anywhere the kidnapper is sneaking these kids inside.

Now PJ is patrolling the main hallway loop. There's a trooper thirty feet ahead of him. Officer Yachuw is thirty feet behind him. They're walking the halls like it's a slow track meet.

At 7:31 P.M., Wendy Rusher wanders out from a classroom into the arms of the state trooper. She's wearing a pink sparkly dress and wire-and-lace fairy wings.

As the trooper carries Wendy to the front where her parents are waiting, PJ storms into the classroom.

It's empty.

White cinderblock walls that need new paint. Tile floor that needs to be swept. An empty closet.

A different trooper runs in behind him. When he sees that it's empty, he gives PJ a look like it's his fault.

PJ doesn't care. He's just glad that Wendy showed up alive.

∽

OUTSIDE, Bob and Joann witness Wendy's reunion with her parents.

The Channel 12 news van is in the parking lot, but the residents of Maple Creek aggressively keep the reporters away from the Rusher family.

Bob records it all. Joann leans on him. She's laughing and crying.

Mary isn't home, but at least there isn't more death.

Bob notes that Wendy's fairy wings are dusty but whole. He's sure that means something but he doesn't know what.

∽

RICHARD STOUTLY HEARS THE SHRIEKING, electronic laughter from outside, and he does not appreciate it, thank you very much.

In all his sixty-eight years, he's never heard something so insensitive.

A boy died last night, a boy who'd been kidnapped last Halloween. Most of this fine neighborhood has the wherewithal not to set up any seasonal decorations—despite Maple Creek's long history of enthusiastically celebrating the holiday—but now it turns out that one of his neighbors has set up some warbling ghost noise.

The damned laughter is as tinny as a greeting card jingle, and Richard is dead sure that isn't because of his hearing aids.

He calls to his wife, "Mallory, I'm stepping outside a moment."

Richard takes his peacoat from the closet, slides his feet into his slippers, and goes out onto the porch.

There aren't many stars tonight. There never are, not since they put in that damned Wegmans distribution center up the road. Richard looks around to his neighbor's yard, trying to spot a ghost decoration, either a blow mold or a plywood cutout, or maybe a bedsheet dangling from a tree. Not an inflatable because Richard doesn't hear a blower motor.

He doesn't spot anything right away.

The laughter comes again. It's from over to his left.

That'd be Wade Greenwood's house. Or Sariah Fisher's house, past Wade's.

He can't imagine sweet Sariah would try to aggravate the neighborhood like this, but he wouldn't put it past Wade.

Richard moseys along his front walk, craning his neck to see into Wade's yard.

Motion-activated lights kick on in his own driveway. His Honda Pilot blocks his view. He's parked it out here since Mallory has her quilting rack set up in the garage, and chivalry says if there's one spot in the garage, it belongs to his wife.

Richard walks around his SUV.

Both Wade's and Sariah's porch lights are on.

There's a dark spot in the grass between Richard's and Wade's driveways.

Someone's standing there.

Richard exhales and grabs his heart when he sees it.

"Shoot, young man, you about gave me a heart attack. What are you doing there?" Richard used to have a VP9 pistol in a hidden box in the coat closet, but it was a long time ago he gave up believing he could quick-draw fast enough to stop a home intruder. As he squints at the shadowy figure in the dark, he wishes he was holding that gun now. "Are you going to answer me?"

The person is perfectly quiet, perfectly still. Might not actually be a person, now that Richard considers it.

He fumbles for his phone. There's a flashlight app on there, if he can remember how to turn it on.

The thing in front of him cackles.

This time Richard really does fear he's having a heart attack. But it doesn't hurt. He hasn't fallen over. Only his heart accelerated faster than he ever thought possible.

It's the damned ghost decoration, that's what's in front of him. He gets his phone light on. It's not as bright as his flood lights, not even as bright as Wade's porch light, so the ghost that he's looking at is dimmer than a white sheet should be. Darker.

There's two eyes on the sheet—not holes cut into it but black felt stitched on with thick orange thread.

It's hanging over some kind of post in the ground.

At least, Richard assumes it's a post. He'll have to lift that sheet off to see for sure.

He reaches for it, then stops to think.

He can't imagine Wade would have put this here. It's facing away from his house, right at Richard's front porch. Must be some teenage pranksters.

They won't catch him unaware. He shines his light down at the grass to make sure he doesn't step in any recently transported dog waste. There isn't any.

So if the prank isn't to get him to step in something, it must be about the ghost decoration itself.

Richard reaches out again. He grabs the sheet between his finger and thumb, has a thought, leans in to sniff. Nothing repulsive, but there is an alcohol smell, like some kind of solvent you might keep in your garage.

Richard yanks the sheet away. He starts balling it up with one hand while he holds his phone light up with the other.

All that's left is a wooden stake with a purple playground ball stuck on top of it.

Where had the laughing sound come from?

Richard starts to circle the stake.

His hand suddenly burns.

He drops the sheet, wipes his hand on his pant leg, but the pain all over his hand only gets worse.

He points the light at his hand. It's wet and red, blistering over his palm and fingertips. Oh, it hurts.

It wasn't just a solvent on that sheet, it was something caustic.

What kind of sick prank is this?

He wipes at his pants again, this time peeling back skin.

"Mallory!" he calls, staggering toward the hose bib, biting his cheek because the pain is so bad.

By the time his wife gets him in the front seat of his Honda Pilot and drives to the ER, Richard can see the white of bone in his middle finger.

OCTOBER 6TH

Bob wakes up to his phone buzzing. He'd set an alarm in case he actually fell asleep, and apparently the events of the last few days wore him out enough that he needed it.

It's 1:30 A.M. The crickets and cicadas of summer are dead, but chirper frogs still sing in the night, loud enough that he hears them through the window.

Joann stirs in the bed next to him. The vibrating alarm has woken her, too, but he knows she's feigning sleep.

He slides out of bed carefully, acting as he would if he really believed Joann were asleep. She wants to avoid admitting that she knows what he's doing, so he'll help her do that. For now, at least.

Bob checks on Sam and Emily. Both are snoozing soundly.

Bob sneaks into his office to grab his backpack. Joann's sister, Polly, is sleeping on an air mattress in there. Bob feels a flash of gratitude. She's said she'll be here every evening until Mary's home.

He puts a small flashlight in his pocket, but it's a full moon and clear skies tonight. He won't need that flashlight until he's inside Old Pine.

Bob opens the back door.

Someone touches his shoulder.

He about jumps out of his skin, whirls around, sees Joann dressed in black sweats and tennis shoes.

"What are you doing?" he whispers.

"I'm coming with you."

Bob is so surprised that when he argues in return, he doesn't even consider all the reasons that her presence will make it more difficult to break in without getting caught. He argues simply based on how surprised he is. "You don't want to go with me."

Joann waves him out the door, follows after, and then shuts it behind them.

Bob isn't sure what's happening.

"Lead the way," Joann says.

The full moon's silver glow makes silhouettes and shadows of their neighbors' houses and of the tall trees in their yards.

Bob doesn't say, *You hate that I leave at night*, or ask, *Did you tell Polly to listen for the kids*? Instead, he says, "This is illegal."

"We decided that we're not waiting for the police to do their job."

Bob's felt that way for the past eleven months. Yesterday, Joann finally agreed with him, but he'd thought it was only about keeping the projector. "Okay," he says.

"I'm not lying awake at home while you're searching for Mary. If my baby's still alive, and she might be in that old building, then I'm going in there with you."

"Yeah, okay. Let's do it." This is nuts. She doesn't have the practice staying out of sight. But he's not going to say no. "Does Polly know she's in charge?"

Joann nods.

"Alright." Bob looks his wife up and down. This will be the most time they've spent alone together in months. "We have to be quiet."

"Obviously."

"I suppose if anyone sees us out in the neighborhood, it'll be less suspicious since we're together."

"Just a midnight stroll."

"Did you bring gloves?" Bob asks. "Don't want fingerprints in the school."

"No. I'll go get some."

"I've got extra in my bag."

"Then why'd you ask?"

Bob shrugs. He offers her his hand and she takes it.

Instead of darting between bushes like he would do alone, Bob walks with Joann down the sidewalk.

They used to go for walks like this when the kids were younger. Had those stopped before Mary disappeared? Bob can't remember. His life is so different now, it's like everything that happened before they lost Mary happened to an older, more naive version of Bob.

They don't talk.

Bob listens to their shoes tapping the sidewalk and he listens to the frogs scream for each other and it's a nice bit of luck that nobody else is out in Maple Creek tonight.

Karl had said there'd be two police cruisers patrolling, but maybe the extra car got reassigned once the kids started reappearing. Maybe both did.

They pass the Rushers' house, and together, Bob and Joann imagine Wendy's parents sleeping on either side of their daughter, determined to never let her out of their sight again, but they keep those thoughts internal and instead of speaking they listen to the night.

Ahead, a wall of trees start out as empty darkness in the night, then as Bob and Joann get closer they can make out individual shapes of branches and a scant few dead, dangling leaves.

Frogs screech louder as they reach the trail that will take them through the woods to Old Pine.

Soft dirt and wet leaves make up the trail. It's not frequented enough to be packed down hard.

Enough leaves have fallen that moonlight shines down through the canopy. The branches highest in the trees are the most exposed to wind, and so they let go of their dead leaves first. Bob feels like they're walking under a chaotic ribcage.

Somewhere off the trail, Bob hears leaves crunch.

He goes still.

Joann breathes behind him. "Did you hear that?"

He answers just as quietly. "Probably a squirrel."

Rodents can sound as heavy as deer when the leaves are dry. The leaves aren't dry tonight.

"Are squirrels out at night?" Joann asks.

"A mouse?" But that's too small. There's any number of nocturnal animals around. But here's the thing: any one of those animals would have heard Bob and Joann coming a mile away and either hightailed it out of there already, or stayed perfectly still until they'd passed on by.

Bob takes a breath. There are a thousand reasons an animal might have ran off just now. He's getting antsy because Joann is with him.

Bob peers determinedly in the direction he heard the noise.

He sees nothing. Whatever it was could be staring straight back at him, gauging whether Bob and Joann are predators.

He still doesn't get out his flashlight. The cops in the Old Pine parking lot might see the light in the woods.

Instead, he moves on, stepping lightly and cursing the screaming frogs that might be drowning out the sound of someone sneaking around.

Joann follows behind, moving even more quietly than Bob.

Soon, bright white light comes through the trees ahead.

The woods end where the parking lot begins, then across that parking lot are the work lights that the cops have put up at the front of the old school.

They're pointed at the doors, so Bob isn't worried about being spotted.

Of course, they can't simply walk across the parking lot and past the two cops on standing-there duty. Instead, Bob leads Joann off the path but still under the cover of the trees. They walk ten feet from the edge of the woods, circling the back of the lot.

It's hard to walk quietly, but the frogs do their part in covering the crunching of leaves beneath their feet.

Joann doesn't say a word. Bob glances back to see her watching the cops. The weight of what they're doing seems to have landed on her now. If they get caught, the best case scenario is that Polly has to bring the kids along to bail them out. Worst case scenario, they get blamed for the missing kids.

As they come around the back of the school, Joann whispers, "What's that?"

Bob looks where she's pointing, deeper into the trees. He sees the tall, straight, dark trunks of the pines, the short, crooked, branches of the sassafras trees, and the thumb-width spiny trunks of a new copse of black locust, but he doesn't see what's caught Joann's attention.

"Over there," she points straight through the black locust trees, and now Bob sees it.

Beyond that spiny stand of trees, at about knee level, is a pink light.

Bob thinks maybe it's the moon reflecting off some broken glass. But that doesn't make sense—how would broken glass be hovering two feet above the ground? "What is it?" he whispers.

Joann shakes her head. She keeps her gaze on the light. "Should we go check it out?"

They can't do that without scratching themselves up on black locust thorns.

But the man in the hoodie carries a jack-o-lantern with a pink glow.

"Is it him?" Joann asks aloud, thinking the same thing as Bob.

Bob leans forward, perched on the balls of his feet. The kidnapper could be standing in the woods, not twenty feet away. The man who took Mary. Who knows where she is right now.

"When I say," Bob tells Joann, "you run for the cops. I'm going after this guy."

"No," Joann says, too loudly.

The pink light bobbles.

Bob isn't missing this chance. "Go get them!" He runs at the light.

The black locusts start closer than he'd realized—he crashes into their outer saplings, waist-high and sharp. His jeans catch and rip. His thighs bleed. But he keeps his eyes on that pink light and charges through the dark woods.

He fumbles for his flashlight. It catches in his pocket as his toes smash into root. He falls forward, catches himself with a quick step, and launches himself back upright.

He looks around for the pink light.

There.

A bouncing glow, heading deeper into the woods.

Now there are shouts behind him and flashlights so powerful they light up the trees around him.

The stupid lights are making it hard to see the retreating pink light.

"This way!" he shouts to the cops and runs on.

But the pink light grows dimmer each time it flashes behind a thick tree trunk.

Bob loses sight of it.

He turns on his flashlight. Under its LED whiteness, the trees reveal their daylight colors, the texture of their bark. It's uncanny.

Bob searches ahead for any movement, but there's no sign of a young man in a hoodie carrying a turnip jack-o-lantern with a pink light.

There's something bright orange on the ground by an oak tree. Bob approaches.

It's a thick plastic bag, about the size of a paperback book. It's got an image of a black jack-o-lantern on the front, and it's stuffed full of something.

Bob kicks it to knock it around and see what's inside.

Candy spills out onto decaying leaves, garishly colored, fun-size bags of M&M's, Skittles, and Reese's Pieces. They're bulging.

Bob squats down to open one up.

Mixed in with the candy are button batteries, the kind that

power wristwatches and greeting cards. The kind that—if swallowed—burn up a kid's esophagus.

As Bob takes in this cruel Halloween trick that he must have interrupted, the cops come crashing up through the woods behind him.

∼

DESPITE THEIR ELEVEN months of emotional distance, Bob and Joann are still cruising on the same wavelength well enough that they tell the same story without even coordinating.

Since Joann's sister was over, Bob and Joann took a nighttime walk to clear their heads. Then they saw the pink light and they remembered what their son had seen last Halloween.

Officer Karl is one of the cops on standing-there duty. He gives Bob a knowing look that Bob interprets to mean that Karl will be sending a condescending message about keeping a low profile.

The cops radio for help to search the woods.

The ever-frowning Officer Yachuw is one of the new arrivals.

While other cops march through the trees, Officer Yachuw and Karl stay with Bob and Joann.

Officer Yachuw dumps a package of candy and batteries into his hand. "Pretty wicked stuff. You said you found this in the woods?"

His condescension is infuriating, but Bob keeps his response friendly. "That's right. I assume the guy we chased off dropped it."

Karl hands Yachuw a clear plastic bag. "Don't handle the evidence, dipshit."

Yachuw's cheeks go red. He points his anger at Bob. "What'd this guy look like?"

Joann answers. "All we saw was the pink light moving like someone was carrying it."

Yachuw keeps his eyes on Bob's. "I thought you ran off ahead of your wife. Why's she answering for you?"

"Was the question not to both of us?" Bob feels himself failing to keep his tone *respectful*.

Karl says, "Go ahead and answer for yourself, Mister Wilson."

"We saw the bobbing pink light. About this high off the ground. I followed it while Joann ran for you guys. I never got close enough to see the guy carrying it."

"But you heard him stomping through the woods?" Officer Yachuw asks. "You must have."

That's actually a good question. Bob thinks about it. He doesn't remember hearing the ruckus that a guy fleeing through thick woods would make. Is that because of his own noise he made chasing after him? Somehow, Bob doesn't think so. The guy fled through the woods, lightning quick, and didn't make a sound doing it.

"I don't remember," Bob says. "There was a lot of adrenaline. I thought it was the kidnapper. I mean, it must have been, right?"

"Possibly," Karl says. "This fucked up candy makes me think it's the prankster who's been fucking with Maple Creek."

"The mousetrap thing?" Bob asks.

"It was worse than that," Joann says.

"Way worse," Officer Yachuw agrees. "Somebody stuck a razor blade to a mousetrap, put it inside a jack-o-lantern, and left it on some teenage girl's front porch."

"Shit." Bob had assumed those rumors were exaggerated.

"And last night," Karl adds, "Richard Stoutly found some Halloween decorations in his yard soaked in acid."

"Did he touch them?" Bob asks.

"Yes, he touched them," Officer Yachuw answers as if Bob's question is ridiculous.

"How bad was it?" Bob isn't friends with Richard and Mallory, but he studied them a bit before breaking into their house, so he feels like he kinda knows them.

"Don't know yet," Officer Yachuw says. "This happened like five hours ago."

"Damn," Bob says.

"Damn is right," Karl says.

"Did anyone see the prankster?" Bob asks.

"No," Karl answers.

At the same time, Officer Yachuw says, "It's an investigation in progress. No details yet."

As if he hasn't just been freely sharing the Stoutly's private business.

Joann asks, "Are the prankster and the kidnapper the same person?"

"No reason to think that, yet," Karl says.

He should know better. Karl knows about the hoodied guy on the TV with his pink light. He should be putting together the pink light that Bob and Joann saw with the battery-candy-surprise.

Bob doesn't push the issue now. Can't give away that Karl is one of Bob's YouTube viewers and has been helping him for months. But he'll be messaging him later.

"We need to get home to our kids," Bob says.

Officer Yachuw smirks. "They're alone?"

"My sister's there," Joann reminds him. "But she'll be worried about us."

Officer Yachuw crosses his arms. "We need written statements."

"Of course," Joann says.

They lean on the hood of a police cruiser to write out what happened.

Bob thinks they're about home free when Officer Yachuw asks, "What's in the backpack?"

Bob can feel Joann looking at him. He waits for Karl to jump in but no help comes.

If he and Joann were on a late-night stroll, why is he carrying a backpack? What answer can he possibly give that won't lead to, "Why don't you let us see what's in it?" And then how he can answer *that* request without sounding guilty?

Joann speaks up. "A blanket. Condoms."

Officer Yachuw gets a gym-locker grin but an altar-boy blush. "Everyone reacts to stress differently, I guess." He barks an insincere laugh.

"Go on home," Karl says. "Try to keep your pants on until you get there."

~

BOB WAKES up way later than he means to.

Last night was disturbing.

This guy who took Mary and the other kids—and killed one of them—is now apparently playing violent pranks on Maple Creek. If he'd dropped those Skittles and batteries somewhere where a little kid could have got them... Bob shudders.

He gets out of bed and goes straight to his office. Before he gets distracted again, he needs to upload his video asking for help identifying the projector.

It takes only a few minutes.

He's eager to see his viewers' responses.

In the past eleven months of looking for Mary, his viewers have been his best source of information.

And it's more than that. These people are on his side. They know Mary is still alive and that his search for her is worthwhile.

Except for a select few who he chats with directly, they don't know that he's broken into at least a quarter of the houses in Maple Creek—it would be beyond stupid to post videos admitting to those crimes—but they know that each scrap of information he obtains is valuable.

Bob's grateful for his viewers, and not just because the ad revenue keeps him from draining his and Joann's savings.

He's grateful because they're something he still needs—a real community.

~

AFTER SCHOOL ON MONDAY, Sam is reading a book in the living room—facing away from the TV—when there's a knock at the door.

Mom's playing with Emily in the girls' room. Who knows where Dad is.

Sam's mad that his parents haven't gone looking for Mary inside Old Pine yet. His sister is in there somewhere.

He's trying to distract himself from all this with a *Choose Your Own Adventure* graphic novel. He'd brought it to school with him and read it at lunch when Jeremy was ignoring him.

But an imaginary adventure under the ocean isn't enough to get Sam's mind off Mary being in that old empty school.

She's over there. He could run there in five minutes. Sure, Mom and Dad told him not to, but they won't care that he disobeyed them if he brings Mary home.

He's scared, though.

He doesn't want to explore a big empty building by himself. And the guy with the turnip jack-o-lantern with those glowing pink lights might be there.

Of course he'll be there. If Sam is gonna rescue Mary, he has to rescue her *from* that guy.

And that's scary.

So when the knock comes at the door, he's distracting himself by flipping from page seven to page thirty-three of *Journey Under the Sea*.

Sam looks up from his book.

The knock comes again. He's not afraid of this knock, but he is surprised by it. Any nine-year-old worth his salt can recognize the knocks of his friends.

It's Jeremy.

Sam opens the door.

Jeremy's got on a Batman t-shirt with a fresh milk stain on the belly. He wears flip-flops with his jeans even though it's probably in the fifties.

His smile is aggressive, which Sam recognizes to mean that he wants to barrel past how he's been avoiding Sam since they found the turnip projector.

Sam's happy with that. He needs his friend. "Do you want to

play?" Sam asks, as if he were the one who'd showed up on Jeremy's porch.

Jeremy says, "I've seen that pink light before. Want to see where?"

∽

MAPLE CREEK'S playground is second-to-none.

There's a kiddie area with a playhouse to climb and two stubby yellow slides—one straight and one curved.

But the real gem is beyond the swings, where a three-story tower stands even taller than the neighborhood clubhouse. You get to the top by climbing into a vertical chute made of really taut netting, which has net platforms stair-stepping their way up.

Sam knows it's perfectly safe—you could only ever fall from one platform down two feet to the next—but it feels like he's scampering up to the crow's nest of a pirate ship.

At the top there's only one slide, but *wow*, what a slide. He's never gone down a slide so steep. Mary never liked it (Emily won't even climb up the netted chute), but Sam loves the staticky prickles on his arm and leg hairs, and he loves how his stomach flies up to his chest when he rockets in a spiral back down to the ground.

The playground is where he and Jeremy have been paratroopers invading Nazi Germany. They've been firefighters responding to a five-alarm fire in the world's biggest toy store. They've been Minecraft avatars tunneling down into a cave to find diamonds and zombies.

Today, as Sam climbs from platform to platform behind Jeremy, he gets a sick feeling that his friend is about to ruin the playground forever. They're going to get to the top and Jeremy will say, *Here's where the pink light comes from,* and then Sam will never want to climb up here again.

He's starting to get a little old for the playground but he's not ready to leave forever yet.

They get to the top platform and there's no pink light.

Sam's eyes go straight to the circular opening of the fantastic slide.

There's nowhere else. Jeremy must be about to say that the evil light is inside that wonderful tunnel.

Instead, Jeremy goes to the wall of netting across from the slide. "Last summer, when your sister was still around but you guys went on vacation, I came up here one night when my dad got home from work and was being an asshole."

Sam manages to hide that he flinched at the bad word.

"Look down there." Jeremy points down from the tower.

Sam looks down at the strip of forest behind the playground. Leaves have turned bright oranges and deep reds. But Jeremy's pointing beyond those trees, to the back yards of the houses beyond.

It's the street behind the clubhouse, where Sarah Stanley from school lives. Jeremy isn't pointing at her house, but at the one next door.

From up here, they can see over the tall white fence and right into the square of grass and fallen leaves.

The sun is behind the trees and will be down in another hour. It leaves this yard in a mild shadow.

Sam doesn't see anything weird about it. They have a deck off the back of the house not much bigger than the blue table that sits on it. Scraggly grass pokes up between the pinky-finger leaves of a big willow oak.

"The old woman—" Jeremy starts to say.

Sam cuts him off. "What old woman?"

"The one who lives there. I don't know her name. When I was out here, I saw her with a shovel and a pick. She was burying something."

"What was it?"

"I'm trying to tell you. Shut up and listen."

With Sam's unspoken permission, Jeremy adopts a storyteller's cadence. "I was up here pretending to spot snipers, and I heard the old lady digging. *Ka-shunk.*" Jeremy mimes swinging a pick.

"Picks are for breaking up rocks," Sam says.

"Or hard dirt. If you dig deep enough it's all clay." Jeremy rubs his finger and thumb together. Sam imagines the feel of grit between his own fingers.

Now Jeremy delivers the killing blow. "The old lady had a black trash bag next to her."

Sam has seen enough cop shows to know why someone would bury a black trash bag. "A body?"

"Bingo. But only about this big." Jeremy held up his hands eighteen inches apart.

"A baby?" Sam is horrified.

Jeremy is equally offended by the suggestion. "Damn, dude. No, it was her cat. Orange fur was sticking out of the bag. She dug that hole and dumped down the dead cat."

"She buried her cat in her own yard?"

"Where else is she supposed to bury it?"

Sam shrugs.

Jeremy goes on. "But it was real shallow. Old ladies get tired quick. She shoveled the dirt on top, and that's when it got weird."

Sam can't stop himself from asking, "What happened?"

"I'm *telling* you," Jeremy says, reveling in Sam's rapt attention. "It got dark before she piled all the dirt back on top of her cat. That's how I saw the pink light."

"Inside the hole?" Sam asks.

This time, Jeremy is happy that he's led Sam to the proper conclusion. "Exactly. Up from beneath the dirt."

"Then what?"

"What do you mean?"

"Did you dig up the cat?"

"In the old lady's yard? Hell no."

"What'd you do?"

"I went home. I figured my dad had cooled off."

"But what was the pink light? Were the cat's eyes glowing like the guy on my TV?"

"How should I know?"

Sam makes a fist. He's been hoping to get a clue he can follow to find the hooded teenager. Maybe some way to search for Mary that won't require going into the empty school. But Jeremy's not delivering. "Why'd you bring me up here just to tell me you don't know anything?"

"I saw the same pink light," Jeremy insists.

"But what's it mean? What do I do now?"

Jeremy's confident storytelling is apparently over. He shrugs.

Sam checks his watch. 4:40. It'll be dark by five. "I'm gonna climb her fence."

But as he says it, the old lady comes out of her back door. She wears soft-looking jeans and a flower-print jacket. A woven sun hat keeps her face in the dark. She stands on her back deck and lights a cigarette.

Sam watches in frustration. By the time she's done smoking, it'll be too dark to search her yard. Unless he comes back with a flashlight. But he suspects that once he goes home, Mom and Dad will keep him in for the night.

"I'm coming back tomorrow after school," Sam says.

Jeremy's eyes go wide. He's obviously scared, but this is the kind of adventure a boy dreams about. "I'll bring a shovel."

⁓

THAT MONDAY EVENING, Bob and Joann watch Officer Karl lead Tiffany Whitt by the hand through the front doors of Old Pine. He'd found her in the cafeteria.

Tiffany is wearing a homemade cat costume. Her face paint is as vivid as the day she disappeared.

The police usher her into her parents' arms and then rush back into the school.

They don't find anything.

Bob's not surprised.

As he and Joann drive home, she says, "I ordered a face paint kit off Amazon a few months ago. Emily got it in her head that she wanted to be a zebra. I painted stripes right on her cheeks. She rubbed them off before dinner."

Bob grunts, letting Joann finish her thought before interrupting with his own. He likes having her as his investigative partner.

"Either that's some marine-paint level makeup," Joann says, "or the kidnapper painted whiskers back on Tiffany before letting her go."

Clever to spot that, Bob thinks. It would have never occurred to him. "That's some bizarre behavior. You think he's some unstable guy who's too obsessed with Halloween?"

"That's where I'd put my money, yeah."

"What do we do with that info?"

"Have you... looked around... the Chester brothers' houses?"

The brothers and next-door neighbors who created last year's Crimson Corridors haunt at Old Pine have also spent the last decade decorating their yards each October. It was always like driving by an inside-out Spirit Halloween. But Greg McIntosh disappeared while knocking on Miles Chester's front door, and they both travel a lot, so Bob's had motive and opportunity to search inside.

"Top to bottom," he says. "I didn't find anything. And anyways, they were both out in their yards when Mary and everyone vanished. Lots of people saw them."

Bob and Joann arrive at home. They park in their driveway and get out. The full moon bathes their yard in silver.

Joann pauses to look up at the moon. "Is there anyone else in the neighborhood who's that obsessed with Halloween?"

Bob shakes his head. Maple Creek is where he lives, but it's not really his community. He couldn't say if any of their neighbors would be crazy enough to kidnap thirty kids and keep their costumes in tiptop shape for eleven months. "I don't know. It's something else we can ask when we talk to the other parents."

"When are we doing that?" Joann asks.

"Tomorrow?"

"Who first?"

"Start with number one," Bob says. "Debbie Meyers' family."
"Will they talk to us?"
"I hope so."
"You mean you haven't asked."
"Not yet."
"I'll reach out," Joann offers.

Bob likes that idea. Joann is way better at the face-to-face stuff.

Mary's not home yet, but with the two of them working together, Bob is getting more confident that she'll be home soon.

OCTOBER 7TH

MAPLE CREEK IS one of many neighborhoods in Sam's elementary school district.

If it were only Sam's neighborhood who attended there, then Old Pine would be plenty big enough. But it isn't, and only one in ten of Sam's classmates are his Maple Creek neighbors.

So at school, the very concept of Halloween doesn't make everyone go quiet like it does back in Maple Creek.

In fact, on Tuesday morning after Dad drops him off at school, Sam walks inside and is bombarded with reminders of how he abandoned his sister.

A poster board skeleton hangs on a kindergarten classroom's door.

Across the hall is a mummy with a smile and a roll of toilet paper at its ankles.

The kindergarten teachers have set up the first Halloween decorations that Sam has seen this year.

He loves Halloween. Or he did.

Now he misses Mary. And when he misses her, he thinks mostly about how he was feeling grumpy and tired and so he wasn't next to her when she disappeared. He could have saved her.

His schoolmates in the hallway around him are getting too

close. He gets bumped by a fifth grader into a first grader. The little girl looks up with wide, scared eyes. "I'm sorry," Sam says and speeds up.

He should leave school right now to go next door to search Old Pine. Or go to that old lady's house where Jeremy saw the pink light. Maybe there's a clue in her back yard.

Those desires rattle with emotions stronger than he understands.

A white poster board ghost with a big smile watches Sam.

These decorations make him want to hide behind Dad. Skeletons and witches and mummies are all mashed up with the moments between when Mary rang that doorbell and when Aunt Polly finally came and took him and Emily home so Mom and Dad could keep searching. It was dark and there were so many grownups who were so scared and Sam wanted so badly to go back and change his decision about skipping the *Nightmare Before Christmas* house.

His eyes blur with tears.

Why do the third grade classrooms have to be so far away? He's afraid to wipe his eyes—someone might notice he's crying.

He's realized something and it makes him want to curl up into a ball.

Until this moment, Sam thought he was avoiding talking about Halloween so Mom wouldn't start crying and Dad wouldn't go all quiet and then be really tired the next few days.

Now he realizes that Mom and Dad have been avoiding Halloween so Sam doesn't start thinking about that night again. About those moments when Mary was suddenly gone and all the adults were terrified.

It's not just the kindergarten classes. The art room has its own door decoration: a witch with a green face and a black dress. Not Elphaba like Mary's costume, but a wrinkly, warty old lady.

These decorations shouldn't be here. It's this dumb Halloween shit that stole Mary away.

Sam stomps over to the bulletin board.

He gets his fingers between the poster and the door, ready to rip down the witch who is definitely not Elphaba, when Jeremy's suddenly behind him.

"What are you doing?"

Sam wipes his eyes to see his friend clearly.

Jeremy has toothpaste spit on the left corner of his mouth. "Want me to help you steal that?"

"No, I want to throw it away."

Jeremy's eyes go wide and his mouth forms an "o." "Because Mary was dressed as the Wicked Witch."

It's so much more than that, but Sam just says, "Yeah."

"I bet you miss her a lot."

It's the most directly anyone has talked to Sam about Mary for months. Right after last Halloween, the whole neighborhood was falling over themselves to say how sad and worried they were. But that died down and then disappeared.

Sam's afraid he'll start sobbing if he answers with words so he nods instead.

Jeremy says, "I knew you did. I kinda miss her and she's not even my sister."

He gives Sam a two-handed shove away from the art class door. It's strong enough that the art teacher comes hurrying into the hallway, but by the time she gets out there, she sees Jeremy's arm around Sam's shoulders. She lets it go.

"I already got my Dad's shovel out of the shed," Jeremy says. "Right when we get home, we'll see what we can find in that old lady's yard."

"Aren't you scared of it?"

Jeremy laughs but it's obviously fake. "I'm scared as shit."

That part's real.

∼

BOB WRESTLES Emily's jacket back over her head while Joann knocks on the door.

"She'll never keep it on," Joann says.

They've walked over to Debbie Meyer's home and onto their wooden porch.

"It's chilly out here. She's already got goosebumps." Bob forces the jacket on his youngest daughter.

Emily refuses to put her arms through the sleeves.

The door opens to reveal Cass Meyers. She stands shorter than Joann's shoulders, with blonde hair closely cropped to her scalp.

Bob had forgotten how young she is. Debbie must have been a teenage pregnancy.

"Hi!" Cass says cheerfully. "Come on in. Debbie's doing some math sheets at the table."

Bob and Joann follow Cass inside. Emily stops struggling to offer a gaping smile to the toys and books strewn across the living room floor.

Cass chatters away as they walk to the kitchen. "I know schoolwork hardly seems like what to focus on right now, but Debbie is somehow fine, it seems like. I'm not sending her to school yet, but she can at least refresh herself on adding and subtracting her hundreds. Turns out she doesn't need much refreshing. She's getting every question right. I'm proud of that. Is that weird?"

Emily wriggles so Bob sets her down. She dashes for a *Bluey*-themed dollhouse.

"Okay if she plays?" Bob asks.

Cass waves and offers a short giggle. "Let her loose."

Debbie is sitting at the kitchen table, legs kicking idly while she does a worksheet. Her hair is in a dozen braids. Bob imagines Cass braiding her hair as an excuse to stay close to her.

"Debbie?" Cass says. "Mister and Missus Wilson are here. They're Mary's mom and dad."

Debbie looks up. "Hi. Who's Mary?"

"She's a couple years younger than you," Cass says.

"We lost her when she was trick-or-treating," Joann says.

"Like me." Debbie puts down her pencil.

"Did you see her?" Bob asks.

"Now hold on." Cass sits at the table and gestures to Joann and Bob to do the same. "Debbie's already talked Detective Otto's ear off."

"Did she see our Mary?" Joann asks. "Is she okay?"

Debbie looks at her mom.

Cass says, "She hadn't been friends with any of the kids she was with. But Detective Otto showed pictures and Debbie recognized a couple."

Bob pulls up a picture of Mary on his phone. She and her siblings are standing on the front porch in their Halloween costumes, ready to get candy, no idea what's waiting.

"Did you see this little girl? The one in the witch costume?"

Debbie leans toward the phone. She shakes her head.

"Where were you?" Joann asks. "Where did they take you?"

Cass holds up both hands. "Slow down. Go easy. Debbie's taking this all really well, but Detective Otto stressed her out and I don't want that happening again. She didn't see who grabbed her. Don't ask about that again."

"He's coming back," Debbie says.

Bob feels his breath catch. Joann touches his leg under the table, for her own comfort.

"Who?" Bob asks.

Cass spits out, "I said don't ask about that."

"Did she tell the police that the kidnapper's coming back?" Joann asks.

"I said-" Cass starts to say.

"She's asking you," Bob says.

Cass inhales. "Debbie, go show Emily your toys."

Debbie picks up her pencil. "I'm not done."

"Go."

Debbie hops down from her chair and pads out of the kitchen.

Cass turns to Bob and Joann. "Listen. I am so happy that Debbie isn't traumatized. I don't know how that could be. And I'm happy to talk to y'all. But Debbie doesn't remember much from where they took her. I told you this on Facebook."

Bob glances at Joann. She hadn't mentioned that.

"But where was she?" Bob feels desperate for answers. They can't have come over here for nothing. "Inside Old Pine somewhere? Somewhere in the neighborhood?"

"She doesn't remember. She says it was dark."

"How'd she end up at the school?" Joann asks. "Does she remember getting brought there?"

"She remembers it was dark, and that's it."

Bob tries to stay calm. "You're saying that in her mind, one minute she was trick-or-treating, then it was dark, then she was walking out the front doors of Old Pine?"

"Yes. No. She knows something happened. I think she must have been drugged."

"For a year?" Joann asks. "What would that do to her body?"

"She's healthy. The doctors said she's fine. She must have had food and water."

"But she doesn't remember," Bob says.

"Right."

"Anything?"

"Right."

He knows she'll throw them out for this, but he can't help himself. "But that's not true."

"Excuse me?"

Joann squeezes his knee. "Bob."

"We all heard her say the kidnapper is coming back."

Behind him, Debbie speaks. "He said I'm the first trick-or-treater and he's the thirty-first."

Bob turns around. Debbie and Emily are standing there with plastic dog figurines. Debbie is looking at Joann, while Emily is making her toy kiss Debbie's.

Cass snaps at her daughter. "Back in the living room."

Emily stumbles backwards. She's not used to the vindictiveness in Cass's voice. Bob gets up to scoop her up before she cries. He doesn't blame Cass. That anger in her voice comes from a place familiar to Bob: fear.

Debbie is shaken. She starts to leave the kitchen until Joann speaks.

"Debbie? Who said he's the thirty-first trick-or-treater? Did you see his face?"

"Don't talk to my daughter," Cass says. "Debbie, don't answer them."

This is getting absurd. "Why not? Did you tell her not to talk to the cops, too?"

"She told the cop about this person and then she woke from nightmares every thirty minutes that night."

Ah. So that's why Cass and Debbie look so frazzled.

"Last night Debbie actually slept three hours in a row. You're not reminding her of that man in the hood."

Chills go down Bob's back. "Is that who took her?"

"Go on and play," Cass says to her daughter. "Can Emily join her?"

Bob lets Emily down and the two girls run off together.

Cass sighs. "I should't have let you come over. I thought you were gonna ask about your daughter. Not all these other details."

"We just want help finding our baby," Joann says.

Bob's plowing ahead now. "This guy in a hood. That's who took Debbie?"

Cass shrugs. "Must be. She doesn't remember that. Only what he said before he let her go."

"That he's coming back," Joann says. "And the police know about that?"

Cass nods. "I don't know why they haven't warned people yet. I see kids running around in the street like it's safe out."

The cops must not have given much credence to Debbie's warning. On the other hand, admitting there's a coming threat would require actually *doing* something about that threat, and Bob has learned in the last year that these cops don't like doing much at all.

"Why's he coming back?" Bob asks.

"To kidnap more of our babies," Cass answers.

"Then why is he letting them go?"

Cass shrugs. "He didn't exactly let Calvin Mitchel go, did he?"

Fear swirls inside Bob. Mary isn't home yet. Mary might not come home alive.

He wants to ask something else, something that will be helpful, that will give him back his Mary. But Cass has said all she knows.

He pulls out the tiny projector from his pocket. Its metal shell taps on the table as he sets it down. "Have you seen one of these before?"

"No. What is it?"

"A projector," Joann says. "Our son saw a video of the guy in the hoodie."

"The Thirty-First Trick-or-Treater," Cass says. "Where'd you get it?"

"It was stuck in a turnip. Someone put it in our living room."

"Creepy," Cass says. "You know, I saw a TikTok that said the first jack-o-lanterns weren't made from pumpkins, but from turnips."

That's a new fun fact for Bob, but he's not sure what he's supposed to do with it. Something to tell his viewers. "Neat," he says.

"I wish I had something more useful to tell you. I honestly thought you wanted some comfort. My little girl has come home so yours will be home soon."

"You've been amazing," Joann says.

They let the girls play for a while before saying their goodbyes.

∼

AFTER THEY HEAD HOME, Bob and Joann sit in the living room.

Bob's fiddling with the tiny metal projector.

Emily is kneeling at the bookshelf, picking out a book, which means they have about thirty seconds before she'll interrupt their conversation, so they both start talking faster.

"Are you worried about the trick-or-treater's threat?" Joann asks. "That he's coming back on Halloween?"

"Is that what it was?" Bob tries to remember if what Debbie shared came with a detailed date.

"Debbie said he called her the first trick-or-treater and himself the thirty-first. The kids are coming home one each day."

"That makes sense," Bob says. He needs to sleep more if he hadn't even put that together yet. "But it feels like a distraction. The crazy person who took our daughter might take more kids at the end of the month. I don't care. I'm gonna find Mary."

"We have two other children. And what about our neighbors?"

"You mean the people who've done jack shit to find Mary?"

Joann tenses up.

Emily runs back from the bookshelf to plop their bent and ripped copy of *Creepy Pair of Underwear* in Joann's lap. "Read it."

"How do we ask for something?" Bob says automatically.

"Please, can you read it?" Emily demands.

Joann puts Emily in her lap and opens the book.

There's still tension thick in the air. Bob's been an asshole. "All I'm saying is one crisis at a time."

"And I'm warning you now, if this guy isn't caught before Halloween, we're taking the kids far away."

"That's fair."

It's all too much, and there's not enough Bob can do. He'll try again to break into Old Pine, but obviously not during the day.

He rolls the projector between his fingers. "I might cut it open. Then there should be some kind of storage we can access to see what Sam saw."

"Unless it was live," Joann says. "Streaming, or a video call, or whatever you'd call it."

"None of my viewers think it's big enough for that."

"But you haven't asked Graham yet."

Graham lives a street over. They'd bought Girl Scout cookies from his daughter Bethany, and in their small talk he'd mentioned he used to work for Best Buy's "Geek Squad." That was two years ago, maybe three.

Bob sighs. "Graham won't know any more than my viewers."

Tatum Carpenter disappeared on Graham's front porch. That was one of the first houses that Bob broke into. Bob doesn't think Graham or his wife have anything to do with the disappearances. And he doesn't think Graham knows a damn thing about one-of-kind, miniature projectors.

"But he can actually handle the thing," Joann argues. "Really check it out. And he's our neighbor. He'll want to help out."

"He doesn't give two shits about us."

He immediately feels the tension return between them. This is a familiar argument.

Joann never once accused him of not watching Mary close enough, and Bob is grateful for that. God knows he accuses himself of it every waking moment. But a few weeks into November, Joann mentioned that she appreciated all the support from the neighborhood, and Bob got livid. No one was helping him look for Mary. As far as he could tell, no one was even looking for their own kids.

Even today, Bob can't understand why the other parents aren't out there every day, checking under each and every rock.

If it weren't Mary, if it weren't any of his kids, he'd still be helping. You don't have to be any sort of magical empath to imagine how much it ruins you to have a child go missing.

But nobody does that for Bob and Joann or the twenty-nine other sets of parents.

Now, when Bob trips into starting that argument again—*Graham doesn't give two shits about us*—Joann deflates.

Bob immediately feels guilty. He wants to unsay it. Joann is finally *home*. She's not soloing her way through grief while Emily plays in the church nursery. Joann has chosen to be here with Bob and he's damn grateful for that but he doesn't know how to say it so he just says it, "I'm glad you're here with me," which is a pretty strange followup to "Graham doesn't give two shits about us," but Joann lets him unsay what he said because she's glad Bob is here with her instead of vanishing into the night by himself.

Another reason she lets the argument fizzle out before it restarts: Emily is smacking her palm against the open book, chanting, "Read this, read this!"

While Joann reads about a rabbit who buys glow-in-the-dark briefs, Bob sits next to them and fiddles with the telescope-looking projector.

"If I cut it open," he says, "we can also check for any transmitting hardware. Bluetooth or cellular or whatever."

"*Shhhhh*," Emily insists.

Joann laughs but keeps reading.

"I'm gonna cut it open," Bob says.

Joann doesn't argue, so Bob takes it out to the garage. He's got a Dremel, but a power tool might get away from him and cut straight through the thing. He instead takes his hack saw out of a toolbox, clamps the projector at the edge of his work bench, and very delicately saws around the outer edge of the cylinder, directly below the lens.

The lens comes free, but it's still connected by wires within.

Bob is holding the lens to one side and shining his phone's flashlight inside the cylinder when Joann carries Emily inside the garage. "Find anything?" she asks.

"Not sure yet." There's a circuitboard in there. Bob doesn't know much about electronics, but he's pretty sure he sees an SD card plugged into a reader that's soldered to the circuitboard. "Gimme one more second."

He cuts the cylinder longways. "Hot dog style," Sam and Mary would say.

He pries it open enough to see that, yes, it is an SD card. There's also a circular battery in a plastic housing, and an LED array that points at where the lens used to be.

"It's a projector with a memory card," Bob says.

Joann sets Emily down. "What's that mean?"

Emily goes straight for the box of wrenches which they leave out as a harmless lure away from more dangerous tools.

Over the sound of wrenches clanking together, Bob says, "It

means that the video Sam saw was stored on here. It wasn't beamed in from anywhere."

"Well, that's better than the alternative, right? It means no one was watching Sam while he watched it."

Emily raises two wrenches above her head, one dangling off the other. "Look!"

"Wow, you balanced them!" Bob praises Emily for her creativity, then says, "I guess so. But someone still put it in our house."

"Now that you say that," Joann says, "How did it turn on?"

"I hadn't thought of that." He inspects the projector's guts once more. "I don't see any sort of switch at all. The wires go straight from the battery to the light. Seems like it should be on all the time."

"Let me see," Joann says.

Bob holds up the cylinder for her. "Any idea what you're looking at?"

"Nope."

"Me neither," Bob says, and they laugh together.

"I see," Emily demands, reaching for the cylinder.

Bobs holds it open for his daughter. She takes an exaggerated look inside and mimics her mom. "Nope."

Joann laughs so hard she cackles. Bob loves it.

"Can you imagine Mary with her at this age? Emily would bulldoze over her."

"No way," Bob says. "Mary can hold her own. You'll see."

They pause and meet each other's gaze.

"Yeah," says Joann. "I want to see."

Neither of them dare say, "Maybe tonight."

And both think of what they fear most, that not every missing child who returns is alive.

"I'm gonna check this SD card," Bob says. He plucks it out of its plug.

"Don't put it in your computer," Joann says. "It could be a virus. I'll get my old laptop out of the closet."

A few minutes later, Joann has booted up her old laptop and turned off its wifi. Bob plugs in the SD card.

There's no video file saved on it.

But there is a single text file. After checking it every way they know how to make sure it's not some kind of malware, they open it.

There's one line of text:

7349 Clearbark Circle

"It's an address," Joann says.

Bob recognizes the street. "That's over behind the playground, isn't it?"

∼

Sam gets home, throws his backpack down and yells, "I'm going out to play with Jeremy!"

He doesn't wait for Mom to tell him to stay home.

School lasted *forever* today. Fortunately, his own teacher, Mrs. Bavin, hadn't put up any Halloween decorations yet, so his brain didn't get all discombobulated thinking about last year again.

But the clock still dragged its hands around the numbers so slowly.

That doesn't matter anymore. The time has arrived.

Jeremy has a shovel, Sam is supposed to think of a plan, and they're going to look for that pink light.

Sam meets Jeremy on the sidewalk on Jeremy's side of the street. His friend has cheeks full of Cheez-Its and a shovel over his shoulder. He's bouncing on his heels. "If anyone asks about the shovel while we're walking over there, I'll tell them we're helping someone with their flowerbed."

"That's what you're worried about?" Sam starts walking and Jeremy falls in beside him. "What about when the old lady looks out her back window and sees us digging up her yard?"

As Jeremy talks, cracker crumbs fly out of his mouth. "You said you'd figure that out."

Sam shrugs. "I've got an idea."

They walk through Maple Creek without any of the passing cars stopping to question them about the shovel. They head toward the playground.

The tower with its netted platforms and iconic slide stands above them as if it's the Maple Creek flag. Sam doesn't know if you can feel patriotism for your neighborhood—there certainly hasn't been any in this neighborhood this year—but if you could, then Maple's Creek symbol of it would be that slide.

He and Jeremy check that no cars are driving by, that no one's taking their dog for a walk, that the moms at the playground are sufficiently distracted, and then they sneak behind the clubhouse, into the thin strip of woods, to the old lady's back fence.

The white plastic panels are a strange interruption of the forest's chaos. Autumn has killed the green of the undergrowth, but brittle vines still tangle with leafless bushes all the way to the fence's flat surface. A spattering of dirt sticks to the bottom of the fence—where rain has splashed up.

Jeremy tugs his ankle free from twisting vines. He's looking straight up the fence. "No way we can climb that."

"There's a gate," Sam says.

"Yeah, and the latch is on the other side. We'd still have to climb it."

Sam finds a dead pine branch and snaps it off the tree. He reaches it through the gap between the gate and the rest of the fence, and then pops up the latch. The top of the gate leans toward them, but the bottom sags into the ground.

"It's stuck." Jeremy yanks at it. The plastic rubs and makes an aggressive squeak.

"Quiet!" Sam hisses.

The gate is open enough for them to slip through, but they wait for any sign they've been noticed. Sam imagines the old lady opening her back door to swoop down into the yard like a witch on a broom.

They stay frozen. Behind them through the trees, toddlers squeal in the playground. Above them, unhappy crows complain.

Sam pokes his head through the gate.

The backdoor of the house is still closed. Horizontal blinds block all the windows. "It's clear," Sam says.

Jeremy pushes through the gate. "We should have checked if her car is in the driveway."

Sam points to one side of the house. "She has a garage."

Jeremy misinterprets what Sam is saying. "Okay, I'll go check." He drops his shovel, ducks forward, and sprints across the yard. The dead leaves are too wet to *crunch*, so he manages perfect silence.

Sam is impressed, at least until Jeremy peeks in the garage window, then turns around to yell, "No car!"

Sam shushes him. He looks over the fence at the neighbors' houses. The house to the left has a big window on the side without any curtains. The sun reflects off it, so he can't tell if anyone's watching. They probably aren't. Besides, if anyone hears kids yelling, they'll assume it's from the playground.

Sam walks out into the yard.

It's smaller than his family's. He could easily throw a baseball all the way across.

The back deck is just as small as it looked from up in the playground tower. From down here, though, Sam can see the supports have gritty termite grooves.

There's a shed to his left, in the back corner of the yard. The roof is green with moss.

Sam looks around for a mound of dirt, or any evidence of the spot where the old lady buried her cat.

Jeremy runs delicately back to Sam. "Where should we look?"

As if there's lots of options in this tiny yard.

"We can look in the shed or we can dig up the cat. I don't see anywhere else."

"Ew," Jeremy says. "I've never dug up anything dead before."

"Then what'd you bring the shovel for?"

"To dig up a dead cat." Jeremy laughs at himself. He points to a patch of leaves that looks just like any other part of the yard. "It was over here somewhere."

"Let's look around first," Sam says. He walks the outline of the yard. He doesn't know what he's looking for, but all he sees is grass and dirt.

Jeremy follows behind him, eyes scanning the ground.

Sam keeps an eye on the back windows while he inspects the deck. He peers underneath. There's nothing but mud and posts.

They walk the fence on the other side of the yard, winding up back at the shed.

"Think it's locked?" Jeremy asks.

Sam tries the door handle. "Nope."

It opens easily.

Dull sunlight comes in through the open door. Dusty garden tools line the back wall.

A push lawn mower sits inside the doorway. Sam gives it a shove to get inside. It's warmer in here.

"Why's it so hot?" Jeremy asks.

"The sun was shining on it."

"The whole yard's in the shade. That's why it's so muddy."

Sam realizes his friend is right. The shed suddenly feels both hotter and darker. There's a tarp off to the right. Sam can't tell what it's covering up, but whatever it is, it's big.

From behind them comes the sound of an approaching car, then the mechanical rumble of a garage door opening.

"She's home," Jeremy whispers.

They both hurry inside the shed. Sam shuts the door behind them.

He's instantly sweating. This jacket is way too hot.

"What are we looking for?" Jeremy asks.

"The pink light." Sam peeks through the shed's dirty window at the back of the house. With the closed blinds, there's no telling what the old woman is doing.

"There's no pink light in here," Jeremy says.

But then suddenly there is.

It's shining out from underneath the edges of the tarp.

Jeremy jumps away. He goes for the door but Sam grabs his hand, which is already covered in sweat. "Wait! I have to look."

What if under that tarp is a pile of dead trick-or-treaters?

No, that's stupid. The missing kids are showing up at Old Pine. They're not dead. Mary's not dead.

But something's under that tarp.

Sam barely registers the sound of the house's back door opening and closing. He's too focused on the pink light.

He steps forward and bends down.

"What are you doing?" Jeremy whispers.

"We gotta see." He hooks his fingers under the tarp and it's got little chunks of mud caked to it. His fingers turn neon pink in the light.

Sam jerks the tarp up.

It's three stacks of buckets—the orange plastic ones from Home Depot. The pink light is coming from the top bucket of the tallest stack. It points at the shed ceiling like a spotlight.

Sam's heart thumps and he feels suddenly cold despite the heat.

He approaches the buckets.

"Don't," Jeremy whines.

Sam leans forward.

The pink light is like a solid beam.

He leans into it. His forehead tingles.

The inside of the bucket comes into view.

Amid the thick light are two deep triangles. Something swirls in that light, like neon hiding in its own glow.

Sam feels those triangles *shift*. They've noticed him.

He stumbles backward, his feet catch on the lawnmower and he's falling.

He sees the ceiling, an image projected up from the bucket. It's interrupted by the roof trusses, but Sam sees the image clearly enough: a classroom without desks or decorations.

Someone's standing in the middle, but a truss cuts right

through them so Sam can't tell who it is. They're wearing black but is it Mary?

Jeremy is helping Sam up, he's fussing about someone coming, but Sam can only focus on the projection on the ceiling and its unmoving figure in black.

The shed door opens.

"Who the hell?" comes a raspy old voice.

Sam's fear of getting in trouble outweighs everything else.

He and Jeremy push past the old lady, run through her yard, and race into the woods.

∼

IT'S BEEN a hell of a day. Bob is exhausted.

Before he drives over to Old Pine, he cruises past 7349 Clearbark Circle.

It's a two-story blue house with a garage. It fits in fine with the rest of the neighborhood, but the maintenance does look a little behind. There's some nail-pops in the roof, but not enough that the HOA has noticed. The front yard needs to be raked, and the white vinyl fence could stand to be power washed.

Bob films the house as he drives by. He's not ready to go knock on the door just yet. He's sent a message to Officer Karl, asking for info about the residents, but he hasn't heard back yet.

He's not super familiar with this pocket of Maple Creek. One of the missing kids—Caroline Newman—has an uncle and aunt at the end of the cul-de-sac. Bob broke into their house a few months back. He found nothing.

He'd like to go inside 7349 tonight, but he doesn't have a clue what he'd be walking into. Could be a "yee-haw" gun nut with an itchy trigger finger.

For now, he goes over to Old Pine.

Joann will meet him there once Polly arrives to watch the kids.

Bob's stomach is in knots, and he expects it to be that way every evening as the numbers on his phone get closer to 7:31 P.M.

Every ounce of his existence is desperate to see Mary, while simultaneously sick with fear that what'll come through those doors is his daughter's dead body.

It turns out that neither his hope nor his fear come true tonight.

While Bob records from his phone with one hand and holds Joann close to him with the other, Officer Freeman carries out a two-year-old named Corben Farmer.

He's the youngest of the missing kids, and as far as Bob can tell, he's perfectly healthy.

OCTOBER 8TH

At lunch, Jeremy and Sam whisper to each other over their square pizza and canned peaches.

It's the first chance they've had to talk about what happened yesterday.

"Which trick-or-treater came home last night? Was it your sister?" Jeremy asks.

Sam shakes his head.

"Damn," Jeremy says. "So we're not done yet."

Sam gets it. That pink light is scary as hell and he'd love to be able to walk away from it.

"But whoever it was," Jeremy asks, "they were alive, right?"

Sam says, "I think so. We would have heard if they weren't."

"Is there pink light behind them when they come out of the school?"

"Nobody said anything about that," Sam says.

Jeremy takes a big bite of pizza and speaks with his mouth full. "I bet there is."

"You ready to go in there with me and look for Mary?"

"There's cops guarding it. We'll get arrested."

"That's not why you're scared, and you know it." Sam points at his friend with his plastic fork, accidentally launching a peach slice at him.

Jeremy gasps and laughs. "You're scared, too."

"Yeah," Sam admits. "But I think she's in there. Will you go with me?"

"I don't think we need to. The cops have searched Old Pine. The missing kids aren't in there. But they've got to be somewhere, right? I bet that pink light will be wherever they are."

Sam digests what Jeremy's saying. "I guess so."

"So we need to find other places the pink light is showing up."

"How?" Sam asks.

Jeremy takes an even bigger bite, then says with a full mouth, "We ask everybody."

Sam motions to the empty seats between them and the rest of their class. "Who exactly are we gonna ask?"

"Our friends."

Sam doesn't hate any of his classmates, and the bullying is rare, but he doesn't have a lot of friends. "Like who?"

"Walter, Jonathan, Mikey, Kenny."

"We don't play with them."

"We do when we play Roblox at my house."

"Oh, yeah." Sam hasn't thought about that.

"Come over after school. We'll get online, play some Tower of Hell, and ask the guys if they've seen any pink lights."

Since Mom and Dad aren't including Sam in their plans to find Mary, this is the best chance he has to help find her. And Dad did tell Sam to ask his friends for information, even if that was an obvious ploy to get Sam to stop asking to help. "Okay. I'll come over."

∼.

OF COURSE, by "Let's play Roblox," Jeremy means, "Watch me play."

But Sam is fine with that. Dad says Roblox isn't a game you buy and have fun with, but instead a sneaky store that tries to keep you spending money.

Sam sits next to Jeremy in front of his computer. The guy on the screen runs all over, dodging little zombies while helping build a bigger zombie.

Jeremy has set aside his gamer headset for his AirPods, which he shares with Sam, so they can both listen and talk with their squad.

"Wanna hear something creepy?" Jeremy asks over the microphone.

Mikey is the first to answer. "Yeah!"

Jonathan is more doubtful. "Is this another dumb story that ends with 'deez nuts?'"

Jeremy bursts out laughing, which makes Sam jump.

"This is real," Sam says.

"Oh shit," Kenny says. "If Sam says it's real, I wanna hear it."

As the squad finishes building their giant zombie, Sam tells them about the TV, the guy in the hoodie with the pink-glowing turnip jack-o-lantern, and the bucket in the old lady's shed.

He tells them how he saw a projected image of a figure in black on the shed ceiling.

The squad goes wild with "ooh's" and "what the hell's." When Walter speaks, Sam realizes he hadn't been reacting with the rest of them.

"I saw a pink light, too," Walter says. "I might have seen that classroom."

"Where?" Sam asks eagerly.

"Last year before Halloween," Walter says. "My mom took me to Crimson Corridors."

"The haunted house?" Sam asks.

"It's not real, dummy," Jeremy says.

"I didn't say it was." Sam had asked Dad about going, but Mom wanted them to wait until Sam was at least another year older. "You saw a classroom there?"

"Of course he did, dipshit," comes Kenny's voice through the earbud. "It's a fake haunted house in an old school. There's tons of classrooms."

Walter replies, "This one was different. It was near the end of it, but before the room with the last big scare where a zombie teacher jumps out from inside a desk. In this one, there was just some spiders hanging from the ceiling and you walked through them. But after we walked back out, I stopped at the water fountain which wasn't on. I looked back into that classroom. Something was lit up all pink inside, on the far side of all those dangling fake spiders. I couldn't tell what it was. So I stepped back into the doorway."

"What was inside?" Jeremy asks, straining to hear every word.

Kenny's crackly voice comes through the earbud. "He's telling you what happened. Let him talk!"

Sam is so caught up in Walter's story he doesn't even point out to Jeremy that they've let their giant Roblox zombie die.

Walter continues. "There was a fan blowing so the spiders would move around a little. A few of them swayed enough that I saw past them."

"What was glowing pink?" Sam asks.

"I couldn't tell. The light was coming from behind a prop. Or I thought it was a prop. All I could see was the outline because that pink light was right behind it. It was a guy in a hood, holding a funny shaped jack-o-lantern."

"Was it shaped like a turnip?" Sam asks, already knowing the answer.

"Could have been," Walter answers.

On Jeremy's monitor, the whole squad is motionless.

"Was the kidnapper staring at me last year?" Walter asks.

"No way," comes Mikey's voice, unsure of itself. "He would have taken you."

"It had to be him," Sam says. "That's the guy I saw when my sister disappeared, and the same guy I saw on my TV."

Sam sits back in his chair. Not only did someone else believe him about seeing the hoodied trick-or-treater, but Walter has actually seen the guy for himself. It's a relief, but a short lived one. It means Sam has to do something really scary.

"No more distractions," he says. "We're going in Old Pine."

"What?" Jeremy smacks his keyboard. "No way. I told you, the cops already searched there."

"But they didn't know exactly where to look. We do."

∼

MOM MAKES spaghetti for dinner and cookies for dessert. Sam doesn't even see any Tupperware containers on the counter, like there are when she's bringing this stuff to church. They actually get to eat it.

Sam can't stop thinking about what Walter said. The hoodied guy was in Old Pine last year, even before Mary disappeared.

Sam imagines what Walter saw, over and over.

Mom's spaghetti actually does a pretty good job of distracting him. He eats himself right into pasta shock.

Emily's cheeks are smeared with tomato sauce and the tiniest bits of ground beef. Sam can feel a little of that on his own cheeks.

Dad checks his watch.

Aunt Polly will be over soon. Mom and Dad will go over to Old Pine to be there for Mary.

Sam doesn't want to be left alone with his new knowledge of what Walter saw when Old Pine was Crimson Corridors last year, so he spits it out. "Last year in the haunted house, Walter saw the orange hoodie guy with the pink jack-o-lantern."

Dad leans forward, ready to ask more, but Mom says, "Please let me and your dad worry about this. You focus on school and playing."

Sam can't believe her. He thought Mom wasn't running away from this anymore. Why doesn't she want to talk about it now? He looks to Dad for support.

Dad glances at Mom, then says, "We know Mary might be in the old school. I'm already on it. Trust me."

Emily has finished her spaghetti and reaches for the big bowl of noodles in the middle of the table. When her little arms can't reach, she instead goes for Sam's plate. He lets her drag away his scraps.

"We have to find her before…" Sam doesn't want to say it out loud. His old classmate Calvin is dead. Mary might end up dead, too.

The hourglass is running out, but the glass is opaque. Mary could die any evening.

"I want to help," Sam says.

"You are helping." Dad uses that serious, soft voice that Sam usually only hears after Dad's fussed at Sam too harshly. "You keep telling us anything you find out. That's how you're helping. But the rest of the time, you go play. How about you get unlimited screens the rest of the week?"

"Hey now," Mom says.

"It'll let him get his mind off things," Dad replies.

"Yeah, I guess that's okay."

Except Sam doesn't want to play Minecraft and Mario right now. Even if he did, he can always go across the street to Jeremy's house where there's unlimited screentime anyways.

He wants to go inside Old Pine to look for Mary.

He's done arguing. It doesn't matter whether his parents take him seriously. He's already decided that he'll go find Mary himself.

∼

THE EVENING CROWD outside Old Pine is getting bigger. It's not just parents anymore—it's rubberneckers, news vans, and who knows who else.

Bob and Joann hold hands while they wait for Mary.

Neither of them say aloud what they're both afraid of: the fourth child to come out of those doors was dead. Today will be the eighth child. Will there be a pattern?

But Dylan Evans wanders outside in his Spider-Man costume. He's alive.

On the way home, they drive by 7349 Clearbark Circle. There are lights on inside. Bob needs to get in there.

"We should go knock on the door," Joann says.

Bob says, "No. I'm going inside. I don't want them seeing me right before that."

Joann goes quiet. This is the first that Bob is admitting aloud to her that he's been breaking into houses. If she'd rather keep pretending it's not happening, he'll go along with it.

But then she says, "Not tonight."

"Why not?"

"Give me a chance to talk to them first."

Now that it's out in the open that he's been committing several felonies per week, Bob's surprised that she's not forbidding it altogether. But if she's on board with only this stipulation, then he'll go along with it. "Okay. Not tonight."

OCTOBER 9TH

Dad drops off Sam at school, and he doesn't notice that Sam's backpack is way heavier than normal, or that something inside is poking against the fabric near the top.

"Love you!" Dad's voice gets cut off as Sam shuts the door. He didn't mean to ignore him, but it *is* Dad's fault that Sam has to do this alone.

He's not alone yet. His schoolmates are funneling into the front doors. He joins the flow.

He's surrounded by kids who like the same games he likes, who watch the same DisneyPlus shows, who have conflicted feelings about Halloween this year. He wishes he were friends with more of them. He's not sure what's wrong with him that's preventing that.

Sam goes in the front doors. The brisk autumn morning breeze is replaced by dry, warm air. The dull sunlight filtered through clouds is replaced by sterile florescent lights.

In the river of his schoolmates, Sam normally passes the kindergarten classrooms, and then turns left toward the third-grade wing.

This morning, he keeps going straight.

The second-grade classrooms are this way, so Sam feels out of place. He's bigger and older than the kids around him, although hopefully not enough for adults to notice.

At the end of the hallway, muted sunlight comes through the narrow rectangular windows of the double doors.

Second grade teachers are standing in their classroom doorways on either side of the corridor. Sam avoids their eyes.

There's Mrs. Crews. She was his second grade teacher and she always says hi. Now she's hugging a kid with a Minnie Mouse backpack. Sam keeps his head down and scoots past.

Then he's out the door, out from under the fake white lights and back into the cool sunlight. Morning chill goes right inside his jacket. It feels like possibility.

The door slams behind him. That'll get the attention of Mrs. Crews and everyone else in the hall, so Sam runs around the corner.

He leans against the school's brick wall. The contents of his backpack clink against the brick. In front of Sam are his school's playground and blacktop. Past those is Old Pine.

Rust-colored brick makes up its walls. The windows are framed in black which has gone gray. Compared to the new school's sand-colored brick and stainless steel window frames, Old Pine makes Sam think of a witch's cottage. A sprawling, maze-like witch's cottage.

Old Pine's doors used to be red. Now that paint is peeling, revealing shiny metal beneath.

Chains wrap around the door handles. Sam knew they'd be there. He's ready for that.

From back around the corner, the door creaks.

Sam's heart sinks.

Someone saw him leave. He'll be caught and Mary will stay missing.

But then the door slams shut again.

Sam listens to the rumble of cars passing by. The noise echoes off the tree line behind both schools.

He tiptoes out from his hiding place.

No one's outside with him.

He's not missing his chance. He runs light-footed across the field, past the playground, over the blacktop.

When he gets to Old Pine's back door, he lets his backpack fall to the sidewalk. The contents clank. He unzips the bag and pulls out Dad's bolt cutters.

The lock itself is thicker than he'd hoped. He's not sure he's strong enough to cut through the chain, and now that he sees the lock he knows he's not strong enough to cut through that.

But Mom says Sam is smart, and Sam knows Mom's right. He's brought two lengths of metal pipe. They'll fit over either handle of the bolt cutters and give Sam extra leverage.

Sam glances back at his school. There are too many windows. The blinds are closed since the sun rises this way, but still, if anyone peeks through, they'll see him.

It's tricky to balance the bolt cutters with the pipes, but Sam manages to get the blades around one of the chain's links.

He squeezes the pipes, flexing his arms and shoulders as much as he can.

Nothing happens.

He adjusts his grip, tries again.

The pipes slip and the bolt cutters drop onto his shoe. Pain zips around the bones in his foot.

Sam hops and curses. He's instantly worried he looks silly, then he's instantly worried someone's looking at him. He checks the windows. It's clear.

He reassembles his lengthened bolt cutter and tries again. No luck.

He tries a different approach. He balances one pipe against the door itself and then pushes with his whole body against the other pipe. It slips. His knuckles crash against the door. Pain explodes in his right hand.

He takes a breath. Nothing broken. He's bleeding, but just barely. He can take it.

But this is pointless.

He felt so proud of himself for thinking of bringing those

handle extensions, but it was stupid. He's not big enough to break a chain.

Sam sits down on the sidewalk. A sob grows in his chest, but he refuses to let it out. He's not giving up. There's gotta be another way inside.

"Hey idiot."

Jeremy's voice makes Sam jump. He turns around and there's his best friend along with Walter.

Walter is in another class. He's tall and skinny and his black hair hangs over his ears. Sam only knows him through watching Jeremy play Roblox, but after yesterday Sam feels like Walter is in on his biggest secrets.

"What are you guys doing here?"

Jeremy scoffs. "I followed you outside. I didn't see you anywhere, but it wasn't hard to figure out where you were headed. I went back inside, texted the guys, and here we are."

Walter rubs his arms as if he's cold, despite his jacket and the morning being mild. "I can't believe we're going ghost hunting."

"My sister's not a ghost," Sam spits out.

"Not your sister, dude." Jeremy holds up his hands. "The guy with the hoodie and the weird jack-o-lantern."

"The Thirty-First Trick-or-Treater," Walter says. "That's what some of the returned kids are calling him."

"Why?" Sam asks.

"Thirty kids went missing. They're coming back one at a time. On Halloween, this guy's coming back. So he's the thirty-first."

"And you want to find him?" Sam's hoping to avoid the kidnapper.

Walter says, "Nobody believed me last year. I'm gonna get a video of it this time." He holds up a cell phone.

Sam looks from his best friend to his newest friend. "We're going to get in major trouble for skipping school."

"You worry too much," Jeremy says. "This'll be fun."

Sam tries to hide the smile that comes unbidden, then notices what he's doing and lets it free. This is awesome. He was about to explore this creepy school alone, but now he's got friends with him.

Except, he remembers dourly, he can't actually get in. "I can't squeeze the bolt cutters strong enough."

"We'll do it together," Jeremy says. "You grab one end and I'll grab the other."

Before Sam can react, Walter picks up the bolt cutters, raises them above his head, and slams them down on the door handle. The curved metal breaks in two, allowing the chain to slide off.

"Okay, now you guys try your teamwork idea," Walter says dryly.

Jeremy tugs at the door. "You broke it. Now we can't close it behind us."

"That was loud," Sam says. "Get inside before teachers start looking out their windows."

Sam stuffs his pipes and bolt cutters back into his backpack, slings it over his back, and goes inside Old Pine, once again thinking how it reminds him of a witch's cottage.

∽

INSIDE, the haunt is still set up.

A fake spiderweb dangles from the ceiling, blocking the entire hallway. It's made of finger-thick rope and is overlain with real cobwebs.

Sam's never liked spiders. But this is just rope and dusty old webs. Not a living spider to be seen.

"Gross," Jeremy says.

Walter checks the window of the door behind them. "I don't see anyone outside. I think we got away."

Sam walks up to the fake spiderweb. He plucks at a rope. "Why didn't the cops take this down?"

"What do they care?" Jeremy asks.

"They searched the whole school, right? Every day for the last week. But here's all this rope blocking the hallway, so they couldn't have searched back here behind it."

Walter comes up next to Sam. He waves away cobwebs to see through the fake web.

Sam peers through the new opening. Sunlight from the windows behind him has to wriggle through the dust and webs. His eyes adjust to the dim hallway.

As they do, he sees the shape of a whiteboard on wheels. It's set up across two-thirds of the hallway, as if it's supposed to shepherd Crimson Corridor visitors through that tight little opening to set them up for a jump scare from a waiting actor.

Wait, that doesn't make sense. There's nothing back here. Nowhere for the visitors to go after they squeeze past the whiteboard.

Maybe it was used to block the entire hallway to keep visitors on a different path.

Walter waves away more cobwebs.

Sam's eyes further adjust.

There's writing on the whiteboard. No—those words are carved in. Compressed wood pokes out from the gashes in the white laminate. Sam can't read it clearly from here.

Walter tugs on the fake web. "I'll show you that classroom. You tell us if it's the one you saw in the projection."

Despite Walter's tugging, the fake web stays connected to the ceiling and walls. "It's stuck."

Jeremy pushes past the taller boy. "The holes are big enough." He kicks away cobwebs near the floor, then crawls through a lower hole in the rope web.

That makes Sam nervous. Watching Jeremy make himself small enough to fit through the web makes the web feel more real.

Walter is next.

If Jeremy is a beetle crawling through the web, then tall Walter is a worm wiggling through.

Sam won't get left behind. He crawls quickly into the hole. The rope catches on his pants' waistband. He tries to pull free, but it's stuck—not tangled—but stuck against his side as if the web isn't made of rope but real spider silk.

Suddenly, Sam wants to move his entire body at once, wants to leap into the air, get out of this web, away from its constricting strands.

And then the thick spider silk lets go, his waistband snaps against his hip, and he's free.

"Did you see that?" he gasps to his friends.

"You get stuck?" Walter asks.

Sam stumbles up to his feet. "The rope was sticky."

"You're carrying that huge backpack," Jeremy says. "Of course it got caught."

"No, it was like glue."

Walter reaches back one of the lower strands. "Hey. Weird." He pulls his fingers free and the rope thrums as it releases. He rubs his thumb and fingers together. "Someone put glue on it."

Jeremy touches a rope. It sticks to his hand. He shakes his hand like he's flicking off a bug. Or like he's the bug, panicking about an approaching spider. The web vibrates until Jeremy's hand is free. "Ew. Who would be in here spreading glue on fake spiderwebs?"

"The police?" suggests Walter.

"You saw him yourself," Sam says. "The guy in the hoodie. The Thirty-First Trick-or-Treater. He's here somewhere."

Even though Sam's the one who says it, the idea still sends icy spiders skittering down his spine. Before he finds Mary, will he have to get past that turnip jack-o-lantern with its glowing pink eyes?

Walter's still rubbing the glue off his fingers. "I saw him last year. That doesn't mean he's still here."

Sam inhales deeply. He chokes on dust and then clears his throat. "If we see him, then my sister could be nearby. You guys distract him so I can get her out." He starts walking toward the whiteboard, angling himself to see around it.

"Hold on," Jeremy says, "We're here to help you find your sister. Not get ourselves kidnapped."

"I'll distract him." Walter holds up his phone. "I'm gonna prove to my family he's real."

As Sam approaches the whiteboard, he can make out the words carved through the laminate and into the particle board.

Detention... of DOOM!!!!!

This is a leftover of Crimson Corridors.

"That's cheesy," Jeremy says.

"It was scary when you were in it." Walter runs his fingers along the word *DOOM*. "At least, some of the stuff was scary. Not this weird threat, I guess."

Sam is the first past the whiteboard, and so he's the first to realize that the whiteboard isn't the only leftover from Crimson Corridors. The whole haunted school attraction is still set up.

They've entered in the middle of the walkthrough, into a maze of rolling whiteboards. Each has terrible messages carved into them.

Eyes on your own paper... or I'll <u>pluck</u> <u>them</u> <u>out</u>.

No talking... or I'll eat your tongue.

No helping each other.

That last one doesn't have a threat attached to it. Strange, but Sam doesn't waste time thinking about it.

"Which way?" he asks.

Walter points to the right and Sam leads the way.

Ahead, a yardstick leans against a whiteboard. Razor blades are stuck into one end.

"Those have to be fake, right?" Jeremy asks.

"I'm not touching them," Walter says. "I don't want a tetanus shot."

They make it through the whiteboard maze and into an area themed like gym class: dodgeballs hanging from chains, soccer nets with big plastic spiders, a dangling jump rope tied into a noose. Lockers have been detached from the wall in order to funnel visitors into a tiny gap and give scare actors a place to hide.

Jeremy kicks a dodgeball. The chain it hangs from jingles. "This is stupid. Why's this in the hall instead of the actual gym?"

Walter is standing with his hands on his hips. "I swear it was. I remember walking through the gym because it smelled like basketballs and dust."

Sam tries to see to the end of this section. The obstacles block his view. "Maybe it leads inside the gym?"

They navigate through the twisted gym equipment and the lockers positioned to allow jump scares, but the gym section ends without reaching the doors to the actual gym.

The exercise and sports equipment gives way to long skinny tables with black tops, littered with beakers and Bunsen burners.

Instead of whiteboards, now it's light brown cork boards blocking the view to allow for jump scares. On the boards are pinned the dried corpses of frogs, front and back legs spread out in grotesque Xs.

"We're moving too slow," Sam says.

"We're exploring," Jeremy says. "We can't race through."

"Where'd you see that classroom?" Sam asks Walter.

"Near the front."

"How do you get there from here?"

"I thought it was this way, but now I'm not sure." Walter pushes a bulletin board to turn it parallel with the hall. "This isn't how I remember it."

Jeremy scoffs. "That's cause you've got holes in your brain."

Sam looks down the hallway past the moved bulletin board, beyond the science class section, beyond what appears to be a Spanish class area, beyond whatever is after that. "How long is this hallway?"

Walter stands on his toes.

Jeremy climbs up onto a science table.

"This doesn't make any sense," Walter says. "They were sending us in and out of classrooms. But everything's in the hallways now."

"The cops must have pushed everything out here when they were searching," Jeremy says.

Sam shakes his head. "This is set up like it's the actual haunt."

"We can try a different way," Walter suggests. "Go back to those whiteboards and go left instead of right."

The hallway shudders like it's a car that's shifted gear.

Far down the hallway, a blurred light turns on. It's pink.

Hope and fear flare up inside Sam. "She's over there!" He races past the science tables, into a display of paper-mache tacos and hand-painted signs that read *"Me gusta el sangre."*

The hallway is so impossibly long, but there's a pink light down there, and that means Mary could be there.

Sam realizes that Walter is by his side, actually slowing his pace to join Sam.

But behind them, Jeremy yells, "Guys, this is messed up. I'm going back."

Sam doesn't care. He's got to find his sister. He runs as hard as he can. His heart pounds and his lungs burn.

After a minute, Walter says, "We're not getting closer."

Sam knows he's right but he's not giving up yet. He's gasping to get enough air but he can't slow down.

Walter speaks clearly, "I don't like this. Maybe Jeremy was right."

"He wasn't," Sam wheezes.

"We need a plan," Walter says. "What do we do when we find the Trick-or-Treater? I'm taking his picture, and after that I'll distract him for you, but for that to work I need somewhere to run away. We're getting too far from the exit."

He's right in more ways than one. The door they came through feels way too far away.

Sam slows down. He breathes deep, chest burning, a stitch in his side. He's never been the best long-distance runner.

Ahead, the pink light isn't just a blur anymore. It's a distinct patch of light spilling from an open doorway.

"That's the classroom where you saw him."

"Maybe," Walter says.

"I gotta see if it's the one I saw on my TV."

Walter looks behind them. "Jeremy's gone already."

"Are you leaving, too?"

"No. I still need a video of this guy."

Sam speeds up again, navigating across a drama-class setup of a stage splattered with rotten tomatoes and intestines. Both smell real.

The doorway emitting the pink light draws closer.

"Does it look familiar yet?" Sam asks.

"No," Walter says. "What about for you?"

"No," Sam agrees.

Between them and the open door, the floor is littered with open textbooks. Crude paintings of faces are on each open page.

They creep between the books.

Sam is approaching the doorway along the opposite wall, trying to see inside.

"Quiet," Walter hisses. "Do you hear that?"

Sam goes still.

The sound of erratic footsteps echoes out from that classroom—a lot of them. A group of people are shuffling around. Sam imagines the missing trick-or-treaters.

Sam can't help himself—he dashes forward. "Mary!"

Walter runs beside him, phone held up, recording.

Then from behind them, Jeremy shouts, "Help!"

Walter disappears from beside Sam. He's stopped.

But Sam has to see inside this classroom. It's the one he saw on the TV. He knows that without even seeing.

Walter yells, "Oh god. Jeremy needs help!"

Sam doesn't care. Mary's around the corner. She must be. But before he can reach it, Jeremy wails like he's in pain.

"Sam!" yells Walter.

Sam skids to a stop. The classroom is only ten feet ahead. Mary.

"Please!" Walter screams.

Sam turns around.

Far back down the hallway, Jeremy is hanging from a bulletin board. His wrists are above his head, strapped to the cork board with clear tape.

Walter is tugging at Jeremy's arms. "I can't get him down."

Sam runs back. "How did he get up there?" And how did he get back to the science class section so quickly?

"I don't know!" Jeremy cries. "Someone grabbed me."

Sam helps him down, then turns back toward the glowing pink classroom.

The entire hallway in that direction is glowing pink now, emanating from a shadowy form in the middle. The light is too bright to make out the shape of the shadow, but it's definitely moving toward them.

"Run!" Jeremy cries.

Sam's plans fly out the window. He can't depend on his friends to distract the Thirty-First Trick-or-Treater. The pink light is too much, too all-encompassing. Sam can't sneak by.

Walter yanks him away from the approaching shadow and its light. Sam wants to stay, needs to find Mary, but he realizes with dread that it'll require going *through* the Thirty-First Trick-or-Treater, not around him.

They flee back through the haunted attraction, back outside.

∽

SAM, Jeremy, and Walter wash off in the hallway bathroom, but their clothes are darkened with dust and the smell of mildew.

Walter goes to his class. Sam and Jeremey manage to sneak in and sit down.

Before library time, Mrs. Bavin notices Sam and asks him when he got there. Jeremy keeps his head on the desk. Mrs. Bavin didn't notice that Jeremy was missing.

Sam doesn't think he can get away with lying, so he tells her the truth. "Twenty minutes ago."

"Did you check in at the office?"

"No," Sam says meekly.

Mrs. Bavin sighs. "There'll be a note going home with you today, Sam. Your parents need to sign it."

"Okay."

She crouches down. "Are you okay? You look worried." On her shirt is a fabric pin in the shape of bird. It's pink—the same shade that was glowing in Old Pine.

Sam worries that if he touches it, it'll stick to him like the thick ropes in that fake spiderweb.

"How'd you get so dirty?" Mrs. Bavin asks.

Sam recites the lie that he and his friends agreed on. "I fell in the flower bed outside."

"Did you hurt yourself?"

Sam shakes his head.

"If you need to talk about anything, we can talk anytime. You know that, right?" Mrs. Bavin says that often.

"I know," Sam says.

"Go get in line. Bring your library books."

And that's it. When he gets home, Mom or Dad will ask about him being tardy, and he can say he felt sad so he walked around before going to class. He might get in trouble, but it won't be severe.

Sam's stunned. It can't be that easy.

For a whole hour, not a single adult knew where he was. In fact, Mom and Dad thought he was one place, when he was actually off looking for Mary.

This is both a terrible and a wonderful realization. Terrible because it's been more than eleven months since Mary disappeared. Sam could have been looking for her every day, despite Mom and Dad keeping close tabs on him. But it's also a wonderful realization, because now he knows he can keep looking for her, no matter where Mom and Dad think he is.

As Mrs. Bavin notices Jeremy and starts a similar conversation, Sam smiles.

The world is still full of strange and important rules, but now there's one less chaining him down.

The Thirty-First Trick-or-Treater has Mary.

Sam can get her back.

The 31st Trick-or-Treater

~

THAT EVENING, when Clara Hill falls out from the Old Pine front doors, she isn't breathing.

The cops storm into the building, as if they weren't already positioned in the lobby.

The paramedics can't bring Clara back.

Bob and Joann listen to her father beg them to keep trying.

Instead of going back to the car, they slip into the dark and look for a simple way inside Old Pine.

They wait in the shadows for an hour, until the cops have given up on their search again.

They make it to a back door, which faces Sam's elementary school. A loop of chain sits on the sidewalk in front of it. The door handle has been smashed.

Bob pulls it open.

It's a long hallway. Backup lights are on, straining against the dark. The hallway is empty. It leads all the way across the school to the front lobby, where cops are beginning another search.

Bob's a little surprised. He thought there'd be at least some leftover haunt decorations from Crimson Corridors.

"We should go," Joann says.

They slip away before the cops notice them.

But Bob isn't done for the night.

Joann couldn't get any response from the owner of 7349 Clearbark Circle.

So tonight, after midnight, Bob's going inside.

OCTOBER 10TH

At 2:00 a.m., Bob and Joann go for a walk.

They pass Clara Hill's house. The lights are still on.

Bob reaches for Joann's hand. He doesn't know what to do with this fear.

That's why they're taking this risk tonight.

Bob tried to convince Joann to stay home—if they both get arrested, what about the kids?

Joann's response: "That's why we're not going to get caught."

Of course, they don't come at 7349 Clearbark Circle from the front. It's got a nice strip of forest behind it.

They navigate the trees and undergrowth in the dark. The fence is white vinyl and the gate is already open.

Bob goes through first.

The yard is smaller than theirs and the six-foot fence makes it feel even smaller. There's a shed off to his left. Ahead, a picnic table fills up most of a small deck.

There are no lights on in the windows or the sliding glass back door. Bob is happy to see it. That style of door has simple latch locks that are easy to jimmy open.

Joann follows him up the deck. He unlocks the door.

"Dang," Joann whispers, sounding impressed.

For a moment, Bob feels like they're in the early weeks of dating again.

He slides the door open as quietly as he can. He and Joann step softly through and close the door behind them.

It's hot inside.

Bob thinks of his grandmother who always had the heat set at 78 degrees.

He switches on his flashlight with red LEDs. Red light draws the least attention from outside, while still letting him see.

"Where to?" Joann whispers.

Suddenly, a lamp turns on.

The light makes Bob's eyes hurt. Joann slides the door back open.

An elderly woman's voice says, "You're not who I was expecting."

She's sitting on a floral print couch, wearing brown slacks and a blouse with even more flowers than her sofa.

"We're so sorry," Joann says, and Bob hears a drunk affectation in her voice. "This is the wrong house."

"That's not going to work. I know what you're here for, even if I thought it was going to be someone else."

Bob's confused. "Why do you think we're here?"

"Because of what I did."

Bob inspects this woman more closely. She doesn't look strong enough to lift a child, let alone kidnap thirty of them.

"What did you do?" Joann asks.

The old woman takes her glasses from an end table and puts them on. She peers closely at Bob and Joann. "You're not the ones who were in my shed the other day. Those were kids."

Joann raises a questioning eyebrow to Bob. He shakes his head in response. *No, I didn't break into her shed.*

Bob asks, "Why was someone in your shed?" If he goes out there, what'll he find? It's too small to be holding all the missing kids, but what if she's dug out some kind of bunker underneath?

No, that's ridiculous. This woman is too frail to dig a vegetable garden.

"I went to Crimson Corridors last year. My grandson was begging for someone to take him. I got turned around one of the classrooms. They had spiders hanging from the ceiling. I've never been good around spiders."

"But you went to a haunted house," says Joann.

"It was for my grandson! But the *Arachnophobia* meets Jackson Pollock was too much for me. I got mixed up which door was which and I went into a bathroom. The toilet was so tiny—must have been a kindergarten classroom at one point. I tripped over it, fell against an old paper towel dispenser, and that smashed into the mirror and shattered it."

The old woman closes her eyes and breathes deep.

Bob prompts her. "So you think you've got bad luck now?"

She opens her eyes. "There was a body behind that mirror."

"Who?" Joann asks.

"I don't know. He was upside down like he'd fallen into the wall from the ceiling. The face was so bloated he looked like a bullfrog."

"Was it a prop for the haunt?" Bob suggests. "Something made to scare you?"

"That's what I thought at first, but no, I was off the beaten path. And there was no way they'd plan on somebody breaking a mirror."

"It was a real body?" Joann asks. "How come we never heard about that? You didn't tell anybody?"

"I ran. Grabbed my grandson and got out of there. For a couple hours, I convinced myself that it was a prop, like you said. But then I thought about the smell and how it made me gag. It was too real."

"Why didn't you call the police?" Bob asks.

"My ex-son-in-law was a cop. I don't trust cops."

"But someone was dead," Joann says. "Their family could have been looking for them."

"I don't trust cops."

Bob's mind races. A body in Old Pine—what does that mean?

Whoever killed that person is the kidnapper? Or is someone seeking revenge?

Joann's mind turns out to be elsewhere. "Why'd you put a projector in our house?"

Bob is so entranced by the old woman's story that he's nearly forgot what led them to this address in the first place. He adds to Joann's question. "And why the hell was it in a turnip?"

The woman crosses her arms. "I have no idea what you're talking about."

"Yes, you do. Our son saw a creepy video that came out of a projector jammed into a turnip."

"What?" she looks genuinely confused.

Bob doesn't buy it. "We found the memory card inside. It had your address on it."

The woman shakes her head. "I've never owned a projector. I don't know who you are or where you live."

Bob pictures this woman uploading the creepy video to the memory card, then squishing the projector inside the turnip. "Our son saw your strange little video. The pink-eyed jack-o-lantern scared the hell out of him. What's your deal?"

The woman groans. "Was a teenager in an orange hoodie carrying this jack-o-lantern?"

"You know damn well there was."

"Shut the door," she suddenly begs. "Did you see him on your way over here?"

Joann obliges, sliding the door shut again. "It's the middle of the night. No one was outside but us."

The woman sighs. Relieved, but still cautious. "He's been following me since I found that body. I've learned to close my eyes as soon as I see a pink light."

"What happens if you don't?" Joann asks.

Bob is so on edge he didn't even think to ask that. He only wants to demand the old woman explain who took Mary and where.

The old woman shakes her head. "He gets closer until I feel him breathing on my face. And I know it doesn't make any sense, but his breath has a color. Pink. If I were to open my eyes and see him that close to me, even once, that would be it."

Bob looks to Joann, hoping to share an unspoken realization. This woman isn't all there anymore. Except Joann only glances at him before she asks the woman, "Do you think he'd kill you?"

The woman laughs sardonically. "Not that bad. And worse than that. Both at the same time." She hugs her chest and shudders.

As much nonsense as she's speaking, Bob sees the fear in her. She can't be the kidnapper because she's too frail. She can't be tangentially involved because she's too crazy to have kept secrets about it—the bad guys in charge would have silenced her long ago.

"I'm gonna take a look around," Bob says. "Keep asking her about the kids. See if anything slips out."

Bobs walks around the first floor. There's a dining room, a kitchen, and a TV room. Nothing suspicious, nothing to search through.

He goes upstairs. Three bedrooms and two bathrooms, with one of those bathrooms in the master. One bedroom is full of fabric and sewing patterns. In the next bedroom, the bed is more accessible. An ancient Nintendo sits atop a big clunker of a TV. There's shelves dotted with fantasy novels and little models of goblins and elves. This was a teenager's room, thirty years ago.

Bob moves on to the master bedroom. The clutter in here is just as bad, but in this case it's clothes. The closet door can't shut all the way for the door rack that's stuffed full of gowns. There are three free-standing racks with dresses taking up every inch. This is the home of someone who loves *QVC*. He doesn't expect to find anything.

There's a photo album on the nightstand. It's a small one—about 20 pages. Bob flips through it, snapping pictures on his phone to look at more closely later on.

That gives him another idea.

After he's sure there's nothing incriminating in the master bedroom, he goes back downstairs.

Joann is asking the woman about the last time she saw the

hoodied teenager. She looks up at Bob. "Her name is Wanda. She's a widow and has two kids and one grandson. They live in Arizona."

"Great to meet you." He turns to his wife. "You didn't tell her your name, did you?"

Joann shakes her head.

"Good." Bob takes the woman's phone.

He navigates to the photos, adds them all to an album and then shares that album with his own phone number.

Then he screenshots her last dozen text chains and her call history from the last few weeks and sends those to himself.

He checks her phone for an email app—doesn't find one—and then social media. He skims it only to find typical lonely old lady interactions—sharing uplifting news stories, commenting on cute animal pictures, oblivious responses to obviously AI images. Nothing suspicious in her messages.

"We're good," Bob says.

Joann smiles at Wanda. "I'm sorry we barged in like this."

"Now hold on. You never said why you're here. If you're not the people I saw in my shed the other day, then who are you?"

Bob answers quickly, before Joann can confess anything. "Just visitors. We'll come back if we have more questions."

She crinkles her brow.

Bob ushers Joann back outside the way they came.

As they walk through the woods back to the street, Joann says, "That was strange."

∿

ONCE THEY GET HOME, Joann checks on the kids while Bob retrieves his laptop from his office, tiptoeing around his sleeping sister-in-law.

He downloads all the photos he'd sent to himself—making sure that the old woman can't remove his access before he gets a chance to search through them.

Joann comes into the bedroom. "Go shower," she says. "You smell like dead leaves."

Bob aggressively scrubs his body. The hot water brings his exhaustion to the front of his mind. By the time he dries off, Joann is asleep in her sweaty clothes on top of their comforter. Bob lays down next to her and starts going through Wanda's recent photos. There are shots of birds and plants throughout Maple Creek.

Bob falls asleep before he gets far through the album.

∼

IN THE MORNING, Bob searches for missing people in the area. Google returns pages and pages about Mary and the other missing kids.

He tells the search to exclude anything that mentions Halloween, but it still comes back with headlines about his neighborhood and conspiracy theories about Democrats and human trafficking in pizza parlor basements.

He adjusts the search to exclude anything in the past year.

Now it leaves out the thirty missing kids to instead show news stories about missing people, but none that he sees are related to Maple Creek.

Well, that should be okay. Maple Creek is the only neighborhood that borders the old school, but the body could have come from anywhere. As Bob scrolls, he realizes how true that is. In terms of population, Hanover isn't huge, but it's part of a metro area of over a million.

Bob can't find out the identity of the corpse by searching for missing people. He needs more details.

He goes to his messenger app to contact Officer Karl. He hesitates. Wanda could just be senile. There might have never been a body inside the walls of Old Pine. Except, she described the same hoodied teenager who Sam claimed to have seen. There's something real here.

The kidnapper—this Thirty-First Trick-or-Treater—started

following Wanda after she found the body in Crimson Corridors. That body is connected to the kidnappings. It could be someone related to the corpse, mad at Wanda for not reporting it. But that doesn't hold water. If it was a loved one and they knew about the body, then they would have reported it themselves.

More likely, Wanda's stalker and Mary's kidnapper is trying to threaten Wanda not to reveal the body. The Thirty-First Trick-or-Treater may have been a murderer before he was a kidnapper.

Although, if Bob was trying to hide the body of someone he murdered, he wouldn't then kidnap thirty kids and let them go in the very building where he'd hidden that corpse.

Still, it's the best lead he's had in ages.

There's one part about it that he hates:

Identifying a missing person is actually something the cops would be better at than him.

Assuming Wanda isn't senile, then the cops can find the body and identify it. Karl can tell Bob who it is, and then Bob can try to find out who wants that body to stay hidden. Whoever that is, that's who's taken Mary.

Bob brings up WhatsApp to send a message to Karl, updating him on Bob's discussion with Wanda.

Karl responds almost immediately. *"She saw the guy with the jack-o-lantern your son saw on Halloween?"*

"Yes."

"Does she still have the video?"

"She never took any video."

"Can't do anything without the video."

Bob wants to strangle him. He's absolutely useless. *"What about the body in the wall? The Trick-or-Treater started following Wanda after she found the body. I bet he's trying to keep the corpse hidden. Get your guys to find the body and find out who it is."*

"They've already searched Old Pine. Every damn night. Dogs and cameras and scanners and everything."

"It's behind a mirror in a kindergarten class bathroom."

"I'm telling you, it's been searched."

"Did they find a broken mirror with space behind it? Tell them to search for DNA or whatever."

Karl takes a few minutes before responding. *"The detectives don't come to me for advice. Go look for yourself. I'll tell you when it's safe. Keep your phone on you the next few nights, because when I say go, you have to go right then."*

That works even better. Bob will have more confidence in his own search.

He'd like to skip waiting for Karl's go-ahead, but with another child murdered, Bob can't risk breaking into Old Pine until Karl says it's safe. Every day he waits there's the risk that Mary comes home not breathing, but if he gets arrested and this whole thing gets pinned on him, then it's guaranteed he won't save her.

As much as he hates cops, now he's depending on one.

∽

Friday evening, at 7:31 p.m., fifteen-year-old Jameson Taylor collapses out from a bathroom doorway into the hallway of Old Pine, right in front of a state trooper.

The paramedics are already inside, part of the constant circle of first responders marching the hallway loop. They can't do anything.

Officer PJ Freeman watches the state trooper captain scream at his men. "How are you missing this intruder?"

He expects his own lieutenant will have a similar speech, once he finds PJ. But instead, he says, "We're bringing guys over from the city. Tomorrow night we'll have eyes in every damn room in this godforsaken building."

∽

Outside, Bob and Joann see the cops come out without a missing kid. They ask for the Taylors. Mrs. Taylor wails in grief. Her husband screams at the cops for being useless.

There's pain in his voice that makes Bob's stomach knot up.

Even through her own emotions, Joann notices that this grief is hitting Bob especially hard tonight. She holds her husband in a long embrace, while the crowd shuffles away and reporters rush the cops at the front door.

Bob and Joann don't have to speak aloud their fear. Two children in a row have now returned murdered. When they see their Mary again, will she be breathing?

∼

At 8:54 P.M., seventy-three-year-old Anna Partridge is walking her Pomeranian, Teddy, when they come across an inflatable Frankenstein lawn decoration blocking the sidewalk.

It's a cartoony monster with big, happy eyes. His arms are a flat image. He holds one finger over his mouth in a shushing pose.

As Teddy sniffs the heavy base, Anna wonders why she doesn't hear a blower.

Frankenstein inflates too tightly. He bulges outward until he's a shape that reminds Anna of that blueberry girl from Willy Wonka.

At 8:55 P.M., Frankenstein pops.

The force of it blows Teddy into the grass, head over heels. It knocks Anna Partridge directly onto her left hip.

Teddy is fine.

Anna's hip and pelvis are shattered.

OCTOBER 11TH

SATURDAY MORNING, Sam is lying in bed.

It's been two days since he saw the pink light inside Old Pine, and since he realized how free he really is. No one's keeping track of him twenty-four-seven.

He's had plenty of chances to sneak away to search for Mary, but he hasn't done it, and that makes him feel like crap.

He pushes aside the guilt. Mary still needs his help. He's got to go back into Old Pine, but Jeremy won't text him back.

If Sam weren't such a scaredy-cat, he could go find Mary right now. March straight into that room with the pink light.

And if he weren't so selfish, then last Halloween he would have rang that doorbell with Mary, and he could have stopped her from being taken in the first place.

He's got lots of flaws that are making things worse for his family.

Sam wants to tell Mom and Dad what he saw inside Old Pine, how he knows exactly what room Mary is in. But he's not sure if they'll do anything about it. What he is sure of, is that they won't let him go back in there. And once they hear that he skipped school to go inside Old Pine, there goes his freedom to sneak around.

No, Sam will go back and find Mary by himself.

He just has to find the courage.

The 31st Trick-or-Treater

∽

IT'S AN UNSEASONABLY WARM MORNING.

Joann has taken the kids to a church activity.

All Bob has to do is wait for Karl's okay to break into Old Pine, and for 7:34 tonight.

The anxiety is making him nauseous.

He walks over to Old Pine again to see if there's a chance to search inside.

No dice.

Now that a third kid has lost their life, the cops are apparently taking this way more seriously. Not the local cops, of course. They're still as incompetent as ever. But now state police cruisers are parked in their own bunch, off away from the county police, as if the parking lot is a high school cafeteria full of cliques.

Bob considers finding a way inside anyways. Mary has to be in there. There's no way someone is sneaking each kid inside.

Or if they are, they've got some secret way inside Old Pine. Which also means that the cops are incompetent at searching.

But if Bob tries to get inside right now, he'll be arrested, and that'll be the end of his search for Mary.

He films himself talking about the arrival of the state police. It's not a lead that he can work with, or that his amateur investigator viewers can work with, but it is a development, and breaking news means more clicks, and more clicks means more people who might see his channel, who might share a random thought that points Bob in the right direction.

When he gets back home, Joann and the kids are returning from their outing.

"Find anything?" she asks.

He shakes his head. "The state troopers are at Old Pine now."

"Maybe they'll do a better job of searching," Joann says.

"Doubt it," says Bob.

"I'm gonna get Emily and Sam's lunch ready, but after that let's look at everything you got from Wanda."

Bob brings his laptop into the kitchen so he can work without being alone. He gets on his WhatsApp group with his most devoted viewers and uploads the screenshots of the old woman's recent calls and texts. "See what you can find out about these people," he types.

Joann sets a plate of chickens nuggets and strawberries in front of Emily, who stuffs her cheeks with the berries.

Sam takes his plate to his room.

Bob watches him go. "Has he been doing that a lot?"

Joann shakes her head. "No. Let's give him a bit of space."

"You sure?"

"Yeah. I'll try to see how he's doing later."

Bob thinks he'll join her in that, but for now, they've got work to do.

Bob looks through the old woman's photos.

There's photos of a little redheaded boy who must be a grandkid, a couple sunsets in the grocery store parking lot, a meticulous album of photographed receipts, and an unorganized smattering of funny license plates.

Then there's the album of teenagers in hoodies.

They affirm Wanda's claim that she was being stalked, but it's pretty clear that it's a different person across the photos.

An overweight guy in a yellow Washington Commanders hoodie, a skinny guy in a black hoodie with illegible heavy metal text, a guy at least six-foot-six wearing a hoodie for the local swim team.

Although.

All these photos are from September. As Bob keeps scrolling back—into August, then July—there are more photos that do look like the same person. These are taken from farther away. The lighting is different between them to the point that Bob isn't sure if it's the same hoodie. Could be red in one photo, pale orange in another. Or it could be the same hoodie in different light.

But that isn't the part that matters.

What matters is that someone was wearing a sweatshirt—with

the hood up—in the Richmond area in July and August. Between the humidity and the ninety-five degree days, that was insane.

Bob shows Joann the strange album.

"So she's not paranoid," Joann says. "She's really being stalked. Can you see his face in any of them?"

Bob swipes back through the images. "No. He's either blurry or in shadow in all of them."

She's looking over his shoulder. "Can't tell anything about him, can you?"

"Nope."

"We keep going. We'll find something useful." Joann already has the screenshots of Wanda's text messages on her own phone. She scrolls through them now. "She was texting a lot with this 'Sheila.' Based on the conversation, sounds like her daughter."

"You said she has two kids, right? What about the other one?"

Joann scans through the texts. "None of these other text conversations read like they're from her kid. Neighbors, friends, automated messages."

"So she's estranged from the other one."

"Maybe. But why's that matter? Do you think her children are involved?"

Bob sighs. "Not really. Weird about her other kid, though."

Joann sets down her phone. "Is this pointless?"

"No! She found a body in the wall of the building where our kids are reappearing. She's being stalked by the same person who Sam saw last year, who sent us a video of himself, and who we almost caught in the woods before he dropped his bag of candy and batteries."

"But how is going through Wanda's text messages helping us find him?"

Bob leans back in his chair. "It's not."

Joann tilts her head. She's thought of something.

"What is it?" Bob asks.

"Wanda didn't say anything about fixing the mirror. Or putting anything in front of it."

"No. She saw the body and ran off."

"But the police never learned about it."

Bob picks up on what Joann's saying. "She can't have been the only one to see the body. Not when Crimson Corridors had people coming through all month."

"It was off the main path," Joann says.

"The classroom was part of the haunt, right? Where the spiders spooked her? And she ran into the bathroom from there. So we're not talking way off the beaten trail. If no visitors stumbled in, then the employees must have noticed."

"Or the owners," Joann says.

"We need to talk to the Chester Brothers."

∼

BOB DOESN'T HAVE a phone number for the brothers who created Crimson Corridors last year, but they're easy enough to find in the Maple Creek Facebook group. He wants an answer quick, so he doesn't hold back.

"Can we talk about the body found in your haunted house? I think it might be related to the kidnappings."

Within a few seconds, his message is marked as *"read."*

Another second and Bob sees pale gray text: *"You are no longer able to message this person."*

Nathan Chester blocked him.

Convenient that there are two Chester Brothers.

He messages Miles Chester, and this time he holds back even less. *"If you block me, I'll talk to the police about the body you covered up."*

Miles takes a few minutes to respond, presumably because he's talking with Nathan. Finally, Bob's phone dings with a message from Miles.

"What do you want?"

Bob responds, *"To talk."*

He gets a message from Nathan, who has unblocked him. "We don't have any money. Leave us alone."

"I don't want any money. I want to know about the body. It might be connected to the kidnapper."

Minutes pass.

Miles sends a message. *"Come on over on Monday. We'll have a Columbus Day cookout—grill some burgers."*

Bob exhales. Finally, some real fucking answers.

∼

SATURDAY EVENING, Bob and Joann say nothing as they walk hand-in-hand over to Old Pine. The sky is clear and the weather is mild. The moon is waning but still bright. They walk through the woods, to the parking lot, to find a small crowd already gathered.

Cops are standing outside the front doors. There's one positioned inside the vestibule, more in the lobby.

There are so many cruisers out here that the building must be absolutely swarming with police.

The annoying Officer Yachuw is outside, on the bullhorn, telling the families of the missing kids to go home. No one pays him any mind.

Bob positions himself and Joann at the front of the crowd. He won't let himself cower after the last two nights. If Mary's about to appear and only have a moment's glimpse before the life goes out of her eyes, then Bob wants her to see her parents.

The clock advances to 7:34 P.M.

Suddenly, there's a fourth cop in the vestibule.

No, not a cop, but a boy in a police costume.

He's got thick glasses and his eyes go cartoonishly wide when a real police officer picks him up and carries him outside.

Bob exhales.

He realizes how scared he's been that there won't be any more living children returning. But it's okay now. There's still a chance for Mary. Still time to find her.

As reporters rush toward the reunited family, Joann tugs Bob away. "Let's not add to their chaos."

OCTOBER 12TH

SAM IS BUILDING a Duplo house with Emily when he gets a text from Jeremy.

"Get your parents to add Walter to your approved contacts. Then tell him to stop texting me."

Jeremy has ignored Sam's attempts to talk about their excursion into Old Pine. It sounds like Walter's been trying, as well.

Emily drops a Duplo brick that she was trying to connect to the roof. She smashes the whole house. Its collapse sounds like glass breaking.

"Don't give up like that," Sam says. He's sure that Mary would be better at playing with their youngest sister, but he's who Emily's got, so he does his best. "Here."

He digs through the bucket and then hands an elephant to his fussing sister. For himself, he picks a lion and then he and Emily chase each other around the jungle of scattered blocks.

His watch dings with another text from Jeremy. *"Did you do it yet? Tell Walter to leave me alone."*

Sam hands the lion to Emily. "Gimme one sec."

As he goes down the hallway, Mom and Dad's tense voices come through the closed office door.

They haven't argued for a while. After last Sunday morning

when they all talked about Mary, Sam thought Mom and Dad might be done with arguing altogether, but apparently not.

He knocks on the door. Mom and Dad go silent. The door opens halfway. Mom is standing there. Her face is red but not puffy. She's mad but hasn't been crying. Dad is behind her in his computer chair. His mouth gets small and tight when he's angry.

"What do you need?" Mom asks.

"Can you add my friend Walter to my contacts?"

Normally, Mom would have a bunch of questions, but this time she wants to get back to her argument. "Yes, that's fine."

She pulls out her phone, opens her version of the app, and Sam tells her the number that Jeremy sent over.

Then he goes back out to the living room.

He wants to text Walter right away, but Emily is once again failing to balance her Duplo pieces onto each other—this time it's a stack of jungle animals.

Sam ignores his watch to play with his sister.

It would be more fun with Mary there, too.

∽

Emily's agitation works itself out. After half an hour of building and smashing Duplos, she's lying on her back, arms in the air, making a plastic jaguar and elephant kiss with loud smooching noises.

Sam sits back against the couch. He's bored of building towers. He taps the screen of his watch. His contact list has updated to now show Walter. Sam taps the new contact and dictates a text message. *"I want to look for Mary again."*

Walter responds immediately. *"Yes! Jeremy's being a pussy."*

Sam instinctively looks over his shoulder, worried that Mom will see he has a mean word on his screen, but she's still in the office with Dad. He messages Walter back. *"Before school starts on Tuesday."*

"Okay, but you need to see this. I saw something in the video I recorded before." Walter sends an Apple Cloud link.

Sam can't open it on his watch, but Mom's left her laptop in the kitchen, so he meticulously types each letter of the link into the web browser.

It brings him to a screen with a video player. He clicks play.

The video shows Sam and Jeremy, navigating the science lab section of the Crimson Corridors haunt. Walter is a wobbly cameraman. Sam watches himself maneuver around the black-topped science tables. He sees the pink glow in the distance, sees himself race ahead.

Then there's the sound of Jeremy calling for help. The camera view looks behind them and there's Jeremy stuck on the bulletin board. The camera points at the floor after this. While Walter yells for Sam to come back and help, and Jeremy screams in fear or maybe pain, the video on Mom's laptop only shows the floor with its yellow tile speckled in brown spots.

Each individual tile doesn't quite touch those which surround it. There's a pattern of lines like a checkerboard, and it's glowing pink. The glow is faint, as if it's coming up through the floor, barely making it through the grout.

But once Sam notices it, there's no denying what he sees. Pink light is shining up from under the floor, between every tile.

How did he miss that before? Was the light at the end of the hallway so bright that he didn't see what was around his feet? Or was the light through the floor only visible on video?

Sam's watch buzzes and he jumps.

Walter's messaged him. *"Did you watch it yet?"*

Sam replies, *"Was that light there on Thursday? I didn't see it."*

"I didn't notice it, either. What do you think it is?"

It's the same light that glows out from the Trick-or-Treater's turnip jack-o-lantern, that came out of the projection on his TV, and that shone up from the bucket in that old woman's backyard shed. Sam considers his answer and then says, *"That's the light from where he's keeping Mary."*

"It's in the Old Pine basement."

Is that a question? A realization? Sam doesn't know. Does the old school even have a basement? Can light shine up through a floor like that? And what about the light from inside that classroom door? That was so much brighter than this light that comes up through the floor—what does that mean?

The answer to that is suddenly apparent to Sam. When you're standing outside a house, what parts of the house let the most light shine through? The windows. And if they're open, the doors.

That classroom has a doorway down to where Mary is being held. He asks Walter his question, *"Were there basement stairs in the room where you saw the kidnapper?"*

Walter replies, *"I couldn't see past him and all that light. But there could have been."*

That decides it. *"Tomorrow morning, as soon as we get to school. Meet me outside the Old Pine back doors."* Sam's going to get Mary, and he's not letting anything stop him this time.

∼

Bob spends Sunday sending messages to the families of the kids returned alive, asking to meet.

Cass Meyers says there's nothing else Debbie can share.

He gets three responses telling him to mind his business.

The rest ignore him entirely.

He's aching for something useful to do.

He messages Karl. *"I'm going into Old Pine tonight. Can't wait anymore."*

Karl responds. *"Not yet. I think tomorrow night will be safer."*

Bob rubs his forehead. What's the smart thing to do? Risk another night where Mary might die? Or risk getting arrested and losing any shot at finding her?

He can't risk it. He's gotta be able to find her, even if that means waiting one more night.

"Okay. But tomorrow I'm going no matter what."

"You gotta wait until I say it's clear."

Bob ignores that last message.

~

SUNDAY NIGHT, a girl in a pink Glinda dress appears right in the middle of the damn hallway.

Thank God it happened far away from PJ so he's not the one getting chewed out. He's been stationed in the school library, feeling creeped out by the decaying carpet and empty shelves.

But then everyone gets called to a meeting in the lobby where the Superintendent of the Virginia State Troopers tears into each and every police officer and trooper who was inside Old Pine.

Two nights in a row now, they've had cops in every single room. And twice in a row, someone looked away and then looked back to see a missing kid suddenly in front of them.

If he's being honest with himself, PJ is starting to get creeped out about this whole thing. Not in a "how can people act this way toward each other" way, but more in a "I'm gonna wear a crucifix to work" kind of way.

He'd ask to be transferred over to traffic duty, but they're filling the school with bodies again tomorrow evening. Someone's gotta see how the kidnapper is getting the kids inside.

OCTOBER 13TH

Miles and Nathan Chester both have kids, but the youngest is a student at VCU and lives on campus.

Bob leaves his own family at home. He lugs over a six-pack and a bag of Doritos to maintain the facade that this is a regular cookout.

As if people have cookouts anymore.

People invite family over on holidays, maybe a few friends make it in there. But the age of neighbors being neighborly just because they're neighbors is long gone.

Sure, everyone's friendly. But there's no relationships like you still see on sitcoms. If he were living in a Stephen King novel, he'd have a cadre of dads and drinking buddies to help him save the neighborhood.

Those are stories from a bygone age.

Community has gone digital. In Maple Creek, camaraderie is on Nextdoor. It's in the neighborhood Facebook groups.

Bob's community, the people who are actually helping him find his daughter, are all online.

But Miles and Nathan have invited Bob to a real life cookout, so dammit, he's acting like it's a cookout.

The Chester Brothers are the only houses to put up Halloween decorations this year, but even they've toned it down. Nets of cobwebs drape over their boxwoods. Fiberglass skeletons stand at the border between each other's yards, posed like football lineman about to smash into each other.

Bob scoffs at that. Sure, the Chesters haven't put up their twelve-foot-tall Home Depot skeletons, but it's not like it's the skeleton's height that reminds the grieving parents of what happened last year.

Bob walks past the decorations and rings the doorbell.

Miles shouts from the backyard, "Come around back!"

Bob goes through the gate, past a wall of privacy evergreens, and here's the rest of their yard decorations. The tall skeletons are posed like they're propping up the branches of an oak tree. Glow-in-the-dark vinyl eyes are stuck to tree trunks. Ghosts made of wire mesh and lace haunt the grass.

Miles and Nathan are on a brick patio, standing by a grill that Bob is pretty sure costs more than his first car.

"There he is," says Nathan, as if they're all great friends who do this every weekend.

"Hope you like brats," says Miles.

To be honest, even if cookouts with your neighbors were still a thing, Nathan and Miles aren't the guys he'd be hanging out with. This bro-ish, slap-your-back-and-laugh-about-your-controlling-wife flavor of conviviality isn't something Bob has ever felt comfortable with. He likes sincerity. Maybe guys like the Chester brothers are sincere about not liking their wives, but that makes Bob want to be around them even less.

Of course, he's not here for friendship.

But he does want answers, so he puts on a friendly act. "Who doesn't love a good brat? You have onions and peppers?" To his own ears, he sounds fake, but they all three know he's here with the threat that he'll go to the police if they don't talk, so who cares?

Miles moves a sausage from the grill to a bun, piles on a colorful cornucopia of peppers and onions, and then hands it to Bob.

"What's with the backyard Halloween party?" Bob gestures with his brat to the decorations.

"We've been decorating for twenty-seven years," Nathan says. "We can read the room, so we didn't put much in the front yard."

Miles finishes his brother's thought. "But it's something we do together every year. We'll keep the wild stuff to ourselves, but we couldn't leave it entirely."

"Sorry if it's offends you," Nathan says.

"He means that," Miles says. "Even if he sounds like a dick about it."

"Yeah, I mean, we wouldn't have invited you back here, but you know, you threatened us."

"We know about your daughter," Miles says. "I can't imagine."

"Then don't." It's been ages since Bob had to put up with forced sympathy. "What you can do is tell me about the dead body you found in Crimson Corridors last year."

"What proof do you have?"

Bob considers lying that he has photos, but the truth might be enough. "To start with, a witness."

"Bullshit," Nathan says. "Nobody saw it but us."

Bob pieces together what he's saying. "You saw the body in the wall, then... got rid of it? No, you wouldn't be so confident there were no witnesses if you went and buried it somewhere."

"We didn't bury anybody," Miles says.

"You closed the wall back up. You stumbled upon the open wall, figured if Old Pine became a crime scene then you'd have to close down and lose all your income, so you left the body there."

Miles and Nathan exchange a look.

"We're not admitting to that," Miles says.

"Because it didn't happen," Nathan says, while his brother shushes him. "But if it did, it'd only be because we couldn't afford to shut down the haunt halfway through October. I took out a second mortgage to pay all the scare actors"

Miles asks Bob, "What do you want?"

"Who was it?"

"The body?" Nathan asks. "I don't know. But it was old."

"It was dry and shriveled, okay?" Miles says. "If anybody was looking for him, they'd given up a long time ago."

That doesn't match the bloated corpse that Wanda described. Who should he believe, an old lady who's losing her marbles, or two desperate businessmen who have every reason to lie?

"I'm looking for him," Bob says. "Who was he? Because someone who wants to keep that body a secret is the one who took my daughter."

"What? Why do you think that?" Miles asks.

Bob considers how much he'll share with these two, but at this point, no one's ratting on anybody.

"You never wondered why that mirror was broken? Why all of a sudden the dead guy in the wall was suddenly in plain view?"

Nathan says, "The room wasn't part of the haunt. No one should have been back there. We figured something inside the wall finally decayed and gave way, letting the mummified dude drop down."

"I talked to one of your visitors. They got freaked out, wound up in that bathroom, and accidentally broke the glass."

"And in nearly a year, they didn't call the police?"

Bob shrugs. "Some people don't like cops."

"They're a criminal, is what you're saying," Nathan says.

Bob resists the urge to argue. Not everyone who distrusts cops is a criminal. Although, he supposes, this past eleven months of breaking-and-entering certainly makes *him* a criminal.

He takes a bite of the brat to give himself a few seconds to think. It's not bad, although the peppers and onions spent too long on the skillet. They've got no flavor except vegetable oil.

"If you think this mystery person is the kidnapper," Miles says, "then why are you talking to us?"

"After my witness uncovered the body, a guy started stalking her. A young man in a hoodie who carries a jack-o-lantern with a pink light inside."

Nathan speaks through a mouthful of sausage. "Is that who the cops are looking for about these pranks?"

"They're a little more severe than pranks," Miles says. "They're goddam booby traps. Someone's gotta do something about this fella."

"Then help me figure out who he is. I think he killed the guy in the wall. If we can figure out who the corpse is, then I can look for who killed them, and that'll be the kidnapper."

Miles asks, "Why aren't you going to the police with this?"

Nathan elbows his brother. "We don't want him to go to the police."

"They're doing things their way. I'm doing them mine." Bob looks for a trace of compassion in the brothers' eyes. Miles might have some. Nathan doesn't. "Please. I need to know who that body was."

"Can't help you, chief," Nathan says, "because we don't know."

"Was it male or female?"

"Male," Miles says, "I think."

"Yeah, probably," Nathan adds. "But like we said, the body was pretty dried up."

"Young or old?"

"You know that Nazi who drinks from the wrong cup in *Indiana Jones*?" Nathan asks. "The corpse was as old as that guy, right before he crumbled to dust."

Nathan laughs at his own joke.

Miles chuckles, but says, "His hair was dark brown, almost black. It was curly and still thick. So I'd guess he was young."

Bob pictures a dried-up corpse with a thick, curly head of hair. It'd be a funny image if the situation weren't so tragic.

"Could you tell his skin color?" Bob asks.

"Probably not black?" Miles phrases it as a question. "Really hard to tell."

"Clothes?"

Miles looks at Nathan. "I didn't notice."

Nathan says, "A bright red polo. I mean, it was covered in dust, but I remember it was bright red, because it made me think of Circuit City clerks."

"Was it a Circuit City shirt? Was it that old?" The electronics store shut down, what, fifteen years ago?

Nathan shrugs. "Could have been."

Bob tries to think of what else he should ask. "Tattoos? Piercings? Gold fillings?"

"I didn't notice any of that," Miles says.

"Me neither," Nathan agrees.

"Anything else you can tell me?"

Nathan closes the grill. "It was just a dead body. It looked ancient."

Miles shakes his head. "I've got nothing else for you. Unless you want to sneak in and take down the plywood we put up."

"It'll be hard with the cops all over the place," Bob says, "but I might have to do that."

The Chesters laugh, but it's forced, and Bob can tell they hear the sincerity in his voice.

Bob's got all the useful info he expects to get from these two. "Well. Thanks for the brat."

He doesn't say that if they tell the cops about his personal investigation, he'll tell the cops that they hid a crime scene. It doesn't need to be said, because the opposite is also true.

That mutual threat is the closest thing to a new relationship with his neighbors that Bob's had in years.

∼

ON THE SHORT DRIVE HOME, Bob feels especially alone.

It doesn't make sense. He still has his community of YouTube viewers, and he can talk with any of his neighbors via Nextdoor or Facebook whenever he wants. In fact, he should be feeling more connected than ever, considering that he and Joann are finally working together.

Maybe it's the powerlessness of not knowing when Mary will return or if she'll be alive when she does.

But he thinks it's also that he just spent half an hour standing around a grill with two of his neighbors, and now he's back in his car alone.

He doesn't especially care for Nathan and Miles, but he also can't fault them for not going to the police about the body they'd found. Best case scenario, the police shut down their attraction. Worst case scenario, they get investigated for murder. Bob hates to think of the dead guy's family worrying about him, but also, when you have the choice to either trust the police or keep to yourself, Bob knows which option he prefers. Maybe he has more in common with the Chester brothers than he'd thought.

Regardless, it was nice to interact in person.

Once Mary's home and all this mess is over, Bob thinks he'll invite neighbors for a cookout on the next three-day-weekend. Maybe even Nathan and Miles.

It's a brief fantasy about how great life will be when he finds Mary, how this constant fear will finally be over.

Bob's phone *dings* with a Facebook message.

It's Miles, saying, *"The in-person meet was a bad idea. If you need to get in touch, use Signal."* Miles sends over his Signal ID.

Bob doesn't have that app.

As he pulls back into his driveway, his home feels like a single warm refuge among the cold, distant houses of Maple Creek.

∼

MONDAY EVENING, Emily vomits all over the kitchen table. It's more food than she could have possibly fit in her stomach.

Sam gets the brunt of it, right in his lap.

Bob puts Emily in the shower while Joann cleans up the kitchen and starts a load of sour-smelling laundry.

Sam showers in the master bath.

Polly arrives at the normal time, but Emily won't let go of Bob, so Polly leaves and Bob stays with the kids while Joann watches Caitlin Powers run out from Old Pine into her parents' arms.

Joann comes home to find everyone in their bed, watching a

Marvel cartoon. Emily is sleeping in Bob's arms. Sam leans on his shoulder.

A pang of sadness hits Joann. This perfect scene of her family isn't complete.

"She threw up twice more," Bob says.

They fuss over whether Emily's keeping down enough water. Bob runs out to get Pedialyte and Saltines.

Bob's alarm goes off at 2:00 A.M.

He's ready to break into Old Pine. No more waiting.

The bathroom light is on. Joann is dry heaving over the toilet.

Bob postpones his outing another night to tend to Joann and Emily.

OCTOBER 14TH

Tuesday morning, Mom drives Sam to school. She's got red lines through the whites of her eyes, and her cheeks are pale, but when Sam asks if she's okay, she says, "I was sick last night but I'm fine now."

They stop on the way to get half-price donuts from the Kroger bakery. Emily stays home with Dad.

Sam worries that Mom's keeping him in the car for longer because she used her app to read Sam's text conversation with Walter yesterday. He watches her from the back seat, noting every movement of her shoulders or head, ready for her to declare, "You're not going to school today because you're not sneaking into Old Pine again."

But instead, they pull into the Kroger parking lot and park. "You can pick two donuts," Mom says. "And two for Emily."

She doesn't say a thing about the rows of bright orange pumpkins lining the front of the grocery store, or the displays of Halloween-branded candy that scream with bright colors.

Sam follows Mom to the bakery section, but he peeks over into the seasonal shelves at the stacks of costumes. If they were doing Halloween this year, he'd want to be Dog Man. Emily can dress up as Cat Kid. Although, Emily really likes Ms. Rachel on YouTube, so she can wear blue jean overalls and a pink shirt, while Mary can be Dog Man's feline sidekick.

Grief hits Sam like a punch in the stomach.

He hasn't done that for ages—think about Mary as if she were still here.

He follows Mom through the produce to the bakery.

Front and center in a glass case are sugar cookies with orange frosting and sprinkles shaped like bats.

Sam's throat gets thick and heavy. The corner of his mouth twitches downward.

He's *not* going to cry in the grocery store. He squeezes his fists and bites his tongue.

Mom opens the glass case with the donuts, and then turns to ask, "Okay, do you want a Boston creme and a chocolate frosted again?"

She sees the tears in his eyes and suddenly she's scooped him up, she's holding him against herself, whispering, "It's okay. I've got you. We're okay. We're still a family. You're safe. I promise, we're all safe."

"I'm sorry," he says and chokes up.

"No, it's my fault. I should have thought about all the Halloween decorations."

This is stupid. Sam loves Halloween. At least, he should be able to love it.

Once he can breathe normal again, Mom sets him down. She fills a box with donuts and then they go check out.

Back in the car, Mom asks him, "Do you want me to drive around before I drop you off? You can eat a donut and let your cheeks dry off some."

But Sam has somewhere to be. "I'll be okay. I can finish my donut before we get there."

Sam meets Walter outside Old Pine's back door. The broken handle still dangles from a single screw. The loop of rusty chain still lies on the sidewalk.

"You've got chocolate on your face," Walter says.

Sam wipes his mouth.

Walter opens his backpack. "I brought a real camera this time. And a big flashlight. I've got some other stuff in here, too, in case we need it."

Since they already busted the door open, Sam only brought a flashlight.

He panics for a second that he's forgotten something, but that's been a common feeling this past year.

He leads the way inside.

It's dark compared to the sunny morning outside. The air feels clammy. Sam finds his flashlight in his backpack and turns it on.

The hallway is empty.

"What in the world?" Walter says behind him. "Where's the spiderweb? Or the whiteboard?"

"Or any of the other haunt stuff," Sam adds.

The door swings shut behind them, cutting off the sounds of the birds in the trees and cars driving by.

"Hold on," Walter says. "Turn your light off."

Sam switches off his flashlight.

They both look at the floor. There's no light coming up between the tiles. In fact, in the morning sun that's coming through the door's window, Sam can tell that there isn't grout between the floor tiles at all. There's no space for it.

"It's different from in the video," Sam whispers.

"We came in through the same door, right?" Walter asks.

"Yeah."

Far down the hallway, a pink light flickers on inside an open classroom.

Sam squints into it, feels that his eyes are still puffy from crying.

He sees the pink light and heads down the hallway, speed-walking at first, and then he breaks into a run.

"Slow down," Walter says, running behind him, fumbling with his bag. "I want a video of this."

But all Sam can see is the pink light cascading into the otherwise dark hallway. Mary will be inside that room, or there will be a staircase down into the basement and then Mary will be down there.

And once Mary's home, then playing with Emily won't feel lonely anymore, and then they can pick out Halloween costumes and eat candy and watch the scary episodes of Mickey Mouse on Disney Plus.

Sam's shoes slap on the tile floor, growing louder until he runs inside the classroom and is enveloped by the pink light.

∼

BOB DOES SOME GOOGLING, but a cursory search doesn't bring up anything about a missing person in a Circuit City uniform.

So he once again relies on his amateur internet sleuths.

He doesn't want to tell them about the body in the wall. He can't yet post that in a way that can be traced back to him.

When he logs in, he's greeted by a barrage of group posts directed at him.

"Stuff finally starts happening, and you go radio silent?"

"Why aren't you updating us? What's happened?"

"Guys, lay off. His daughter might die."

To see that spelled out on the screen makes his stomach twist. It's butterflies in his gut except the butterflies have razor blade wings.

Maybe that's why he crosses the line that he just set for himself.

He makes a post:

I found a body in a haunted school's walls.

It's clickbaity, but that's how he's learned to get attention since he started his channel.

He tells them how an old woman saw this body. He keeps his promise to the Chesters not to reveal how they found and rehid the body, but he does find their description more trustworthy than Wanda's, so he says that the body was dried and withered.

Once he starts typing out the truth, he writes out everything. He'll make a video to match it later, but for now the words cascade from his fingers.

My son saw a teenager in a hoodie holding a turnip jack-o-lantern with pink light...

The old woman started seeing this same stalker after she found the body...

I believe this hoodied teenager is the kidnapper, and that he's the one who killed the body in the wall.

He even starts to write about all the houses he's broken into and his plan to break into Old Pine, but maintains enough clearheadedness to at least hold back the explicitly illegal stuff.

He's satisfied with the draft. It even includes several turns of phrase that'll add an attention-keeping flair when he turns the post into a video.

Guilt flashes through him. Bob hates the cold-hearted, clickbaity machinations of trying to get views. But that's how he keeps the attention—and thus the assistance—of his team of internet sleuths.

And right now, he's going to end his post with a request:

I believe the corpse in the wall was a person who went missing while wearing a Circuit City shirt. Can anyone find any news stories about him? I need a name.

∼

As Bob posts that request, Joann walks into his office, phone in hand. She's tense.

"I thought you were feeling better?" he says.

"Have you checked your phone?"

Bob reaches for the spot on his desk where it usually sits, but he's left it in the kitchen. "No, what's up?"

"I got one of those automated messages from the school. It says Sam is absent today."

A hot spike of dread stabs Bob in the chest. "You drove him, right?"

"Of course. We got donuts from Kroger and then I dropped him off. I watched him walk inside." Joann taps at her phone. "I'm calling them."

Bob gets up. "I'm going over there. Text me if it's a false alarm."

He drives to Sam's school and tries to storm inside but the front doors rattle in place. He follows a sign that says, *"These doors locked during school hours. Ring bell by the office door."*

He rings the bell. Through the window he sees a young woman who speaks to him through an intercom. She's got her hair in a messy bun and wears thick, large glasses. "Hello?" is all she says.

"I got a call that my son isn't here." Bob wants to yank the door open, but that'd mark him as a crazy person and get the school resource officer called. Plus he's not strong enough.

The intercom clicks. "Come on in." The door unlocks.

Bob flings it open and walks inside.

Before he can say anything, the young woman says, "Your wife just called. Sam's class is in the cafeteria right now so I can't call Mrs. Bavin through the intercom, but my coworker is running over to check right now. I'm sure it's just a paperwork mistake."

But those assurances fall flat when the school resource officer walks in and asks the woman, "Hey Jackie. What'd you need?"

Jackie looks at Bob like she's wondering how to whisper to the cop without Bob hearing. But that's obviously not going to happen, so she says, "Hopefully nothing. Barbra's going to check on a student who was marked as absent but his mom says she dropped him off."

The cop smiles at Bob. "I'm sure everything's okay." He's even worse at fake assurances than Jackie. He wears his kevlar vest like a child wearing a lifejacket to swim in the kiddie pool, and his tool belt like a kid trick-or-treating as Batman. There's nothing he can say to make Bob think Sam is okay.

"I'd like to go check on my son," Bob says. He doesn't expect the tremor in his own voice, but there's no masking the fear. Once it's out, it swirls around him and constricts.

"Barbra will be right back," Jackie says.

A woman in her sixties walks in. Without acknowledging Bob or the cop, she says to Jackie, "He's not with his class in the cafeteria. I found Mrs. Bavin and she says he wasn't here at all today."

That fear constricts even tighter. "My wife watched him walk inside this morning. Where's my kid?"

Barbra pipes up. "I'll go check with the other third-grade teachers."

"And the library," Jackie says before her colleague runs out the door.

Bob tries to slow his breathing. "How did you lose my son?"

The cop raises his hand as if Bob is threatening him. "Calm down, sir. Everything's under control."

"Bullshit. You should be looking for him, not playing your typical act of 'who's got the most testosterone.'"

To his credit, the cop says, "Yes, we'll figure out where your son went. Should be easy enough. My name's Officer Randy. Come look at the security tapes with me."

Bob follows the cop deeper into the front offices. While they walk, Officer Randy radios to other cops to come help search, which sounds way more serious than how the man is talking to Bob.

He leads Bob into a small office, sits in front of a computer, and motions to an extra chair. "Bring that over here and tell me when you see your son. We'll find him right quick."

On the computer is a view from the ceiling of the school's front lobby. Kids lug their backpacks through the front doors and into the main hallway. The size discrepancy between fifth graders and kindergartners is almost imperceptible from this awkward angle, but Bob is perfectly capable of spotting Sam. His son is wearing his brown Carhartt jacket that's getting too small for him. Bright green shirt sleeves stick out by his wrists. In the video, Sam is walking in a hurry, getting in an awkward skip every few steps.

Dread twists in Bob's gut. Sam is nervous and excited. He's planning something.

"That's him," Bob says.

"Got it." Officer Randy switches the view on the monitor from the lobby to the main hallway. He moves the video forward until the timestamp matches the first camera.

Bob spots his son walking away from the camera, down the hallway. He attended Sam's back-to-school night, so he knows that it's a left turn to get to Sam's classroom. But Sam doesn't turn left. Sam keeps right on walking.

"Where's he going?" Bob asks.

Before the cop can answer, they both watch Sam walk to the end of the hallway and straight out the door.

Bob looks up from the computer, at the wall in the direction Sam went, as if he could see straight through it.

Officer Randy says, "Give me as second. There's a camera out there, but I gotta see which one it is."

But Bob doesn't need to see. He knows where that door leads and he knows where Sam went. Bob gets up to go after him.

"Hold on a sec, here he is," says the cop.

On the screen is a view of the asphalt square where the kids have recess. Sam is walking across it with a kid Bob doesn't recognize. In the corner of the screen waits Old Pine. There's the door with the broken handle that Bob opened the other night.

Has Sam already been in there? Is that why the handle was broken?

As the screen shows Sam and his friend disappear inside Old Pine, the cop says, "Well damn. Let me speed it up and we'll see if he's already come back out."

Bob knows Sam is still in there. He runs out of the office to get his son.

∼

Bob sprints down the hallway, following his son's route.

His feet slap on the tile floor.

A teacher sticks her head out the door, then quickly shuts and locks it.

Officer Randy chases after Bob. He's slow.

Bob bursts out into the autumn day. There's enough sun to make the world bright but the air chills Bob's cheeks and dries his eyes.

Kids laugh and scream on the blacktop, playing dodgeball and foursquare.

Bob runs through the games, straight for Old Pine.

He flings open the door, accidentally ripping off the broken handle.

The hallway is dusty and dark. He runs inside before his eyes can adjust. "Sam!" His shout bounces down the empty hallway.

His eyes adjust enough to see sunlight coming into the front lobby at the end of the hall. He runs, shouting, looking in classrooms at random, but the rooms are as empty as the hallways. There's nothing left behind from when this building was a functioning school, and nothing from when it was Crimson Corridors.

Where would Sam have gone?

Bob frantically tries to think of what Sam knows. He came in here to look for Mary—there's no doubt about that. But Sam doesn't know about the body in the wall. He can't be looking for the kindergarten bathroom where the old woman broke a mirror and the Chester brothers sealed it up. So he must be searching the whole place. Where would he have started? How long has he been at it?

Instinct or anxiety or some dark voice tells Bob that his son would have found his way to that kindergarten bathroom, regardless of whether he knew about the body. He runs straight ahead to where Wanda described the classroom to be.

Officer Randy must have radioed to the guys on standing-around duty outside the front doors of Old Pine. Doors squeak and two cops run inside. One of them is a sneering Officer Yachuw.

Bob ignores them to check a kindergarten classroom. The room is empty. There's a closed door on one wall, which Bob opens. A kid-sized toilet is on the floor, facing a kid-height white porcelain sink. Above it is a mirror.

The Chester brothers said they covered the hole with plywood. It's not this room.

Bob sprints out into the hallway. The cops have almost reached him. They've each got one hand raised toward him, one at their holstered guns.

Bob puts his hands up. "I've gotta find my son."

The first cop says, "You're one of the parents?"

"That doesn't give him the right to come charging in here," says Officer Yachuw.

Behind Bob, Officer Randy's boots pound on the floor. He's out of breath. "Ease up guys. His kid's missing. Not one of the thirty—just happened this morning. The kid's on camera running in here."

The other cops relax, which gives Bob the chance to dart into another classroom, across the hall.

Officer Randy yells, "Goddammit, Bob!"

The room is the same as the first he searched, only reversed. Bob runs for the bathroom door. He tears it open as the cops charge into the classroom behind him.

There it is—little toilet, low sink, and plywood nailed to the wall.

Bob digs his fingers into the drywall around the plywood. He gets a grip and pulls. If angry bros jacked up on Monster and creatine can punch through walls, then he can rip one apart.

The plywood has rotted. A corner rips off unevenly. Bob reaches in for a better grip.

For a second he feels like a monkey caught in a trap, closed fist unable to withdraw. But he doesn't want to get free—he wants to break this wall apart. The plywood is slimy on the interior side. He jerks off a piece with a crumbly edge. He drops it, breaks off another.

The cops rush in and grab him. They yank him by both arms,

throwing him to the ground. His butt hits the tile hard and pain spikes up his spine.

"Go easy," Officer Randy says.

"Look!" Bob points at the hole he's made in the wall.

"Hands on your head!" Officer Yachuw stomps down on his arm.

A bone snaps and Bob gasps from the pain. His vision blurs then returns.

"Chill!" shouts Officer Randy.

"This is probably the killer," Officer Yachuw responds.

"Look in the wall," Bob cries. "There's a body."

The third cop rolls Bob over and mashes his wrists together to handcuff them, yanking his broken arm.

Bob passes out from the pain.

OCTOBER 15TH

Early Wednesday morning, Bob is still in the hospital, still handcuffed to the bed railing.

He's got a cast around his left arm and not enough pain meds in his blood.

He suspects the doctors would have discharged him by now, but the cops keep coming in to ask questions.

They won't let Joann in to see him.

Anytime he asks for a lawyer, the cops leave without saying anything, only to come back an hour later to start asking questions again.

He doesn't know if they found a body. Doesn't know if Sam came home.

Hell, Mary could have come home last night, for all he knows.

He pushes the button to call for a nurse.

Officer Randy walks in. The man is disheveled in every sense of the word. His uniform is wrinkled. Salt-and-pepper stubble covers his thumb-shaped face.

Bob doesn't wait for him to say why he's here. "Did you find Sam?"

Officer Randy shakes his head. "He isn't in Old Pine."

Grief hits Bob like an icy wave.

He pushes against it. Not grief. Sam isn't dead. Mary isn't dead. *But his little boy.*

He wants to squeeze Sam against him, hear him say, "Can you talk with me, Dad?" while he's lying in bed unable to sleep.

Bob tugs against the handcuffs. "Let me out. I gotta find him."

"Take a breath," Officer Randy says. "I helped in the search myself. I couldn't do anything less for one of my kids."

That rankles Bob—Sam is *his* kid, Joann's kid. But he does appreciate Officer Randy's enthusiasm.

"When I heard they'd detained you here, I went straight to the lieutenant. I vouched for you."

Bob says, "Thank you," before he can stop himself.

"You've got plenty of alibis, but there's a pretty damn big question you do gotta answer."

"Not without a lawyer," Bob says.

Officer Randy waves off Bob's objection. "I'm a school resource officer. I'm not bringing in the heat lamps to interrogate you. But the guys gotta know—how'd you know that wall was hiding a dried out body?"

Bob isn't going to rat out the Chester brothers. If he did, they'd tell the cops that Bob's running his own investigation, and then the noble boys in blue would get in his way.

He could tell them about Wanda and her experience in Crimson Corridors. Even if she tells the cops that Bob and Joann broke into her house, her obvious dementia would make it impossible to convict them of it. But the accusation might be enough to get him charged, and would definitely be enough to get him watched like a hawk.

Although, that's already gonna happen, regardless of what he admits to now.

"Lucky guess," Bob says.

Officer Randy scoffs. "Even with your arm getting broken, you were gung-ho about us looking behind that wall."

Bob bites his tongue at Officer Randy's passive phrasing of his injury. "Like I said, lucky guess."

"Listen Bob, if you want to get out there and look for your boy, you need to make sure you don't get locked up. Because the way they're gonna see it at the station is that you personally knew where a murder victim was hidden, that just happened to be where three more murder victims have appeared in the last two weeks."

Bob hates that the cop is making sense. "I was tipped off."

"By who?"

Bob shrugs. "People in the neighborhood. They know I've been looking for my daughter."

"Your daughter? Jesus Christ, you lost a kid last year? If I were you I'd have been out of my mind today." Officer Randy pats Bob's shoulder. "That's even more reason why you need to be a hundred percent open. You gotta be there for your wife. Do you have any other kids at home?"

Bob glares at Officer Randy. He's not getting buddy-buddy with the guy looking the other way about his colleague breaking Bob's arm for the hell of it.

Officer Randy sits down next to the bed. "Sam is a good kid. He says 'hi' to me in the hallway. I'm gonna help find him, but if you want to help, then you need to be wide open. You say someone told you about the body. Who was that?"

Bob can't keep up his belligerence. He wants to get home to Joann and Emily. He wants to go look for Sam and Mary.

But he's not stupid. He knows that's exactly how the cops will try to wear him down, to make him say something accidentally incriminating, and then he won't ever get home to his family. He needs a lie that the cops will believe, and that will neatly snip off any investigative thread into Bob.

"I told you. Someone in the neighborhood told me."

"And I asked you: Who?"

"I don't know. It was a note taped to my door." Bob tells himself that's a good lie.

"Do you still have the note?"

"No."

Officer Randy raises his eyebrows, but he doesn't press that issue. "Do you have a doorbell camera?"

Bob's stomach flips. He does. He sees Officer Randy notice his fear, so Bob rubs at his cast and exaggerates a wince. "Sorry. My arm's screaming at me. I have a doorbell camera, yeah, but only at the front. The note was on the back door."

"No security cameras out back?"

"It's a safe neighborhood." Bob shrugs, and this time winces for real.

Officer Randy *hmm*s.

"Maybe the neighbors across the street? I don't know them real well, but our kids play, so I could ask." Our kids *played* Bob mentally corrects himself, and then shuts down that dark thought. Sam is still alive.

"I'm sure the detectives will be asking the neighbors about it." Officer Randy says that as if it's the final word on the matter, and Bob thinks maybe his note-on-the-door lie has worked. But then the school resource officer says, "I know you're trying to pull one over on me, and to be frank with you, son, you're doing a piss poor job of it. I don't know how you knew about that body, but I bet you thought it was a step on the path to finding your kids. Am I right about that?"

Bob stares the man calmly in the eye.

"I'll take that as a yes. So here's what I'm going to offer you. I'll do what I can to make sure my colleagues don't point the finger at you, if and only if you agree to stop whatever investigation you're on. You gotta leave it to the professionals."

Bob almost loses it. The cops have had nearly a year. They've accomplished nothing. For the past two weeks, a missing child has walked or fallen out the front doors of Old Pine Elementary, and still these worthless uniforms with more ego than self-control have accomplished fuck all. And now he's supposed to trust them to find both Mary and Sam?

But Officer Randy is offering Bob a chance to get out of this hospital and go home. One more lie won't hurt.

"You've got a deal," Bob says.

OCTOBER 16TH

IT TAKES until Thursday for the cops to actually let Bob go home.

But it turns out that Officer Randy has plenty of sway, because it's Officer Yachuw who comes to unlock Bob's cuffs, and he's not happy about it.

"I don't care what the old babysitter says." He manages to bump Bob's cast while he unlocks the cuffs, which hurts like crazy. "I saw you charging down that hallway and I knew you had something to do with all this."

Bob rubs his cast. "I just want my family back."

"You're probably the one who killed them."

Bob doesn't have any delusions that he could win a fight with this cop, but he almost goes for it. There's a heavy plastic cup on his side table that he could smash against that stupid buzzcut.

But Joann and Emily need him to come home. Mary and Sam need him to bring them home.

"Am I free to go?" Bob asks.

"So you can go kill more kids?" Officer Yachuw spits, but this time it sounds like a whiny middle-schooler not getting their way.

Bob stays quiet. He gets up off the bed, his legs sore from sitting there the last day. He gets dressed, and then without a look back at the fuming cop, he walks out to find a phone to call Joann.

~

JOANN PICKS him up from the hospital.

Her eyes are puffy and her cheeks are red.

Bob looks in the empty backseat. "Is Emily with your sister?"

She nods.

"Any news?"

"Franklin Duncan came home Tuesday. Rachel Isington last night. Both alive."

Bob knows someone would have told him if Mary had returned, but his heart still sinks. "And what about Sam? Do you know anything yet?"

"The other boy is named Walter. His parents said Walter's been scared of Old Pine since they went to Crimson Corridors last year. They blamed Sam—said Walter would have never gone in there without someone forcing him—but they couldn't muster the energy to get angry about it."

"They're still in there," Bob says. "They've gotta be."

"They aren't."

"The cops told you that? I'm sure they searched it just as thoroughly as they have each day this month."

"I searched," Joann says. There's no trace of lie or exaggeration in her tone.

"You snuck in there?"

"They sure didn't roll out the red carpet for me. I looked in every classroom, every closet, every bathroom. I knocked out ceiling tiles and stuck my head up there. There's nowhere that a kid could be tucked away, let alone fifteen more of them."

"What about a way to smuggle them in? They're appearing each night somehow."

Joann shakes her head. "I looked for that. Tunnels or something. But there's not even a basement. If there's a trapdoor into a tunnel somewhere, I couldn't find it."

Bob is impressed. He has a year's experience breaking into

empty houses, and he's still been worried about going into Old Pine with all the cops around.

Joann went straight in.

"What do we do next?" she asks.

Bob isn't sure. But when they pick up his things from the police station, he's got a dozen notifications on his phone.

He checks the first one. It's a message from one of his YouTube viewers.

"I know who your dead guy is."

∼

Bob opens up the message.

"What's it say?" Joann asks. "Who's it from?"

"BlueBlackControl69," Bob tells her. "He's been a viewer since the beginning. He sends me theories."

"Do they make any sense?"

"Sometimes." Bob skims the message and then reads it more slowly. "A teenager ran away in 2002. Lived in Maple Creek."

"That must have been when the neighborhood was brand new."

"Not even done being built," Bob says. "The family never heard from him again, but because he'd finished high school, had a drug problem, and argued with his dad, the cops assumed he ran away."

"So why is this our guy?" Joann asks.

"He worked at Circuit City."

"Is there a picture?"

"Gimme a sec."

Bob downloads the attachment from BlueBlackControl69. It's a senior photo of a teenager in a tuxedo. He's got a pointy chin, acne, and a nose that's been broken and healed crooked. His smile is forced, which Bob can tell by his sad eyes. He's got curly brown hair that covers his ears. The same hair that the Chester brothers described.

He shows the picture to Joann.

"He's a baby. What was his name?"

Bob checks the message. "Martin Donovan."

"Donovan?" Joann asks. "As in, Wanda Donovan? Let me guess, the address where he lived-"

Bob reads it for her, "7349 Clearbark Circle. And his parents' names: Jim and Wanda Donovan."

∽

PJ IS NOT AN IT EXPERT.

That doesn't stop his lieutenant from assigning him camera 32, positioned on a tripod and aimed at the north entrance to Old Pine, from the outside.

There are cameras all throughout the building, each manned by someone untrained in how they work.

PJ's happy to get an evening standing under the stars, instead of marching in a circle through the old school, waiting to stumble onto a trick-or-treater who wasn't there two seconds ago.

At 7:31 P.M., there's a commotion inside. It sounds excited rather than defeated, so PJ assumes the kid is alive. That's a relief.

But later on, when the video gets passed around, PJ considers walking off the job.

The video shows the short hallway leading to the side entrance of the cafeteria. The cafeteria doors are propped open, and you can see an officer's boots in the corner of the frame. As the time advances to 7:31 P.M., there's suddenly someone else in the shot.

It's a boy in a fireman costume. When he appears, he's whipping his arms around. He kicks and falls over, then jumps back up before he realizes there's no one to fight against.

PJ's watching the video on his phone. He rewinds and plays it in slow motion. One second the doorway is empty. The next, the little fireman is there.

PJ takes the crucifix hanging from his neck between his thumb and finger.

People have started calling the kidnapper the Thirty-First Trick-or-Treater. A couple of the returned kids have said he's coming back. There were thirty missing kids, so it stands to reason that if this Thirty-First Trick-or-Treater has plans, they're for the thirty-first. Halloween.

PJ might need to find a new career before then.

OCTOBER 17TH

Bob and Joann have been watching Wanda's house since yesterday. They're parked in a driveway of an empty house down the street.

Earlier, Bob went by to look in the garage. Her silver Mazda was in there. She's home.

They've done some digging and confirmed that Martin lived at 7349 Clearbark Circle, the second child of Jim and Wanda Donovan. They find an obituary for Jim from 2019.

Bob's antsy. "I don't want to wait any longer. I'm going in and getting some answers."

"Easy," Joann says like she does when the kids are seconds from a tantrum.

"Kids are dying," Bob says. "She might kill Mary tonight. She might have Sam locked up in there."

"We don't know that she's the kidnapper."

"But she lied to us. Why wouldn't she tell us the body she found was Martin?"

"Maybe she didn't recognize him. She said it was rotted and bloating."

"Oh, come on. She just happened to stumble onto her own son's corpse?"

"I admit it's hard to believe. That's why I'm on board with

watching her house. But we're investigating this strangeness, not assuming that she killed her son, or that she has Mary and Sam."

Bob keeps his eyes glued to the house. "What if they're in there right now?"

"They're not. You searched it. So if she has them somewhere, then she's got to leave the house to go there. Let's stick to the plan. We wait until she goes somewhere, and then we follow her."

Bob grinds his teeth. Joann's right, but he hates waiting. "The whole creeping dementia thing has to be an act, right?"

"Seems that way," Joann agrees. "But that still leaves the question: How?"

"How'd she kidnap thirty kids?"

"Exactly. If she did it, how was it even possible? I mean, you barely looked away and Mary was gone. That's how it happened for everyone. And at the same time? How was she thirty places at once?"

Bob doesn't like the conclusion that question leads to. "She's not the only one involved."

"She said she has a daughter."

"Sheila," Bob remembers. "But their most recent texts were pretty benign."

"Who else has she talked to?"

"Let's see." He pulls up Wanda's profile on Facebook. It's not locked down, because that would require knowing how to navigate settings and menus. She doesn't have her family or any other personal details listed in her profile.

She reposts a ton of old-people bait. Pray for this sick kid. Click "like" to support our troops. Get outraged at what the "Demon-rats" are doing to our country. For every ten of these posts, there's one photo of a sunset or flower—the pictures Bob already sent himself from her phone. These don't have many likes or any comments, but through his social media experience, Bob knows that only means her barrage of reposts doesn't get anyone slowing down to look at them, so when she posts something real the algorithm doesn't show it to anybody.

There's no way to search for any comments she's made on other people's posts. Sometimes Google will bring up something, but this time it doesn't.

"Her Facebook doesn't say much," Bob says. "Only that she gets angry when the algorithm tells her to."

"Conspiracy memes?" Joann adjusts in her seat. "That's strange. If she's pretending her mind's addled to hide that she's the kidnapper, wouldn't it be easier to delete Facebook?"

Bob shrugs. "She could be legitimately losing it."

"Not if she masterminded the kidnapping of thirty kids."

"You know," Bob says, "I guess that number is thirty-two now."

In the silence that follows, Bob aches to see his son and daughter. He almost throws the car into gear to drive over to Polly's house to hold Emily, but he's not letting Wanda drive away without them seeing.

Joann fidgets with the window controls, which do nothing since the car is off. "I feel like I can't be still."

"I feel that a lot."

"I've got enough self control to not charge into her house and give up our chance to follow her to Sam and Mary," Joann says, "but our babies are gone and everything about everything feels wrong."

"I know." Bob puts his hand on her knee. "We'll find them."

"We will," she squeezes his hand.

It's nice to be next to her. He holds no resentment that she grieved Mary. It's harder to be as understanding about Joann spending so much time away from him and Sam this last year, but if he'd believed their little girl was dead, maybe he'd have wanted promise about heaven. Regardless, if he needs to work through something in how he perceives his wife, he can do that later on, after they bring home Sam and Mary.

He looks at her and wonders if she thinks similarly of him—aware of resentment she'll eventually need to address, but in her case, about his leaving her alone in bed so many nights so he could go chasing after—what was in her mind—an impossible dream.

Before he can ask, Joann's eyes go wide. She points. "There she is."

Wanda Donovan's garage door is open. She's pulling out in her Silver Mazda.

Bob cranks the engine. "Let's see where she's going."

∼

Bob's never tailed someone before, but he's pretty sure that mid-afternoon isn't the best time to do it.

"She's drifting all over the place," Joann says.

The Mazda rides the white line and then it's back over the yellow. Wanda's curly hair sits too low in the front seat. "How can she see over the wheel?" Bob asks.

"I'm not sure she can."

It'd be funny in any other circumstance, but right now, Bob just wants Wanda to lead them to Mary and Sam.

"Don't let her spot you," Joann says.

The situation is too much. All their anxiety and fear and exhaustion manifests in peels of laughter.

To Bob, it feels manic, but then, everything since Sam disappeared has felt manic.

"She's turning," Joann says.

They follow Wanda down a suburban thoroughfare of strip malls. It's getting close to rush hour, so traffic moves slowly.

"What if she's going for groceries?" Bob asks.

"Then we wait and follow her some more."

But Wanda turns down a side street. Townhome complexes line either side. They pass the library and a business park.

Wanda speeds up.

"She's been five under the speed limit this whole way," Bob says. "Did she spot us?"

"Not a chance," says Joann. "Not with how low she's sitting."

Wanda's silver Mazda goes five over, ten over, fifteen. Wheels hit the shoulder, gravel sprays. Bob eases off the accelerator, expecting

Wanda to spin out, but the car's computers must be top notch because her driver's side wheels compensate. She gets back on the asphalt.

Bob speeds back up. "Did she spot us?"

"I'm telling you she didn't. She keeps looking out her side windows."

"Probably sees us in her mirrors."

"I swear she's watching the woods and parking lots as we pass. Look, there she goes!"

Sure enough, the silhouette of Wanda's hair has turned left but she's leaning to the right, as if she's trying to get away from someone pounding on her window.

Her passenger side wheels go off the road again. The shoulder is low and the car tilts. Wanda overcorrects. Her front wheels jump back onto the asphalt but her rear wheels slide along the shoulder for a dozen feet before bouncing back onto the road. The Mazda fishtails too much for its computers to control. It spins around off the left side of the road, falling into a ditch in front of a strip of townhomes.

Wanda ends up sitting crooked, facing Bob and Joann.

Bob brakes.

"Keep going," Joann says. "If the cops find us following her, they'll get even more suspicious."

Bob pulls into the townhome complex. "They don't know about Wanda. And we'll be gone before they get here."

He throws the car into park and runs down to Wanda's car. Joann is behind him.

Cars pass by. No one stops to help, since everyone carries a cellphone and can call for whatever help they need. That's the assumption, anyway.

As Bob runs to Wanda's door, she sees him through the open window. Her hands fly up as if he's going to beat her.

"Leave me alone!" she cries. "You're not real!"

She looks closer at him, through her splayed fingers. She hesitates.

"I'm your neighbor," Bob says. "You wrecked. Are you okay?"

Wanda swings her head around, permed hair swaying. "Where'd he go? Don't let him near me."

She's acting delusional.

Except, it can't just be delusions. She described the exact hoodied figure who Sam saw. Even Bob and Joann saw the pink light in the woods. The Thirty-First Trick-or-Treater is real. He has to be.

Bob looks behind him, at the townhouses and the scant landscaping. Is the kidnapper watching him right now?

"The guy stalking you—did you help him kidnap our kids?"

Wanda covers her face with her bony hands and lets out a trilling sob. "He won't leave me alone."

"Who? Who's the Thirty-First Trick-or-Treater? Who killed your son?"

Wanda drops her hands. She's looking at Bob with earnest, gray eyes. "Martin's at school. He'll be home after chess club."

Bob's not having it. "Quit your dementia act. Your son was dead inside the Old Pine Elementary School walls. Who killed him? Who took our kids?"

The old woman wails. "Martin isn't dead! Those cops today were lying! He's going to Reynolds in September."

Joann catches up. She says to Bob, "That can't be right."

It's already October, for one. And Reynolds Community College changed its name four or five years ago.

"Bob," Joann says softly. "She really does think her son is still alive. Sounds like the cops identified Martin and talked to her already."

Bob's anger is flowing too hot. He pounds his cast on the car roof, sending waves of pain into his arm. "Where are my kids? Where'd you take the trick-or-treaters?"

"The missing children?" Wanda asks.

Joann takes Bob's hand firmly. "She doesn't know. She's being harassed by whoever killed her son."

Sirens wail in the distance.

"We should go," Bob says.

Joann leans in to the old woman. "Wanda. Who's the man in the hoodie?"

"I don't know," Wanda sniffs. "He follows me."

"When do you see him?"

"Throughout the day. Mostly at night, outside my windows."

"Let's go," Joann says.

Bob follows after her. "Is that it?"

"Get in the car before the cops show up. We have somewhere else to be tonight."

∼

BOB DRIVES them out the back way through the townhome lot and they head for home.

Leaves have faded from bright yellows, oranges, and reds to rotting brown. The coziness of early fall is over.

"You have a plan," Bob says.

"That poor woman is half-senile and fully convinced that her son will be home from school any minute."

"Right."

"But the Thirty-First Trick-or-Treater is a real person. Not something she's imagining."

"Agreed. Sam saw him. He's real." Bob's heart constricts at mentioning his son.

Joann winces, but she's in this plan now, not willing to slow down. "If he's looking in Wanda's windows after dark, then we were watching her house at the wrong time of day."

"You want to go back tonight," Bob says. "Let's do it."

∼

THE DISAPPOINTMENT ONLY GETS WORSE.

Friday evening, Bob and Joann watch Olivia Dalton walk out from Old Pine.

It's getting harder to be happy for the other families instead of devastated that his family is still torn apart.

They don't go home. Instead, they drive over to Wanda's street.

On the way, they notice another house has put up Halloween decorations—a Maypole with little plastic skeletons holding the end of each ribbon, posed in the act of skipping.

They park in sight of Wanda's house.

For the next four hours, they watch the shadows around her windows, her porch, her front door. There's nobody.

~

KENNY MOON OPENS his front door to see exactly what he knew was coming:

Someone's put Halloween decorations in his front yard.

Limping from an old softball injury, he storms out onto his porch.

Kenny holds his Ruger down at his side, against his hip. He doesn't want to get charged with brandishing a firearm. But he's also not gonna let this prankster—this so called Thirty-First Trick-or-Treater—get the better of him.

In his front yard is some kind of pagan bullshit. One of those big poles with the ribbons stretching down to the ground. Only in this case, eight little skeleton fellas are circling the pole, tied to the ribbons.

The prankster has jabbed holes in Kenny's perfect lawn.

"Who's out there?" He shouts.

All his neighbors' porch lights are on, but there are still plenty of shadows to hide in: Under his truck, in the rhododendrons, behind the boxwoods.

Someone's got to do something about this violent prankster. The police are busy with the missing kids and their murders—as they should be—so it's got to be the people of Maple Creek standing up for themselves.

Kenny walks down his porch steps, onto the grass. He leaves plenty of space between him and the nearest skeleton.

He knows damn well this setup might have hidden razor blades, or be coated in acid, or swing around to knock him on his ass. The Thirty-First Trick-or-Treater is out for blood.

Shadows move inside the rhododendrons. Its big leaves hide something. Or someone.

Kenny circles the skeletons, creeping toward the bushes.

From within the branches, a stick snaps.

This guy is in there, all right.

Kenny keeps his finger off the pistol's trigger, but he's ready to whip it up and fire if he needs to. He reaches the bushes, kicks at the lower branches. "Come on out. I know you're in there. You're staying here with me while I call the cops."

There's a sound behind Kenny, like more sticks breaking.

He turns around.

One of the skeletons now hangs halfway up the pole, dangling by its neck from a ribbon.

"What the hell?" Kenny stomps back toward the pagan decorations, still giving them space, but trying to see who the hell strung up the plastic skeleton.

There's nowhere anyone could hide. It must have been automatic.

"Go ahead," Kenny mutters. "String up another. Let me see how it works."

He watches the remaining seven skeletons standing there motionless, with the one swaying in the slight breeze, tapping against the metal pole.

Rustling comes from the bushes.

Kenny whirls around. There's a twinge in his bad knee but he ignores it.

As soon as he gets the rhododendrons in his sights, there's once again that noise of sticks breaking. He turns back to the center of his yard.

Now there's only one skeleton still standing on the grass, its ribbon leading up to the top of the pole. The remaining seven have been hanged.

Kenny thinks maybe he should have called the police to start with.

"You're not gonna get me." He backs toward his porch. He raises his voice. "We're gonna find you. We're not pansies around here. You're messing with the wrong neighborhood."

Something smooth and cold against the back of his neck. A ribbon.

Before Kenny can step away, the ribbon whips around his throat. It jerks him to one side. He keeps his balance but the pressure on his neck hurts.

He manages to get his left hand up to grab the ribbon, take the pressure off his neck.

The ribbon leads from his neck up to the top of the pole. The eighth skeleton is lying neglected on the grass.

How did the ribbon get over to him?

Kenny doesn't have time to puzzle that out before it yanks him toward the pole. It slips through his fingers so the impact is all on his neck.

He gasps but can't get air into his lungs. Blood gets heavy in his cheeks and behind his eyes.

Scrabbling at the ribbon with his free hand, Kenny raises his pistol with the other. He fires at the ribbon, twice, three times. All three strike true, but the holes punched in the silk are too small to weaken it. He fires four more times, emptying the gun, hitting his target three of those. It's still not enough. He can't rip apart the ribbon, even with the bullet holes.

The dark neighborhood goes blurry. Neighbors' porch lights glisten like stars drawn by children.

Kenny's chest burns.

His keys! In his pocket. He doesn't have a knife on his keychain anymore, but the house key itself might be jagged enough to cut through.

He drops his pistol into the grass, fumbles for his keys, pulls them free. He hacks at the ribbons, stabbing a key into the bullet holes and ripping.

The ribbon tears halfway across.

It's miraculous, but the tautness around his neck hasn't let up.

He hacks at it again and it rips into tiny threads.

Kenny falls back onto the grass.

His knee screams in pain but his lungs fill with sweet, cold oxygen.

Kenny scrambles for his pistol.

It's empty, but the Thirty-First Trick-or-Treater doesn't know that.

Kenny can't spot him.

He backs up to his front door, this time glancing behind to make sure there aren't any more surprises.

He gets inside, engages the lock and deadbolt.

This is out of control.

The citizens of Maple Creek are going to have to put the fear of God into this prankster. Kenny's the man to make it happen.

OCTOBER 18TH

SATURDAY MORNING, Bob is in his office, checking messages from his YouTube viewers.

Condolences about Sam flood his inbox.

Some clickbait blog site must have made an article about him. "This conspiracy YouTuber linked to the Maple Creek Trick-or-Treaters just lost ANOTHER child."

More viewers is always good, but whenever something like this goes viral, there's always a week or two of inundation with comments and messages from new viewers who will disappear in a couple weeks. It's great to boost his videos' reach, but it doesn't translate into the sort of viewer who wants to help with his investigation.

While Bob's skimming the well-wishes, he gets a *ding* which means someone's messaged him on Facebook. He switches tabs to check it out.

It's from a Paul Keller. He knows that name.

"I'm Walter's dad. Can we talk?"

Oh, that's right. Sam's friend. *"Sure. Do you want to come by?"*

"Messenger is fine."

Bob's a little put off. Both their kids vanished three days ago. If ever there was a reason to meet together in person, this is it.

On the other hand, Bob hasn't reached out to him, either. He responds, *"What can I do for you?"*

The three dots appear that mean Paul is typing. They disappear, then appear again. Finally, a message comes through. *"Do you know anything? Anywhere your son liked to hide?"*

Bob sighs. Paul has nothing useful. Just flailing in the misery of a missing child. Bob responds, *"No. What about you?"*

"No."

This is pointless.

Bob goes back to skimming messages from his viewers.

Paul dings in again. *"How are you guys holding up?"*

Bob doesn't have time for this. He closes his Facebook tab, goes back to YouTube messages.

He finds a message from a viewer with a screenshot of the Wayback Machine, a website that saves a sporadic history of the internet. In this case, it's an old discussion forum about a tabletop miniature game. In the viewer's message, they say that Martin Donovan posted here.

Bob skims the forum discussion.

There's a user named "DarkElfDonovan," but they're asking about painting techniques. Even if it's him, it's not a clue about his murderer.

The rest of the messages are equally useless. If they're not simple condolences about Sam, then they're absolutely bizarre tips.

There's another *ding* from his computer. A tab in his browser is blinking: Facebook.

He could have sworn he closed that.

He clicks over to see a new message from Paul Keller. *"What did Wanda Donovan tell you?"*

Chills go down Bob's back.

He types out, *"How do you know about that?"* then thinks that he shouldn't admit to anything. He hits enter anyways.

Is this guy following him? Was Walter's dad watching Bob and Joann while they watched Wanda?

Those three dots that say "someone's typing" put a knot in Bob's stomach. Then Paul sends his reply. *"Walter's friend Jeremy said he and Sam snuck into her backyard. Something spooked them but I wasn't clear on what."*

Bob parses all the names and pronouns in Paul's message.

Sam had been in Wanda Donovan's backyard?

"What happened?" Bob asks. Why hadn't Sam told him about it?

"That's everything I know. I was hoping you'd know more about it."

Bob doesn't respond because he's already marching across the street to Jeremy's house.

∼

WIND SWIRLS DEAD LEAVES, brown and gray.

Bob hasn't bothered to grab a jacket. Chilly air quickly seeps beneath his clothes.

He jogs across the street and knocks on the Appleman family's door.

Jeremy opens up.

Bob's never been a big fan of Sam's needly-nosed and weasly-personalitied friend, but Sam thinks the world of him, and so Bob keeps his mouth shut.

"Is your mom or dad home?" Bob asks.

"My dad, yeah." Jeremy stares up at Bob.

"Mind going to get him?"

Before Jeremy can disappear inside, Bob adds, "And I've got a question for you, too, when you get back."

Jeremy's cheeks burn crimson, telling Bob that Paul's message was at least partly true. The boy leaves the door cracked as he goes to find his dad.

A minute later, Bob hears heavy footsteps and then the door swings open.

Vince Appleman fixes forklifts at the Amazon warehouse, as evidenced by his grease-stained fingertips and the stiff way he moves his neck.

"Hiya Bob," Vince says. "Any news on Sam?"

That throws Bob off. Why would he share news about Sam with this near stranger? But then that thought feels odd, because Bob wishes he did have that sort of relationship with at least a few of his neighbors, and not just via Facebook groups or Nextdoor.

"No," Bob says. "We still can't find him."

That garners a tilted head from Vince, since Bob didn't say that the *police* haven't found anything yet. "What'd you do to your arm?"

"I fell." Bob continues. "Paul Keller was telling me that before Walter and Sam disappeared, Jeremy had told Walter that he and Sam had a strange experience. Something in Wanda Donovan's backyard?"

Vince looks down at his son.

Jeremy shrugs. "I don't know who that is." But his cheeks are so red they look ready to burst.

Vince looks back to Bob. "Sorry. We can't help."

"Hold on," Bob says. "I'm not accusing anybody of anything. I just want to know if there's anything weird that happened. Wanda Donovan is an old lady who lives on Clearbark Circle. That's the cul-de-sac behind the clubhouse and playground."

Jeremy's eyes go wide.

Vince asks his son, "Do you have something to share? Don't confess if it's a crime."

"It's nothing bad," Jeremy says, "except sneaking into that lady's yard."

"What'd you see in there?" Bob asks. "What creeped you out?"

Jeremy looks to his dad. Vince cautiously says, "Go ahead."

"I saw a pink light from under the ground," Jeremy says, "but that was last year. That's why we went and looked in there—Sam thought the pink light would lead us to Mary."

"Oh Jesus," Vince whispers to himself.

"We didn't see any pink light in the dirt," Jeremy says, "but in the shed, it came out of this bucket and shined a picture on the ceiling of a guy in a hoodie with a jack-o-lantern."

"A turnip jack-o-lantern," Bob says, not a question.

"Yeah. With pink light coming out of the eyes."

Vince says, "Wait, was the light doing the projecting pink, or was the image that it projected pink?"

"I don't know," Jeremy says. "It scared the hell out of me."

"Don't swear," Vince says. He glances behind him, probably checking that his wife didn't hear.

"What'd you do next?" Bob asks.

"We ran. Nearly ran over the old lady on our way out of there."

"And after that?"

Jeremy grimaces. "Walter told us he saw that guy inside Old Pine, last year when it was Crimson Corridors. Sam wanted to search it. Me and Walter caught him about to sneak inside."

"If you went inside," Vince says, "don't admit to that."

Jeremy goes quiet.

"What'd you see in there?" Bob asks.

"You gotta understand why he can't talk about that," Vince says. "People are getting suspicious of each other. The cops are ready to investigate anybody."

That reticence would make Bob suspicious of Vince, but he's broken into his house twice in the past year, and he's confident nobody in that family is hiding anything.

"How about I come inside, I leave my phone outside, I don't record anything? You tell me what happened, and I keep looking for Sam and Mary?"

"No," Vince says.

"I wanna help Sam," Jeremy says. "I was too scared to go with them the second time, but maybe I can still help."

"You can," Bob says. "And you don't even have to do anything scary. Just tell me what happened."

Jeremy looks up at his dad. "Please?"

Vince's shoulders slump. "Okay. But you leave your phone outside, Bob."

"Deal."

Bob goes inside and listens to Jeremy's story of an abandoned haunted attraction with fake spider webs, dissection equipment, and a pink light shining out from a classroom at the end of the hall.

~

"You're sure you searched in there?" Bob asks Joann while they drive to Old Pine.

A sliver of moon does little to light the evening around them.

He's filled her in on Jeremy's story about the boys going into the school and seeing a classroom emanating pink light. Based on Jeremy's description, it sounds like the same room where they found Martin Donovan's corpse.

"Positive," Joann says. "I saw the bathroom where they removed Martin. They opened up the whole wall."

He wants to see it for himself, but that's desperation talking. He trusts Joann. If there were anything strange to find in that room, she would have seen it. Whoever lured Sam and Walter there didn't stick around after taking them. "There's gotta be a hidden way in and out."

"Not from that room," Joann says. "I thought the same thing—maybe the boys found a secret tunnel that the kidnapper's using to bring in the kids each night—but I zeroed in on that room. The floors are solid. The walls are whole."

"Maybe in a room nearby?"

"Must be."

They pull into the Old Pine parking lot. It's a madhouse.

Local and state police cruisers, news vans, and so many more cars than there are grieving parents. It's becoming a circus.

They park and walk to the front of the crowd. The faces around them are familiar now. They see them every night.

There's the Fuentes family, who live a few doors down from them. Their missing daughter's name is Sofia. She's Mary's age.

There's the Newmans, waiting for their daughter Caroline. Next to them are Peter and Hannah Smith. Their missing son's name is Ted.

Bob and Joann join them in hoping for a miracle, terrified of what will happen at 7:34 P.M.

As their clocks advance to a minute beforehand, the newsmen point their cameras to the front doors.

And here comes Ted, wearing black sweats and a gray striped scarf. Bob wouldn't recognize the costume except he's read that the eleven-year-old disappeared dressed as Gru from *Despicable Me*.

Peter and Hannah run to their boy.

Bob and Joann walk back to their car.

"You didn't film it," Joann says.

"No." Bob doesn't give more answer than that. Does his YouTube channel need another video of a missing trick-or-treater coming home who isn't Mary or Sam?

Something else occurs to him. Should he expect Sam to reappear in Old Pine, or are those rules only for the original missing thirty?

He and Joann leave behind the commotion of reporters jostling for questions and cops swarming like ants.

They drive back over to Clearbark Circle to settle in for another night of watching Wanda's house, desperate for some breakthrough.

OCTOBER 19TH

IT'S AFTER MIDNIGHT, and Bob is restless. "She's delusional. The Thirty-First Trick-or-Treater isn't looking in her windows."

His back aches from sitting in the parked car for the past four hours. Joann is at his side, dutifully watching down the street at Wanda's house.

Twice they've left their car to walk the Clearbark Circle cul-de-sac, so they could see the other side of Wanda's house. They found nothing.

"What if you can only see him from inside?" Joann asks.

"I thought we both agreed he's a real person, not a delusion."

"He is," Joann says. "I'm not saying it's magic glass. But maybe she's seeing him from certain angles, like he's over in a neighbor's yard and we can't see him from here."

"Yeah," Bob says, "that could be it."

He gets out of the car.

Joann follows suit. "What are you doing?"

"Going inside to look out her windows."

"Right now?"

"I'm not waiting anymore."

They walk as casually as possible through the night. They go down Wanda's driveway like they belong. Bob opens the gate and they go inside the back yard.

"It looks more run down than I noticed the first time," Joann says.

Bob agrees. "Especially the shed."

The shed's roof is warped into waves so that shingles are popping off. The wood siding is black with dirt and mold. The door is open.

He thinks of his conversation with Jeremy. "Let's look in there, first."

Bob and Joann head for it. He pushes the shed door all the way open.

Inside, the plywood floor is as warped as the roof. A push mower sits on the floor, accessible to the door. The rest of the shed is filled with scrap wood, buckets, shelves of hardware, and unfolded tarps. It all smells of motor oil and cut grass.

Joann points to a stack of orange buckets, caked with dirt. "Those the buckets Jeremy told you about?"

"Looks like it."

They both wade through the junk. Bob peers down into the top bucket carefully, like he's looking down the barrel of a gun.

It's an empty bucket.

"Jeremy described it like the turnip projector in our living room?" Joann asks.

"Yeah," Bob says. "He saw the Thirty-First Trick-or-Treater in a video on the ceiling."

They both look up. Plywood droops beneath each sagging rafter.

"There's gotta be another projector in here, right?"

"Not sure whether it'd still be here," Bob says.

"This guy's sneaking projectors in and out? How'd he even know the boys would be here?"

"Maybe it's someone they know? We can go back and ask Jeremy if they told anyone else what they were doing."

"What if," Joann says, "what if it's Martin Donovan?"

"You think he's still alive? It was someone else in the wall?"

"No." Joann doesn't look like she's teasing.

Is she really suggesting what Bob thinks she is? "Did that church convince you ghosts are real?"

"Ease up. I'm just saying, we've been asking why the kidnapper did what he did and where he's stashed the kids. But we're avoiding the *how*."

"How they're sneaking a kid into Old Pine each night?"

"Sure, but moreso, how did they kidnap thirty kids at once?"

"We've been over this. There's probably lots of people involved."

"And not a single one was spotted?"

"That's what happened. No one saw anybody take the kids. That's a fact we can work from."

"And I'm saying where we go from that fact is that maybe something weirder than we can explain is going on."

"Like ghosts." Bob bites his tongue. He wants to call his wife crazy, blame her church community for opening her up to spooks and ghouls. But he reminds himself that the only real problem he needs to worry about is slowing down their search for Sam and Mary.

"Yes, like ghosts," Joann says.

"I'm trying not to sound like a dick when I ask this, but where did the ghosts take our kids?"

"I don't know. The afterlife?"

Bob's stomach twists. Mary and Sam aren't dead. "They go to the afterlife and they come back into Old Pine?"

Joann throws her hands up. "They're not in the school. The cops have searched. You've searched. I've searched."

"They have to be," Bob says.

"They're not. But they're still showing up there, one at a time."

"Then the kidnapper is sneaking them in!"

"There's cops at each entrance! In every room in the building! But somehow, all of a sudden, a missing trick-or-treater is walking down the hallway."

Bob thinks, *Or collapsing onto the floor*, but doesn't dare say it aloud.

Joann must be thinking the same thing, because she goes quiet.

"Okay," Bob says. "What do we do about it? Let's say that's the case. Someone hid Martin Donovan's corpse in that school, and then Martin came back to haunt his mom and steal our kids. If that's what's happening, then what do we do about it?"

"We find him," Joann says. "Make him give the kids back."

"There's another question. He is giving the kids back, one per night. Why?"

"And why have four of them died?" Joann concedes.

"If it's a ghost who's doing it," Bob asks, "does that answer any of these questions?"

"Martin Donovan could be angry that he's dead. He blames our neighborhood and especially his mom."

"Okay, that could be the case. But what do we do with that info?"

Joann closes her eyes.

Bob breathes in the oil and cut grass smell of the lawn mower.

Finally, Joann says, "I don't know."

It's too much. "Why did you bring up ghosts if there's no point?"

"It feels like there's a point," Joann says, "but I don't know what it is. We need to expand what we're doing."

Bob hears himself answer too harshly. "Expand it how?"

"I don't know," Joann snaps back. "You're the one who's been working on this for the past year."

"And where were you?"

"Grieving our daughter."

"She's not dead!"

"Missing children don't come back. After she was gone two days, there was a ninety-nine percent chance she was gone forever."

"That one percent should have been enough to keep looking!"

"Don't you accuse me of not caring. Where have you been for Emily and Sam? Sneaking around at night, sleeping through the morning and then making videos in your office the rest of the time!"

"And you've disappeared to church, leaving Sam at home."

Joann goes quiet.

His last accusation lingers in the shed, but so does hers. They'd both abandoned Sam, while their whole family was missing Mary.

"We fucked up, didn't we?" Bob says.

"Oh god. That's why Sam went off on his own. Why he didn't come to us."

Guilt roils Bob's gut. It blends with the ever-bubbling panic he's felt since Sam disappeared, and both strike a powerful blow to the determination he's felt since losing Mary.

Before they can continue their argument, the shed fills with a pink glow.

Bob looks down into the stack of buckets and then up to the ceiling, but the pink light isn't brighter in any one place.

"Where's that coming from?" Joann asks.

In the junk of the shed, there's no single point that's brighter than any other. Bob kicks down the stack of buckets. He tilts the lawnmower over. He tries to toss a tarp to one side, but it's caught under a bag of mulch. He yanks at it, losing his calm. "Get out of the way, goddammit!"

Joann kicks the bag of mulch. It falls over but stays on the tarp. She kicks it again with a guttural shriek. That frees the tarp and Bob turns his whole body to throw it to the other side of the shed.

Roaches scatter from their lost shelter.

The pink light that fills the shed grows brighter.

"Where is it?" Bob topples a sheet of curved plywood that was leaning against the wall.

He's not even sure what he's looking for—a pink lightbulb, a projector, a turnip jack-o-lantern?

Joann picks up a leaf blower and throws it. It crashes into the shed's door, knocking it open.

Fresh air fills Bob's lungs. His head spins then slows.

Why did they trash Wanda's shed? The source of the pink light couldn't be hiding beneath a tarp or behind a sheet of plywood. Throwing a leaf blower certainly didn't help.

Bob staggers outside.

The light over Wanda's back door still pushes back against the night, but now there's a pink tinge to everything it reveals. Thin grass is the color of wilting roses. Both the rotting deck and the dead leaves look orange. The fence should be white but is undeniably pink.

There's no texture to these new colors. They haven't been painted or stained. It's as if a projector is pointing in all directions, reaching every corner and crevice without casting shadows.

Joann stumbles out from the shed. "What's going on?"

"You feeling better?"

"I think so. What happened to us?"

"I don't know. Something about this light."

"Everything out here is pink, too. Not the trees, though."

Bob looks up. Joann is right. The strange light is limited to Wanda's yard.

Before Bob can comment, a scream comes from inside Wanda's house.

∽

"That was Wanda!" Bob races for the back door.

Joann is at his side. "Be careful. Something weird is going on."

The sliding glass door is unlocked. Bob flings it open.

Pink light fills Wanda's living room, even brighter than in her shed. It discolors her floral patterned couch and the family photos on the walls.

"Wanda!" Bob calls into the house.

Joann runs in beside him. "Is she okay?"

"I hope so, but I'm after whoever's scaring her." Bob runs through the living room to the foyer. Finally, after a year of searching, he's in the same house as the kidnapper. Martin's murderer and the violent prankster who's been terrorizing Maple Creek—Bob is so close to catching him.

He turns the corner, Joann close behind. Wanda is at the top of the stairs, her back to Bob. She's standing at the very edge, her heels over the top step.

It's all bathed in pink.

Joann pushes past Bob, heading up the steps. "Wanda, get away from the stairs."

Wanda screams again, raises her hands in self-defense against someone down the upstairs hallway. She flinches—the aggressor around the corner must have lunged. She falls backward, flinging her arms above her head.

Joann leaps up three steps at a time. She lifts her hands to catch the old woman. Wanda is light but she's already building up momentum. Joann isn't ready for the impact.

Wanda knocks Joann down and to one side. Bob jumps up to catch his wife. There's a terrible clatter as Wanda flips past him.

Joann falls into Bob and he does his best to fall straight down instead of backwards, only partly succeeding but it's enough to lessen the impact of their fall. They hit the steps and then slide down.

Everything's still.

"Are you okay?" Bob breathes.

"I'm fine." Joann sits up. "Oh god."

Bob does a mental check of his own body. His butt and right hip hurt, but he's otherwise fine, broken arm included.

"Wanda?" Joann asks.

Bob looks over.

The old woman's left leg is bent at three right angles. There's a break in her left arm so bad that her forearm is dangling by skin. Blood pools on the wood floor beneath her, red tinged pink.

Wanda opens her eyes. Moans.

Bob jumps to his feet. Joann can help Wanda. Bob's not letting the kidnapper get away.

He sprints up the stairs three at a time. There's a scuffling sound above, he's sure of it. He runs up and around the corner.

He flips on the light. It's a bright, narrow hallway, painted yellow but the colors are now all polluted.

Three closed doors line the hall, which leads to a half-open door at the end.

When Bob searched this house in the dark, the doors had all been open. And he could have sworn there were only two doors in the hallway, not counting with the master on the end.

Now's not the time for self-doubt.

Bob charges straight ahead. Each pounding step sends a jolt of pain up his right leg. He throws the master bedroom door open. It crashes against a bedroom wall.

There's a perfectly made bed with nightstands on either side covered in a layer of dust.

A dark window reflects the room.

Bob rattles it, but it's locked tight from inside.

He searches the room.

Nothing under the bed except for clear totes with Christmas wrapping paper. The closet is full of untouched clothes on hangers, the same as he saw before.

Bob grabs an armful and tosses them to floor. Against the back wall of the closet are stacked shoeboxes. There's no one in here.

Bob goes back into the tight hallway. The pink glow feels like a fog, heavy and damp on his skin.

The three doors remain closed. Two on the left, one on the right.

He can't remember which one wasn't here the other night.

He pushes away that thought. It's ridiculous. Still, Joann's suggestion of something beyond the normal weighs heavy on Bob's mind.

Adding to his discomfort: Whoever scared Wanda—whoever made that scuffling noise Bob heard on his way up—is still here.

He opens the first door on the left.

It's a bathroom. All the porcelain is a faded salmon, now colored a deeper pink by whatever's infecting the air.

Nowhere to hide in here.

Bob moves on to the next door. He tries to remember what will be in here. This one—across from the bathroom, between the stairs and the master—should be a small bedroom.

He opens the door to discover he's right.

Of course. He remembers the teenager's room from before.

Martin's room.

A twin bed sits against one wall. An ancient TV with an original Nintendo on top. A bookshelf full of brightly colored epic fantasy paperbacks.

Bob opens the closet. It's empty except for a graduation robe and a red Circuit City polo. The polo hangs by stretched shoulders from a hanger.

Wanda's kept Martin's room the same, almost thirty years later.

Bob looks for a journal but no luck. No computer that might have digital journal entries.

Bob hesitates at another shelf. This one is lined with hand-painted miniature elves and goblins.

It's sad to think that the corpse in the wall was once a teenager passionate enough about something to get this talented at it. The miniatures are so full of detail that Bob can see the whites and irises of the elves' eyes and the serrated edges of the goblins' daggers.

He feels like there must be some answers in here, but there's nothing else to find.

From downstairs, Joann calls up, "Bob? Are you okay? Is anybody up there?"

He goes out into the hallway. "One more room to check. You should get out of here."

"I'm staying with Wanda. I've called 911. We were over for a late visit, she went upstairs, and then we heard her scream, okay?"

"Got it."

This isn't good. The cops will have serious suspicions.

Unless the intruder is still here.

The first intruder—not Bob and Joann.

Bob goes to the final door. He pictures the house from the outside. There won't be much space behind this door--it'll have to be a closet only as deep as the bathroom.

It's locked.

But these are hollow core doors held in the frame by a latch and quarter-inch screws. Bob's read online how to break down a door. He tries it now.

He raises his left foot, leans back, and then throws all his weight forward, slamming the bottom of his foot against the door, right next to the doorknob.

The latch cracks and the door swings open.

Momentum carries Bob stumbling inside the room.

It takes him five or six steps to catch his balance.

Darkness envelops him but that darkness is somehow pink. He holds his good hand up in front of his face. He can't see it—only pink.

He turns around and there's the open doorway. Through it is the hallway, and across the hall are the stairs. The door is a bright rectangle in the dark pink fog.

How can he be so far away from the door? The house isn't this big.

Bob raises his hand in front of his face, scared that it won't block his view of the hallway and stairs, that it's not the room that's too dark but instead he's faded from existence and nothing is real anymore.

His hand silhouettes against the door. Its shadow is pink instead of black, but his hand still exists nonetheless.

Bob's heart leaps into his throat—there's still an intruder in here somewhere. He whirls around, sees nothing but the pink dark.

He hears a police siren. He starts back for the hall until he hears something behind him that sounds like a sigh or a whimper. He turns back.

He sees only the single, solid color, but under the wail of the siren he can hear whispers.

Bob goes still and listens.

Not whispers. The voices don't have the breathiness of whispers.

Not murmuring. The words aren't blurred. They would be crystal clear if only they were louder.

But they're so quiet, as if it's a recording played back with the volume turned down.

Bob listens, trying to hear the voices despite the approaching siren.

He walks deeper into the room.

"Mary?" he calls. "Sam?"

The voices get the tiniest bit louder.

They're kids.

Bob's stomach flips. He yells for his children. Are they here? Has he finally found them? He runs into the pink darkness. "Mary? Sam?"

The chorus of children separate into distinct voices.

A little boy—not Sam—says, "Stay still. He's coming."

A girl—older than Mary—answers, "He'll find us even if we hide."

Bob can't tell which direction they're coming from. He turns a full circle.

Light from the doorway blinds him. It's only a few feet away, even though he'd ran at least twenty feet into the room.

"What the hell?" he whispers.

Suddenly, there's a shape in the pink darkness. The motion of the color is all emanating from this shape. It draws near—a turnip with a face carved into it. Triangle eyes, a toothless grin.

And behind this turnip jack-o-lantern is a young man in a hoodie.

The Thirty-First Trick-or-Treater. The kidnapper. The violent prankster. Martin Donovan's murderer.

But the hood tilts back to reveal a face that Bob has seen in photographs online. A round jawline. A sparse mustache. Eyes that Bob now realizes aren't full of sadness but anger.

It's Martin Donovan himself.

Not bloated and rotting. Not dry and shriveled.

Before Bob can react to this specter before him, a small hand shoves him in the back, through the open door, into Wanda's upstairs hallway.

Bob trips, falls.

A little body falls onto his back.

Bob rolls over, catching his son.

∽

BOB SQUEEZES Sam against his chest. A million words try to pour of his mouth at once. He lifts Sam by his shoulders. "You're okay. Sam. Are you okay?"

It hasn't been determination, Bob realizes. It hasn't been hope. He hasn't kept searching out of any noble emotion, but out of fear, out of stubbornness covering up that fear.

But now Sam is okay.

His boy wriggles out of his grasp. "Where's Mary? Did I hold on for long enough?"

Sam hops up.

Bob jumps to his feet, well as he can. Elation at having Sam back is swirling together with hope to see Mary again.

But it's only him and Sam in the hallway.

The door into the pink room is gone.

There's only the drywall and a framed photograph of Martin Donovan as a child Sam's age. He's got his hands on his hips and his foot on a soccer ball.

"Where's Mary?" Bob asks. This can't be possible.

"She was with me," Sam is crying, sobbing, overwhelmed. "I had her with one hand, pushed you with the other. I don't know where she went. I held on. I did."

Bob picks up his little boy who's much too large to be picked up.

"You did great. You're wonderful. I missed you so much. You did so amazing."

"I lost her again," Sam babbles.

Bob's heart breaks for his guilt-ridden son. "You didn't lose her. You did your best." Bob can't keep it together.

Sam is back.

Was Mary almost back?

She was in the pink room. The pink room was right through this wall.

Below him, Joanna yells, "What's going on? Did you find him?"

She's asking about the intruder, Bob realizes.

"Sam," Bob yells back, a sob forming in his throat stops him from saying more.

"Mom," Sam says, not loud enough for her to hear. He steps for the stairs, a mama's boy who's been without his mama for too long.

But then he turns back to the wall. "Mary's still in there."

"I'll get her." Bob kicks at the drywall, hurting his toe. He turns around, kicks with his heel, exposing a hole between two studs. He drops to his knees to look through.

Black wires are squished against pink insulation. This is an outer wall. There's nothing behind it but the back yard.

This can't be real. Bob squeezes Sam's hand, then he moves down a few feet, kicks another hole in the wall.

Nothing but wires, studs, and insulation.

Sam gets on his hands and knees to look through. "Where's the hillside?"

Downstairs, cops pound on the door.

Bob hears hinges squeal as Joann lets the cops in.

"Someone attacked Wanda," she says from downstairs. "My husband went upstairs to see if the attacker is still here."

Boots storm up the stairs.

In the lead is Officer Yachuw. His hand is on his gun at his belt. He holds his other hand out to Bob. "You?"

"I don't know where the guy went," Bob says. "I looked everywhere."

The second cop goes down the hall.

Officer Yachuw looks at Sam. "This is your missing son, isn't it?"

"He was up here." Bob hears how fake that sounds, but he can't say what really happened, that there was a door to a strange pink darkness full of children's whispers. Bob speaks louder out of a hope that volume will add to credibility. "Wanda was yelling at someone up here right before she fell. I ran up to find the intruder and I found my son."

Joann's voice from down below. "Sam?"

There's a pounding on the steps and then Joann is lifting Sam into her arms, holding him against her, pushing his cheek against hers, whispering that she'll never let him out of her sight again.

The second cop comes back down the hall. "There's no one else here."

Officer Yachuw chews his lip and eyes Bob. "Yeah. I figured there wasn't."

∼

It's Sunday evening by the time they get home from the police station.

Bob and Joann shepherd Sam into their bed. Joann goes to get Emily from her bed and the four of them sleep close together.

Or rather, Bob tries to sleep. His mind replays the last night and day.

In Wanda's house, Officer Yachuw had launched into aggressive questioning.

Bob told him the truth but not the whole truth. After Wanda fell down the stairs, Bob ran up to confront the intruder. He found Sam stumbling down the hallway.

A long shot story, but Wanda backed it up. Before the ambulance arrived, she was conscious enough to describe the man who attacked her.

"This man here?" Officer Yachuw asked.

"No," Wanda scoffed through her pain. "This man was younger. He looked like my son."

"I saw him, too," Bob had said, still processing the insanity of seeing the young man who had most definitely died twenty years ago. And that was it, wasn't it? Martin was still *young* when Bob saw under that hood. How was that possible?

Officer Yachuw had responded with giddiness. "I thought you said you ran upstairs and only saw your son."

"Martin was running away," Bob said. "Or the guy who looked like Martin."

"To where?"

"The master bedroom." Bob knew there weren't any unlocked windows in there, but what else was he supposed to say?

That's when the paramedics arrived, and everything became about getting Wanda into the ambulance.

In bed now, Bob drapes his arm over Sam and Emily. His little boy is home. There's shame in the relief he feels. A year of fruitless effort to find Mary, and Sam came home after being missing five days. He tries not to have a favorite child. It's an absurd thought, but he's overwhelmed and exhausted.

After Wanda got carried off in the ambulance, and cops swarmed Maple Creek to look for the intruder who looked like Martin Donovan, Bob's Sunday consisted of sitting in the police station with Joann and Sam.

It wasn't until late afternoon that someone finally came to talk to them.

A gray-haired, fit man in a black polo shirt and a badge on his belt identified himself as Detective Otto. He ushered the three of them into an interrogation room that was made comfortable with a leather couch, a glass-doored mini-fridge filled with soda cans, and a basket of packaged snacks.

His questions for Sam were curt. Sam answered in kind.

"Where were you?"

"A hillside. There was pink fog everywhere."

"Outside Mrs. Donovan's house?"

"No. I don't think so. Me and Walter went down the stairs in Old Pine."

"What stairs?"

"In that classroom near the front."

Detective Otto wrote with an electronic pen on his iPad. "Can you show us where you found stairs?"

"Yes."

"Was your friend Walter with you?"

"Yes. Lots of kids were there."

"Did you recognize them?"

"Yes. The kids who disappeared last year."

"Your sister?"

Sam nodded. "I tried to bring her with me."

"Why didn't... why *couldn't* you?"

Bob appreciated the detective's attempted tact.

"I don't know. I tried."

"Tell me more about what happened. How did you end up in Mrs. Donovan's house?"

"I don't know." Sam wiped his eyes. He often does that when he's lying. He'd heard Bob's story to the cops and didn't want to contradict it.

Bob felt both pride and guilt that his son was lying to the cops.

"If you left this pink foggy place, why didn't any of the other kids?"

"I wasn't there very long, but several kids did leave."

"Where's Walter?"

Sam sniffed. "I wanted to stay together. But then I found Mary so I stayed with her and Walter wanted to keep searching."

"Searching for what?"

"The Thirty-First Trick-or-Treater. Walter wants to prove he's real."

At that point, Joann cut in. "You're not getting any clear answers because he's scared and exhausted. Let us take him home, give him a shower and some rest, and then we can talk again tomorrow."

Detective Otto smiled grimly. "Time is a factor. There are eleven kids still missing."

His dismissal of Joann's concerns angered Bob. "One of those missing kids is our daughter."

"I'm Sam's mother," Joann said. "I'm telling you the best way for him to help your investigation is for him to first get some rest."

Detective Otto put his hands behind his head. He looked down at Sam. "What do you think, son? You need a nap?"

The man's condescending tone made Bob want to leap to Sam's defense, but he let his son answer.

Sam nodded.

"Alright then. Let's all go home. We'll have an officer parked outside your house in case the kidnapper still has their eye on Sam."

Sam's eyes widened. Joann put her arm around him.

Bob sighed. "You didn't have to say that in front of him."

The detective's cheeks reddened. "Sorry about that."

A cop capable of feeling shame. Now Bob had seen everything.

The detective cleared his throat. "Everyone get some sleep. I'll be by your place around noon tomorrow."

At home, Bob tried to ask Sam questions, but Joann shot him a look. "After we sleep."

"But Mary," Bob said.

"Sam says she's still okay. He wants to help, but he needs sleep. He needs to feel safe again."

"I thought you said that to the cops so we could keep our own investigation going."

"Only partly. Sam really does need rest."

And now they're in bed. Bob listens to Sam's heavy breathing and Emily's little snore.

He notices that Joann's breathing is still irregular.

The day has gone by too fast for Bob to digest what's happened.

He walked through a door that wasn't there, into a pink fog where Sam had been trapped.

He saw beneath the hood of the Thirty-First Trick-or-Treater. He saw Martin Donovan.

What does that mean?

The body in the wall wasn't actually Martin? Except Officer Randy said the cops had identified him, so it had to be.

How then, did Bob see Martin in the early hours of this morning? Even more disturbing—Martin had looked how he did in his missing photos. Those were from more than twenty years ago.

Sam mumbles in his sleep.

Is Sam dreaming about angry ghosts?

Because Bob suspects that if he ever gets to sleep, it'll be ghosts haunting his dreams, too.

OCTOBER 20TH

SAM WAKES to something cold and wet on his inner arm.

He's in a soft bed. Morning light is coming in through yellow curtains.

The curtains in Mom and Dad's room.

He's home, in his parents' bed. Emily is still asleep, drooling on his arm.

Yesterday's events flood back into his mind.

He almost brought Mary back with him.

Had that been yesterday?

Everyone said that today is Monday, but it was only yesterday that Sam and Walter went back into Old Pine, and that had been Tuesday.

He thought once he had a good night's sleep, things would make sense, but he still can't believe that so much time has passed.

Sleeping didn't take away the guilt, either.

He was *there*.

He'd found all the missing kids. He'd found Mary. He'd tried so hard to bring her with him, but he'd failed. He was a bad person for leaving her behind.

Sam hears breakfast sizzling from the kitchen. Mom and Dad can make him feel better. They'll tell him this isn't his fault.

Part of Sam knows that they'll be right. Yes, he accidentally left his sister behind, but now he knows how to get her back: The stairs in Old Pine, in that classroom where Walter had seen the guy in the hoodie.

Sam carefully slips his arm from under Emily. She murmurs but stays asleep. He runs down the hallway to find Mom frying bacon. Dad's on his laptop at the kitchen table.

"I know how to get back inside," Sam says.

Dad gestures to the chair across from him. "Let's talk before Detective Otto gets here."

"I've made french toast and bacon," Mom says.

Sam doesn't need breakfast. He doesn't need to talk. He needs to go get Mary. "Me and Walter went downstairs in Old Pine. The basement was dark except that darkness was pink. And it wasn't a basement but a hill outside. That's where all the kids are. That's where Mary is."

Dad opens his mouth to ask more, but Mom interrupts him. "Sit. Please." She sets four plates on the table and serves food.

She's not taking him seriously. "Dad? Get up. I can take us to Mary."

Dad closes his laptop. "Let's talk."

"I'll tell you whatever but please, let's go back for Mary."

Dad takes a bite of bacon. "You did a good job in that interview with Detective Otto. Now let's talk about everything you didn't tell him."

Sam wants to tell Mom and Dad everything, but that can happen after they go get his little sister. "Please, I want to try again. I can get her back this time."

"We'll go find her," Dad says. "I promise. But what happened the first time? You went down those stairs, onto a hillside that was covered in pink fog."

"That's right," Sam says.

"Was it fog or just solid?"

"What do you mean?"

"Could you see through it at all?"

"A little."

"Strange. And then what happened?"

Sam makes himself think of that creepy place. "Me and Walter ran through it. There were other kids."

"Who'd you see?" Mom asks.

"I don't know their names. They were in their Halloween costumes, though. We kept running until we saw Mary. I grabbed her hand. She was scared about the Thirty-First Trick-or-Treater coming back. Then I saw a door open and you stepped through, Dad. I kept my fingers tight around Mary's hand—I swear I did. We ran to you and I pushed you back into that door so we could get out. I didn't let go of Mary, I swear! But then she was gone."

Mom hugs him. She's warm. "I know. You did so good."

"I'm proud of you," Dad says, and it's a mental relief.

It feels so good to hear Mom and Dad say he shouldn't be ashamed of failing, even though they're only partly right. "Can we go get her now?"

Dad asks, "Where did you find those stairs?"

It's exasperating. Sam already explained this with the police yesterday. "In a classroom up near the front lobby."

"That building's been searched top to bottom," Dad says. "The cops looked all over, your mom snuck in there, I even charged in the day you disappeared."

"Then you've seen the stairs that go down through the floor."

"No," Mom says.

Dad shakes his head. "There aren't any stairs."

"Then you're not looking in the right place. It's scary in there. I went in twice and it was different both times."

In the middle of cutting his french toast, Dad puts down his fork and knife. "What do you mean?"

"The first time, it was all the decorations from Crimson Corridors. When we went back it was a regular old hallway."

"Someone cleaned it up?" asks Mom.

"Maybe," admits Sam. "But it felt weirder than that."

"Things are pretty weird," Dad says. He looks at Mom. "How

could he have stumbled upon a staircase that nobody else has found?"

"It's hidden really well," suggests Mom, "but the kidnapper uncovered it to lure him in."

Dad nods. "Yeah, could be. Or. It disappeared like the door in Wanda's house."

Mom sits next to Sam but she and Dad are in their own conversation now. "Detective Otto will want Sam to show him where he found the steps."

Dad nods. "Do we trust the cops not to screw it up?"

"We're not breaking in again," Mom says. "They're already looking for ways to pin everything on you."

"I might need to risk that. We're running out of time."

Mom says, "We'll go with them today. If you want to go back and search on your own later, we can figure that out."

Dad turns to Sam. "What do you think? When Detective Otto gets here, can you show everyone where you found those stairs?"

Sam nods. He'll do whatever it takes to get his sister back.

∼

A KNOCK COMES at the door earlier than Bob expects.

He goes to open it to find Paul Keller standing there. "Where's my son?"

Walter's dad smells like he hasn't showered. His black ponytail is greasy. His John-Lennon glasses are smeared. His flannel shirt doesn't look warm enough for the cold wind.

"Hey Paul." Bob steps out onto the porch, closing the door behind him.

Dry, brittle leaves are swirling through the air. Bob hugs his arms around his chest.

"Can I ask Sam where Walter is?"

Bob's not letting that happen, but he doesn't see any harm in being up front. "He said they went down some stairs in Old Pine. Sam was looking for Mary, and Walter wanted to prove that the

Thirty-First Trick-or-Treater is real. The cops are coming by to ask Sam some more questions in a bit. I think we're gonna go look for that staircase."

Paul blinks. He rubs his hands. "Stairs?"

Bob can't get a bead on whether Paul is manic and grieving or manic and angry. "Yeah, that's what Sam remembers. But you're right, it's a one story building, no basement. That's why Sam's gonna show the cops where these stairs might be."

Paul's eyes narrow in on Bob's. His left pupil is totally obscured by the smear in his glasses. "Sam came back. Why didn't he bring Walter with him?"

"Hey, he didn't bring his own sister, either. He's a kid. He did his best and we're not done trying. Talk to the police, but for now, you gotta leave." Bob steps back toward the door but Paul grabs his arm. He's surprisingly strong.

"Did Sam see the kidnapper? Who was it? We can go get him."

Bob's not talking about ghosts to a grieving father on edge. "He didn't see anybody. Like I said, you should talk to the cops."

"Guys around the neighborhood are ready. The kidnapper is the same as this violent prankster, right? We've had enough. We're gonna find him and deal with him."

Bob knows he should walk away, but he's pissed at Paul grabbing his arm, and ready to make him feel stupid. "How are you gonna do that when you don't where or who he is? Wait until Halloween? The kids will all be back by then."

"Halloween?"

"Yeah, some of the kids have called the kidnapper the Thirty-First Trick-or-Treater, said he'll be the last one to come back. There's thirty of them, so he'd be coming back on Halloween."

Paul's nodding along. He lets go of Bob's arm. "Then that's when we'll find him."

"No, I wasn't suggesting—"

An SUV pulls into Bob's driveway. Detective Otto steps out.

Paul says, "Thanks for your help, Bob," and approaches the gray-haired cop.

Detective Otto steps back as Paul approaches, lifts his hand ever so subtly toward his gun, but then Paul stops a respectable distance away.

Bob can't hear their conversation over the wind, but it's short and it's satisfying enough for Paul to shake hands with the detective and then walk away down the sidewalk, nodding to himself.

Detective Otto turns to Bob. The man does not look happy.

Bob waves him over and inside.

∽

Detective Otto's visit is uneventful.

He talks to Bob first, asking why they were visiting Wanda so late (they were chatting and lost track of time), if Bob's sure that the intruder he saw looked like Martin (he is), and how this intruder could have slipped out of the master bedroom if the window remained locked from the inside (Bob has no idea).

Bob gets the sense that Detective Otto doesn't believe him, but that's fair because Bob isn't telling the truth. It's just that the truth involves a disappearing doorway to an impossible location where Bob heard the missing children and where he saw Martin Donovan —not a guy who looks like Martin, but actually the dead guy himself in the not-so-dead flesh. Or the ghost of his flesh. Either way, if he shares that with the detective, they'll think he's crazy enough to play violent pranks, kidnap kids, and kill some of them.

Detective Otto moves on to questioning Sam. It's the same questions as yesterday, and Sam gives the same answers: he and Walter went down the stairs to a hillside with pink fog. He doesn't remember how he got out, only suddenly he was in Wanda's upstairs hallway. He didn't see the kidnapper.

The detective asks him the same questions six ways from Sunday, but Sam sticks to his guns.

When Detective Otto asks Bob and Joann if their son ever has trouble telling real life from imagination, Joann answers curtly. "He lost his sister, got stalked and harassed by the kidnapper before getting snatched away, and then escaped to make his own way back home. You'll have to forgive him if his nightmares have seeped into his memory of reality."

"My apologies," the detective says. "If there's nothing new you can tell me, maybe we reschedule this for another time."

"No," Sam says. "Let me show you where the stairs are."

∽

SAM IS scared that the inside of Old Pine will be full of the Crimson Corridors props again.

He holds Mom's hand as they walk past cops in uniform, through the front doors. Dad is on Sam's other side, carrying Emily. The intimidating Detective Otto walks in front.

They all walk into the lobby.

It's a normal school. Well, one that's been closed for ten years. Dust is caked into the corners. The glass trophy case on the back wall is full of cobwebs.

Sam's heart races at the thought of spiderwebs.

But there's no spiderweb made of sticky rope. No whiteboards carved with warnings to turn back. No science tables littered with dissected frogs.

There's not any pink lights coming up between the tiles, either.

Sam relaxes his grip on Mom's hand.

"You doing okay, honey?" she asks.

"I think so."

Detective Otto clears his throat. "Well? Which way?"

Sam points down the hall to their left. This isn't the way he came in last time, but he still feels confident where he needs to go. It's on the left, two doors down from the lobby. Four, if you count the boys and girls bathrooms.

Detective Otto goes first. He stops at the first door on the right. "This one?"

Sam shakes his head. He points across the hall, down another twenty feet. From this far away, he can just barely see inside the room. A black chalkboard needs cleaning.

The detective walks to the right door.

Sam doesn't move. What if the stairs are gone? What if there's no way back to Mary, and Sam's wasted everybody's time making it even harder to find the missing kids before they get killed?

Emily wiggles in Dad's arms. He says, "Nope, you're staying up here."

Mom says, "You can do it," and leads him to the classroom.

Sam stands in the doorway.

He knows this room. It's not the one he saw before. That was filled with pink fog and had a glowing staircase going down into the middle of the floor.

This one is a dusty room with cinderblock walls painted white and faded. There are two doors in here--one is open to reveal a kindergarten-sized bathroom. The other is a sliding wooden door that's a coat closet.

The room is empty, except for a single desk against the back wall. It's the kind with a cubby under the desktop.

Although the lights are on and the window is letting in sunlight, inside that cubby is as dark as nighttime during a power outage.

Sam knows this classroom, alright. It's where he first saw the Thirty-First Trick-or-Treater, on that video projected onto the TV.

Sam's eyes are glued to the desk, to that deep, black rectangle beneath the desktop.

Detective Otto says, "Well?"

Sam jumps a mile.

"Sorry for that, son. What do you think? Do you remember where you found those stairs?"

Sam takes a step into the room, toward the desk. "It's different."

Mom asks, "Are you sure this is the right one? Every kindergarten classroom looks pretty similar."

"It's this one."

"Maybe the stairs got covered up," Dad stomps around the

room, but each stomp sounds the same. Nothing hollow underneath.

Sam creeps closer to the desk. Something weird about that cubby. It's too deep. And it's angled downward, even though below it, the outer bottom of the cubby is parallel with the floor.

"What'd you spot?" Detective Otto asks.

Dad freezes, looking at the bathroom which is right next to the desk. He thinks that's what's grabbed Sam's attention.

But Sam doesn't care about the bathroom. He wants to see inside this desk.

He walks closer, bending down for a more direct view. Darkness inside, but something more, something pink.

Sam picks up his pace.

"Wait," Dad orders, racing him to the bathroom. But since Dad's going to the wrong spot, Sam makes it to the desk unimpeded.

He drops to his knees too hard. It hurts, but Sam ignores the pain. He puts his face up to the cubby.

Deep into the darkness, farther than Sam can throw a baseball, there's a hint of foggy pink.

It's the hillside.

It makes no sense, but this opening into the desk leads to where Mary is.

Sam reaches his arm in, tries to lift his foot and climb through.

Mom pulls him away. "What are you doing?"

"Mary's down there!"

"It's just a desk," Mom says.

Detective Otto crouches down to peer inside. He reaches in. Sam hears his knuckles rap the bottom of the desktop, his fingernails scrape dust from the bottom of the cubby. "Am I missing something?" he asks.

But Sam still sees that pink fog, so far deep within the darkness. "Do you see it?" he asks Mom.

She shakes her head, tears welling in her eyes.

"Dad?" Sam asks.

Dad squats awkwardly, still holding Emily. "It's a desk," he says.

Emily looks inside, lets out a sound that's between a squeak and a moan, and then buries her face in Dad's shoulders.

"She saw it," Sam says. "Mary's down there. I'll go get her."

But even if Mom let go of him, there's no way he'd actually fit through the opening. His head's too big.

Detective Otto says, "How about we look around some other rooms?"

They think he's crazy, but who cares? He can see the pink fog as if this desk is a window onto that creepy hillside.

He's too big to fit through, but maybe Mary isn't.

He leans in, pushes his face sideways against the opening so the desktop pushes into his right cheek and the metal bottom of the cubby pushes into his left one. He yells for his sister. "Mary! This way! You can get out over here!"

"Okay," Mom says too calmly. She picks up Sam, lifting him up to her shoulder, whisking him out of the classroom.

She won't believe him. He yells over her shoulder and she flinches since it's too close to her ear but he can't think about that right now. He's got to yell loud enough for Mary to hear so she knows where to escape.

He's still yelling his sister's name when Mom carries him outside, with Dad following close behind.

∼

MARY'S HUDDLED in a pink fog, arms around her knees, sitting in the exact spot where Sam's hand slipped out of hers.

She hears her brother's voice from up the hill.

OCTOBER 21ST

MARY SQUINTS, trying to see through the thick pink fog.

She heard Sam's voice, she's sure of it. Loud at first, then quieter, but definitely there.

He didn't leave her. The thought fills her with so much excitement that she almost forgets about her friend, Sofia. But she doesn't forget, because Sofia isn't just Mary's friend. She's her *best* friend.

The way home must be toward Sam's voice, but first she has to go back for Sofia.

Only a second ago, Sam had run up to her where she sat with her best friend. He'd grabbed Mary's hand, yanked her to her feet, and started running.

Then they'd seen Dad and a way out but suddenly Sam's hand wasn't holding hers anymore and she was alone.

No, not alone.

That man was suddenly there, the man with too many names. Jack of the Lantern. The Thirty-First Trick-or-Treater. Stingy Jack. Marty.

He'd been looking down at her, both with the face inside the darkness of his orange hoodie, and with the face carved into his big, white turnip.

"You're not the nineteenth trick-or-treater," he'd said. "Not your turn yet."

"Which one am I?" she'd asked, too scared to look up.

He didn't answer. When she finally gathered the courage to open her eyes, he was gone.

And then Sam had shouted for her.

Mary stands. She's scared to go up the hill. The kids who the man takes up there don't come back. But that's how she'll get to Sam, and Sam will keep her safe. He's her big brother.

"I'm coming," she yells so Sam will keep waiting, then she goes back for her best friend.

Thin pink fog lingers around her. A few hours ago, when she got here, she could hardly see through it, but now it adds color to everything rather than blocking her view.

The field around her is like the hill beside the playground, next to the woods. Here there aren't any woods, though, just grass as tall as Mary's waist. A few kids got scared when the man came for them and they ran down the hill.

But Mary's afraid of whatever's down there, even more than she's afraid of going uphill. Worst of all, on this hillside, there's nowhere to hide. All Mary can do is sit in the mist and hope she's small enough to not get noticed.

She looks around for her friend Sofia.

Mary didn't know Sofia before going trick-or-treating, but now she loves her. Sofia is also four—just like Mary. She has curly hair like Mary's, but hers is a dark shiny brown.

For the past few hours, since they all got stuck here in this pink room, Sofia has sang songs and played games with Mary.

As Mary walks back, she worries that Sofia might have found a new best friend. Or what if she walked downhill, or the Thirty-First Trick-or-Treater came and took her away?

There are other kids on this hill, but none of them are Mary's best friend. She'll be alone. She doesn't want to march up the hill alone.

But Mary finds the spot of grass they'd flattened together, that they'd called their "nest," and there's Sofia.

Sofia's eyes are puffy. She's been crying, which makes Mary worry.

Mary runs up to her friend. "What's wrong?" She thinks maybe another kid got taken away.

"You left me!" Sofia cries.

Mary doesn't quite understand. Sofia's the one who's been taking care of Mary, helping her not be too scared, helping her stay away from the Thirty-First Trick-or-Treater. Why would she be scared that Mary left? Still, Mary says, "I'm sorry." She doesn't want to make Sofia sad.

"Where'd that boy go?" Sofia asks.

"Sam's my brother."

"Where'd he go?"

"There was a door. My dad was here but Sam pushed him out the door."

"A door in the grass?"

"Above the grass. In the air."

"You didn't want to go, too?"

The question makes Mary sad. "I did want to go. Sam held me tight but the door closed."

Sofia gasps and grabs Mary's hand to inspect it. "Did you squish your fingers?"

"No," says Mary, suddenly grateful. It does hurt when a door slams on your fingers.

"Do you want to pretend like you did squish them, and we can play hospital and I'll be the doctor?"

"Yes!" That sounds fun. This is why Mary likes being best friends with Sofia. But then she remembers, "I heard Sam up the hill. He's yelling for me. Let's go find him."

Sofia frowns. "You said he went out a door."

"He came back."

"What if Stingy Jack comes?"

This is why the idea makes Mary nervous, but she has a plan. "We'll hide in the grass."

"Does your brother know how to get home?"

Mary considers this. "He must. He went away but now he came back, so he must know how to get home."

Sofia nods, which Mary appreciates. She wasn't sure about her faith in Sam, but Sofia agrees, so it must be okay.

"We can go find him," Sofia says.

Mary waits for Sofia to walk in front, but Sofia's waiting for her. They hold hands and walk together.

They pass an older boy who's got his arms wrapped around his chest real tight. He's singing the song from *Mickey Mouse Clubhouse*. Mary thinks maybe he's nice if he likes that song, but when she slows down, Sofia tugs her along.

"When we get to your house," Sofia says, "we can call my Mom. I remember most of her phone number."

But the hillside keeps going.

There's a group of three older girls. They're sitting in a circle with their eyes closed, all whispering. It's kinda creepy to Mary, but Sofia says, "They're praying. We have to whisper."

As Mary and Sofia go by, one of the older girls opens her eyes and sees them. "Have you been here the whole time? Do you need help?"

"We're going home," Sofia says. "To her house."

"Come sit with us," the older girl says.

Mary doesn't want to.

Sofia whispers to Mary, "Can they come to your house, too?"

Before Mary can decide, the older girl screams.

Mary frantically looks around. Sofia squeezes her hand so hard it hurts.

The older girl's friends join in the screaming.

Sofia points up the hill.

Mary looks, already knowing who she'll see.

The first thing she sees is a face glowing pink—triangle eyes and a smiling mouth. It's up in the air, taller than even Dad, but

Mary's been tricked by this before. She squints to look deeper into the pink mist, and there's the man in the orange hoodie that hides his face. He turns his funny-shaped jack-o-lantern back and forth, aiming the glowing face first at Mary and Sofia, and then at the circle of older girls.

When those triangle eyes point at Mary, she feels cold like when she opens the freezer to sneak ice cream. She tries to hide behind Sofia, but Sofia tries to hide behind her, and so they end up hugging each other which is okay, too.

Mary closes her eyes and listens to the Thirty-First Trick-or-Treater's tennis shoes *shush* through the grass, getting closer.

Sofia whimpers and Mary feels herself making the same noise.

She hears those footsteps right behind her, close enough for the man to put the jack-o-lantern right in her face, to let those triangle eyes stare right into hers. Then he keeps on walking past.

The older girls scream. One of them yells, "Carolyn!"

The girl who invited them over screams loudest of all, her voice jerked around.

Sofia pulls on Mary and they're running up the hillside, away from the terrified older girls behind them and the trick-or-treater who's taken someone else.

Mary can't hold back the sobs anymore. She's running and the pink hillside is blurry from her tears and she can't breathe from her nose for the snot and she's choking as she tries to gasp but they have to run and get away from the Thirty-First Trick-or-Treater before he grabs them, too.

OCTOBER 22ND

"Wait for me!" Mary can't keep up with Sofia. Her friend is running too fast, still holding her hand but now Mary is reaching as far forward as she can, holding tight but it feels like Sofia isn't holding on at all.

Sofia looks back. She's got tears all over her cheeks and snot running over her mouth. She jerks her hand out of Mary's.

Panic explodes inside Mary. She screams and sobs and reaches for her friend. She thinks Sofia will run away and leave her behind but Sofia slows down. Mary's not expecting that so she crashes into her. Their heads bump and they fall to the ground. The dirt sinks enough so the fall doesn't hurt but they start to roll downhill.

Mary can't go downhill.

Other kids went downhill to get away from the Thirty-First Trick-or-Treater, and they never came back up.

Mary kicks her toes into the dirt, her new black shoes digging in enough to stop her roll. She holds tight to Sofia's hand.

Sofia immediately pushes herself up to look uphill. "He's gone," she says.

Mary turns around. Through the mist, she can make out a pair of older girls weeping together.

The nice one is gone.

Mary and Sofia sit far away from the older girls but they cry with them.

Mary cries until she can't anymore.

It was only a few hours ago that she was trick-or-treating. The yard with Jack the Pumpkin King and Sally and Zero was so *cool*. Sam would have said it's *skibidi* if he liked it, but *Nightmare Before Christmas* is Mary's favorite movie, not Sam's.

Anyone who decorated their yard like that had to be giving out amazing candy. Sam was tired and didn't want to knock on anymore doors, but Mary wanted to go. Even though she was nervous to go by herself, she did it, which Dad was really happy about.

But Mary's not sure what happened next. She ran through the yard, between Jack and Sally, rang the doorbell, and then she was here.

She's still wearing her Elphaba costume that Mom made, but she doesn't have her candy bag anymore—one of the older boys took it.

Now it's been hours and that scary man keeps taking kids, and Mary is so tired and she wants Dad to pick her up and take her home.

The shoulder of Mary's dress is wet with Sofia's tears and Sofia's shoulder is wet with Mary's tears.

Mary's sobs drift away. She's still sitting here on this hillside.

Sam might still be uphill, waiting to take her home.

"Come on," she says and gets up. Her butt is wet from the ground.

Sofia looks up the hill, checking for the trick-or-treater. "Do you remember where you heard your brother?"

"This way."

Even though Sofia is braver, Mary leads the way into the pink fog.

∼

THEY'VE WALKED TOO FAR.

Grass is breaking under Mary's feet. Her shoes push into the soft dirt, releasing a smell like when Mom cleans the kitchen sink drain.

Mary slows down.

Sofia's hand is warm in hers. Her best friend turns back to see why she's slowed down.

"He didn't sound this far away," Mary says.

Sofia looks back into the pink fog. "Did we pass him?"

"I don't know which way to go," Mary says.

From uphill comes the soft sound of dry grass breaking.

Mary freezes. Sofia gasps so loudly that Mary wonders how far the sound travels.

The sound of dry grass breaking becomes more distinct. There's a rhythm to it: footsteps.

"He's coming again," Mary hisses.

They run, hand in hand, and Mary thinks how they're running farther away from where the door was, away from where she heard Sam yelling. They're not running downhill or uphill, but along the hillside. Mary hasn't thought about what's this way.

The footsteps grow faster, louder.

Sofia cries out, "He's getting closer!"

Mary runs faster than she ever has before. She tenses her thighs, pumps her left arm (her right hand is holding tight to Sofia's left), even lowers her head—all the things that Sam says make you run faster—but Mary looks back up the hill to see glowing pink triangle eyes and a toothless grin bouncing through the air, swooping down on her like a hungry bird.

Mary collapses, covering her head but refusing to let go of Sofia's hand, so she pulls her friend on top of her.

They bonk heads but her pain is small compared to her terror.

Sofia lifts off her, not getting up but being picked up by the trick-or-treater. Mary clings to her friend's hand, grabs for her dress, but the man jerks Sofia away.

Mary lunges after them.

The man is too fast, even though he's not running, only taking big, loping steps, left arm held forward above his head with the jack-o-lantern dangling from his hand.

Sofia wiggles in his right arm.

He squeezes her tighter. It looks like it hurts.

Mary runs after them. The man terrifies her but being left on this hillside without her best friend is even scarier.

She doesn't have any clue what'll happen once she catches up. Still, she runs up the hill, after the fast-walking man and her struggling friend.

Mary's legs start to burn. She's never run uphill for so long. She ignores the pain. She won't let Sofia out of her sight.

The man is moving faster than she can. His form becomes less clear as he moves farther away in the fog. She's losing him. She's losing Sofia.

Mary lets out a loud sob, too loud. The man will hear her. But he either doesn't or he doesn't care.

He keeps right on marching up the hill, jack-o-lantern held high against the fog, Sofia tucked firmly under his arm, until they disappear completely.

Cold fear washes over Mary. She's alone.

But she keeps running. She won't be left by herself.

The hill is so steep and her legs are so tired. She slows down until she's nearly walking but it's the fastest her muscles will carry her.

Dad would say, "If you need to do something hard, keep your head in your head and your body in your body, and push right on through it," and so Mary climbs up through the pink darkness, pain in muscles she's never once thought about.

The fog thickens around her. She feels pink moisture on her cheeks and her hands. Her eyes sting.

It's so bright.

No. There's brightness coming from up ahead. It's not all of the fog—just a long and low rectangle.

Mary climbs closer.

There's a line of glass doors in the field. Dry grass and pink fog press up against the glass on this side. On the other side is a sidewalk. It's nighttime but there's yellow light from street lamps. There's a crowd of people. Mary sees her preschool teacher, Mrs. Eikhorn, and there's the mom and dad of one of her friends she plays with on the playground. Are her own mom and dad out there? Are Sam and Emily?

She lifts one heavy foot and then the other, aiming herself at those doors.

The Thirty-First Trick-or-Treater is already there. He's still holding the jack-o-lantern in the air. Now he's standing sideways to the doors, Sofia still struggling under his arm, and he's trying to work the door handle with his hand at hip level. It reminds Mary of Mom trying to open the car door handle while holding Emily.

The man gets the door open. Cold wind blows from the other side. Then he does something that shocks Mary: he puts down Sofia. He keeps a firm hand on her shoulder so she can't run. Then he ushers her through the open doorway.

Mary is still plodding her way up the hill, as fast as she can, when Sofia goes all the way through. The people outside all yell when they see her.

Mary won't be left behind.

She closes her eyes, keeping her head in her head and her body in her body, and pushes her legs as fast as she can. She's running for the door before the man can close it. Her sense of balance flutters like a butterfly. She'll have to open her eyes before she gets close so she can slip past the scary man, but if she opens her eyes now then her head and her body will get all mixed up and her legs will give up and she'll fall over and she'll lose Sofia.

Mary crashes into something hard. It's the trick-or-treater's leg.

His voice is higher and soft. "What the hell?" His hood tilts forward as he looks down at her.

Mary still only sees shadow under that hood. She's not sure there's anything else there.

But she only looks for a moment before she's running past him, using her hands to push off his legs to get some actual momentum since her legs are so tired. She runs beneath his jack-o-lantern.

He grabs at her with his other hand, reaching across his body too slowly. "You're not the twenty-second!"

The glass door swings closed behind Mary, colliding with her shoulder, knocking her through.

There's a soft hiss as the door closes its last inch.

Mary's caught up to her friend. "Sofia," she says.

Sofia turns around. Her face is smeared and puffy from crying. There's blood at her fingertips from scratching at the trick-or-treater. The corners of her mouth are turned down and quivering. "He said he's coming through soon."

People are shouting and it's loud but Mary's so glad she caught up to Sofia. She steps toward her friend and her legs completely give out. She falls to the floor, which is cold tile.

Doors open up both behind and in front of the girls.

Mary panics that the Thirty-First Trick-or-Treater is coming after them but the doors don't go back to the pink hillside anymore. Now they open up to a dirty school.

It's a policeman coming through the doors, who must be the biggest hero in the world.

More grownups approach from the other direction. Someone really happy says Sofia's name and then Sofia is lifted off the floor.

The hero policeman kneels down next to Mary.

"Can you hear me? Are you hurt?"

"My legs are tired," she says.

And then Mom's face is over hers. "Mary? It's you! Are you okay? Is she okay? She's breathing isn't she?"

Dad's face is there, too. "I'm so sorry I didn't go with you. I'm so sorry."

"She's okay," the hero policeman says, "the others were gone as soon as they arrived. She's not like them."

"Are you sure?" Dad asks.

"I... look, here's the paramedics."

More grownups crowd around her. Based on their blue shirts

and skinny flashlights, these are the doctors who come to your house in ambulances. But she thought they were for emergencies, not for when your legs are tired.

Mom and Dad hold her hands as the paramedics put her onto a stretcher.

Now that she's with her parents again, everything will be okay.

Except there's still two things she's worried about. She tries to sit up but a paramedic gently holds her down. "Stay still, babygirl."

"I want to go with Sofia."

Mom looks over her shoulder. "Is Sofia the girl you came back with?"

Dad answers for Mary. "Sofia Fuentes. They're two houses up from us."

Mary didn't know that. Maybe Sofia can come over and play.

"We're all going to the hospital," says Mom. "Sofia will be there, too."

Dad frowns at Mom but Mary isn't concerned about that right now. She's got another problem she wants Dad to fix for her.

"An older boy took my candy bag."

Dad laughs and leans down to hug her, prompting a frustrated sound from the paramedics. "I'll buy you all the candy in the world."

OCTOBER 23RD

Bob can't stop kissing Sam on the top of the head, or squeezing Joann's hand, or picking up Emily to hug her.

Of course, in this hospital room that smells like antiseptic and is bathed in garish fluorescent lights, he also keeps a hand on Mary, in her big bed with its stiff white sheets.

His relief is manifesting as gratitude for the whole world, and that's manifesting as physical affection for his family.

Mary's been sleeping fitfully. She wakes and holds Bob's hand, or lets her fingers explore the roughness of his cast.

Joann sits in the armchair beneath the white curtains which hold back the night. Sam is squished in next to her, head propped back against her arm. Emily sits sideways, butt on Joann's lap, legs across Sam's. She's asleep against Joann's chest, hair sweaty and matted on her forehead.

Joann is still awake. It's not the middle of the night anymore but there's not quite sunlight coming through the window.

Bob catches his wife's eye, over top of their daughter who has come back to them, who is fine, who was dehydrated and exhausted but who is fine.

He and Joann sink into each other's smiles, expressions that say,

"If I weren't attached to our children right now, I would hold you tight," but that also say, "My life is perfect in this moment because we are attached to our children."

Their nurse's name is Claire. She comes in and Bob has to remove his hand from Mary's. Claire is younger than Bob by at least ten years—she can't be more than a few years out of school. But this is Claire's kingdom and Bob is appreciative that she's here to once again check the monitors and say that Mary is okay. He's also looking forward to an hour from now when Claire will return to do it all again.

As they checked into the hospital, Detective Otto approached them in the waiting room to say that he wanted to interview Mary once she was recovered. That part, Bob isn't excited about. He doesn't want to ask Mary to relive the eleven months and twenty-three days she was gone.

But even as he has that thought, he knows he can't commit to it.

There are seven children still missing. Bob knows that he and Joann will let Detective Otto interview Mary and he knows that he'll ask her plenty of questions himself.

But for now, while Mary sleeps, and Joann cradles their other kids, and the nurse comes every hour to declare that everything is fine, Bob sits still and appreciates life.

~

THEY SERVE donuts with breakfast in the hospital. Sam thinks that's weird. Aren't donuts unhealthy?

Sunlight had avalanched through the thin curtains to wake them up. Sam feels sweaty and stiff from sleeping sitting up in the chair, so he's doing jumping jacks. Emily copies him but she hasn't finished her donut so she flings crumbs everywhere.

Mary is looking past the nurse, who's reattaching black velcro to her arm, which Mary apparently took off before she was supposed to. "I want to get down," she says.

"In a few minutes," Mom tells her.

Mom is next to Mary's bed and Dad is in the armchair asleep.

Sam hasn't talked to Mary yet. He kissed her on the cheek last night, after Aunt Polly got him and Emily out of bed to take them to the hospital, but Mary was already asleep at that point.

Now she's awake and Sam thought he'd want to play with her but he feels nervous. One way he deals with nervousness is by acting like a good big brother. He picks up Emily and brings her over next to the bed. "This is your sister, Mary," he tells Emily. "I told you about her."

Mary's eyes widen. "Emily?"

"That's right," Mom says. "You remember your little sister."

Mary shakes her head. "She's too big." Mary looks at Sam. "You're too tall."

Sam looks down at himself, as if he'll spot whatever strangeness his sister is seeing.

"Everybody looks perfect," Mom says.

Nurse Claire finishes putting the velcro cuff on Mary's arm. She pushes a button on a tower of electronics and computer screens, and there's a rumbling hum as the cuff inflates. "You know," she says, "you two girls could almost be twins."

Sam's hit with memories of strangers often saying that about Mary and Emily. He'd always thought it was stupid. Yes, they both had blonde hair, but Emily's was curlier, and the most obvious thing was that Mary was a lot older than Emily—almost two whole years! Emily's always had chubbier cheeks and her head looks bigger compared to her body.

But now as Nurse Claire says his sisters look like twins, she's *right*. Emily's hair is still curlier, but now Mary doesn't look so much older. Emily's cheeks aren't so chubby anymore, and her ratio of head size to body size is less *toddler* and more *little girl*.

Mom notices the same thing. "They're looking more like each other as they get older." But she says it funny, because she sees it, too.

Emily is older than the last time they saw Mary, but Mary isn't.

Her Halloween costume from last year is on a table in the

corner. She was still wearing it. He goes over and picks up the black dress, gives it a good sniff. It doesn't smell dirty.

"Mary, how long were you gone?" he asks.

"I don't know," Mary says.

"All the kids have been confused about time," Nurse Claire says. "I assume it takes a few days to feel like everything's normal again."

Sam talks through Nurse Claire's excuses. "Mary, how many days was it? How many times did you sleep?"

When he ran down those stairs in Old Pine, he'd seen Mary, grabbed her, seen Dad, and then ran for him. But when he'd left that pink, misty hillside, several days had passed.

So Sam isn't surprised when Mary answers, "I didn't sleep. Me and Sofia played."

Mom's getting Sam's point. "How long did you play?" she asks.

Mary says, "I don't know."

Mom clarifies the question. "How many movies could you have watched?"

"We didn't watch movies."

"But if you did, how many could you have watched in the time that you were gone?"

"When I was with Sofia in the pink place?"

"Right."

Mary smiles nervously. This is a silly question that has an obvious answer so it must be that Mom is playing a joke. "Three?"

Mom gasps ever so softly. "Not a hundred?"

That's supremely funny to Mary. Sam loves her giggle so much that he joins in. Emily—who has continued to act shy of Mary up to this point—loosens up in Sam's arms and adds her own belly laugh.

"No," Mary says. "Not a hundred. That's so many movies."

"Oh thank God," Mom whispers, then more loudly she asks, "So you weren't alone and scared for a year. Only a few hours."

Sam recognizes the silly shrug that Mary gives. Usually it's when Dad asks her some adult question that she doesn't know the answer to, like "should I claim the standard deduction on my taxes?" and Mary knows the proper response is to join in the joke.

But Sam also hears the content of Mom's non-question: it's a good thing that Mary wasn't gone a whole year.

Sam gets a deep fear that he's been wishing for the wrong thing this past year. He's been wishing he could find Mary, and that wasn't enough. If he found Mary just normal then she would have been scared forever or starved to death. So this is even better than finding Mary. She's scared but it's only been a few hours and so she won't be scared forever. And obviously she didn't starve to death.

But she could have.

But Mary thinks Mom's questions are a joke and that means she's okay. It doesn't matter how close it came. Everything is okay now.

Except.

Walter is still gone.

All the other kids are still gone. They'll come back one each night—hopefully alive—but what about Walter? Does he get to come back, too?

Sam tries to remember what happened to his new friend once they went down those stairs and onto that pink hillside.

"Is he here?" Walter had asked, talking about the hoodied teenager who he'd seen in Crimson Corridors last year and been mocked for telling people about.

When they'd run along that pink hillside and Walter asked that question, had Sam answered?

He doesn't think so. He'd seen Mary right away, sitting next to another little girl. Was Sam a bad person because he hadn't tried to help her, too? Not that it ended up mattering. He hadn't even been able to help Mary.

Sam reminds himself that he's standing next to Mary right now. He wasn't the one who'd brought her back. He hadn't fixed his mistake of letting her trick-or-treat that house by herself, but she was still back.

He asks, "Is Sofia the girl you were with when I grabbed you?"

Mary says, "Yes! Is she okay? She's my best friend."

Mary looks at Mom, who looks at Nurse Claire.

Nurse Claire nods. "You can ask her for yourself. She's two rooms down."

Mary starts to get up.

Nurse Claire says, "I meant your brother. You stay in bed until the doctor comes. Once he checks a few things, then you can go home."

She motions to the door with her eyes, but Sam doesn't move.

"Ask her if she wants to come play," Mary says.

Mom shakes her head. "Wait until Dad wakes up. I'm not ready for any of you to be out of my sight just yet."

Nurse Claire says, "Oh, I'm so sorry. I should have asked before suggesting he go wandering off. Your daughter's friend is doing great. Nothing wrong with her, but don't tell anyone I told you that. HIPAA, you know?"

"Of course," Mom says. "Thank you."

Mary's extra happy now, but Sam's got a knot in his gut. It's growing.

It was his fault that Mary got taken away, but it's *really* his fault that Walter is gone. Walter got into this whole mess because of him.

But even that's not the core of what's bothering him. There are other kids still missing, and they might not come back alive. He can't leave them all alone, either.

Dad will understand. When Dad wakes up, Sam will talk to Dad, and they'll figure out what to do next.

∽

BOB WAKES up in the stiff hospital armchair.

Someone is screaming.

Sam and Emily are sitting on either side of Mary on her hospital bed. They're watching cartoons. Or they were, but now they're wide-eyed, looking at the door.

Joann is in the plastic chair next to the bed, twisted around to look at the door herself.

It's cracked open, which lets in the scream crystal clear.

Mary tries to get up. "That's Sofia!"
Joann holds her down.
Sofia's scream descends into frantic crying.
A nurse runs past the door.
Bob stands up.
"Leave them be," Joann says. "What are you going to do?"
"Shut our door." But Bob's not sure what his intentions are. He walks across the room. Sam hops down from the bed to join him.

His son had been searching for Mary, too. He's as invested as Bob is, so Bob doesn't tell him to stay.

Someone who was there with Mary is having a meltdown. He's heard that some of the children freak out after they're home. Bob wants to know why.

So he doesn't close the door. He goes out into the hallway. Out here the lights are garish. The tile floor is yellow and speckled and the walls are decorated with children's art.

Sam is at Bob's side. In a strange way, Bob feels like he's got another partner at his side. An in-person partner, not his amateur investigator YouTube viewers and not Officer Karl via messaging apps.

The door to Sofia's hospital room is wide open. Her sobs are pouring out from it.

Nurse Claire rushes past Bob and Sam, into the room.

There's a chorus of adults in there, cooing that everything's okay now.

But Bob and Sam hear Sofia's words.

This is the commotion that they've heard about—what happens in the hospital after the kids come back.

Bob and Sam stand in Sofia's doorway.

There's four adults at her bedside—parents and step-parents. The little girl has curly brown hair and bangs and thick glasses. She's clinging to a round woman in sweats, who's sobbing and promising her daughter that everything's okay.

Sofia is looking around frantically. She's blinking and covering her eyes like she just woke up, and that's probably what this is—

she's been asleep until now, but upon waking a horrible memory has returned.

"He's coming back," Sofia cries. "He wants everyone in Maple Creek!"

～

A DOCTOR with too many patients and too little time evaluates Mary.

"Water, Gatorade, rest. Stretch those legs. I don't mean exercise, I literally mean stretching."

Bob hears Joann say, "Got it," and then ask a question which Bob doesn't hear because he's messaging Officer Karl.

"What the fuck? When were you going to tell me that the COMMOTION these kids are causing when they come back is that they're warning that the damn kidnapper said he's coming for everyone?"

The doctor answers Joann's question, more background noise.

"Okay," Joann says. "Okay."

Bob still has his messaging app open when Karl responds. *"They're kids. They're scared of their kidnapper. It's a non-issue."*

Bob starts to type a furious response, then realizes that both Joann and the doctor are looking at him, expectantly. All three of his kids, too. "Um, sorry. I wasn't listening."

"You alright?" Joann asks.

"Fine."

"I was saying that it's a miracle your daughter is okay. And it seems she's skipped the commotion that all the other kids have gone through."

"You've told the police about that, right?"

"Of course," the doctor says.

"Is that what they've all yelled?" Bob asks. "That the Thirty-First Trick-or-Treater is coming back for everyone this Halloween?"

The doctor adjusts his collar. He looks at his iPad. "I can't disclose details about other patients."

"You mean the answer is 'yes.'"

"I didn't say that at all."

"If the cops aren't warning people that the same thing is about to happen this Halloween, don't you think *you* ought to?"

"These are children with trauma. It doesn't mean it's real."

Bob can't believe this guy's denial. "Where do you think they've been for the past year? Something *real* had my kids until they got away."

Joann touches Bob's arm. "Hey."

The calm of his reunited family brings him back to himself. His daughters are on the bed, eyes wide with fear at their dad's outburst. His son is next to him, leaning forward to soak in Bob's righteous indignation.

"Sorry," Bob whispers.

Things are different now. His kids are home. It's no longer okay to plow through whoever gets in his way. Now there are means that the ends won't justify. His family is safe, so now his biggest duty is to keep them safe, and that doesn't require hopping over social guardrails like he had when Mary and Sam were missing.

His family deserves to feel safe, so he can't be screaming at other adults in front of his kids.

"Let's step outside," Bob suggests to the doctor.

"I've got six other patients to see in the next half-hour," the doctor says. "You're welcome to send me an email. You can find the address on the hospital website."

Bob says nothing as the doctor leaves.

"Thank you," Joann calls after him.

Bob takes a deep breath. It's easy to push away the anger because this room is still full of his healthy, safe family. "You guys ready to go home?"

"Is Sofia okay?" Mary asks for the twentieth time.

"She had a nightmare." Bob tells himself he's only slightly exaggerating. "But she's okay now."

"Can she come over and play?"

"Not today, honey," Joann says.

"When?"

"Soon," Bob says. "Let's get home. I'm sure Emily would love to show you her most recent birthday presents."

Emily springs up in excitement.

She's treating Mary like she does any visitor who she doesn't know: shy nervousness progressing to excitement about the novelty of a new friend.

Bob is simultaneously heartbroken that his daughters don't know each other anymore, and ecstatic that Emily gets to slowly realize that her new friend will be hers for life. "Alright. Everybody up. I want to go home."

There's a knock at the door. Detective Otto walks in.

∽

SAM IS sick of Detective Otto.

He hasn't believed a word Sam has told him. He made Sam feel like a baby for screaming for Mary into that desk.

Detective Otto wears jeans and a black shirt instead of a uniform. His badge is on his belt. He's bigger than Dad—taller and wider. His voice booms a little like the Wizard of Oz's, but without the echo.

So when Detective Otto claims the plastic chair next to Mary's bed, Sam climbs up onto the sheets next to his sister.

Dad stands next to Sam, arm overtop of him with his hand resting on Mary's shoulder.

"Sam," Mom says. "Come on over here."

Sam shakes his head. He keeps his gaze on Detective Otto, staring him down alongside Dad.

"It's fine," the policeman says. "Sam's heard a few of these questions already since we talked a few days ago."

Dad says, "We'd like to get home. But I'll admit I'm a little worried that there's a threat to the entire Maple Creek neighborhood that you've been ignoring."

"You mean what the returned kids have been saying?"

Sam feels anger radiate off of Dad at such a dumb question. "Of course that's what he means," Sam says.

"Sam," Mom snaps. Her tone is scarier than Detective Otto.

Sam zips his lips. For now.

"We haven't been ignoring any threats," the policeman says. "Do you know how much overtime we've been paying to have constant patrols up and down your streets? And trust me, on Halloween, there won't be a spot you can stand in Maple Creek without seeing two different officers."

Sam looks up at Dad. Those sound like good promises to Sam, but he's not sure.

Dad blinks real slow. "Oh my god. You're counting on the kidnapper showing up on Halloween. That's why you've been dragging your feet in this investigation. Why risk scaring him off now if you can set a trap for him on the thirty-first?"

"No, Mister Wilson. That's not what we've been doing. Children are dying. We've been searching. The state troopers and FBI are assisting us—at our request. We're taking this very seriously."

Sam looks up at Dad again. His mouth is a short, straight line. He doesn't believe the policeman. Sam looks back at Detective Otto. Of course Dad doesn't believe him. Look at his face. Nobody who's telling the truth has an angry smile like that.

"If you're done with your questions," Detective Otto says, "then I have a few I'll ask your daughter."

"Go ahead." Dad walks out.

"Bob," Mom says, and for a moment Sam is scared that she's going to follow him, leaving Sam the only one to protect Mary from Detective Otto, but then Mom sighs. "I'm sorry about that. It's been a shitty year, you know?"

"One hundred percent okay," Detective Otto says. "No offense taken. I always say, once you've been shot during a routine traffic stop, there's no words anyone can say that'll hurt too bad."

He laughs. Sam doesn't like how it's all scratchy and loud.

"Mary?" Mom asks gently. "Are you okay to talk to Detective Otto for a minute?"

Mary shrinks sideways into Sam's arm, which he lifts to put

around her. Sam doesn't try to convince her that everything's okay. After all, a large, loud man just laughed largely and loudly right in their faces. But Mary does relax.

The policeman begins his questions.

"Where'd you go when you disappeared while trick-or-treating?"

Mary doesn't answer, but this time Sam whispers, "It's okay."

Mary says, "A field with pink grass. On a hill."

Detective Otto nods. He's heard this before. "Who was there?"

"Sofia," Mary says.

"I spoke with Sofia. She says you were a great friend to her when you both got scared. I'm sure your mommy and daddy are very proud of you."

He's talking to her like a baby, which make Sam hate him even more.

"Did you see this boy?" He shows Mary a picture on his phone. It's of Calvin from Sam's class last year, who came back dead.

Mary nods.

Detective Otto leans forward in his chair. He's excited. No one's answered 'yes' to that question before. "Can you tell me about when you saw him?"

"He took my candy."

That's not a surprise to Sam. Calvin wasn't a close friend for a reason.

"What happened after he took your candy?"

"He ran away with it."

"And after that?"

"I saw him go down the hill."

"*Down* the hill? Didn't the trick-or-treater take kids *up* the hill?"

Mary didn't say that, so he must be going off what other kids have said. Sam doesn't think he's asking questions in the right order. He's starting to understand Dad's comments about the police, the ones that Mom shushes.

Mary nods. "Nobody took him down the hill. He just went."

"What happened once he went down there?"

"I don't know."

"Did you see him again?"

She shakes her head.

Detective Otto shows her another picture. "Did you see this little girl?"

Sam recognizes her as another of the dead kids.

Mary nods again. "Only for a minute. She looked scared."

"Did she go down the hill?"

"I don't know. I didn't see."

The detective goes through several more photos with Mary, all of the dead kids. Mary recognizes two of them, but only saw one go down the hill.

Sam sees where the detective is going with this, and it makes sense to him. There's a pattern to which kids came back dead—they went down the hill. Mary didn't see all of them because you can't see for shit in that pink fog, but Sam is pretty sure that Detective Otto has nailed it.

He moves on to another subject of questions. "Who took you to that place?"

"I don't know," Mary says.

"The trick-or-treater?" he prompts.

"We were all trick-or-treaters. He said he's the thirty-first."

"When he grabbed you, did you see him?"

"He never grabbed me. I chased him when he took Sofia."

"And that was very brave of you. But I'm asking about when you were trick-or-treating and he took you there at the beginning."

"I didn't see him until I was already in the field."

He's visibly disappointed. "The kids who were with you—not the ones in the pictures I showed you, but everyone else. How did they leave?"

Sam can tell he already knows the answer to this question.

"The Thirty-First Trick-or-Treater came and took them up the hill."

"What does he look like?"

"He has a candy bucket. It looks like a pumpkin."

"A jack-o-lantern?"

"Well, not really. It's not orange. It's white. And it's shaped like a heart."

"A turnip," Sam says.

Detective Otto glances over at Sam blankly. Sam takes it as instruction to stay quiet, which he resents.

The detective asks Mary, "Why do you call him the 'Thirty-First?'"

She crinkles her eyebrow. "I told you. He said it."

"Oh right. And did you see his face?"

"No," Mary says.

"You called him 'he.' Are you sure he's a boy?"

"Yes."

"Why?"

"Because he's a boy."

"Did he talk to you?"

"Yes. He said it wasn't my turn."

The detective tilts his head. "He didn't say anything else before he pushed you through the doors?"

"He didn't push me. I chased him when he took Sofia."

"Oh, that's right." Detective Otto gives Mary an open mouth grin. He looks over at Joann. "You've got a brave little girl. Nobody else has done that."

Mom nods. "She's something else."

"I guess that explains why two of you showed up on one night."

Mary withdraws into Sam. He realizes that she doesn't know what the detective is talking about. To her, she was only there for a few hours.

Sam's proud of Mary. She's shy, but she's not afraid of doing what she wants.

"One more really big question," the detective says. "Can you tell me anything else about this trick-or-treater? Anything else he said, or what he sounded like, or smelled like, or where he went when he wasn't grabbing one of you?"

Mary stretches her mouth to the side when she thinks. "He's really mad."

∼

BOB LEAVES MARY'S ROOM, letting his family and Detective Otto think that he's storming out in anger.

He goes over to Sofia's room, taps his knuckle on the frame, and slips inside.

The bed looks as big around Sofia as Mary's does around her. Sofia sits on the edge, lollipop turning her mouth blue. A woman with the same lifted nose and dark brown hair sits next to her—Sofia's mom.

A man with Sofia's curved jawbone sits on the couch, next to a woman whose angular features mark her as the stepmom. That's Carlos, who lives on their street.

The stepdad who Bob saw earlier isn't here anymore.

Sofia and her parents look up at Bob as he walks in.

"Who are you?" Sofia's mom asks.

"I'm Mary's dad."

Sofia's face lights up. She leans forward to see around Bob. "Where's Mary?"

"A couple rooms down. I'm hoping you can tell me about what you saw when you were gone. Especially what you heard."

Carlos stands up. "Sofia already talked to Detective Otto. Who did you say you are?"

"I'm Mary's dad. Apparently, our daughters kept each other safe when they were gone."

Sofia's mom says, "Let's get them together. But right now we're about to go home. My husband is getting the car."

"I'm worried the kidnapper—the trick-or-treater—isn't done yet."

The stepmom scoffs. "Then talk to Detective Otto. Leave our baby alone."

Sofia speaks up. "Is he coming back to get me again?"

Carlos steps toward Bob. "Get out."

"What did he tell you?" Bob asks Sofia.

"He wants everyone in Maple Creek," Sofia says.

Now both mom and stepmom are on their feet and there's three adults corralling Bob back toward the door.

"Why?" Bob asks.

"I don't know. He sounded so mad."

"At who?"

Sofia's mom positions herself in between Bob and her daughter, blocking his view, but the little girl still answers, "At everyone who left him inside the wall."

A thousand more questions jump into Bob's head. *Everyone?* How many people were involved in his murder?

"Who left him there?" Bob asks.

Mom, dad, and stepmom now physically push Bob back toward the door.

"Wait," Bob begs. "If she knows something, we can rescue the other kids. We can stop it from happening again, or stop whatever worse thing he's planning for Halloween."

"Ask your own daughter," the mom says.

Carlos adds, "After you get out."

Sofia is apparently enthusiastic about preventing Martin from coming back. She shouts over her parents. "He's mad at the lady with all the Halloween dollhouses!"

Bob remembers, twenty-three days ago, looking inside Sariah Fisher's house, the woman who was never away from home until that night. And what did he see in the basement but a model Halloween village, porcelain and plastic figurines of haunted houses, spooky carousels, and classic ghouls. There was even an electric train with a ghost conductor.

He doesn't have any idea why Martin Donovan would be angry at Sariah Fisher, or why that anger would have inspired him to kidnap thirty children and kill several of them.

Sofia's parents take advantage of Bob's confusion to push him out into the hallway.

The elevator dings.

Bob barely notices. He's got to tell Joann. He needs to ask Officer Karl if he knows anything about Sariah or how she's connected to Martin.

Sofia's stepdad walks out of the elevator, happily tossing his keys to himself. He smiles at Bob. "It's Bob, right? Helluva good day, isn't it?"

OCTOBER 24TH

FRIDAY MORNING, Bob wakes to Mary asking to watch *Fancy Nancy*, a cartoon that hasn't been on in their house for over a year.

Bob says yes. After a night of restless dreams, Bob's happy to get out of bed early. No more nightmares about Martin Donovan and his strange jack-o-lantern with its pink light inside. Now it's just plain old terrifying thoughts about what Martin's got planned for Halloween.

He sits with Mary on the couch while she eats dry cereal out of a cup.

She nestles into him.

It seems that for Mary, only a few hours passed. But that's still enough that he's worried for her mental health.

"I've got you," he says. "You want to stay home all day?"

"Can Sofia come over?" Mary asks.

That'll require Bob groveling and apologizing to her parents. "Yeah. We can invite her." He'll never liked eating his words, but Mary's home. He'll do anything for her.

∽

A FEW HOURS LATER, they're all five playing with Legos while a Disney princess album plays on the stereo.

Bob knows he's got major decisions to make, but it's so much easier to set them aside and build a little plastic house with his family.

Joann isn't as easily distracted. She catches his eye. "How about helping me make some lunch?"

"Sure." Bob's stomach twists as they go into the kitchen.

"Mind cutting up some veggies?" Joann asks.

While Bob is rinsing a bell pepper in the sink, Joann says, "We've got to decide what to do."

"What do you mean?"

"You know exactly what I mean." Joann gets out the bread and peanut butter.

"Yeah," Bob admits. "Should we go stay with my parents until November?"

It's not what he wants. His animal instincts want revenge on Martin Donovan, whatever he is. But he knows his biggest duty is to his family, so if Joann wants to leave, he'll force himself to be on board.

But Joann is surprised at his suggestion. "What? No. I mean, sure, maybe we'll send the kids there."

Bob slices up the pepper. "You don't think we should leave?"

"This is our neighborhood. These are our friends. If this guy— or his ghost—is going to take more kids, shouldn't we try to stop it?"

The sound of falling Legos comes from the living room. Mary giggles.

"We've got to keep our own kids safe," Bob says.

"Will we be safe if we leave? Do you really think he's confined to Maple Creek?"

"He certainly seems to be targeting us."

"Exactly. We're already in his sights. Yes, as we get closer to Halloween, we should send the kids to stay with Polly across town. Or if we decide that's not far enough, then yeah, with your parents."

Joann aggressively spreads peanut butter on bread. "But we've got to do something assertive. Not just run and hide."

Bob gets out three plates, appreciating that it's three and not two, and sets a small handful of pepper slices on each. "What do we even do? I can't believe I'm saying this, but Martin Donovan is dead. This is his ghost we're dealing with. How do we stop a ghost?"

"Is that what we're saying?" Joann asks.

"Are you doubting the supernatural now?"

"No. He's a ghost. But I'm making sure you've accepted it."

"It's ridiculous, but I can't deny what I've seen." Bob shakes his head. "What can we do against that?"

"Salt his corpse and burn it. That's what they do in *Supernatural*."

"Karl doesn't have the sway to get us into the morgue. I don't even know where the morgue is."

"I can get my pastor to do an exorcism."

"Would he do that?"

Joann plops jelly on top of the peanut butter. "No. He'd probably refer me to a psychologist."

"Plus, Martin's not possessing anybody," Bob says. "Can you do an exorcism for a whole neighborhood?"

"Probably not. What about salt lines? Ghost can't cross salt, right?"

"I think that applies to any ghostly thing that wants to hurt you."

"So that's something to consider."

Bob wants to laugh at how matter-of-factly they're approaching this. "But where do we put the salt? Around every house in the neighborhood?"

"Maybe around Old Pine. Keep him in there."

"That's still a lot of salt." Bob considers what she said. "You think he's coming out from there each night he pulls his violent pranks?"

"Don't you? When we ran into him in the woods and he

dropped those Skittles and batteries, what else was he doing but going from the school to the neighborhood?"

"Okay, yeah. We can try a big circle of salt around the school."

"Or a line through the woods."

"And if that doesn't work?"

"I don't know. We'll try the salt first." Joann puts a sandwich on each plate. "Kids! Lunch!"

It takes a few more invitations before the kids pull themselves away from their play.

While they're eating, Joann suddenly pops up her head. "Unfinished business."

"What?" Sam asks, eager to be involved with his parents.

"Nothing," Joann says. "Your dad and I will discuss it later."

"Go ahead," Bob says. "He's been thinking about this as much as we have. Maybe he can help."

Joann looks at their son, as if recognizing for the first time that he's not as little as his sisters anymore. "In a lot of stories, ghosts linger because they have unfinished business. More specifically for our case, angry ghosts hang around because someone hurt them and hasn't seen justice yet."

"Did someone hurt the Thirty-First Trick-or-Treater?" Sam asks.

Mary stops chewing her sandwich, her little mouth slowing until it it's hanging open.

Bob tries to get Joann's attention. Maybe they shouldn't be talking about this in front of everybody.

Joann doesn't notice their daughter getting worried. "His name's Martin Donovan," she tells Sam. "His body was found in the walls inside Old Pine, in the classroom where you found the staircase. Someone must have killed him."

Bob scoots his chair closer to Mary. "Let's talk about this later."

Sam asks, "If we find his murderer, he'll leave us alone? He won't do anything in Maple Creek this Halloween?"

Joann sees Mary leaning into Bob and quickly wraps up the conversation with a mother's reassurance. "Exactly. Me and Dad are doing that so you guys never have to worry about him ever again."

Bob likes her confidence, but now he's confused. "Are we still doing the salt thing?"

"Yes. This evening."

Bob's doubtful it'll work, but he's open to it.

And if it doesn't, then they'll fix Martin's unfinished business. Find the person who killed him.

They don't have many leads—maybe the old folks the pranks have been targeting, definitely Sariah Fisher who Sofia said Martin is mad at—and they only have a week before Halloween. But that's enough to solve a twenty-year-old murder, right?

∼

BOB SPENDS the afternoon buying every pint of salt in every grocery store within five miles.

He makes a line through the woods, starting at the road, between the trees, across the foot path, and only ending it when he runs out of salt, fifty yards past the edge of Maple Creek.

He inspects his handiwork. It's a white line overtop leaves, roots, and dirt.

But is it enough to stop an angry ghost?

Feeling doubtful, Bob heads home.

∼

SUSAN SWAINSTON LIKES HAVING the news on the TV, even while she's cooking dinner or getting ready for bed. It's nice to have some noise in the house, ever since Frederick passed.

Tonight, Sean Hannity is warning about some threat or another while Susan plays sudoku on her iPad.

She gets a notification from Facebook.

Someone in the Maple Creek group has made a new post.

Susan taps the notification.

It's Peter Householder. She plays Spades with Peter at the library on Tuesday mornings.

The post starts out with, *"I'm furious!"* Peter is usually the nicest man, so this must be serious.

"Another wretched trick, this time dropping a car on Ben Richards' arms while he was changing his oil. It's felony assault is what it is. The police and justice system are too good for this so called Thirty-First Trick-or-Treater. We need to band together to scare him off for good."

Susan's not sure she agrees. She taps out a response to his post. *"Nobody knows where he is."*

Peter Householder responds within a minute. *"He's telling his kidnapping victims that he's coming on the 31st. If we can't find him before then, I say we get him at Old Pine on Halloween."*

Susan waits to see what someone else in the neighborhood thinks about that.

While she's waiting, there's a *THUMP* from the basement.

In its wake, the house feels eerily silent, even with Hannity lecturing a guest about TDR.

The clothes in the washer must have gone all wonky and started the machine walking. Susan will have to go down there.

She stands up. Her knees audibly pop, although it's her lower back that hurts. Each step down into the basement always sends a little jolt of pain up her spine. Susan's son Daniel has offered to move the washer and dryer up to the first floor, but Susan isn't handicapped. She can handle stairs.

Susan approaches the basement door. It's a hollow core door, and the front panel has come loose at the bottom corner. That's a leftover from her cat Georgiana, who was a destructive little beast, and whom Susan misses severely.

Another *THUMP* comes up the basement stairs. It rattles the door's bottom corner.

Maybe she should call Daniel.

The washer has gone imbalanced and walked before. It was a sharper, quicker sound. This thumping makes Susan think of something loose and heavy being dropped on the ground, like a dump truck full of mulch or a laundry basket full of clothes.

Susan relaxes. That's probably what it was. Her basket full of towels got vibrated off the dryer.

She opens the basement door. There's a landing and then stairs going down into the dark. Susan reaches in to flip on the light.

Two bare bulbs reveal cinderblock walls, exposed ceiling joists, and a dusty red rug that sat in her living room back when it was new.

The washer and dryer are directly beneath the stairs, so she can't see them from up here.

Susan starts down.

Another *THUMP*.

She leans over the railing.

The railing snaps.

She plummets, too fast to even register that she's falling.

A pile of damp towels cushions her fall.

Heavy fear washes over Susan. Daniel was right. She shouldn't be going into the basement anymore.

Her wrist hurts. No, the skin on her wrist hurts. The broken railing has scratched her. She's so scared of breaking bones—there'll be no convincing Daniel she can live on her own if she starts breaking bones—but it seems the pile of towels has saved her from that humiliating conversation.

Susan stares up at the ceiling joists, at the black wires and copper pipes going through them.

Why is there a pile of towels on the floor?

She'd carried the basket down twenty minutes ago, thinking the washer was already done. It wasn't, and so she'd left the basket on top of the dryer.

How did it get on the floor?

THUMP

It comes from behind her. She's lying on her back, so it's more like the sound came from above her head. She's not flexible enough to look in that direction, over there beneath the stairs, past the dryer.

Carefully, painfully, Susan rolls onto her hands and knees. Her lower back protests. She lifts her head.

In that back corner is a tangled nest of orange string lights, something that those Chester boys might use to decorate their yards. There's enough to fill the space from the floor up to the landing at the top of the stairs.

Another *THUMP*. It comes from inside the thick tangle of string lights. The lights bulge outward, plastic bulbs clicking against each other.

This is the work of the prankster, the Thirty-First Trick-or-Treater. Susan hasn't heard of pranks inside people's houses, but it must be him.

She reaches up to the dryer for something to hold onto and help get back to her feet.

A cold, boney hand grips hers.

She tries to scream but she's already out of breath from her fall so it comes out as a crackly wheeze.

The hand yanks her to her feet and suddenly Susan is staring into pink triangle eyes.

A voice drifts out from a still, toothless grin. "Your fault."

Susan is whipped around into the nest of clicking, orange lights, which are much sharper and hotter than she expects.

OCTOBER 25TH

SATURDAY MORNING, Bob sneaks out of their crowded bed to his office.

He checks the Facebook groups. Susan Swainston had an accident in her home. She's in the hospital after getting tangled in orange string lights. Foul play is suspected.

Bob's salt line didn't stop the ghost.

That leaves one option: solve Martin's murder.

He navigates over to YouTube.

Yesterday he posted an update video, thanking his viewers for their help, and sharing that Mary was home.

Within a few hours, so many people commented their congratulations that the video went semi-viral. That's the kind of attention he could have used when he was still looking for Mary.

But he still has a use for it.

He makes a post asking for anyone who knew Martin Donovan to get in touch.

The wacko theories arrive first. He was killed by villains from some shadow world called the "Periphery." He was human trafficked by pizza delivery boys. He was eaten by clowns and puppets. That last one neglected the fact that Martin's body was found in one piece.

Then come the messages from his regular viewers, sharing less out-there theories. It's gotta be Martin's mom. Or a jock who was bullying him. What about his sister?

It's Bob's old pal *BlueBlackControl69* who asks, "How did he die?"

Bob realizes he doesn't know. He messages Karl to ask.

Karl responds right away. *"They haven't told me. I'll see if I can find out."*

Bob hears Joann sneaking out of bed and whispers to her. "Hey, come here."

"The kids are sleeping hard," she whispers back. "I want coffee before they wake up. You come this way."

Bob obliges, speaking as they go to the kitchen. "Karl is finding out how Martin died. I want to talk to Sariah Fisher."

"The lady with the Halloween village?"

"Right. Mary's friend said Martin's mad at her."

"Today's Saturday. Let's go knock on her door."

"Just go over there and ask, 'Why is Martin Donovan mad at you?' Are you a murderer? Accomplice? Ex-lover?'"

"We should phrase it a little gentler," Joann says. "Maybe let me do most of the talking."

"What if she won't talk to us? If Martin's got a real reason for being mad—if she killed him—she's not going to let us in to ask about it."

Joann thinks for a second. "We'll bring the family."

"To a potential murderer's house?"

"We're making a point to meet our neighbors. That's what we'll say."

"But it's dangerous."

"No," Joann says. "I've met Sariah briefly. She's around thirty. That means she was a little kid when Martin disappeared. She didn't kill him."

"I can buy that," Bob says, "but I'd still rather take the kids to Polly's first."

"She's gone this weekend for work," Joann says. "So unless you want to wait until Monday..."

Sam wanders into the kitchen, rubbing his eyes. "What's on Monday?"

The hallway echoes with little thumps as Emily stampedes toward the living room. She clips Sam with her shoulder and goes face-first onto the rug. Emily screeches in pain and frustration.

Mary's coming down the hallway behind her. "Oh no!"

She and Sam both run to Emily's side. Sam helps her up even as she pushes him away. When you're three, pain makes you lash out like a hurt puppy.

Mary pats Emily on the back. "It's okay. It'll only hurt for a minute and then it stops."

Bob knows that three siblings under one roof will go right back to being more chaos than moments of love and support, but there will also be plenty of moments like this. He sees Joann with her hand over her mouth, tears welling in her eyes as her daughters hug for the first time in a year.

This is their family.

Bob thinks of Walter and the other kids. And of every other family who might be at risk when Martin comes back on Halloween.

Waiting until Monday to talk to Sariah isn't an option. Ninety-nine percent chance she's not dangerous, and if she is, she's tiny. Bob and Joann can handle her.

"Everybody eat some cereal and then put your shoes on," Bob says. "We're going to see a neat Halloween village."

∽

It feels like they're knocking on a relative's door, about to enjoy a Thanksgiving dinner.

Bob can't remember the last time he stood on a porch with his whole family. There was trick-or-treating last Halloween, but Joann stayed home for that. There have been some family get-togethers this year, but those were without Mary.

The girls cling to his legs—one on each. Sam stands in front,

The 31st Trick-or-Treater

head tilted up so he'll be looking right at Sariah when she opens the door.

Which she should, Bob thinks. Her car is in the driveway. It's early for a weekend, but not too early.

Sure enough, he hears the floor creak and then the door opens.

Sariah Fisher is in her early thirties. Curly brown hair is tied up into a messy bun, with almost imperceptible streaks of gray. She's wearing a Winnie the Pooh sweatshirt with honey-yellow sweatpants.

She looks wide-eyed at Bob, Joann, and then the kids. "Hi," she says.

Bob says, "Morning! We're your neighbors. I'm Bob..."

"I'm Joann. These are Sam, Mary, and Emily."

"My neighbors?" Sariah looks over to the houses next to hers.

"From the neighborhood," Bob says. "Over on Cedar Lane. We've been trying to meet more of our neighbors, get to know everyone in Maple Creek."

Sariah loosens up a bit. "Seems like a nice idea."

Bob suddenly realizes that they should have brought pastries or something. He's not sure how to get from this introduction to sitting down with Sariah to ask her what she knows about Martin Donovan.

Fortunately, Joann is better at this than him.

"Can we come in and get to know each other a bit?"

Well, she's more assertive about it, anyway. Bob's not sure her approach is less awkward than his would be.

But Sariah takes it well. "Oh. Sure. I have a niece and nephew I haven't seen forever. This'll be nice."

She backs away from the door, raising her arm to present her living room.

Sam has been staring down Sariah this whole time, but now he sees what she has paused on her TV. A *Mario Kart* game on the Nintendo Switch. Scratch that—the Nintendo Switch 2.

"Whoa!" Sam says. "Are you being Bowser Junior?"

Mary twists against Bob's leg. She's excited but still feeling shy, wants to play but doesn't want to ask for it.

Today, Bob wants Mary to have every little thing she wants. "Hey, do you think our kids could try out a race?"

"Oh," Sariah says. "Sure. Let me finish this one so I don't screw up my ranking."

Bob feels like he's made a bigger *faux pas* in this request than Joann did with inviting them all inside, but he's not sure why.

As Sariah stands in front of the TV, pink controller in hand, driving her go kart across the finish line, Joann whispers to Bob, "Let me take the lead."

Now he's sure he shouldn't have asked for kids to play on the Switch, but he's still not sure why. Regardless, he's ready and willing to shut up.

Sariah navigates menus on the game. "I have two extra controllers. You can all play."

Sam's excitement about the game is manifesting as bouncy feet. "At our house, Emily pushes the 'home' button too much when we're playing."

"It'll be fine," Joann says.

"I'll leave her controller unplugged," Sariah gets the kids set up in a race and then sits down on her couch. She gestures for Bob and Joann to sit down as well, which they do. "I gotta say, this is a little strange..."

"I'm sorry," Joann says.

Sariah waves her off. "I hate that it's strange, is what I'm saying. We live in the same neighborhood. It shouldn't be weird to stop by to visit and introduce yourselves. Ourselves."

Bob likes what she's saying, but he's following Joann's instruction to shut up. He nods enthusiastically.

Joann pats Bob's knee. "That's how we feel, too. No way to deal with it other than push through the awkwardness, right?"

"I guess so." Sariah laughs.

Mary giggles at something in the game, prompting Sam to make an exaggerated groan of defeat. There's an explosion on screen.

"Hey," Sariah says. "Your daughter was one of the thirty trick-or-treaters, wasn't she? And your son disappeared for a few days?"

Bob can barely keep his mouth closed. Sariah is practically inviting them to start asking their questions. But he trusts Joann.

"That's right," Joann says.

"Wow," Sariah whispers. "I can't imagine."

"We couldn't have either," Joann says. "Not until it happened."

"You must be over the moon that they're back."

"Of course," Joann says.

"Are they... okay?"

"All things considered," Joann says, "yeah."

"Wow," Sariah whispers again. "Can I ask... I mean, Mary came back three days ago, right?"

"You've been following the news," Joann says.

"Are you really going around, knocking on doors to meet people? Three days after your girl is home?"

"What do you mean?" Joann asks. Her cheeks turn red. She must have had a specific conversation path she'd intended to travel before getting to the real questions, and Sariah's own direct questioning is throwing her off.

Bob jumps in. "We have some questions for you."

Sariah raises her eyebrows. "For me? About what?"

Sam interrupts. "Can I see your Halloween village?" *Mario Kart* has soothed his suspicion of Sariah.

"Sure!" Sariah says, and this must be a special interest because she's so very enthusiastic about sharing it with her guests. "It's in the basement."

"Come on." Sam pulls Mary to her feet. "She has a Halloween train."

Mary hops up excitedly. Emily joins in being excited, carrying her unplugged Switch controller with her.

"This way," Sariah says.

They follow her down basement stairs, and Bob insists on going behind her, his family behind him. He's leading his family down into the basement of a woman who might be a murderer, but he'll at least put himself in the lead. Besides, Martin Donovan being mad at Sariah does not mean she's the one who killed him. Martin Donovan is obviously mad at a lot of people.

And like Joann said, Sariah couldn't have been more than ten when Martin went missing.

As they walk into the carpeted basement, Sariah flips on the light. The walls are covered in horror movie posters and there's a huge table in the middle of the room. It must be four or five tables under that tablecloth. On top is a model train set that goes through a village—all horror themed. Not anything extreme, but classic Universal monsters, ghosts on carousels, skeletons on a rotating dance floor.

The kids squeal to each other and run from piece to piece, inspecting the fun spookiness right at eye level.

"Careful," Sariah says. "Don't touch. Everything breaks way too easy."

"This is impressive," Bob says. "It's laid out the neighborhood, isn't it?"

"Yeah, I thought that'd be fun."

Bob still thinks it's strange, but he lets it go.

"How'd you know about it?" Sariah asks.

Bob freezes.

Joann offers a lifeline. "The missing little girl who Mary escaped with. She said their kidnapper is angry at the lady with the Halloween village."

Sariah blinks. "Okay. That's a lot. I have questions about that. But it doesn't explain how you knew I made this."

Bob clears his throat. "You posted about it on Facebook."

"Are we friends there?"

"You posted on the group."

"I might have in a horror themed group. Are you saying I did in our Maple Creek group?"

"You must have," Bob digs in with his lie. "I remember seeing it."

Emily picks up a porcelain Frankenstein. "This is my honey," she says.

"Put that down," Joann orders.

"But she's my honey."

"Down."

Emily sets it down with a clink.

"Sorry," Sariah says. "I'd let them play with the pieces, but they're really fragile."

"Don't apologize. You're an angel for risking them even looking at it." Joann points a silent threat at Emily, who freezes mid-reach for a clown with bat wings, and then says to Sariah, "Can you circle back to the thing about the kidnapper?"

"The kidnapper's mad at me? I didn't realize the cops know who the kidnapper is."

"They don't," Bob says.

"But you do?"

"Maybe. Mary and her friend saw him face to face."

"I didn't see his face," Mary says while peering into a firehouse manned by mummies.

Bob hadn't realized she was listening. He feels a pang of guilt for letting her hear his recap of her trauma.

"I don't know why he'd be mad at me," Sariah says. "I don't think I know him."

"If you don't know who it is, how do you know you don't know him?"

"I work seventy hours per week writing code. I guess it could be somebody I play games online with. Did they say their name?"

Bob goes all in. "Martin Donovan."

Sariah fails to hide a tiny gasp.

"You know him?"

"Not anymore. I did, before he disappeared."

"You know about his disappearance."

"Sure. I lived in the neighborhood as a kid. Not in this house, but over on Clearbark."

"You were neighbors with Martin," Joann says.

"Down the street from him. I was... twelve when he disappeared. He was seventeen or eighteen. It scared the hell out of me." Sariah glances at the kids. "Sorry. It scared me real bad. The idea of someone not being there anymore. Not that he'd died. Not that he'd left home. But no one knew what had happened, and that scared me. I was the right age to start worrying about death, which believe me, I was, but Martin vanished and his mom didn't know where he went and to me that was even scarier than death. What if the same thing could happen to me?"

"Did he ever contact you?" Joann asked.

"No, we weren't close. He would say hi to me sometimes. But he was kinda mean to me when I was younger, so mostly I stayed away from him."

"Sounds like he impacted you, though."

"You could say that. I made flyers for his mom. Well, not for his mom, I guess. I didn't even give them to her. I went around the neighborhood, knocking on doors and handing them out. What really impacted me was that nobody seemed to give a shit. Sorry."

The kids aren't listening to her, they're too engrossed in exploring the Halloween village. Bob looks at Mary. Or maybe they are listening. Who knows?

Sariah continues, "Martin was a tough looking teenager. To me, I saw a scary guy disappear and that was scary. But all the adults in Maple Creek saw a troubled teenager who probably ran away. You know, I even went looking for Martin."

"What do you mean?"

"I went on adventures. I crawled through drain pipes. I hiked through the woods between Maple Creek and the old elementary school. As if I might find him sitting by a tree, waiting for someone to come happen by and say, 'Hey, your neighborhood noticed you were gone. They're worried.' Like that would ever happen."

"What would never happen?" Bob asks. "You'd find him sitting by a tree, or someone in the neighborhood would be worried about him?"

"Either one," Sariah says.

Emily and Mary have found a train tunnel through a cliffside, and they're watching the ghost-conducted train disappear inside. They run to the other side of the mountain, then cheer as a yellow light appears in the dark of the tunnel, vanguard to the clicking and whirring of the train itself appearing.

Sam's not watching the train. He's explored the Halloween village and now he's more interested in the adults' conversation. "Why didn't anyone care that he was missing?"

Sariah asks, "Is it okay to talk about this in front of him?"

"Go ahead," Bob says.

Sariah shrugs. "They were busy with their own lives. The neighborhood was pretty new, the Donovan family were the newest. They didn't really fit in. Wanda is a socially weird lady, the dad was a bit of a jerk, and Martin himself was somewhere between a skater and a goth. Super obsessed with Halloween."

"That's why he's mad," Sam says.

"Martin's mad?" Sariah asks. "You guys are saying Martin's the kidnapper?"

Bob had hoped for more answers from Sariah before they broached the topic of ghosts. "Martin's dead."

Sariah sighs. "I figured. How do you know? I've never found a news story about it."

"The cops found his body in Old Pine this month." He leaves out the fact that Martin's own mom was the first to find the body, a year earlier.

"He came back and died in the school?"

"No. He was stuck inside a wall. He'd likely been in there since he went missing."

"Oh geez." Sariah shakes her head. "As I got a little older, I heard rumors that the older kids before us had been into trespassing and building hacking. He must have been exploring and got stuck."

Is that all it was? No murder, just a terrible accident? "If that's the case," Bob asks, "why is he mad at you?"

"You said he's dead." Sariah's expression changes to one of

surprise and disdain. "A minute ago you said the kidnapper is mad at me. Are you saying that Martin Donovan's ghost is mad at me?"

Bob feels embarrassed. Is he really saying that? He waits for Joann to bail him out, but it's Mary who speaks up.

"He's real." Mary's voice sounds too little to approach such a big topic.

Joann starts to tell Mary not to dwell on that, but Bob puts his hand on Joann's arm. "Let her."

"He's really scary," Mary says.

She doesn't know anything about Martin as a person, but when she was on that pink, foggy hillside, she knew about him as a ghost.

Sariah reverently asks, "Where were the kids for the past year?"

"I don't know," Bob says. "I saw the place, stepped inside, but I couldn't tell you what it is. The afterlife, maybe."

"You saw Martin there?"

"Yes," Bob says.

"Mary saw him lots of times," Sam adds.

"How do you know it was him?" Sariah asks. "You saw his face?"

Bob's uncomfortable with Sariah interrogating his daughter. "Sorry to be blunt, but whether you believe us or not isn't a big deal. What I want to know is why he might be mad at you."

"I have no idea."

Joann, who's been quiet for a bit, speaks up. "Have you seen him?"

"I already told you—the last time I saw Martin Donovan was before he disappeared twenty years ago."

"He doesn't show his face anymore," Joann says. "He wears a hoodie pulled down real low. It's a dark orange. And he carries a funny shaped jack-o-lantern with pink light coming from the inside."

Sariah's face pales.

"You've seen him," Bob says.

She nods. "Outside at night."

"Watching you?"

"Yeah. I thought it was someone with poor taste trying to

spook the people who lost kids. I even called the cops once, thinking it might be the prankster who's terrorizing the neighborhood."

"How many times did you see him?" Bob asks. "When did it start?"

Sariah walks over to her Halloween village. "The first day of October. I remember because I laughed to myself, 'just in time for spooky season.' The most recently I saw him was last night, a little before eight. He was standing at the edge of my driveway."

"Watching you?" Joann asks.

"Hard to say for sure, what with the jack-o-lantern glowing so I couldn't see past it into his hood. But yeah, I'm pretty sure he was."

"You think he's trying to scare you?" Bob asks.

Sariah shrugs. "There's a lot scarier stuff in this world than a weirdo with a glowing pumpkin."

"Turnip," Sam says.

"Big turnip," Sariah responds.

"Did you tell anyone you saw him?" Bob asks.

"I called the cops."

"But you didn't tell your neighbors? Wasn't Richard Stoutly one of the first prank victims?"

"He was, but I don't really know him."

"You didn't even post in the Maple Creek Facebook groups?" Joann asks.

"I called the cops, okay? Was it my job to tell everyone around that I saw him? I work seventy hours each week. When I step inside my house at night, I'm only interested in decompressing. Maybe I should be a better neighbor, I don't know."

Mary tugs on Joann's shirt. She and Emily have wandered over to their parents now that the conversation has grown volatile. "Can we go home?"

"One second," Joann says. She looks at Sariah. "Is he getting any closer when you see him?"

"No. More like farther away."

"Toward Old Pine?" Bob asks.

"Yeah. I hadn't realized that, but yeah. Should I follow him? Would that help?"

"No. I wouldn't follow the trick-or-treater. Especially not, considering he's mad at you."

"I don't get why he'd be mad at me," Sariah says.

Bob's phone buzzes. It's a response from Karl. *"The coroner wasn't positive because the corpse is so old, but there's not any visible trauma. No violence against the body. Martin most likely died of heart failure after getting stuck upside down."*

Bob's mind swirls around this revelation.

Joann answers Sariah. "You don't think he's mad at you? You just said the whole neighborhood ignored his disappearance. Sounds like he's mad at all of Maple Creek—you included."

"But I looked for him!"

"He's an angry, irrational teenager. You failed to find him."

Bob lets them argue.

Last night, this seemed so simple. Find Martin's murderer, no more unfinished business, Martin's ghost moves on.

But there was no murder. Martin was exploring the school building, got stuck, and died terribly.

Except.

He took thirty kids. Killed some of them.

And now he's made threats through the returned kids that he's the Thirty-First Trick-or-Treater—that he's coming back on Halloween.

He wasn't murdered but he's still vengeful. Furious at the neighborhood who didn't bother to look for him while he was stuck and dying painfully.

That's not a wrong Bob can right. There's no single villain to apprehend.

So now how do they stop Martin?

"We'll get out of your hair," he says to Sariah, cutting off her argument with Joann.

Sariah quickly softens her tone. "You don't have to go yet."

"We have a few things to do." His stomach is already twisting from this internal revelation, this new question of how to keep his family safe.

"Let's keep in touch, though," Sariah says. "I do want to be part of the neighborhood. Not only online."

Joann and Sariah exchange numbers while Bob shepherds the kids back upstairs and outside.

As they walk home, Bob gets lost in his head. How in the world are they going to stop a ghost who's angry at everyone?

OCTOBER 26TH

Bob wakes on Sunday morning with an uncomfortable thought: there are only five days left until Halloween.

Joann is already awake. Once she notices that Bob's eyes are open, she doesn't give him time to dwell on his nerves. She invites him to church with her.

"I really want to go today, but I don't think I can handle everyone in the congregation telling me how happy they are that Mary's home."

"You want me to play interference against your friends who are happy for you?"

"You get it. Will you?"

"Okay. Yeah." Bob suspects he might still have some deep resentment toward's Joann's church attendance and how she gave up on Mary still being alive in favor of hoping for a reunification in Heaven. But fuck it. Let's go to church. "Do I wear a tie?"

An hour later they're packed into the minivan, driving to West Hanover Presbyterian. Joann turns on a playlist of instrumental piano music. It's calming, but Bob's pretty sure this one is a cover of Michael Jackson's "Human Nature."

Sam tells them about a dream he had. He found a secret closet in their hallway and it was overflowing with bags of gummy orange slices.

Yesterday after their visit to Sariah, Bob and Joann set aside their problem of how to stop Martin. They felt like they'd stressed out Mary, so they spent the afternoon and evening getting ice cream, playing at the neighborhood playground, and then playing boardgames. The girls chose Candy Land and then Sam chose King of Tokyo.

Emily wanted to sleep in their bunkbeds, rather than everyone squishing into Mom and Dad's bed, but Mary looked nervous about that, so Bob laid down with Mary on the top bunk. Sam and Joann squeezed in with Emily on the bottom.

"Not sure how this is better than our room," Bob said.

But the five of them fell asleep quick.

Bob blinks. He's still driving. Now that his family is together again, it's wild how easy it is to relax and drift off.

He reminds himself that they have to act. Running away isn't guaranteed to keep their kids safe, so they have to do something about Martin. He just doesn't know what, and so anxiety is like a constant swarm of wasps inside his body.

They arrive at Joann's church, and Bob's whirlwind of thinking comes to a screeching halt as the carpeted lobby is full of well-wishes and tearful, joyful smiles.

A teenage boy wearing a Looney Tunes tie gives Joann an enthusiastic hug. "Congratulations," he awkwardly says.

An old lady with thick glasses and even thicker makeup bends down to Mary. "We prayed for you, darling."

Bob steps up to Mary's side. He puts his hand on her shoulder. He doesn't like all these strangers acting like they know her. Mary rests her head on his thigh, not enjoying the attention either. Bob picks her up one handed to avoid hurting his broken arm. She hides her face in his chest.

"We're going to sit down and enjoy the service," Joann tells her friends.

As a family, they go into the sanctuary doors, pick a pew toward the back, and sit down.

Bob hasn't been to church since he was a kid.

The preacher talks about Jesus while Mary draws on a donation slip. Emily rips a dozen slips off the pad, one by one.

Bob doesn't much go for the preacher's excited moralizing, but he gets into singing the hymns. He hears Sam's cautious voice singing about being friends with a deity, and it grows more confident as the song goes on. Mary puts her hand inside Bob's palm, then uses her other hand to close his fingers around hers. Then she puts her other hand in Joann's and relaxes between her parents.

Emily watches her family sing from their hymnals. She grabs her own hymnal and blesses the pews in front of them with off-key vocalizing.

A proper-looking woman winces.

After the hymn, Bob notices a familiar face in the next row. Vince and Patty Thacker, whose nine-year-old son, Cody, is still missing.

Tears are freely flowing down Patty's cheeks.

Bob knows firsthand how hard it is to watch other families reunite when your child is still missing, to be happy for them but also so immensely envious.

His mind goes into problem-solving mode. If he can get back onto that pink, foggy hillside, he can bring Cody home. Maybe if he goes back to Wanda Donovan's house, or he could break into Old Pine.

But he's powerless. He knows that door won't be there anymore. That staircase won't show itself to him.

Based on Mary and Sofia's stories, Cody will come back when the Thirty-First Trick-or-Treater decides to send him back. Unless Cody goes down the hill. Then only his corpse will return.

And there's nothing Bob can do about it. He's stuck on this side of the door, this end of the staircase. Martin Donovan is angry at Maple Creek. He's harassing the neighborhood, taunting them with their own children, threatening his return on Halloween.

And what then?

Bob isn't sure yet. He's got to assume Martin intends to kidnap their children again—even though it doesn't make sense. Why would Martin return the kids just to take them again? For that matter, why is Martin returning the kids at all?

He checks the time on his phone. There's another twenty minutes in this church service.

Time passes excruciatingly slowly. Bob needs to talk this through with Joann. They're running out of time, and he has no idea how to stop whatever Martin's planning for Halloween.

Bob forces himself to pay attention to the sermon. It's on Jesus' parables about lost children, animals, and coins.

The people in Jesus' stories need to do a better job at keeping track of what's important to them.

∼

THE PASTOR ENDS his sermon encouraging his congregation to be a "light in the darkness."

This sticks in Bob's head as they sing the closing hymn. He repeats it to himself as more well-wishers intercept his family in the lobby.

On the car ride home, he asks Joann, "What's that mean, 'light in the darkness?'"

Joann hands a picture book to Emily, who's fussing in her carseat.

Bob thinks she's going to ignore his question, until eventually she says, "It's like being there for someone. I'm pretty sure the intention of the metaphor is that in the darkness, a light would be like a beacon for people to find. So when the pastor says it, he means we should live the kind of life that brings others to happiness. But personally, I feel like sometimes the dark is okay. Maybe you're trapped in it, or maybe you want to be in it, but it's still reassuring to see that there's light in the dark somewhere. You know you can go to it if you need it. That's what I try to be with my friends. I don't know how good I am at it, but I'm trying."

Bob thinks about that. Is he a light for his friends, someone they can go to when they need him? He doesn't have many in-person friends. This past year, his entire social community has become his team of internet sleuths. None of them have reached out to him for emotional help, but he hopes they would if they needed to.

Sam speaks up from the backseat. "The Thirty-First Trick-or-Treater carries a light in the darkness."

"That's not the same kind of light," Joann says.

"It's a jack-o-lantern," Mary says. "That's why his name is also Jack o' the Lantern."

Bob glances back at his little girl. "What do you mean? His name is Martin. Did he tell you a different name? I know he told some of the kids he's the Thirty-First Trick-or-Treater."

"That's not a name," Mary says. "That's just his day."

Joann carefully asks, "Did he tell you his name is Jack o' the Lantern?"

"Yep. And Stingy Jack."

Joann mouths that name to Bob, who shrugs. He's heard of the first name, but not the second one.

They leave it until they get home and can talk in private.

Once the kids are eating lunch and listening to music, Bob and Joann talk quietly in their room.

"We need a way to stop him," Joann says. "Do you know anything about those names?"

"Jack o' the Lantern is the Halloween guy, right? Something to do with why we trick-or-treat, but I don't know the details off the top of my head. I've got no idea about Stingy Jack."

"That's the extent of my knowledge, too. Let's see what we can figure out."

Then Mary is screaming that Emily hit her, and it's back into the moment-to-moment of daily life, except now Bob's got a goal, a path to follow, and something he hasn't yet felt today: hope.

OCTOBER 27TH

MOM AND DAD keep Sam home from school on Monday.

They say he's having his "Fall Break," even though school is still going on.

Of course, Mary's staying home, too. No one's mentioned when she might go back to school, and Sam understands. He still wants to be close to Mom and Dad. He can't imagine how Mary feels, since he only had a fraction of the experience that Mary had.

Mom and Dad are in Dad's office, talking with the door closed. Emily's sitting in the hallway, leaning her forehead against the door and singing songs from *Frozen*.

Sam's sitting on his bed, figuring out how to phrase a text to Jeremy, when Mary walks in. She's holding a piece of printer paper and a handful of colored pencils. "Can you draw with me?"

"Um." Sam fiddles with his watch. He's been thinking about texting Jeremy all morning. But if he's being honest with himself, he wasn't about to do it. "Yeah, let's draw."

Mary sits on his rug, splaying her legs and putting the paper in between. The pencils tap together in her fist. She picks a red one and starts coloring shapes.

Sam takes a blue pencil and draws on the far end of the paper. "What are you drawing?" he asks.

"Sofia," Mary says. "She's my best friend."

Sam takes a look. His sister has colored two oblong shapes. "Who's the other person? Is it Walter?"

"Who's that?" Mary asks.

"He's my friend. He came with me when I tried to find you. He's still there."

"When's he coming home?"

"I don't know. I'm scared for him, though."

"Why?"

Sam tries to remember if Mary knows that some of the missing kids died. If she doesn't, he's not going to be the one to tell her. "It's scary over there. You know that better than me."

Mary nods. "I hope your friend comes home."

"Thanks. So who's the other person you're drawing?" Sam asks.

"Stingy Jack."

Sam remembers the car ride home from church yesterday. "You said the Thirty-First Trick-or-Treater called himself that name."

"Yeah." Mary colors pink eyes on one of the shapes.

"Why?"

Mary shrugs. "He picked it."

Sam colors a beach scene on his end of the paper. "Is he named after somebody?"

"What's that mean?"

"Did he pick that name because someone else had it first and he likes that person?"

"I don't know." Mary's sitting more stiffly. Her strokes with the colored pencil are more jagged.

Sam's stressing her out. He drops his questioning to enjoy coloring with his sister.

∼

"Should we let her in?" Bob asks Joann.

They're sitting at Bob's desk, waiting for responses to a post Bob made.

Emily is singing against the closed door to his office. It sounds like her mouth is right up against it.

"No, she's having fun," Joann says. "But we've got maybe ten minutes until she starts fussing."

Bob's laptop *dings*. The discussion over Bob's post has begun.

He's told his internet sleuths that the ghost of Martin Donovan —the Thirty-First Trick-or-Treater—has claimed to be "Jack o' the Lantern" and "Stingy Jack."

Bob and Joann parse through the responses saying that Bob has lost it, believing in ghosts.

But others in his community are taking it seriously.

One response reads:

"Stingy Jack is the same person as Jack o' the Lantern. He's from Irish mythology. Stingy Jack was a trickster figure, like Anansi or Coyote. He trapped the devil up a tree and only let him down once the devil agreed to never let Stingy Jack into hell. But when he died, all his dishonest deeds kept him out of heaven, so he wanders the edge of the afterlife. That's when he became Jack o' the Lantern. The devil gave him a single burning coal. He hollowed out a turnip and made it into a lantern. Supposedly, he's always wandering, but the veil between us and spirits is thinnest on Halloween, so that's when people see him."

Bob turns to Joann. "Martin's not an old Irish spirit. He's a kid who died tragically twenty years ago."

Joann scrolls further through the comments. "Here."

She's found an argument between sleuths along the lines of Bob's same concerns.

"It's not Stingy Jack. It's Martin Donovan."

"Maybe his ghost got wrapped up with Stingy Jack's."

"It's Martin pretending to be Stingy Jack."

"Not pretending, just mimicking, like a copycat serial killer."

"What do you think?" Joann asks.

"Hell if I know. Does it make a difference?"

"Probably not," Joann says.

Bob types his own comment on his post and then pins it. *"How do we keep him from doing something on Halloween?"*

The answers flood in.

"Put up jack-o-lanterns."

"The Irish used jack-o-lanterns."

"A jack-o-lantern on each porch."

"That's where the Halloween tradition comes from. Jack-o-lanterns keep Jack o' the Lantern away."

Bob thinks aloud, "But he carries a jack-o-lantern."

Another comment has made this same response, and someone answers. *"It's like a scarecrow for evil spirits. The tradition is from the Celts. It's older than Halloween. Stingy Jack carrying a jack-o-lantern is a mockery of the tradition, like Christian demons using inverted crosses."*

Joann types in her own question. *"How many jack-o-lanterns do we need to protect a whole neighborhood?"*

Nobody can agree on the answer.

"One for each house."

"A line of them between you and Old Pine."

"One wherever Martin is going to appear on Halloween."

"What do you think?" Joann asks. "Is it like a charm that protects your home, or is it a barrier he can't pass?"

"Why does that matter?"

"Because," Joann says, "that decides what we're doing on Friday night. Do we need to convince everyone in Maple Creek to stay home and put out a jack-o-lantern? Or can we make a big circle of them around Old Pine to keep Martin trapped inside?"

Bob imagines a ring of glowing jack-o-lanterns around the empty school. "That'd be a hell of a sight. Is there some way we can test it, whether we can actually ward him off with a pumpkin and a candle?"

Joann says, "I mean, we make a jack-o-lantern, find Martin, and see if we can chase him around with it."

Bob laughs. "I'll bring the Bluetooth speaker to play the Benny Hill theme."

"You up for it? We'd have to find somewhere Martin is guaranteed to be."

"He's playing his violent pranks almost every night, which

means he's coming out from Old Pine almost every night. But we can't try to intercept him too close to the school because there are still four more kids who haven't come home yet, so it's pretty crowded around those front doors."

"We can try to cut him off in the woods," Joann suggests.

"That's like a football field's worth of space to try to catch him. And besides, I think we only see him when he wants us to." Bob scrolls through the comments but doesn't find anything else useful.

Joann snaps her fingers. "We already know who he wants to see him. Sariah Fisher. He's mad at her, and she keeps seeing him outside her house."

"Not every night," Bob says.

"You have a better idea?"

"Nope. Let's do it."

Bob stays with the kids while Joann goes out to buy a pumpkin and a candle. They decide not to make a family event of it, since reminding Sam and Mary of Halloween still makes them anxious.

After the kids are in bed, Bob finds himself carving a jack-o-lantern in the garage.

Joann texts Sariah to let her know what they're up to.

After midnight, Bob carries his jack-o-lantern out into the dark.

OCTOBER 28TH

Bob doesn't bother hiding in the car like when they were watching Wanda's house. They've got Sariah's permission, and if any of the neighbors call the police, Sariah will vouch for him.

Plus it's crazy dark tonight. Cloudy, and the moon is barely a sliver of light. No one will notice him.

He sets his pumpkin down on the sidewalk in front of Sariah's house. He bends over to light the candle inside, and then he walks to her porch to sit down.

The jack-o-lantern faces the road, but Bob can see the orange glow on the sidewalk and grass.

He waits an hour, decides that if it's working to keep Martin away, then he's not going to see Martin, so he won't know if it's working. He collects the jack-o-lantern, blows out the candle, and brings it back to the porch with him.

The early days of fall have passed. It's cold out here. Bob's coat keeps him warm, but the cold of the brick under his butt seeps right through his jeans.

He thumbs his lighter, stopping short of making it spark.

Suddenly, there's someone on the sidewalk, a silhouette against a distant porch light.

As Bob tries to see whether it's Martin in his hoodie, a pink light flickers to life. Bob can no longer see the silhouette of the body—now there's only the pink glowing face: two triangle eyes and the gaping, toothless mouth.

Bob flicks his lighter. He reaches into his own jack-o-lantern, lights the candle, and carries it off the porch.

His heart pounds with fear. He wants to retreat to Sariah's porch, hiding behind his jack-o-lantern, but he needs to know if this will work away from people's homes.

Halfway across the yard, fifteen feet from where the pink face watches him, Bob places his jack-o-lantern carefully in the grass. He aims the orange glowing face at its pink sibling.

"What do you think, Martin?" Bob asks into the dark. He tries to sound confident but hears his voice waver. "I made myself one, just like you."

The pink face moves forward. The ghost is advancing.

Bob backs up. Slippery mud squelches under his shoes.

The floating pink jack-o-lantern advances, those triangle eyes taking up more of the night's darkness.

Bob bumps into the bottom step of the porch.

The phantom reaches Bob's own jack-o-lantern. Orange candlelight reveals Martin's ankles. He's wearing navy jeans and black Converse sneakers. They look as real as any shoes that Bob owns.

Bob wonders if ghosts are supposed to be translucent, and then those pink eyes and toothless mouth are past his jack-o-lantern, advancing through Sariah's yard, backing him up to the front porch, against the door.

He tries the doorknob. Locked.

"Dammit," he breathes. He jams the doorbell and strikes his knuckles on the door.

But Sariah's windows are dark. Did she say she'd even be home? Did she really go to bed knowing that Bob would be out here confronting Martin?

Then he notices there's light from the basement windows. She's downstairs. Maybe he can get her attention.

Martin advances onto Sariah's front walk, into the yellow glow of her porch light. The fierce pink light is pushed back inside the turnip. Clumps of dust are caked onto Martin's dark orange sweatshirt, remnants of his time spent inside the walls of Old Pine Elementary. He keeps his head pointed down, his hood blocking Bob's view of his face.

Bob's not about to get cornered up here on the porch. He dashes down the steps, around the ghost.

Martin turns to come after him. He's not especially quick, but it doesn't seem that death has slowed him down at all.

Bob flees across the yard. The grass before him turns pink as Martin raises his jack-o-lantern to give chase. That light also reflects off the back of Bob's pumpkin. He scoops it up.

Banking on a hunch, he whips around, holding his jack-o-lantern up with two hands.

They're two figures in the dark, raising lanterns against each other.

Bob holds his breath as Martin approaches. "Stop," he whispers, "you gotta stop. You can't get past the jack-o-lantern while I'm holding it."

Martin is getting closer, he's an arm's length away, his turnip jack-o-lantern and its pink light are inches from Bob's pumpkin.

And then he stops.

He raises his head, revealing deep shadow beneath his hood. This close, the glow from Martin's turnip keeps his face hidden, but Bob can feel the perpetual teenager's hatred seething out.

Bob's heart pounds like he's run a marathon. "You don't like it, huh?"

Martin backs away a few steps.

Bob walks toward him, pressing his advantage. "Whatever your plans are for Halloween, how about you cancel them? Give us back the rest of the kids and go away forever."

The pink eyes and mouth blink out.

Bob frantically searches the darkness, now using his jack-o-lantern as an actual lantern. Staring into those pink eyes temporarily worsened Bob's night vision.

His eyes adjust to Sariah's front yard, lit only by his own candle and the neighbors' porch lights.

Martin has vanished.

It worked.

Martin couldn't pass Bob's jack-o-lantern when he was holding it.

Bob breathes in the night air. Adrenaline dissipates, leaving behind exhaustion, but that's blended with excitement.

They now have an actual plan for stopping Martin on Halloween.

As Bob walks home, pumpkin under his arm, he considers whether he should have been taunting Martin. He's a kid who went exploring, got stuck in a wall, and then slowly died while his community ignored that he'd vanished.

Then Bob thinks about his family's life the last year without Mary, about Mary being scared on that pink hillside, and about the kids who didn't make it home alive.

If there were a way to trap Martin inside a wall for a second time, Bob would be first in line.

∽

JOANN HAS FALLEN asleep by the time Bob gets home.

He doesn't blame her. This whole month has been one debilitating punch in the gut after another. And now they've got one chance to stop it all from happening again. It all takes its toll on body and mind. Sleep has a constant appeal.

Any given moment, Bob can look at his kids and the relief that washes over him is enough that he can easily konk out.

Which is exactly what he does upon arriving home.

He sleeps in until the sunrise, and then finds Joann sipping coffee in the kitchen.

He sits across from her. "It worked. Martin wouldn't pass the jack-o-lantern, but I had to be holding it."

"What do you mean?"

Bob tells her how the ghost stepped right over the jack-o-lantern when it was on the ground, but then when Bob picked it up, the ghost stopped in its tracks.

"Weird," Joann says.

"Yeah, who knows. But it works, so we can stop Martin on Friday."

"How many people do we need?"

Bob hasn't thought through this yet. He'd been so excited that he'd found a way to stop the psycho that he hasn't considered how they'll actually put this discovery to work. "To circle the whole school? I don't know. How tight does the circle need to be, do you think? If it's a complete circle can he not pass? Or do we need to block every possible path?"

"It's gotta be the complete circle thing."

"Based on what?"

"We'll never get enough people to make a complete three-hundred-sixty degree circle around Old Pine. So it's gotta be that a complete circle works, even if we're not shoulder to shoulder."

"And if it's not?"

"Then our plan doesn't work. Martin takes another thirty kids. Or the same thirty. Or he does whatever he's planning to do as the Thirty-First Trick-or-Treater."

"Unless Maple Creek manages to lynch him first."

Joann huffs. "They're gonna string up a ghost? Honestly, I'm hoping it's all talk. It won't surprise me if they don't even show up."

"I don't know, people are *pissed*."

"And rightly so. But that anger isn't useful. All it can do is get in the way of the people who are actually trying to help."

"Agreed," Bob says. "We need to talk about potential failure a bit more."

"Is dwelling on the negative helpful?"

"It's necessary. Sam, Mary, and Emily. Are we sending them to Polly's? To my parents?"

Joann gets up to pour Bob a cup of coffee. She sets it in front of him, then sits back down. "I want them close so I can protect them."

"You can go with them," Bob offers. "I'll handle everything at Old Pine."

"No. That dead asshole hurt my kids. I'm gonna help stop him."

Bob awkwardly adjusts his mug, carefully phrasing his next question. "Are you saying you want the kids with us on Friday?"

"Of course not. Or maybe. I don't know. The thought of dropping the kids off somewhere terrifies me. Leaving you alone on Halloween makes me worry for *you*. What if I go with the kids and then you're one person short for your plan to work? But if the other option is bringing the kids with us, that feels monumentally stupid."

Bob gets up to put a frying pan on the stove. "We don't have to decide yet. Let's make breakfast."

~

SAM'S HAD a knot in his stomach all day.

He's lying on his bed, *Calvin and Hobbes* comic open, but not really reading it.

Walter still didn't come home last night. Since he wasn't one of the original thirty kids taken last year, will he actually get to come home?

Even if he does, he might not be alive. Sam knows that.

But it's Sam's fault that Walter went to that foggy hillside. Yes, Walter wanted to prove that the Trick-or-Treater is real, but he never would have gone without Sam recruiting him.

Sam slams his fist down on his pillow. He's so stupid. He spent a whole year feeling awful that he didn't go with Mary onto that porch, and now Mary's home but it's his fault someone *else* is missing.

This time it wasn't because he was a coward—but once he saw Mary, Sam totally forgot about Walter. So, he's stupid.

He wants to fix it but he doesn't know how.

Even if Mom and Dad would let him out of their sight—or out

of Aunt Polly's sight—what's he going to do? Old Pine is too locked down for Sam to sneak in there again.

Even if he broke in, there's no guarantee there'd be a way onto that hillside again. He never found any rhyme or reason to when or why those stairs were there.

So here he is, another day feeling bad about Walter and being completely unable to do anything about it.

That's when Jeremy finally texts him.

"I want to go look for Walter."

Sam double checks that the message is from Jeremy. His friend has been too afraid to even talk about Walter, and now all of a sudden he wants to go looking for him?

"Why now?" Sam asks.

"I'm scared for him. We should go back into Old Pine."

No, Sam is positive he does not want to go back there. But Jeremy didn't answer his question, so Sam asks it again. *"What changed? Why do you want to go now?"*

It takes Jeremy several minutes to respond. *"I'm scared for him."*

Oh. Jeremy's in the middle of a bad moment. He's reaching out to talk because he doesn't know what else to do. If Sam were to agree to sneak into Old Pine again, Jeremy would probably back out. But instead of trying to talk his friend out of it, Sam messages back, *"I bet he'll come home tonight."*

"What if he doesn't? We should help him."

Maybe Jeremy really would be willing to sneak into Old Pine. The idea makes Sam's stomach turn. Jeremy went with Sam when Jeremy was scared. Does that mean it's Sam's turn to be brave for his friend? Except, this isn't about being scared. Sam's been over there now, where the Trick-or-Treater has the missing kids. He tried to bring Mary home and it didn't work. She had to find her own way home. Jeremy's idea is no good.

Sam responds, *"He'll come home. Today, tomorrow, or the next day."*

Sam takes off his watch. He doesn't want to see Jeremy's next message, because he knows what it'll be.

"What if Walter comes home dead?"

OCTOBER 29TH

Time for the awkward requests.

Bob brings his laptop to the couch while the kids are watching *Wish*.

Joann has reached out to everyone she knows in the neighborhood, including Sariah Fisher.

Sariah is one of six people who've said they'll join on Friday night. Two of them are from Joann's church. The last three are people Joann met in the school pickup line or while the kids played on the playground.

Bob's reaching out to his own connections. For him, there's not many face-to-face friends he can ask.

He posts in his group of amateur internet sleuths, "Anybody local? Or local enough to come to Old Pine on Halloween? We're doing your jack-o-lantern plan and we need as many people as possible."

By the end of the kids' movie, he has four people saying they'll be there.

That's ten total. Not enough.

Who else can they reach out to?

Bob scrolls through his recent messages.

The Chester brothers. Bob messages them both, laying everything on the table. Miles responds: *"We'll be there."*

Sam is next to Bob on the couch, eyes glued to Bob's phone screen. "Can I play a game on your phone?"

"Not right now," Bob says. Twelve people still isn't enough. Who else can he ask?

"Please?" Sam asks again.

Bob doesn't feel like saying no to his kids. Not after Sam had been missing for days and Mary for a year. He idly wonders how long these feelings will last while handing Sam his phone.

Joann has already gone into the kitchen to get the kids' lunch ready. "You want your laptop?" she asks. It's on the counter.

Bob looks out the window. "I don't even know who else to ask."

"You could post in the Facebook and Nextdoor groups."

That doesn't feel worthwhile—he hasn't interacted enough on those sites. But he could make a general post to his YouTube channel, instead of just his inner circle of sleuths.

"Or if you don't want to," Joann says, "I'll do it."

"Sure," Bob says. "Go ahead."

Mary is at his side. She tugs at his arm. "Can you read me a book?"

"Not right now," Bob says, which pains him.

"Then can I play with Sofia?"

A fully formed idea pops into Bob's head.

"Yeah! In fact, let's go knock on their door right now and see what she's up to."

∼

TEN MINUTES LATER, after wrestling with shoes and coats, Bob is knocking on the Fuentes' front door.

He's holding Mary's hand in his left hand, and Emily's in his right. She insisted on coming, which is alright by Bob, because the chaos she carries with her should help distract the kids while Bob chats with Sofia's dad and stepmom.

The door opens. Carlos Fuentes blinks at them with groggy eyes. A flash of recognition as he sees Bob. "What do you want?"

There's a happy squeal from behind Carlos' legs. "Mary!" It's Sofia, thrilled to see her friend.

Mary runs past Carlos and inside.

Her confidence shocks Bob, but he's excited for her.

Emily leans in, stops, looks back up at Bob, and then dashes inside before Bob can encourage her.

"My little girl missed your little girl," Bob says.

Carlos turns around. "Come on in, then."

Bob follows him inside.

A small TV sits on a massive table. Mismatched couches are too big for the room, but provide lots of space for the girls to bounce around. Hot Wheels cars and stuffed animals are scattered around the carpet.

"Forgive the mess," Carlos says. "I worked until midnight last night. Nicole left for work before sunrise."

"I've got kids, too," Bob says. "I get it."

They stand there awkwardly while the girls bounce and laugh.

"I can keep an eye on them if you have things to do," Carlos says.

"Actually, can I ask a favor?"

"A big one?"

"Sort of."

"Let's hear it."

Bob hasn't actually thought about how strange it'd be to talk about ghosts face-to-face. "What has Sofia told you about the kidnapper?"

Carlos goes stiff. "You know how kids are. Seeing spooks and phantoms."

"She said he's coming back on Halloween. A lot of the kids did."

"Like I said, kids make up scary stories."

Bob decides to lay it all out. "My wife and I have seen the kidnapper in the neighborhood. He's the one who's been pulling those violent pranks. I believe his threats to come back this Halloween are real, but a group of us have figured out how to stop him."

"I'm not joining an angry lynch mob."

"No, that's not us. We're not part of them. You can't beat up a ghost."

"A ghost?"

"His name is Martin Donovan. He died in an accident in Old Pine twenty years ago. He blames Maple Creek."

"You're serious?"

"I've seen him."

Carlos rubs his eyes. He turns to the kids. "Sofia, your friends said they have to go now."

"Take this seriously," Bob says. "It matches what your daughter's said, doesn't it?"

"She's a child!"

"And it explains how our kids vanished last year. It never made sense because it wasn't rational. The Thirty-First Trick-or-Treater is a ghost."

"Then where was Sofia for the past year? A hill with pink smoke, that's what she told me."

"I don't know what that place is. I was there, for a few seconds. It's not anywhere around here, I can tell you that."

"And you want to go in there, after this ghost?"

"No. He'll be coming out, somewhere inside Old Pine. I want to keep him trapped in there so he can't take our kids again."

"Why would he do that?"

"I told you. He blames everyone in Maple Creek for his death."

"But if he had our kids already, why release them only to take them again?"

"I don't know. Maybe he's planning something else. If that's the case, I'm sure it's just as terrible as what he did last year."

Carlos watches the girls play. After a minute, he asks, "You really believe this?"

"Yes."

"What would I need to do?"

"Hold a jack-o-lantern. Stand in his way."

"The ghost can't get past jack-o-lanterns?"

"That's right."

"How do you know?"

"I tested it out last night."

Carlos squints at Bob. "You sure you're not crazy?"

"Fairly sure, yeah."

"Okay."

"Okay?"

"Tell me when and where."

"Friday at seven in the Old Pine parking lot. Thank you." Bob steps toward the door.

"Hold on," Carlos says.

Bob pauses, hiding his disappointment. He thought he'd convinced him.

"Our girls need some time together. Sofia has asked about Mary every day."

~

IN THE AFTERNOON, Bob, Joann, and the kids walk around the neighborhood, knocking on the doors of families with returned kids.

Several slam the door in their face.

Several more listen until Bob brings up ghosts, then they invite them to leave.

Others aren't home, and based on the stack of mail in their mailboxes, they've gone out of town. The people most likely to take Bob and Joann seriously are also most likely to take Martin's threats seriously and get the hell away.

By the time the sun sets, Bob and Joann have two more families committed to joining their efforts on Halloween.

They make it home and usher their kids inside.

"What is that?" Bob asks. "Twenty?"

"Twenty-one," Joann says. "Five people I know personally, then there's Sariah Fisher, the Chester brothers, six parents of missing trick-or-treaters, four from your internet sleuths group, and three from my posts on Facebook and Nextdoor."

"That's not enough." Bob tries to picture twenty-one people circling Old Pine. They'd be a hundred feet away from each other.

"How close do we need to be?"

"I don't know. Enough that it feels like a complete circle."

"Which means?"

"Close enough that Martin won't think he can pass between us without us moving to cut him off."

"What are you basing that on?"

"Vibes."

Joann laughs. "What are we doing?"

"Protecting our kids."

"Most everyone else doing that has fled town."

"I don't think we can run away from him," Bob says. "And there's a hundred families with kids in Maple Creek who aren't getting out. We have a shot at protecting them, so that's what we're doing."

"We're out of our depth."

"No argument here."

Mary complains about being hungry and Bob can't believe it's already time to fix them another meal. "Come on, let's find something to eat."

After dinner, they distract the kids with iPads so they can talk in the kitchen.

"If I'm estimating the size of the school right," Joann says, "We need like a hundred more people."

"I'm tapped out," Bob says.

"What about the rest of the neighborhood?"

"We've already asked all the parents of missing kids. You want to go door to door?"

"We can try," Joann says. "But you don't think it'll work?"

"No."

"You look like you have another idea."

"Not one I like," Bob says.

"What is it?"

"Post about it publicly. Not in the chat group with my investigators, but right on my YouTube channel for all my viewers."

"How many people is that?"

"Ninety-thousand."

"How many are local?"

Bob shrugs. "Last time I went through my backend stats, three percent of my viewers live in Virginia."

"So somewhere south of three thousand people who live close enough."

"Some might be willing to drive farther."

"How many is 'some?'"

"Not three thousand, but if we need a hundred, I bet we'd get them. I don't have close friends around the neighborhood. These viewers are my community. At least some of them would turn out, if I asked them."

"Then what's the holdup?"

"It's public. A conspiracy YouTuber whose daughter was missing for a year calls for his viewers to descend upon a crime scene. It'll be on the news. The neighborhood will hate us. The cops will hate us. I might get arrested before we can do anything."

"Put it at the end of a video."

"What?"

"Most people only watch the start of a video, right? Only your biggest fans watch to the end. Those people will be less likely to report it to the police or the news."

"It's still risky. What if I get arrested?"

"Your viewers will still come. I'll get everything set up. Or if they arrest me, too, then I'm sure Sariah will make it happen. We need more people, you have access to more people, and I don't see another way."

"Okay. I'll do it."

After the kids are in bed, Bob records a simple video. It's the same explanation, the same request he made in-person to his neighbors today.

He considers checking in with Karl, getting his feedback on this plan, but then decides to plow ahead.

Bob uploads the video and gives it a title: "A request."

"Let's see how crazy it gets," he says to Joann.

OCTOBER 30TH

Bob's phone buzzes. It's a message from Karl.

His stomach flips. Karl saw his video and won't be happy about it.

"What's this I hear about threats of arson?"

That's not what Bob was expecting. He responds, *"No idea what you're talking about."*

"The department says they're seeing online chatter about burning down Old Pine, after the last kid comes home tonight."

"Why?" Bob asks the question, but he kinda gets it. Old Pine has been an eyesore for the past decade. Now in the last month, it's been forever linked to Maple Creek's greatest trauma. He doesn't blame anyone for wanting to burn it down. In fact, maybe that would banish Martin Donovan's ghost.

Karl's next message drips with frustration. *"Why are you asking me? They're your people threatening it."*

Bob responds without thinking. *"The fuck they are. Nobody in my groups has said a thing about it."* Karl should know that since he's in all Bob's groups.

"They're not talking about it in front of you, but it is the same people."

"Who?"

"They haven't told me."

"Who hasn't told you? You haven't seen this for yourself?" Bob tries to process what Karl's saying. "Your bosses told you these people are connected to me? They've been watching my groups online?"

"Of course they have. You were publicly investigating their biggest case for a whole year. They kept tabs on what you were doing."

"And you never bothered to tell me? Are you part of their surveillance? Have you been helping me at all?"

"Cool your jets, champ. How many times did I give you a heads-up when you were sneaking around the neighborhood?"

He's got a point. Bob takes a breath. "They think I'm going to burn down Old Pine?"

"They know someone wants to. They suspect you're involved."

Bob throws his phone on the bed. Of course the damn police department who've done nothing to find their kids now want to get in the way of Bob protecting this all from starting again. He paces the floor and then picks his phone back up. "What am I supposed to do about this? I'm not calling everybody off. Martin's going to come out of that school tomorrow evening and take our kids again, unless we're there to stop him."

"The department is looking for a potential arsonist. If you all show up with lighters and matches, you're getting arrested."

Bob swallows his rage. "Then give me a solution."

"I don't know. This is your show."

"You live here, too, asshole. If we don't use lit jack-o-lanterns to keep Martin Donovan from charging back into Maple Creek tomorrow evening, then how do we stop him?"

"I'm not saying not to do your plan. I'll help with your plan. I'm just saying don't have fifty people show up with matches and lighters."

"If I'm the only person with a lighter, then does that shine the spotlight on me? Am I getting arrested for planned arson?" That might not be the end of the world. If everybody else still makes the ring around the school, then Martin will be trapped inside, even if Bob spends the night in jail.

"You'll probably be fine. You bring a lighter, tell everyone else not to. Light some candles, then use those to light the rest."

Bob thinks of a better idea. *"Any chance you'll be on duty at Old Pine tomorrow night?"*

"Yes, otherwise I would have got my own pumpkin today to join you."

"Then you bring the lighter. And when it's time to light the jack-o-lanterns, I'll come get it from you."

"That works."

Bob sits on his bed. He rubs his forehead and listens to the kids play in the other room. He wants to find a cop to scream at. While the police are standing around, waiting for something to happen, Bob's organized a group of people to actually do something about Martin's threats.

But it's fine. He's got everything worked out.

Tomorrow is Halloween, the last day they'll have to deal with Martin Donovan.

At least this year.

Maybe the whole arson idea isn't terrible. But that's a thought for another time.

∼

"Alright," Joann says. "Tomorrow's the day. What are we doing with the kids?"

Bob raises an eyebrow in response. His gut is still aligned with Joann's—he wants to scoop them up and run away. But his head says they need to stop Martin if they can, otherwise their kids will be in danger wherever they are. He hates the idea of them being out of his sight on Halloween, but he still says, "I'd rather them be at Polly's house."

Joann nods. "That's far enough away? We don't need to send them to your parents?"

"Honestly, I think if Martin gets out of Old Pine, he can go after them wherever they are. They won't be any safer whether it's with Polly, my parents, or with us. I just don't want them at the school where they'll be a distraction from what we need to do."

Joann looks at her feet. "Yeah. I wanted some magic way we

could guarantee their safety. But the only way we'll do that is to trap Martin where he is. The kids can go stay with Polly. Anyways, I don't want them seeing the angry mob who'll be at Old Pine, thinking they're gonna kick a ghost's ass."

Sam calls from the living room, "Don't say 'ass.'"

∽

WHILE THEY'RE all playing in the girls' room, Mom and Dad say that Sam and his sisters are going to Aunt Polly's house tomorrow night.

Sam barely registers the news. His attention is on the window, which is getting darker by the minute. Only a couple hours until Walter comes home.

Last night, it was Carly Farmington who they found in Old Pine. She was okay, which Sam was happy to hear. It's been a while since one of the kids returned dead. Sam's not sure if that means it's more or less likely that Walter will be alive tonight.

Sam's stomach twists just thinking about it. Only a few more hours until they find out if Walter is dead or alive—if Sam should have listened to Jeremy and tried to go save their friend.

He reminds himself that he couldn't have done anything. He tried to save Mary and all he did was get Walter taken.

"Sam?" Dad's looking at him. He asked something, but Sam's not sure what.

"Can you grab the book from your room?"

"Which one?"

"*Where Do Diggers Sleep?* The one Emily asked for."

Emily jumps to her feet. "I get it."

She's pinned in the corner by a block tower she and Mary have built.

"No, I got it," Sam says, to keep Emily from crashing through the blocks and upsetting Mary.

He runs to his room.

His watch buzzes on the dresser. He doesn't want to check his text messages. It'll be Jeremy worried about Walter, and Sam doesn't need any help worrying about their friend.

Sam checks his watch anyways.

There's a notification on the screen. The name at the top isn't Jeremy. It's Walter.

With his heart in his throat, Sam taps the notification. The message appears.

"I need your help."

Sam wants to feel hope. He heard wrong—it wasn't Carly who came home last night, but Walter—except he knows that's not true.

Sam messages back, *"Where are you?"* He already knows the answer. Walter is still with the Thirty-First Trick-or-Treater.

His watch buzzes again. *"I'm where you left me."*

"No," Sam says aloud. It's not his fault. He doesn't want it to be his fault.

But this is a good thing. If Walter is asking for help, then maybe there's a way Sam can help him come home before this evening and totally avoid the risk of Walter coming back dead.

"How do I help you?" Sam asks. His mind races with plans. Will Mom and Dad go along with sneaking into Old Pine last minute like this? Will Sam need to sneak out the front door while everybody's in the girls' room?

Walter responds. *"Don't believe what happens tonight."*

Sam answers right away. *"What do you mean?"*

There's no answer.

Dad yells from down the hall, "Did you get lost?"

Sam sends a followup text, just a question mark.

He straps on his watch, grabs the book that Emily wants, and runs back to his family.

Mom sits on the floor and reads the book. The girls crowd together on her lap. Sam stands behind her. He's too old to be read to, but he still likes it sometimes.

Every time Sam adjusts how he's standing, he thinks his watch has buzzed and checks it.

After Mom finishes the book and Emily runs for a new one, Dad leans over to quietly ask him, "Are you waiting for a text?"

"No." Sam hears himself answer too quickly.

Dad says "okay," but then pulls out his own phone. He can see Sam's text messages from the app. Sam watches him scroll.

This is it. Dad's going to see that Walter texted him and then he'll take away Sam's watch and Sam won't be able to help no matter what Walter needs.

Dad puts away his phone. He doesn't say anything about what he saw.

That doesn't make sense. Walter is still missing. Dad should be freaking out that he texted Sam. But Dad goes right back to building Mary's block tower.

Sam looks at Walter's last message again. *"Don't believe what happens tonight."*

He asks Dad, "Can we go to Old Pine? I want to see Walter."

Mom and Dad exchange a glance that they think is subtle, but Sam sees Mom shake her head ever so slightly.

"Let's give his family some privacy," Dad says.

They're afraid of Sam seeing Walter come back dead.

∽

At 8:30, Sam crawls out of bed and tiptoes down the hall.

The girls' door is cracked open and dark inside. Mom and Dad's light is on. Sam pushes open their door.

Dad's in the bathroom but Mom's sitting on the bed, typing on her phone.

She notices Sam. "Can't sleep?"

"Did Walter come home?"

Mom sucks in a little gasp. "Oh my god, I'm sorry. You must be so worried." She taps more at her phone. "I was so caught up in something else, I haven't asked anybody or seen the news."

While Mom searches for the answer, Sam feels like he can't get a full breath. This is it. He's about to know whether he should have tried to help Walter, no matter how scared he was, no matter how pointless it felt.

"I think he's okay," Mom says. "I'm still trying to find what the news says, but there's plenty of people posting how happy they are that all the kids are home now. Oh here we go. Somebody mentioned Walter by name. He's safe. He's home."

Sam sucks in a chestful of air. It's all done. Everyone's home. He messed up but it's okay now.

He's crying, which doesn't make sense because he's happy, he's relieved, and Mom picks him up into her lap on the edge of the bed. He sobs onto her shoulder.

"I know," she says. "It's been a stressful year. It's a lot. But you're okay. Everybody's okay now."

Except the kids who aren't, Sam thinks. But Walter's home, and Mary's home, so Sam doesn't have to feel guilty anymore.

But then Walter's last text pops back into Sam's mind. *"Don't believe what happens tonight."*

What does that mean? Is he not supposed to believe that Walter really came home?

Mom walks Sam back to bed.

"Do you want me to lie down with you for a while?"

Sam nods.

His exhaustion outweighs his stress and he falls asleep while cuddled against Mom.

OCTOBER 31ST

Up until 6:12 P.M., it appears to be a normal Halloween in the neighborhood of Maple Creek.

Houses are decorated, albeit far fewer than last year.

There's even a handful of trick-or-treaters—new move-ins and ignorant folks who drive in from other neighborhoods since Maple Creek is one of the few who still has enthusiastic trick-or-treating. At least, they did before this last year.

But at 6:12 P.M., the sun finishes setting.

The half-moon has been visible since mid-afternoon, and now it offers pale light to the sudden flurry of movement throughout Maple Creek.

A dozen cop cars arrive and start patrolling the street.

Folks switch off their porch lights to let trick-or-treaters know they won't be home. They march to their cars and then drive out from the neighborhood, down the main road, and into the Old Pine parking lot.

Others walk along the Maple Creek sidewalks, toward the west edge of the neighborhood and the trail through the woods.

Many of them carry jack-o-lanterns.

Trick-or-treater visitors from other neighborhoods notice the exodus. One concerned parent hurries his little superheroes back to the car and speeds back home.

Maple Creek residents who haven't been on Facebook or Nextdoor peer through their curtains to see their neighbors all heading in the same direction, a spread-out crowd that's hardly acknowledging each other. Those out-of-the-loop folks let their curtains fall closed, deciding to keep their heads down.

The small army of patrolling police radio to each other about the strange crowd that's angry, determined, and jittery. They warn their colleagues at Old Pine that a river of anger is heading their way.

Out from the neighborhood march its residents.

And so, despite its normal beginnings, this year's Halloween in Maple Creek has quickly turned into something no one has ever seen before.

∼

Across town, Sam, Mary, and Emily are in Aunt Polly's townhouse.

Aunt Polly has a box of dress-up clothes, so they each have a costume while they hand out Halloween candy.

"What are you picking next?" Aunt Polly asks Sam.

He's still got Snickers between his teeth, but Aunt Polly is trying to distract him from how stressed he feels.

Today's the day the Thirty-First Trick-or-Treater has been threatening to do... something. Mom and Dad are going to Old Pine, trying to stop it. He's scared for them. Angry that they wouldn't let him come.

"You keep your sisters safe," Dad had said.

Mom had elbowed Dad. "Aunt Polly is keeping everyone safe. Sam, you just have fun. Eat lots of candy."

Sam checks his watch, pulling back the billowy sleeve of a pirate shirt. No texts.

"How about some Laffy Taffy?" suggests Aunt Polly.

"I want it!" Emily snatches away the candy rope. She's wearing a glimmering pink princess dress.

"Me too," Mary whines. She's got on a monkey costume, complete with brown furry gloves.

"I've got another one here," Aunt Polly digs through her candy bowl.

The doorbell rings.

"Trick or treat!" Emily yells.

"No," Mary corrects her. "They say it to us."

Aunt Polly leads the way to the door.

Sam's watch buzzes. It's a text from Walter.

Sam has texted him several times today, asking if he's okay, but this is the first he's texted back.

"I still need your help."

Sam replies. *"Why?"* He's home, isn't he? Shouldn't he be spending time with his parents, happy that everything's okay?

"The door is closing tonight. It's my last chance."

The message holds Sam's eyes captive as Aunt Polly and his sisters hand out candy.

He responds. *"You came home last night."*

"I told you not to believe what happened."

All the guilt from the last year comes rushing back into Sam. Walter's not actually home. He still needs help. It's still Sam's fault that he's trapped.

Aunt Polly shuts the door. "Did you like their costumes?" she asks Mary and Emily.

"Yes!" Emily shouts.

"I forgot something at home," Sam spits out.

Aunt Polly doesn't believe him. "What did you leave?"

He's not sure what to say. "My blanket."

"You still sleep with a blanket?" Aunt Polly's disbelief quickly turns to embarrassment. "Sorry, I didn't mean it like that. You didn't think to bring your blanket?"

"Can we go get it?"

Aunt Polly looks down at the big bowl of candy in her hands.

"Let's wait a while. We'll get plenty more trick-or-treaters before your bedtime."

"I want it now," Sam says. "I get nervous without it."

Aunt Polly checks her phone. "I guess we can go and be back pretty quick."

∼

THE CHAOS outside Old Pine shocks Bob.

All the missing trick-or-treaters are home, and yet there's a crowd outside the school's front doors, bigger than ever before.

And they are *angry*.

Bob and Joann stand at the back of the parking lot. Their minivan is full of pumpkins. Bob's hand still aches from carving so many jack-o-lanterns yesterday.

"What are they thinking?" Joann asks. "They're going to beat up a ghost?"

Bob says, "Did you see some of the discussions online? People are pissed about all the pranks."

"I'm not saying he doesn't deserve mob justice. I'm asking what exactly are they planning on doing to him?"

More cars pull up and park. More people walk out from the woods.

Bob moves pumpkins from the back of the van to the asphalt. He climbs in to move the rest closer to the open back door. "They're riled up. Hell, maybe it'll work. Martin will walk out the front doors, and before he can do anything, our neighbors will beat him back to death with their fists."

"You're not serious," Joann says.

"Nope. But it's okay, because we'll keep him trapped in there," Bob projects more confidence than he feels. "Then tomorrow, Halloween is over, and the barrier between this life and the next gets nice and thick again. Real thick."

Joann laughs. "Why'd you say it like that?"

"Because I make stupid jokes when I'm anxious." Bob pats his pocket, even though he knows it's empty. He looks over at the crowd around the front doors. As they move amongst each other, Bob catches a glimpse of the two cops at the entrance.

There must be more on the way, now that they've seen the angry crowd, but it's a huge failure of an incompetent police force to pack up and go home a single day after the last kid returned.

It's Karl and a young guy on duty. Bob's pretty sure it's the one named Freeman.

Bob's going to have to fight through the crowd to reach Karl and borrow his lighter.

"Where is everybody?" Joann asks.

As she does, Sariah Fisher walks up. She's got her own jack-o-lantern. "I'm ready. You brought matches, right? Remind me again why I wasn't supposed to?"

"Threats of arson," Bob says, reciting what Karl warned him. "The cops think someone's coming to burn down Old Pine. If a bunch of us show up with lighters and matches, we're going to get the cops upset and we won't be able to do our thing."

A truck door slams. Carlos Fuentes steps out. "Makes me happy to see you sent your kids away. My Sofia is with her Great Aunt in Maryland." He gets a jack-o-lantern out from the truck bed.

"Did you bring matches?" Sariah asks.

Carlos raises his eyebrows toward Bob. "Bob said not to."

"We'll get everyone's candles lit," Joann says. "Once everyone gets here, we'll light each one and send you all to your positions."

Sariah asks, "A big circle, right?"

"How many are coming?" Carlos asks.

"Enough," Bob says.

Carlos turns back to the school and the maddening crowd. "Are you sure?"

Bob checks the time on his phone. He thought more people would be here by now. Not even all the Maple Creek folks are here yet.

Joann reaches over to squeeze his hand. It's a small gesture, but it's comforting. They're partners in this. Their separate paths—hers through grief, his through manic searching—have led back together.

Cars keep entering the parking lot. People keep walking out from the woods into the parking lot.

Most go to the angry crowd.

Police sirens wail in the distance. The cops are rectifying their mistake of underestimating how many people would be here.

A car parks nearby and a gray-haired couple get out. Bob recognizes them from church with Joann.

They have their own jack-o-lanterns.

A small group of people emerges from the woods and breaks off from the rest of the arriving crowd. They come to join Bob and Joann. They're four of the parents of missing kids who agreed to come, plus they've recruited three more people. They've each got their own jack-o-lantern.

Real confidence alights inside Bob. This might actually work.

Sirens grow louder as three police cruisers appear up the road. They block the parking lot entrances.

"No," Bob whispers. He's hoping for a hundred of his viewers to show up, but the cops are about to shut everything down. It's all going to fall apart. Martin's going to walk out of that school, past the angry mob who won't see him, and into Maple Creek.

Joann gasps. "Look!"

There's a line of cars outside the parking lot. They're pulling over onto the side of the road. People are getting out, leaving their cars there, and walking over to Bob and Joann. Many of them are carrying jack-o-lanterns.

It's not a hundred, but it's at least half that.

The newly arrived cops scream at Bob's YouTube viewers, but only manage to stop a handful.

"They're gonna try to shut us down," Bob says. "Between the threats of arson and the lynch mob over there, they're gonna try to make us leave."

"Let's move quick," Joann says. "I'll get people in place. You go get the lighter."

The 31st Trick-or-Treater

Bob jogs across the crumbled asphalt. He pushes through the crowd of his neighbors. They're yelling around him, demanding the cops get out of their way. Bob's pretty sure some of these people aren't even from Maple Creek. He reaches the front of the crowd.

Karl and Officer Freeman stand in front of the Old Pine front doors. Yellow barriers are between the two cops and the angry mob, but they're flimsy plastic things that someone could shove aside at any moment.

Bob tries to get Karl's attention, but his friend is currently telling a woman in a yellow peacoat to step back.

"Karl!" he yells.

Karl finally looks over.

Bob opens his palm and beckons with his fingers. *Hand it over.*

Karl gives Bob a look of confusion. He goes back to trying to convince the woman in the peacoat to give him space.

Bob pushes up next to the woman. "I need the lighter," he tells Karl over the noise of the crowd.

Karl replies, "Sir, you all need to go home." He's still acting like he doesn't know him.

Bob swallows his frustration. "Just give me the lighter."

"Sir, I'm not giving you anything. Please go home."

It's too much. Bob snaps at him. "I didn't bring my own, just like we decided, so give me your damn lighter and quit playing dumb."

Karl motions for Officer Freeman to deal with the lady in the peacoat so he can move closer to Bob. There's sincerity and a bit of compassion in his expression, like he's honestly worried about Bob's mental health. "Sir, I've never spoken to you in my life."

∽

SAM LOOKS out the window of Aunt Polly's car as they drive through Maple Creek.

The backseat is crowded with carseats.

There's a lot of grownups walking down the sidewalks. That's weird.

Sam's watch buzzes. Another text from Walter. *"We're running out of time. Are you going to save us?"*

Who is he talking about? Sam thought it was only Walter still there. Was it fake when other kids came back, too?

"Who are you with?" Sam asks.

"A little girl named Sofia."

Mary sees the screen on Sam's watch. "That's my friend's name."

"I think she needs help," Sam says.

Aunt Polly talks loud over the *Frozen 2* soundtrack. "What are you guys talking about back there?"

"Halloween!" Emily shouts.

"What's wrong with Sofia?" Mary asks.

"Nothing," Sam says. "Forget I said anything. She's fine."

"Is she okay? Is she back in that pink place?"

Sam doesn't answer.

"Is she back there?" Mary asks again. "Are her mom and dad going to get her?"

"I don't know," Sam says.

Aunt Polly pulls into their driveway. "I've got my key. Let's run inside and get what you need, then we'll go right back to handing out candy at my place."

Sam unbuckles. Out of habit, he reaches over to unbuckle his sisters.

They all three hop down from the car.

Sam looks down the street, toward the path through the woods that leads to Old Pine. He's made it this far but the next step makes his stomach twist.

"In we go," Aunt Polly says.

"Are you going to help Sofia?" Mary whispers.

"Who's Sofia?" Aunt Polly asks.

Now's the time. Aunt Polly is about to get suspicious that Sam doesn't need his blanket to sleep anymore.

He runs.

Across the grass, to the sidewalk, toward the woods.

Aunt Polly yells behind him. "Sam! Stop!"

Behind Sam, footsteps slap on the pavement. He didn't think she would chase him, since she's still got to take care of Mary and Emily. Sam looks back.

It's Mary running after him. "I want to help!"

"No!" He stops dead. "You go back. It's too dangerous."

Mary catches up. She grabs his hand and tugs him along. "I want to help my best friend."

Aunt Polly has scooped Emily into her arms and is now giving chase. "Both of you, stop now!" Her "serious" voice isn't nearly as scary as Mom or Dad's, but she is an adult, and if she catches them, she'll easily stop them.

Sam starts running again. Mary, too.

"Go back to Aunt Polly," Sam says.

"I'm gonna help."

And that's how they enter the woods, Sam leading the way, Mary giving her all to keep up, and Aunt Polly running behind them both, carrying Emily who's squealing joyfully at the fun they're all having.

∼

BOB INSISTS that Karl repeat himself, even though he knows what he heard.

"We haven't spoken before," Karl says. "I'm sorry for that, since we're neighbors, and I was heartbroken for your daughter. But we haven't had a conversation about a lighter. Or about anything."

Bob's head is spinning. He can't make sense of what Karl is saying. "You saw my video about people bringing jack-o-lanterns tonight. You messaged me that there's a threat of arson and told me not to bring lighters or matches. I told everyone not to bring them because you agreed you'd have a lighter."

"Mr. Wilson," Karl says, "That conversation never happened."

Bob pulls out his phone, navigates to his last chat with Karl. For a moment, he's afraid that he's gone completely insane, that he'll open the app and Karl will be right. But the messages are there, ending with Bob saying, *"I'll come get it from you,"* and Karl responding, *"That works."*

He shows it to Karl.

Karl squints. "That's my profile picture but that's not me. Did you make a fake account?"

"Stop playing stupid." Bob looks over at Officer Freeman, who is fully distracted by the woman in the peacoat and someone who must be her husband. "It's just you and me."

"Look." Karl pulls out his phone and brings up his own messaging app. Holding the phone so Bob can see it, Karl searches for Bob's ID. The app asks if he wants to add Bob to his friends list.

That's impossible. They're already friends.

Bob suddenly feels overheated, despite the chilly air.

He's been messaging with Karl for nearly a year. On his own phone, Bob goes to Karl's profile page. It says they're friends. He shows Karl.

"What the fuck?" Karl takes Bob's phone. "That's my profile. See, the URL is the same. But I've got it locked down. You shouldn't be able to see all this if we're not connected."

"We are," Bob says. When Bob was searching through his neighbor's houses, Karl was sending him warnings about police patrols. When Bob felt he'd hit a dead end, it was Karl who encouraged him onward. Karl's one of few people who Bob personally knows.

At least, he'd thought so.

Karl shakes his head. "We're not friends from my end. I don't know what to tell you. Someone's fucking with you. But you and I have never talked before tonight."

"Then who the hell have I been talking to?"

Behind Karl, through the smudged glass of Old Pine's front doors, a pink light flashes to life.

∾

Bob backs away into the crowd.

His neighbors roil about him. He doesn't process their words, only their anger toward Martin Donovan.

His mind spins.

He's never spoken to Karl.

It was only Martin manipulating him.

But to what end?

Martin took Mary but then he helped Bob investigate? He encouraged Bob to keep going. He saved Bob from getting caught breaking-and-entering. Why?

A single voice in the crowd rises above the others. It's someone near the front. "Look! The prankster's jack-o-lantern!"

Pink light burns in Old Pine's front lobby.

Everyone in Maple Creek knows that the prankster, the kidnapper, the Thirty-First Trick-or-Treater, carries a jack-o-lantern with a pink glow, and so everyone knows what it means when pink light fills the lobby like a still, impenetrable fog.

"He's in there!"

The crowd surges forward. Someone shoves Bob in the back. He stumbles but stays on his feet.

There's a sharp clattering as the plastic barriers hit the sidewalk. Karl and Officer Freeman shout to everyone to stay back.

Jingling noises trill in the crowd. Low buzzes. Phone notifications.

A man next to Bob checks his phone. Bob sees the screen. A text message reads, *"He's inside!"*

Rectangles of light burst to life amidst Bob's neighbors, people checking their phones, even as they charge the school.

A cold realization washes over Bob. The anger in the Maple Creek Facebook groups, on Nextdoor, in text messages—it grew ever more heated until it boiled over—but it was never the Maple Creek residents alone, riling each other up. Martin's been there the entire time, making each person see whatever would make their heart beat the fastest, make their brain swim in adrenaline and cortisol.

They've watched his violent pranks, complained online, and

now been pointed at Old Pine on Halloween, when the barrier between this life and the next is so very thin.

The Thirty-First Trick-or-Treater isn't here to take the children of Maple Creek again. He's here for the adults.

∼

Bob plants his feet to force the crowd to go around him. He fights against the flow.

He has to find Joann.

She's thinking the same thing, apparently.

As Bob pushes past angry neighbors, he sees his wife beneath the street lamps. She's holding a dark jack-o-lantern and heading toward him.

Their recruits tail behind her, spreading out in a sporadic V, all holding carved pumpkins that aren't lit. There are at least of fifty of them. A few are craning their necks to look through the bigger crowd at the glowing pink lobby. Some are checking notifications on their phones.

Bob stops, his mind still racing.

"Did you get the lighter?" Joann asks.

"It's not real," Bob says.

Joann points to the school. "Inside Old Pine looks like lit up cotton candy. Of course it's real."

Bob stumbles over his words. "I never talked to Karl. It was Martin."

"Then he's trying to stop you from lighting the jack-o-lanterns." She turns to their recruits behind her. "Does anybody have a lighter? Matches?"

A few get passed forward.

"That's not the problem," Bob says, still working it out in his head. "Martin doesn't want to leave Old Pine. He's not trying to get back into Maple Creek."

"Yes he is," Joann says. "He's furious at our neighborhood because nobody looked for him twenty years ago."

"Yes," Bob says, "but he doesn't have to leave the school. He's lured everybody here. And we've helped him."

One of their recruits, a younger guy with blonde hair and a ski jacket, steps forward. "The jack-o-lanterns aren't going to work?"

"No," Bob insists. "I think they were just part of Martin's plan to get us all here."

"That guy needs to get what's coming to him," the young man says. He checks his phone and then puts it in his pocket. "I'm going in there."

He drops the pumpkin and jogs to catch up with the crowd. A few more recruits—all people Bob doesn't know—go with him.

Bob grabs one of their shoulders. "Wait. This is what he wants."

The online recruit looks Bob in the eye. He raises his phone. "We're doing what you told us to."

"I never told you to go in there."

The recruit points at Bob and grins. "You warned us about this." And then he's gone, part of the crowd pushing into Old Pine.

"What's happening?" Joann asks.

"Martin was in all our online communications. He lured the angry mob here because he's mad at Maple Creek. He lured everyone he could because he's mad at the world."

Carlos and Sariah come up beside Joann. "He's taking adults this time?"

"It's always been about the adults," Bob realizes. "The kids were only part of the lure."

"He murdered kids just to make people angry?" Sariah asks.

"To trick them into coming here tonight," Bob says.

"Why not take the adults last year?" Carlos asks.

"He must need everybody closer to where he died. That's where he's most powerful. He could reach out and take thirty kids last year, but he wants so many more than that."

"What happens when they go inside?" Carlos asks.

Bob watches another handful of people make it past the cops. "He traps them where he took our kids."

"The edge of the afterlife," Joann says, "if he really has made himself like Jack o' the Lantern."

"What do we do?" Sariah asks. "We can't let people go in there."

The crowd outside the doors tightens as people pack in.

"What *can* we do?" Bob says. "I don't think they even all have the same reason. My own viewers think I told them this was some sort of backup plan. Martin's convinced everyone individually."

Joann gasps. She drops her pumpkin and races for the school.

Bob follows. "What are you doing?"

But then he sees.

Sam and Mary are slipping around the edge of the crowd, heading for the pink light of the lobby.

∽

BOB RUNS BEHIND JOANN. He shouts to his recruits behind him, "Stop as many people as you can!"

By the time Bob and Joann reach the crowd, their kids have already made it inside. The crowd is too thick this close to the doors. Joann yanks at an old woman who shakes her off to continue screaming and pushing.

"Mary!" Joann yells. "Sam! Get back here!"

But there's no way the kids can hear her over the angry shouting.

Bob tries pushing his way through the crowd but it's too packed. The only option is to join the slow rush.

"No," Joann says. "We won't catch up. We have to convince people to leave."

Bob jumps straight into it. "You're all walking into the prankster's trap!"

Nobody pays him any mind.

He sees the parents of Tiffany Whitt—one of the first kids to come home. Bob's only ever talked to them online. "Hey! Tiffany's not in there. What are you doing?"

The 31st Trick-or-Treater

Her dad looks back at Bob. "We're stopping this from happening again."

Bob's taken aback. That's what Bob thought he was doing with the jack-o-lanterns. How many people in this crowd have been conducting their own investigations, strung along by someone online who was secretly Martin Donovan?

"It's a trick!" Joann says, but the other couple continue on and the crowd stays too thick to push through.

They're in the thick of it now—a mass of neighbors has closed in around them.

Body heat and odor hang thick in the air.

As they near the doors, Bob sees Officer Yachuw standing next to the door, outside. He's ordering people back, but he's given up trying to physically stop anybody. Instead, he's yelling into a radio for more help.

Bob's sick of the local cops' eagerness to give up. "Martin's going to kill these people if we don't turn them around!"

Officer Yachuw sneers at Bob, but then gives another look at his surroundings. The pieces must fall into place in his head, because he steps into the flow of people to block their paths, and he shouts for them to stop.

Bob's lost track of Joann but he finds her nearby, tight in the crowd, talking into the ear of someone from her church. The person actually listens.

Bob searches the crowd for more people he knows, people who might actually listen to him.

There are Calvin Mitchel's parents, still grieving over their son's death, now out for revenge. Bob has messaged with them several times. He manages to get close.

"You have to stop! You can't hurt this guy. He's tricking you into going inside."

Tina Mitchel turns to regard Bob. There's hate in her eyes and not much else.

Bob backs away. He doesn't want to contemplate how he'd be if Mary or Sam didn't make it back.

Joann has made it farther ahead in the crowd. She's inside the lobby, in the haze of pink.

Bob tries to push past the people in front of him. It's the Chester brothers. He realizes that they never showed up to the corner of the parking lot where they said they'd meet. Martin must have got to them.

Bob's heart sinks. The Chesters are boorish and overconfident. He'll never convince them to leave. But he has to try.

He smacks Miles Chester on the shoulder. "What are you guys doing?"

Miles turns around angry but that changes to surprised as he recognizes Bob. But it's Nathan who speaks up first. "Keep your voices down. If we don't get that body out of there, the cops will pin the murder on us."

Bob shouts back, "Listen to yourself! They found the body weeks ago. It's not there anymore. It's Martin who's tricked you into coming back."

Miles says, "But you said-"

Bob cuts him off. "Martin's infected all our messages. I'm telling you now that you need to run. Get anybody who will listen to you to leave."

"Right, okay," Miles says.

Nathan offers the pink fog another glare, but then follows his brother sideways through the crowd. Their departure makes a space ahead for Bob to push forward, a few steps closer to his kids.

Then he's through the front doors, into Old Pine, into the pink haze.

~

THE FOG IS as blinding as it was behind the impossible door in Wanda's house.

But instead of soft earth under Bob's feet, it's definitely the hard tile floor of Old Pine's lobby.

The crowd has spread out.

Bob looks behind him. There's the wide rectangle of the open front doors with the crowd pushing their way inside. They're silhouettes against the yellow street lamps. Around that rectangle is only pink.

Bob shouts for his family.

He hears the angry yells of his neighbors, now separated from each other to the point that they each sound ridiculous.

"We're going to kill you!"

"You'll never hurt a child again!"

"I'll beat your face in!"

Bob doesn't think his own shouts are any more effective than these, but he nonetheless keeps calling for his family.

Someone grabs him. "You're Bob!"

Bob doesn't recognize him, but since it's a male under thirty, he assumes it's one of his viewers. "Have you seen my family?"

"We're all here for you. We'll get the Trick-or-Treater."

"No! You can't do anything to him. He's already dead. He only wants to take as many people with him as he can."

"We'll get him first. I promise. It's an honor to meet you in person." The young man runs off into the fog.

"Come back!" Bob yells after him. His viewers are supposed to be his community, but he can't even get them to run away from an angry ghost who wants them dead.

With the viewer gone in the pink fog, Bob keeps calling for his family.

More people force their way into the lobby.

Bob estimates the proper direction and heads for the hallway, toward the classroom where Martin Donovan's body waited for years to be found.

∼

SAM AND MARY are holding both each other's hands.

It's awkward reaching across each other, but there's no way that Sam is losing her again.

They're back in the school. The pink fog from the hillside is moving past them, up the hallway, out from the classroom where Sam found the staircase. Its movement is subtle, but Sam notices it well enough to follow it to its source.

"I can't see," Mary says.

"Me neither."

"How do we find Sofia?"

"She and Walter must be down the stairs."

Sam carefully steps forward, feeling with his feet. They're in the classroom now. There are people around, heading the same direction as Sam and Mary.

As Sam taps his foot into the fog, he feels the floor fall away.

They've found the stairs.

"Here it is," he says to Mary.

A grownup pushes past them to run downstairs. As soon as she steps onto the first step, Sam loses sight of her.

"Is she helping, too?" Mary asks.

"I think so," Sam says.

They walk carefully down the stairs, still holding hands in their awkward manner.

He hears more adults run along the floor behind them, but when they reach the stairs, their footsteps vanish.

Halfway down, the fog begins to thin. Sam can see the stone steps leading down to the grassy, sloped field.

Behind them, Mom suddenly yells. "Sam! Mary! Stop!"

Mary stops. "Did you hear Mom?"

"Yes," Sam says, "But she doesn't know Walter and Sofia need help."

"She sounds mad," Mary says.

"You go back. I'll get our friends."

"Maybe Mom will come with us."

Sam looks behind them. The pink fog is thicker that way. The stairs seem to go up for farther than he and Mary have walked.

Mom yells again, and she sounds farther away than before. "Come back!" Her voice rumbles as she runs down the stairs.

But if she's running, why can't they see her yet? They haven't walked very far.

"Maybe we should go back," Sam says.

A new voice from down the stairs.

"Your friends still need your help." It's a male voice, higher pitch, kinda whiny.

Mary squeezes Sam's hands. "That's him! Stingy Jack!"

The fog thins but at the bottom of the stairs, a pink glow remains. It clears into a face: two triangles and a wide, toothless grin.

The Thirty-First Trick-or-Treater stands on the bottom step, jack-o-lantern held high. His sweatshirt hood hides his face.

Sam gathers his courage. "Let Walter go. And Sofia."

"You have to come down to save them. They're in between, just like I am."

"I don't like him," Mary whispers.

As much as Sam needs to save Walter, to not be responsible for him being missing, he can't bring himself to get any closer to the Trick-or-Treater. Not when Mary is with him.

"Please," Sam says to the kidnapper. "I want Walter to come home. I didn't mean for him to get stuck there."

"But it happened," the hooded man snaps. "Now get down here. Your parents are getting close, but it won't be close enough if you don't come down here."

That doesn't make any sense. Walter texted Sam for help. Why is the kidnapper acting like he also wants Sam to help?

Mom shouts from above, closer than before, but not by much. "Come back!"

Sam holds Mary tight, unsure which direction to go.

∼

BOB RUNS BEHIND JOANN, down the stone steps of the impossible staircase.

"Come back!" Joann yells. She exhales, gasping to Bob. "How are we not catching up to them? They don't sound that far away."

From down below comes Sam's voice. It's scratched and scared. "I have to help Walter!"

Bob shouts back, "Walter is home!"

He's faster than Joann, wants to run past her, but there's no space for that on this staircase.

Sam yells up through the fog, "He texted me that he still needs help."

Joann answers, "It's a trick! The kidnapper sent those texts!"

"He tricked me, too!" Bob adds. "He tricked everybody."

Joann lets out a sob. "Where are they?" she says to Bob. "We've gone so far, why aren't they getting closer?"

"Sam," Bob yells, putting authority in his tone, "Bring your sister back upstairs."

"Not like that," Joann hisses.

∽

MARY SQUEEZES Sam's hand too tight, but he doesn't let go.

Dad's words squeeze his chest.

Sam needs to bring Mary back upstairs. He's the big brother, and now he's brought Mary right back into danger. He should have done more to keep her from following him.

The Trick-or-Treater calls up from the bottom of the stairs. "Walter and Sofia still needs your help. Don't let it be your fault that they're stuck here forever."

He can't let Walter down. He can't let Mary down by abandoning her best friend. "We have to keep going down," he says.

∽

THEY'RE both out of breath but they keep running down the stairs.

In front of Bob, Joann shouts, "It's not your fault. Walter is home, but him being missing was never your fault."

Sam shouts back, words drenched in grief. "It's my fault. Just like Mary."

Regret surges through Bob. He's spent the last year trying to bring Mary home, never noticing that Sam wasn't only swimming in grief—he was drowning in guilt.

Joann shouts, "Martin Donovan took your sister. It's not your fault."

"You're a good big brother," Bob yells. "The best."

"I didn't go up with her to that porch. If I held her hand, then she wouldn't have gone missing."

Bob feels the shame that's been in his son for so long. The regret Sam feels, the fear that he hadn't been who he was supposed to be. It breaks his heart, those cyclopean emotions in his small, fragile little boy. "It was a long night. You were tired. It wasn't your job to protect Mary from kidnappers. That was my job."

∼

SAM DOESN'T LIKE the way Dad's voice cracked.

"Is Daddy crying?" Mary asks. She pulls Sam up a step. Sam lets her.

"Get back here," the Trick-or-Treater snarls. "Bring them closer."

He stomps up the steps.

Mary screams.

Sam runs up the stairs, still holding both hands with his sister.

The Trick-or-Treater is so much bigger than them, he should be gaining on them so quickly, but each awkward step that Sam and Mary take up toward Mom and Dad, their pursuer gets farther away.

Suddenly, Sam feels himself lifted into Mom's arms. He sees Dad pick up Mary.

"Are you sure Walter isn't down there?" Sam manages to ask.

"I promise," Mom says. "It was all a trick. The kidnapper doesn't even want you, he just wanted me and your dad to follow you."

Back upstairs, Mom and Dad keep Sam and Mary in their arms. They run through the pink fog in the hallway, bumping into other adults.

Sam buries his face in Mom's shoulder, clinging to her and to his parents' promise that everything's okay, that it wasn't ever his fault.

∼

BOB RUNS through the foggy Old Pine hallway, holding Mary tight, her face against his chest so he can shoulder his neighbors out of his way without risking knocking Mary into anybody.

He checks that Joann and Sam are behind him.

His mind swirls with how close he came to losing his family forever, or to getting yanked away from them forever.

"Keep going," Joann says.

They make it into the lobby. Too many people push through the thick, pink fog, all headed for the classroom that Bob and his family are coming from.

Their anger roils in the air.

"You can't do anything," Bob cries to everyone and no one. "He wants you all dead!"

He sees neighbors he recognizes only from Facebook pictures, young strangers who must be his YouTube viewers. No one will listen to him.

"Wait!" Joann yells.

Bob stops and looks back. With Sam still squeezed against her, Joann is frantically warning someone to turn around. It's a woman who Bob vaguely recognizes as an HOA board member. He's pretty sure Joann argued with her about their landscaping.

Whatever Joann says to her, she abandons her plan for neighborhood vengeance and instead turns around to follow Joann and Bob.

Ahead, Bob spots the rectangle of glass doors amidst the pink fog. People still shuffle inside, silhouettes against yellow street lamps.

Bob pushes through, forcing a path, making sure Joann is right behind him. Joann's newfound follower is behind her.

Bob crashes into Paul Keller, Walter's dad.

"What are you doing here?" Bob can't believe he's not home with his son. It's barely been twenty-four hours since Walter came home.

"Making sure this doesn't happen again."

"No, that's a trick. Whatever you think you're going to do to stop the kidnapper, it's a trick to get you closer."

Mary looks up from Bob's shoulder. "Walter's home," she says.

"He is," Paul agrees. "And I'm going to keep it that way."

"Please," Bob says, "my kids were gone, too. I know you blame my son for Walter getting taken, and I know you don't like me. But I'm on your side. We were manipulated. The kidnapper wants to take you away forever. Don't leave your son."

Paul shrinks, overcome with doubt.

"Come on," Bob says. "Go home." Relief weakens Bob as Paul turns around, pushing through the crowd.

He follows him outside.

The cops are shoving people back, getting overwhelmed.

But it only takes a second for Bob and Joann's little caravan to clear the crowd. Most of the angry mob and many of Bob's recruits have already gone inside. A few others mill about their cars, watching the chaos around Old Pine's front doors. He sees Sariah, Carlos, the Chester brothers, and strangers who are happy to see him—they must be his viewers.

Bob spots Polly, who's carrying Emily.

He and Joann run to her.

Tears have smeared Polly's makeup. "Are they okay? I'm so sorry! They ran off and I couldn't keep up."

"It's okay. Everyone's okay," Joann says.

Not everyone, Bob thinks. He watches the rest of the angry

crowd force their way inside the school. The cops grab the last four or five people, but so many make it past.

Bob couldn't help barely anybody.

The pink light inside the lobby flickers out.

The cops run in, but Bob expects they'll find the school empty.

Martin Donovan got his revenge against the neighborhood of Maple Creek. He got everyone's attention by taking thirty children, then let them out, one by one, to lure the neighborhood to Old Pine on Halloween—the exact time and place when he'd be most powerful. How many people has he now taken away to the edge of the afterlife? A hundred? Two hundred?

Bob holds Mary tight, hoping that Martin is satisfied with his revenge, that he's gone for good.

"All those people," Joann whispers. "Why didn't they believe us?"

"We're safe," Bob replies. "Our kids are safe."

"Can we go home?" Sam asks.

"Of course," Bob says.

Instead, they all go to Aunt Polly's and spend Halloween night together on the couch, far away from the horrors of Maple Creek, Old Pine, and the Thirty-First Trick-or-Treater.

ARE YOU A STRANGE READER?

Hello Strange Reader,

Stephen King has "Constant Readers." But you just read a book about a Halloween ghost dragging a neighborhood to the edge of the afterlife, so I figure you'll happily wear the title of "Strange Reader."

I'd like to invite you to visit my website where you'll find some exclusive bonus material for 'The 31st Trick-or-Treater.'

I'll ask you for your email address so you can be part of my "Strange Reader Newsletter," but you're welcome to unsubscribe at any time.

To access the bonus content, scan this QR code with your phone's camera app:

Are you a strange reader?

Printed in Dunstable, United Kingdom